# HIDE AWAY

# OTHER BOOKS BY JASON PINTER

## HENRY PARKER SERIES

*The Mark*
*The Guilty*
*The Stolen*
*The Fury*
*The Darkness*
*The Castle*

## FOR CHILDREN

*Zeke Bartholomew: SuperSpy!*
*Miracle*

# HIDE AWAY

JASON PINTER

THOMAS & MERCER

This is a work of fiction. Names, characters, organizations, places, events, and incidents are either products of the author's imagination or are used fictitiously. Any resemblance to actual persons, living or dead, or actual events is purely coincidental.



Published by Thomas & Mercer, Seattle
www.apub.com



ISBN-13: 9781542005906
ISBN-10: 1542005906

Cover design by Rex Bonomelli

Printed in the United States of America

*To Dana, Ava, and Lyla*
*My girls, my world, my everything*

Everyone has three lives: a public life,
a private life, and a secret life.
—Gabriel Garcia Marquez

# CHAPTER 1

The night her family was ripped apart, the woman stood by her oven, watching the chicken cook through the glass, thinking to herself there was nothing on earth more terrible than a burnt casserole.

She stole a quick glance at the baby monitor sitting atop the counter. She could see her six-month-old daughter's chest rising and falling ever so slightly, the child's peaceful slumber a salve for a mother's anxiety. Her son, now six, had always managed to escape from his swaddle—her little Houdini, she'd called him—but since birth her daughter had melted into the soft cloth, tucked in and content. *Our little burrito,* Brad had said on the day they brought her home.

Her son had gone to play at Zachary Bloomfield's house around the corner on Fox Hill Lane after school. He'd sworn to be home by 6:30 p.m. for dinner. Given that the Bloomfield residence was just two blocks away, she allowed him to return on his own. It was now 6:38. She considered calling Zachary's mother, Mallory, for a status update, but she had promised Brad that she wouldn't worry until there was something worth worrying about.

Their son had a whirling dervish of a social life: every afternoon brought a playdate or a birthday party or peewee soccer practice. Keeping up with him while simultaneously maintaining a relatively clean household *and* taking care of an infant left her drained, but she was pleased he was so active, so sociable. Half his classmates whittled away beautiful days lost in the glare of an iPad. Deep down, she was glad he was late. Of course, she couldn't let him know that.

Besides, the casserole needed another ten minutes to bake. The salad was already prepared and waiting to be tossed with her delicious homemade italian dressing. A side of israeli couscous sat in a warm pot. Brad worked eighty-hour weeks, but he'd sworn to eat at least one dinner a week at home with their family. And tonight was family night.

Most evenings she ate alone with her son, glancing forlornly at Brad's empty chair, the baby in a bouncer on the floor next to her. Her son talked her ear off: chew and talk. Chew and talk. There was no detail too small or too insignificant to share. He regaled her with tales of bad cafeteria food, which friends he chose to sit with and why, and whose birthday party had the best (and worst) cake. And she sat there and listened, riveted, a blissful smile on her face.

And as soon as his plate was clean, her son shot from the table like a lit firework. She never stopped him but always silently hoped he might stay just a little longer. She cherished the company. With a loving husband who worked long hours to provide and two wonderful, healthy children, she felt guilty even thinking it . . . but was she lonely?

Most nights Brad got home exhausted, tossed his clothes into a pile on the bedroom floor, and collapsed into bed. A three-minute *How was your day* and a chaste peck on the lips, and suddenly it was the next morning. They hadn't been intimate since their daughter was born. She had been anxiously waiting for him to make the first move, longed for him to slip a gentle hand underneath her tank top. She missed his touch, feeling his weight on her, the roughness of his stubble on her face. She knew Brad was pushing himself all day, every day, for them. They had struggled to make ends meet for as long as they'd been together. Brad brought home $80,000 a year, barely enough to pay their mortgage while providing for a family of four. Their three-bedroom, two-bathroom house was meant to be a starter home, but with finances stretched to their limits, they wouldn't be moving anytime soon.

Brad worked hard and needed rest. But she still found herself yearning. And not just for physical intimacy. Not that long ago she'd graduated as class valedictorian, captained the field hockey and swim teams, and plowed through college with a 3.9 GPA. She vacillated between med school and law school, knowing she could excel at either. Her mind was sharp, work ethic unparalleled. The world was hers if she wanted it. And she did.

When she got pregnant with her son soon after graduation, it was a surprise but not an unwelcome one. Her ambitions were put on the back burner, where she assumed they would stay warm. But seven years later, her career aspirations had grown as cold as their marital bed. Suddenly she was a stay-at-home mom at thirty. She felt too old to go back to school, but the thought of draining her remaining youth waiting on casseroles made her want to jump off a bridge.

She still had boxes upon boxes of reference books in a storage unit, buried underneath old high school yearbooks and jeans that would never fit again. Medicine. Law. History. On nights like tonight, when she was standing alone in front of the stove, they called out to her. The books were her whetstones, her mind a blade grown dull. Her son was in school, and her daughter would soon be old enough for day care. Perhaps it was time to revive her senses.

In the interim, she needed to rekindle the fire with Brad. Her son had a birthday party down the block on Saturday, and it would take a nuclear explosion to wake her daughter from her afternoon nap. She would drag her man into bed, kicking and screaming if need be. She would end their dry spell—with prejudice.

But in the meantime, the casserole was ready.

She took the dish from the oven, removed the foil, and let the meal stand. She plucked a blonde hair from the bubbling cheese and chastised herself for not paying closer attention. She checked her watch. 6:51. No sign of her husband or son. Now she was growing irritated. And slightly worried.

The table was set. Dinner ready to serve. She called Brad's cell. It went straight to voice mail. That was odd—Brad never turned his phone off.

She did a loop around the dining room table, straightening out the silverware, smoothing out the napkins. Just when she began to dial the Bloomfield's phone number, she heard the front door open.

"Mom?" her son shouted from outside. "Can you come here?" There was concern in his voice. And something else . . . a tremor of fear beneath it that sent a shiver up her spine.

"Hon? Everything OK?" she shouted back, chalking her fear up to ordinary mother anxieties. He was fine. Everything was fine. "I'm in the kitchen. Go wash up for dinner. Your father should be home soon."

"Somebody left something on the porch," he said, his voice shaky. "Something in a bag. Mom, come here."

Something in a bag? She hadn't ordered anything online recently—certainly nothing that might be delivered in a bag. "Is it the dry cleaning?"

"No, it's not that kind of bag. There's . . . there's something wet on it," he shouted. "It's red."

*Red?*

"Hold on, sweetie. I'm coming."

Her heart began to thrum in her chest as she went to find her son. The front door was open. She found him kneeling on the front step, untying a large brown burlap sack.

"Honey, stop," she said. "You don't know what . . ."

Then she saw what he saw—a spot of red. Not a spot, more like a stain. But the stain appeared to have soaked through the sack from the *inside.*

"Baby, don't . . ."

But he had already finished untying it. She watched as he pulled apart the strings and opened the sack.

The look on her son's face when he saw what was inside would be forever burned into her memory.

His eyes grew wide, wider than she thought possible, his lips trembling, his mouth spread into a horrible O. At first there was no sound. But then a scream welled up from deep within him, a horrifying, anguished howl that rattled her bones.

He fell backward onto the porch, still screaming. She gathered her son in her arms and held him tight, pressing his face into her chest, his screams muffled by her thick cardigan. His whole body shook; his mouth opened so wide she felt his teeth sinking into the flesh of her arm. She tried to pull him away, worried he might choke. He hooked his fingers into her back and continued to wail as she ran her fingers through his hair. Then she looked down into the open sack.

And she began to scream too.

# CHAPTER 2

***Seven Years Later***

Rachel Marin's heels clacked on the dark, iced-over cobblestone street as she hurried home, shielding herself against the bitter December wind. Her afternoon sitter, Iris, had already threatened to quit twice if Rachel didn't start getting home on time. She was expected home by 7:00 p.m. It was already 7:42.

The thread securing the top two buttons on her coat had frayed, the cold wind slipping inside her jacket, chilling her to the core. It was hardly beyond Rachel's skill set to sew a loose button, but unearthing ten spare minutes between her children and her job was like squeezing chocolate milk from a brick.

With a brutal winter having descended upon the city of Ashby, Illinois, vacant cabs were nonexistent, the public transportation system was overloaded, and the nearest UberX was twenty minutes away. The lack of transportation options reminded Rachel why many people referred to Ashby as "Budget Chicago." Ashby was the kind of city you moved to when you were priced out of metropolitan areas, content to live with an abundance of strip malls and a lack of cultural options: one (run-down) cinema, a local theater company, and more burger joints per capita than anywhere else she'd been. But culture was not why they had moved to Ashby. Nor were they strapped financially. This unassuming small town had allowed Rachel and her children to restart their lives. And a fresh, clean start was all that mattered.

So Rachel found herself barreling down a snow-dusted sidewalk under a darkening sky, her purse swinging wildly as she slalomed between pedestrians, trying to avoid catching her heel in a pavement crack and taking down a slew of poor souls like puffy-coated bowling pins. And with just five blocks to go, Rachel was in the home stretch. She'd beg forgiveness from Iris and maybe, just maybe, get home in time to read her daughter a bedtime story.

She didn't see the man step out in front of her until it was too late.

He was big and solid with a bald freckled head and red cheeks, and Rachel caromed off him like a tennis ball from a cement wall. She fell backward and landed sharply on her tailbone, a lightning bolt of pain shooting through her pelvis. She could feel slush seeping into her pants.

The man, all 250 pounds of him, reached down, pulled her up by the elbow, and whipped her into an alley. Rachel landed hard on her hands and knees and reached for her purse. The man grabbed Rachel's wrist and held it briefly, as if to say *Don't do that*, then threw her up against the brick wall. Her back, hands, and knees were covered in sludge and snow. The man pressed his body firmly against hers and placed his forearm into her neck. His breath smelled of onions and beer.

"I could crush your windpipe like a packet of ketchup," the man whispered into her ear, his stubble searing her cheek. "You make a sound, and I'll squeeze until it pops."

He allowed just enough slack to permit her to breathe but maintained enough pressure on her throat to let her know it wouldn't necessarily stay that way. With his free hand he slipped her pocketbook from her shoulder, pressed the brass clasp to unlock it, and took out her wallet. He then turned the purse upside down and shook it until all Rachel's belongings fell onto the grimy street.

Out went her lipstick, tampons, mirror, hairbrush, a KIND bar, a pack of sugar-free gum, and her makeup kit. He dropped her purse into the muck, then unzipped the wallet. He smiled when he saw a thick wad of twenties nestled inside.

"That's to pay my sitter," Rachel said.

"*Was* to pay her," the man said, stuffing the bills in the pocket of his dark-green bomber jacket.

"Please, don't do this."

"Consider yourself lucky if I only take the money," he said, pressing his arm against her throat just a little harder. Rachel struggled beneath his bulk.

"Please," she said, croaking out the word. "I just want to get home to my children. Just walk away now, and we can forget this ever happened."

He stared at her. She saw the slightest twitch in his eyes, like he was considering her plea. Then he glanced down the alleyway. It was empty. And it was dark. She felt something rub up against her leg and instantly knew what was about to happen.

"It'd be a shame to end the night early," he said, dragging her farther into the alley. "Scream, and I'll open you up where you don't already have any holes."

She dug her feet into the ground and said, "Sir, I'm begging you, don't do this. You'll regret it."

"*I'll* regret it?" he said with a hearty laugh. "Beg all you want; it'll be more fun if you do."

"Please. Don't make me do this."

The man stopped. Looked back at her, amused. He still held her by the wrist.

"Make *you* do *what*?"

Rachel sighed. Before the man had a chance to take another breath, she brought her wrist up so that her palm was facing her nose, forcing the man to straighten his arm, forearm up, to keep his grip. She then snapped her free hand upward against his elbow, hyperextending the joint and tearing the radial and ulnar collateral ligaments. He howled in pain and grabbed his injured limb. She was free.

Then Rachel turned the flat of her hand into a knife's edge and jabbed her fingers into his throat. The man made a choking sound, his eyes went wide, and he fell to his knees, gasping for air. Tears streamed down his cheeks. When he staggered back to his feet, Rachel used his forward momentum to slam his head against the brick wall. He crumpled to the ground. Rachel then pressed the point of her heel into the small, soft crook in his ankle where the tibia bone met the talus bone.

"If I press down any harder," Rachel said, "I'll split your ankle in two. You scream, and I'll pop it like a ketchup packet."

"What do you want?" the man spat between moans.

"What do I want? Hmm. Let me see . . . what do I want . . . ," Rachel said sarcastically. "Well, I *wanted* to get home in time to read my daughter a story before bed, but you ruined that, so thanks."

Rachel knelt down, keeping pressure on the man's ankle, and slid her hand into his jacket pocket. She took her money back. In one pocket she found his wallet. In the other, she found a small folding knife. She flicked the blade open.

She examined the steel. It was old, dull. A careless weapon for a careless man.

She pressed the knife tip into the small of the man's back, just above his pelvis. He went rigid.

"Please," he said softly.

"This part of your spine is what's known as the cauda equina," Rachel said. "It's a group of nerve endings that controls everything from motor and organ function to your lower limbs. Point being: I could make you a paraplegic in the time it takes you to sneeze." She pressed the knifepoint in, harder. Mucus and blood and tears pooled together and dripped down his face into the slush.

Methodically, Rachel reached down and deposited each of the scattered items back into her purse. She opened the Camera app on her cell phone and snapped several pictures of the brass clasp. Then she opened his wallet and slipped out his driver's license.

"Reginald Bartek," she said, "of 115 Sycamore Lane, in North Ashby."

Rachel scanned Bartek's license, confused.

"Wow, you live in a real nice neighborhood, Reggie. A two bed, two bath will easily run you a million four in that part of town." She sniffed the air. "And that Tom Ford cologne you're wearing runs a hundred bucks a bottle. You need my money like I need a submarine."

She ran her fingers over Bartek's wallet.

"This little indent here," she said, caressing the leather, "is where you usually keep your condom. But you don't have one in there at the moment. Which means you took it out so your wife wouldn't find it. Or you used it and forgot to replace it. So you're married. And that jacket you're wearing is old, but the colors haven't faded much. Grangers detergent, I'm guessing. And I'll bet your wife is the one who keeps it in good condition. You don't strike me as someone who believes cleanliness is next to godliness." Rachel paused. "And you have a daughter."

"How in the hell do you know that?" Bartek said. The menace in his voice had been replaced by unease.

"You have flecks of pink nail polish on your right ring finger. You removed most of the polish, but you missed a spot. You let your young daughter paint your nails last night."

"I don't have a daugh—"

"Yes you do. You tried to scrape the polish off before work, using a file rather than nail polish remover, which is why it flaked. You were sloppy." She ground the knifepoint harder into Bartek's back. "Sloppy. Imagine that."

"You made your point; now leave me alone," he said. Bartek's entire body was stiff. A sudden movement or even a twitch could inadvertently plunge the knife into his skin.

"I will," Rachel said. "But I can't just leave you like this. You didn't need my money. You're not desperate or hungry. Which means you're either a sociopath or a thrill seeker. Am I warm?"

"I got nothing to say to you."

Bartek squirmed. Rachel pressed her knee into the back of his hamstring. Hard. He stopped squirming.

"You got unlucky tonight choosing me. But you'll be back tomorrow. You'll find someone else. Guys like you are too dumb to quit. You know, I could have the cops haul your slimy ass in."

"So why don't you?" Bartek said.

"Aside from the fact that I don't really trust them—rich pricks like you always seem to skate—somebody once told me that I'd be faced with choices like this," Rachel said. "And that I'd sleep well at night knowing I made a choice to prevent things like this from happening to people who *can't* defend themselves. And they were right."

Rachel drew up Bartek's left pant cuff and, with a quick stroke, slid the folding knife blade across the back of his ankle and partially severed his Achilles tendon.

Bartek screamed and flopped about on the ground like a fish on a boat. He cradled his injured arm and maimed leg and curled up into a sobbing, bleeding ball. Rachel wiped the knife with a tissue and tossed it into a sewer grate. She removed a ballpoint pen from her purse and wrote four words on the back of Bartek's driver's license.

"I'm taking your driver's license," she said. "I want you to see what I wrote on it." Rachel held the license up to Bartek's face so he could read what she'd written.

He shook his head and tried to crawl away.

"I can cut your other heel. Read it. Out loud."

Bartek raised his head, looked at the ID, and choked out, "Attempted robbery. Attempted rape."

"Good." She slipped his license into her purse. "I'm going to keep this somewhere safe. You also did me the favor of leaving a perfect thumbprint on my purse, which I now have photos of. So if anything ever happens to me, or if I ever see you again, people will find the license and the print photo. Now ask yourself, Reggie: Are you smart enough to come up with a logical explanation for why I'd have your license and why your fingerprints would be all over my purse?"

"You assaulted *me*!" Bartek howled.

"Look at me and look at you, Brutus. You outweigh me by a whole other me. *You* made the first move. Remember that. This is all on you."

Bartek was silent.

"Now, you'll heal, but you'll never run quite as fast. And just think what the next person might do to you," she said, turning away. "And fuck you for making me late for my sitter."

◆◆◆

As Rachel took her keys from her purse, she noticed a smudge of Reginald Bartek's blood on the sleeve of her coat. She hid the stained cloth against her chest and opened the front door slowly, watching for Iris or the kids. When she confirmed the foyer was empty, Rachel quickly opened the closet door and put the coat on a hanger. It promptly fell to the ground. She hung it back up, with the dirty sleeve facing inward. She would need to get it cleaned professionally—blood didn't come off easy. Then Rachel took a deep breath to settle her nerves and went to find her family.

Iris was seated on the living room couch with the dregs of a cup of jasmine tea next to a Jodi Picoult novel. Iris was in her late fifties but nimble enough to chase around children a fourth of her age. She wore dark-green pants and a thick red wool sweater that itched Rachel just to look at it. Her hazel eyes could switch from sweet to serious in an instant. Rachel had come home to find serious.

"Iris, I am *beyond* sorry," Rachel said. "I got held up at work. Steve dropped a pile of work on my desk right as I was leaving, and it had to be done before the weekend."

Iris looked at Rachel with a mixture of irritation and disappointment. She put the teacup in the dishwasher, tucked the paperback in her pocketbook, and walked to the front door without responding to Rachel.

"Megan is asleep. Eric is doing his homework," she said.

"Thank you, Iris."

"You were late last Tuesday," Iris said. "And the Wednesday before. And that previous Friday. In fact, you're late often."

"All I can do is apologize and promise to try harder."

"I have a family too," Iris said. "My husband makes lasagna on Friday nights, and then we watch a movie on TCM. But by the time I get home, the food will be cold, and the movie will be half-over."

"I'm sorry. That sounds like a lovely evening," Rachel said. A pang of loneliness radiated in her chest.

"Other families inquire about my availability constantly," Iris said. "My references are impeccable. I stay with you because I care about those kids, and I can imagine how hard it is being a single mother. But if I can't get home to *my* family when they expect me, I'll need to find different work. I hope you don't force my hand."

"I do respect your time. This kills me, Iris. The kids love you. I'll make this work, I swear."

"Please do, Ms. Marin," Iris said. "I've given you plenty of chances. There won't be another."

Iris slipped on a pair of black rubber boots, cinched up her gray L.L.Bean lamb's wool coat—all its buttons neatly attached—and left. A frost hung in the air as the door slammed shut.

Rachel stood in the entryway for a full minute, gathering herself. She still felt the adrenaline from the Bartek encounter coursing through her. She took her shoes off, tied her hair in a ponytail, and went upstairs. She knocked on Eric's door, heard a muffled and slightly irritated, "What?"

She took that as an invitation and opened the door. Her son was hunched over his desk, a textbook open in front of him. His walls were adorned with plaques, accolades, and certificates: Math Olympics.

Spelling bee champion. Junior debate team. They were bereft of movie posters, photos of favorite athletes, or pictures of friends. There was a lack of joy and youth in her son's room that ate at Rachel every time she entered. Once, a lifetime ago, she could barely keep track of his thriving social life. Playdates and birthday parties and endless smiles. There was nothing wrong with being a bookworm . . . but she ached for him to throw a baseball, bike around town, show any sign that he had a life beyond academia. She wanted him to be a kid again. But the truth was, since that terrible night, he'd never been the same. He'd thrown himself into his studies with a zeal that would have most parents overjoyed. But Rachel knew it was to stave off the nightmares, to shield himself from the cruelty of the outside world.

Rachel wrapped her arms around her son and kissed the top of his curly dirty-blond mop of hair. He wrenched himself free without turning around. Eric was thirteen, his once-plump cheeks losing their baby fat. He was beginning to stretch out, lean out. In a few years he would be taller than his mother and go from "cute" to "handsome" overnight. He had his father's sparkling blue eyes, the color of the Mediterranean Sea. Looking at them made her heart swell and ache.

"I'm studying," Eric said gruffly. He spun around in his chair. "Why are your pants all dirty?"

Rachel looked down. She was still covered in grime from the alleyway.

"I fell. Your mom is a klutz." He raised his eyebrows as if to say *duh*. "So what are you working on?"

"History," Eric said, spinning back around.

"Studying anything in particular?"

"We have a quiz on Tuesday. I have to memorize all the US states and capitals."

"Will you be ready?"

Eric shrugged.

“Wyoming,” Rachel said.

“Cheyenne,” Eric replied.

“Delaware.”

“Dover.”

“Nevada.”

“Carson City.”

“Puerto Rico.”

Eric snorted dismissively. “Puerto Rico is a territory of the United States, not a state itself. But it’s San Juan since you asked. Nice try, Mom.”

Rachel smiled. “When did you get so smart?”

“I’ve always been smart,” Eric said.

“Yes, you have. How’s your sister?” She hated speaking to the back of his head.

“Annoying.”

“She’s seven. How annoying can she be?”

“She told me she was going to cut my hair off and cook it for dinner as spaghetti. Then she found a pair of scissors that Iris had to take away from her.”

“Iris let her get a pair of scissors?”

“Megan is a lot faster than Iris,” Eric said.

Rachel laughed. “I bet she is.”

She reached out, stopping just short of tousling his hair. Rachel remembered the day he had come into the world. Scarily early, at thirty-two weeks. Tiny, at just over four pounds. He spent five weeks in the NICU, the five longest weeks of her life. But when they brought him home, he grew. Lord, did he grow. Rachel resisted the urge to wrap her hands around this young man and squeeze him as hard as she could. After everything he’d been through, she just wanted to protect him, to make sure he knew he was loved.

“Do you like it here?” Rachel asked. “In Ashby.”

Eric shrugged again. "It's fine." He spun back around. "Do you think we're going to stay?" His voice was hopeful and lanced Rachel's heart.

"I hope so, sweetie. I hope so. I'm going to check on your sister." She paused. "Vermont."

Eric thought for a moment, then said, "Montpelier. Now let me study."

"All right, kiddo."

"Hey, Mom?"

"Yes, hon?"

"Remember to check."

Rachel sighed. Every night over the past nearly seven years, Eric had asked her to check the front porch. Rachel's heart felt heavy as she said, "I'll check."

Eric nodded and went back to his computer.

Rachel went down the hall and eased open the door to Megan's room. She was sprawled out on her daybed, a tiny angel tucked under *Max & Ruby* sheets. The seashell-shaped night-light beside her bed cast a warm glow. Megan was wearing her favorite red Wonder Woman pajamas, her long blonde hair splayed across the pillow.

Rachel leaned down and gently kissed her daughter's warm cheek, the small body beneath her stirring ever so slightly. Papers were strewed over the floor, pictures and words she couldn't quite see in the dark. She could make out one page that read *A Mystery Book by Megan Marin*. Rachel's heart swelled. She'd ask her daughter about it tomorrow. She crept out of Megan's room and eased the door shut.

Rachel went to her bedroom, stripped off her work clothes, and hung them up neatly. She looked at herself in the mirror. She'd gotten used to the brown hair, which was not natural, and the crow's-feet, which were. She was thirty-seven, with two children and a full-time job, so keeping her body and mind in the kind of shape necessary was a constant struggle.

And it *was* necessary.

Both children had been delivered via C-section, and she was proud of that scar. Her arms were sinewy and strong, blue veins visible running down her biceps and across her shoulders. She'd worked hard for that vascularity. If Reginald Bartek had seen what Rachel did to her body every night after the children went to bed, he would have considered his target much more carefully.

When she removed her undershirt, Rachel ran her finger over the thick two-inch-long scar just below her rib cage that resembled a bulging pinky finger. Rachel had told the emergency room nurse she'd been randomly slashed by a teenager participating in a gang initiation. She'd lied. Even filled out a police report.

Shockingly, they never turned up any suspects.

Because of that scar, Rachel wore only one-piece swimsuits when she took the kids to the communal pool. Her children had never seen the scar, and she would prefer they never did. If they saw it, she would have to lie again, and Eric had a first-class lie detector.

Once, only once, had a man seen it. A fling with a local obstetrician that had turned into something more. Their first time in bed, she was too caught up in the moment to hide it, her judgment clouded by just how long it had been since she had felt a man's touch. Years. He'd gasped when he removed her shirt.

"Did you get mauled by a bear?" he asked. She told him she had her gall bladder removed when she was young. He seemed to accept the explanation, or simply not care enough to probe, and they carried on. But the ease and comfort with which the lie came shocked Rachel. For the remainder of the relationship she insisted on wearing a T-shirt or tank top when they had sex. And when the dalliance ended, part of her had felt relieved.

Rachel put on a pair of blue sweatpants and a comfy old fleece. Then she removed Reginald Bartek's driver's license from her wallet.

Examined it. It was a good photo. He was smiling. Freshly shaven. Kind eyes. He looked like a decent man. A family man.

*Sometimes behind the kindest eyes lay the darkest hearts.*

A lawyer had said those words to Rachel once, as she'd sat in a courtroom staring across the aisle at another man who'd also had kind eyes.

Rachel flipped the license over and reread her words.

*Attempted Robbery. Attempted Rape.*

She opened the closet and pushed aside a row of blouses and blazers. A large black safe was mounted to the wall. She entered the combination and opened the metal door. Inside was some jewelry, her passport, an engagement ring, a wedding band, her children's birth certificates (real and fake), and a loaded Mossberg 500 shotgun with four boxes of double-aught buckshot shells.

The diamond on the engagement ring was about the size of a caper and set in a sterling silver band. It wasn't worth more than $1,500, but when it had sat on her finger, Rachel had felt like the richest woman alive. She used to remove it only when exercising or showering. But now, every time she opened the safe, she regretted each moment she had left her finger bare.

Rachel picked up a small brown cardboard box bound tight with rubber bands and opened it. The box held half a dozen driver's licenses, passports, and various government-issued ID cards. She'd had some of the licenses for so long they'd expired. One of them had a reddish-brown smudge obscuring half the man's smirking face.

There was a small plastic bag at the bottom of the box. It contained a single piece of jewelry. A bracelet. It did not belong to her. Rachel stared at the piece for a moment, then placed Reginald Bartek's license inside the box, closed the lid, and wound the bands back around the box.

"Mommy!"

Megan was awake and calling for her.

"Just a second, sweetie!" she shouted.

Rachel locked the safe and went to put her daughter back to sleep.

◆◆◆

Two hours later, after checking the front porch for Eric, Rachel turned on the television in her bedroom and flipped the input to HDMI-8. The split screen feeds came through in sharp high-def black and white.

The left feed displayed Megan's room. The right feed, Eric's room.

She'd mounted the CCTV cameras herself. Nearly a dozen others were installed throughout the house, hidden well.

She ran through the different cameras. Megan's bed. Megan's door. Megan's window. Eric's bed. Eric's door. Eric's window. Front door. Back door. Kitchen. Living room. Her own bedroom.

Rachel watched the feeds for a few minutes until she was certain she was alone and the children were fast asleep. She listened to them breathing. Knew their rhythms. Then, Rachel tiptoed to the basement door.

She entered a six-digit code on a silent keypad. The door unlocked. She'd told her children that under no circumstances could they ever go downstairs. She'd said the basement had asbestos and the lock was for their protection. The first part was a lie.

Rachel crept downstairs while her children slept. Her adrenaline began to surge.

She had work to do.

# CHAPTER 3

"Dispatch says the scene is a mess," said Detective John Serrano. "Lieutenant George says the body was found on *top* of the frozen river. Forensics is on scene. Bridge is closed down. Harbor patrol has a boat out."

"A boat? Isn't the river frozen?" replied Detective Leslie Tally.

"Solid," Serrano said. "I can't imagine many worse ways to go."

It was just after 2:00 a.m., and the roads around Ashby were nearly empty. The Crown Victoria was silent aside from the hum of the road and the wipers brushing away snow.

Detective Serrano held a paperback book on his lap. He thumbed the cover, opened it, read a few pages, and closed it again.

"Life would suck if you were an orc," said Serrano. "You're born ugly. You grow up ugly. There are a billion of you, and you're *all* ugly. Has there ever been an attractive orc? Like, has a boy orc ever looked at a girl orc and said, 'Whoa, that is one *fine-looking* orc lady'? And then what do you do to pay the bills? Your whole life is spent either dragging heavy stuff around to build massive weapons of death or in battle, where you're basically just cannon fodder for your bosses, who would feed you to a troll before giving you the time of day. So basically you're born ugly, with bad breath and terrible skin, and then die having never been laid, ever."

"I don't know how you can read in the car with no light without throwing up," Tally said. "Even the tiny-ass text on the GPS makes me queasy."

"My eyes adjust," Serrano said. "Makes you thankful, doesn't it? We're pretty lucky to be human. We could have been born orcs."

Tally took her eyes off the road for a moment to roll her eyes at her partner. "You have problems, John. Deep-seated problems. You should see a therapist about this goblin stuff."

"Orcs," Serrano said. "Not goblins. Anyway, this *stuff* helps me think."

"If you don't stop talking about orcs while I'm driving, I'm going to *think* us right into the river."

"You know, I'm willing to bet that Claire and the kids would love these books," Serrano said. "At least you were smart enough to marry someone who's open minded, even if her good traits don't rub off on you."

"Claire is open minded about Spanish wines and British sitcoms. Books where the main characters have hairy feet and don't wear shoes? Hell no. And why don't they wear shoes? They wear clothes, don't they? So why no shoes? There are rocks in Central-earth, right?"

"It's Middle-earth," Serrano said. "But I'll give you points for trying."

"Spending twelve hours a day chained to your goofy ass doesn't give me a choice *but* to pick up some of your nonsense. Read a real book."

"I'm going to pretend I didn't hear you say that."

"Enough of this crap," Tally said. "We're almost there. Dispatch says word from Lieutenant George is that it looks like a suicide."

"Wouldn't be the first to go off this bridge," Serrano said, "and probably won't be the last."

Snowflakes drifted onto the windshield like powdered sugar and disappeared beneath the wiper blades. The sky was a rich tapestry of inky black with hues of dark blue. Serrano listened to the wind. Gentle, calming.

Ashby winters could be brutal, but Serrano relished the frigid months. While some people came down with seasonal affective disorder, the cold made Serrano feel alive. Summers sapped his energy. Gorgeous, sun-dappled days brought back memories he had tried long—and unsuccessfully—to forget.

Partnering with Detective Leslie Tally had been a blessing. It was more than a partnership to Serrano. She was his family. Tally had brought him back from the brink on more than one occasion. And if you'd told twenty-two-year-old recruit John Serrano that he'd one day be reading thousand-page fantasy novels and his best friend and only family would be a younger, black, gay detective with three stepchildren, he would have laughed.

Serrano saw the Albertson Bridge looming ahead, a ghostly vision in the dark night.

"Here we are," Tally said. "Could this night get any eerier? Wait, I take that back. Given the stuff you read, you could probably say yes."

"No evil clown sightings yet," Serrano said.

"Now, even I read that one."

The Albertson Bridge had been erected in 1928, its steel truss standing 148.5 feet above the 1.2-mile-wide Ashby River. At night the bridge was a beautiful sight, and the midpoint was a favorite spot for couples to get engaged. On the eastern side of the bridge you could see clear across the river into Woodbarren Glen, which contained a thousand acres of lush foliage, hiking and running trails, and bridle paths. When Serrano was younger—much younger—he could comfortably run the 5.4-mile jogging trail around the Glen in under thirty-five minutes. Now he was content to walk it while listening to audiobooks and podcasts. The Ashby River itself flowed north one hundred miles into Iowa near Cedar Rapids and cut southwest, ending in northern Missouri.

Tally pulled the car to the side of the riverbank. The water beneath the Albertson Bridge was frozen solid, a thin dusting of snow covering it like icing. Serrano could hear a steady whup whup whup across the river as a harbor patrol boat cut through the ice. Most older patrol boats had been retrofitted with icebreaker technology. The reinforced bow was strong enough to cut through solid ice, but the specially designed hull pushed the broken ice away from the boat so as not to damage the propulsion system. The wind from the propellers swirled the snow around like a wintry cyclone.

Portable Nomad 360 Scene Lights had been set up on both riverbanks. The spotlight from atop the patrol boat shone a white circle that illuminated an area underneath the bridge. Serrano could see two forensic techs taking photographs and samples. Between them was a seven-foot-long, three-foot-wide yellow tent staked into the ice. The tent was there to prevent the elements from doing more damage to the body underneath.

Serrano and Tally each put on a pair of Caterpillar Drover Ice+ boots and exited the car. Serrano heard the whup whup from the icebreaker slow and then come to a full stop. A strong wind bit into his face. The patrol boat needed to chop through the ice to get close enough for its lights to illuminate the scene. But get too close, and it risked fracturing the ice to the point where the crime scene itself might not only be disrupted—but disappear beneath the surface.

"Careful," Serrano said, as he and Tally gingerly stepped onto the frozen river. Forensics had determined that the ice on the eastern shore of the Ashby River was five to seven inches thick. It would support the weight of the detectives, and possibly even a light vehicle such as a snowmobile. They were still trying to figure out how to remove the body without jeopardizing the lives of the crime scene technicians or destabilizing the ice shelf to the point where the body itself could slip under. Airlifting the body off the river via helicopter could cause them to lose potentially valuable trace evidence, making it out of the question.

Serrano wiped the frost from his face and blew his nose into a tissue. He heard a crack, his heart lurched into his throat, and Serrano stopped in his tracks.

"It's from the boat, you big ninny," Tally said.

"I fell into a frozen pond in Woodbarren Glen as a kid," Serrano said. "Would have died if a couple guys ice fishing hadn't seen me go under. Rather not go through that again."

The scene in front of them was a beautiful nightmare, a three-quarter moon hanging over the leafless trees of Woodbarren Glen and glowing off the iced-over Ashby River, the illumination from the boat and police spotlights bathing it all in a sheet of harsh yellow. Two forensic technicians wearing heavy coats with *Ashby PD* in yellow lettering stitched on the back worked the scene about two hundred yards out from the eastern riverbank. Isaac Montrose, one of the techs, saw Serrano and Tally approaching and slowly crossed the ice to meet them. Serrano greeted him with a handshake.

Montrose nodded at Tally. He was big and burly—six four and on the other side of two fifty—with a shaved head hidden under a thick wool cap and a long bushy goatee that made him look like a member of a biker gang rather than a forensic investigator. Montrose had been hired away from the Peoria PD the year before, where he'd been working as a blood-splatter analyst. He wore extra large latex gloves that fit over his insulated mittens. Montrose was the size of a small rhino, but Serrano had witnessed him working crime scenes. The man's hands had the finesse of a violinist. He could catch a wasp in midair with a pair of tweezers.

"So Detective Tally, you haven't killed Serrano yet?" Montrose said. "You two might just work out."

"The X factor being *yet*," Tally said. "I'm still learning how to say, 'Shut the hell up and let me drive in peace' in Orc."

Montrose laughed. "He tried to push some of those spells and dragons books on me last year. Gave them to my son. Now he's hooked. He was never much of a reader. Guess I should say thanks?"

"You're welcome," Serrano said. "So what are we looking at?"

Montrose led them over to the body.

"Caucasian female. Forty-two to forty-eight years old. No identification. She'd been out in the elements for several hours before the

911 call came in. A couple of teenagers were hanging on the pedestrian walkway on the Albertson Bridge, seeing if their spit froze before it hit the ground. They hocked a loogie and saw the body. She might have been here until morning otherwise. Fingerprints are going to take some time."

"How come?" Tally said.

"The blood vessels are thinner in your extremities," Montrose said. "Fingers, toes. The cold may have expanded her capillaries significantly, which would distort her skin shape and texture. We'll have to wait for the liquids to thaw to get accurate prints. But we'll need to get her back to the lab quick because her organs have already begun to freeze. Human plasma is made up of fifty percent water. So when the blood freezes, it expands, and it can start to destroy surrounding tissue. And that's when my job gets *really* hard."

"Do we have a preliminary cause of death?" Serrano said.

"Hard to tell out here," Montrose said. He pointed up at the Albertson Bridge, then whistled and mimicked his finger falling, making a splat sound when it hit his palm. "She did a header off the pedestrian walkway. That's almost a hundred and fifty feet up. It . . . doesn't look good. Fall from that height, exact cause will depend on how and at what angle she landed, which we won't know until we get her to the lab and examine the body without worrying about losing her beneath the ice. Could be blunt-force trauma if her head hit first. If she landed flying squirrel style, arms and legs spread, she could have shattered every rib in her chest and impaled her heart and lungs with the bone fragments."

"Christ," Tally said, shaking her head.

"ME is on the way. They'll take her down to Hector Moreno at the morgue once we're done," Montrose said. "But I'm not sure how we're going to move the body yet without destabilizing the ice around her."

"I'll call Lieutenant George," Tally said. "He might have a suggestion."

Serrano said, "Let's have a look."

"I'll stay here," Montrose said. "The ice surrounding the body is thick enough to bear the weight of two more people. But three or four, we risk losing the body and maybe one of you too. And I'd prefer not to become a two-hundred-and-sixty-pound ice pop."

Serrano thanked Montrose, and he and Tally headed for the tent covering the body. Another forensic tech, a guy Serrano didn't recognize, was hunched beside the tent. When he saw the detectives, he stood up and greeted them.

"Ryan Beene," he said. Beene was young—Serrano guessed twenty-nine; he was five ten with hollow cheeks and dark circles under his eyes. He stripped off a pair of latex gloves and shook Serrano and Tally's hands. He sniffled nonstop and was working hard to stop his teeth from chattering.

"Not from around here," Tally said, "are you?"

Beene laughed, then turned to the side and sneezed into his elbow. "Reno," he said. "We don't get winters like this."

"Welcome to Ashby," Serrano said. "Get your flu shots, make sure you always have tissues on hand, and next time you're documenting a crime scene on a frozen river, wear thermal underwear."

"See, that's useful information they left *out* of the department handbook," Beene said. He gently undid the tent flap and lifted one side. "Well, here she is."

The woman's body came into view. Serrano felt a shiver run up the length of his spine, and not from the cold.

She was lying stomach down on the frozen surface of the Ashby River, her face still partially submerged.

Serrano studied the mangled body splayed out before him. Her right arm and leg were both bent at horribly unnatural angles, which led Serrano to think she had landed face-first with her body tilted slightly toward the right.

Six inches in front of her head was a rough oval-shaped gash in the ice. A smear of blood had frozen at the edge. It sparkled like red lipstick in the spotlights.

"We think she landed cranium first," Beene said. "Her head drove through the ice, but the rest of her body stayed above the surface. Like a macabre bobbing for apples. Her head was submerged for at least an hour before the 911 call came in."

Serrano examined the hole in the ice by the woman's head and the blood at the edge. "You pulled her out?"

"Just removed the top of her head from the water," Beene said. "If all the liquids in her face froze—blood, mucus, eyes, brain—it could make getting accurate tox and tissue readings like trying to put a cow back together out of hamburger patties."

"Have some respect," Tally said. "This is a woman you're talking about."

Beene nodded in apology. "I'm sorry, Detective."

"Did you photograph her body, her positioning, before you took her out?" Serrano asked. He already knew the response.

"No," Beene said.

"Goddamn it."

Beene turned white. "Don't tell Montrose," he pleaded. "I've only been here a month."

*So I get the newbie,* Serrano thought. If this was a suicide, like Lieutenant George suspected, it likely wouldn't matter. At this point, Montrose and Beene would have catalogued everything they needed: hair, fiber, blood. There was nothing left to worry about disturbing.

Serrano knelt down next to the woman and felt her fingers and joints. Her body was stiff to the touch, a combination of rigor mortis and the liquid in her body freezing.

"Her blood and organs are starting to solidify," Beene said. Serrano nodded. It was like touching a block of ice zipped into a down jacket.

"We need to get her out of here," Serrano said. "The longer she stays, the longer the body takes to thaw, and the less accurate the tox screen will be."

Serrano went to turn the body over to see her face but noticed the fur-trim lining on her jacket had frozen to the ice. He took a TAC Force folding blade from his boot and began to saw away at the lining. The TAC Force had come in handy on numerous occasions and could punch out the window of a car if need be. But this was the first time Serrano could recall using it to detach faux fur stuck to the surface of a frozen river.

Once the lining was separated, Serrano leaned down and gently rolled the woman onto her back. Her face was a ghostly white. The damage to her head was tremendous. The front of the woman's skull was flattened from the top of the frontal bone above her eyelids to her mandible. Her nose had been crushed, jawbone dislocated.

Still, despite the damage, Serrano recognized her immediately.

"Holy hell," Serrano said. "It's Constance Wright."

"No way." Tally came closer. She sighed when she saw the woman's face. "Shit."

"You know her?" Beene said.

"Yes, we know her," Tally said. "She was the mayor of Ashby not too long ago. A damn good one until she got railroaded. I voted for her. Twice."

"What happened?" Beene said.

"Let's just say that some people fall from grace," Serrano replied. "Constance Wright plummeted into the Grand Canyon."

Tally looked at Serrano. "John?"

He turned away. "Look, I'm sorry she's dead."

"Detective Serrano and Mayor Wright had a bit of a history," Tally said to Beene.

"She did what she had to do," Serrano said. "I've moved on." His voice made it clear he had not.

"Yeah. Moved on like a tree," Tally said. "What happened between you and Mayor Wright wasn't personal, John."

"It was a long time ago," Serrano said. "I don't hold grudges."

"I know it's barely five degrees out, but your pants are on fire."

They heard the sound of tires squealing along the riverbank. Three television vans rolled up, skidded on the icy slope, and nearly rammed into each other while jockeying for position. Serrano cursed under his breath. Tally cursed over hers.

It was common for TV crews to arrive at potential crime scenes almost simultaneously with law enforcement. Deep-pocketed media producers offered cops cash for tips. And on a cop's salary, taking into account alimony and child support and the occasional gambling debt, an extra grand to buy Christmas presents could be too good to pass up.

Still, they had to keep Wright's identity confidential until a proper ID was made and any next of kin notified.

"I don't see a purse or pocketbook," Tally said. "Did you and Montrose find one at the scene?"

"Nope. What you see is what we found."

"It could have slipped into the water after she landed," Tally said.

Serrano shook his head. "Impact crater is the size of the victim's head. No other scrape marks around. And no footprints around the body other than ours," Serrano replied. "So doubtful we have a grave robber. It's also not uncommon for suicide victims to lack identification or money. Where they're planning on going, they figure they don't need to bring credit cards or house keys."

Tally knelt down and slid her hand into Wright's coat pockets. "Empty."

Serrano waved Montrose over. "I want a full tox workup. BAC and screens for prescription and illegal drugs."

Serrano watched the TV vans with contempt. Camera operators were already setting up for live shots. The reporters themselves were hidden, waiting by the heat vents until it was time for their close-up.

"ME is ten minutes out," Montrose said. "How do you want to handle this?"

"Ice is too thin for the wagon," Serrano said. He pointed at the patrol boat. "And if the boat comes any closer, this whole sheet could crack."

"Snowmobile," Tally said.

Serrano nodded. "Good call."

Tally continued. "Have them attach a litter basket stretcher to the back of a snowmobile. The basket will prevent her body from dragging along the ice. We need to get her out of here, without any further damage to the body."

"I'll call it in," Montrose said.

"What about them?" Tally asked, motioning over to the news vans. Serrano sighed. He didn't especially enjoy live shots, especially in this kind of weather, when there was a decent chance of a high-definition booger making it into viewers' living rooms. A small crowd of onlookers had begun to gather on the bank of the river. At this time of night, they were mainly rubberneckers, drunks, and vagrants.

"Call dispatch," Serrano said. "Tell them we may need crowd control. And with the media already here, Lieutenant George will want me to make a brief statement. *Nobody* gives Wright's identity to the press."

Tally nodded. "You know, if you asked me a few years ago, I would have said Constance Wright had a shot at the White House."

"Me too," Serrano said.

"Even after what she did to you?" Tally said, surprised.

"Even after that."

Tally offered a weak smile. "Go get 'em, Tiger."

Serrano trudged off to the bank of the Ashby River, where he planned to tell the assembled media crews absolutely nothing of substance. Still, one question gnawed at him. It had been two years since Constance Wright's life had gone up in flames. The woman had endured indignity, malice, mockery, and cruelty on an unfathomable level. But she'd kept on living. Two years, and nothing.

So why would she suddenly decide to end it all now?

# CHAPTER 4

Eric finished his breakfast in silence and left the table without so much as a thank-you. Megan, thrilled to have her mother's sole attention, gushed about the new book she was writing.

"It's a mystery *and* an adventure story," she said. "Like Wonder Woman meets Dora the Explorer."

"I would totally read that book," Rachel said, completely serious.

"It's going to be a whole series. My character's name is Sadie Scout. She's superstrong and has a pet tiger."

"Of course she does," Rachel said. "And what's her pet tiger's name?"

"Roxy."

"A pet tiger named Roxy. And where does Roxy sleep?"

"In the bed with Sadie, of course," Megan said, annoyed that her mother even had to ask such a silly question.

"I should have assumed the tiger slept in bed with Sadie. So when do I get to read the first Sadie Scout story?"

"When I'm *done,*" Megan said, slipping off her chair. "And not a minute before."

"Well, I'll be waiting."

Eric came downstairs, slinging his backpack over his shoulder.

"Have a good day!" Rachel shouted. Eric said nothing, merely nodded and put on his headphones. Then he was gone. Minutes later the school bus pulled up. Rachel knelt down so Megan could wrap her little arms around her, planting a kiss on her daughter before she sped out the door. Rachel watched as she climbed aboard and took a seat next to her best friend, Simone Watson.

*When did my peanut become a kid?* At least she'd outgrown her previous favorite toy, something called a "Blingle," a kit that allowed children to design their own glittery, sparkly stickers, which could then be affixed anywhere within reach. Rachel was convinced Blingles must have been invented by a pure sociopath, given that they essentially gave your child the ability to make your home look like a low-rent strip club. It wasn't long ago that Rachel had opened the toilet seat lid to find a bedazzled unicorn staring back at her.

When both kids were gone, Rachel planted herself at the kitchen counter; made an egg white, spinach, and feta frittata; brewed a pot of french press coffee; took a stool at the counter; and streamed the news from her laptop while she ate.

She tuned in to Channel 8. The weatherman, sporting a tan that no December sun could have possibly bestowed on him, informed viewers that temperatures would top out this week at fifteen degrees, with a windchill factor around zero. Rachel grimaced as she sipped her coffee.

They cut back to the local anchors: a fiftysomething man with a wavy blond comb-over and chin sharp enough to cut glass and a smiley young brunette whose early-morning perkiness had to either be espresso or meth related.

"Now to follow up with our top story, breaking news from late last night," the man said. "A body was found at the base of the Albertson Bridge in the early hours of the morning. Ashby PD was on the scene, as was our own Charles Willemore."

Rachel put her coffee down and leaned in closer. The stream on her computer was choppy. She hoped it wouldn't cut out.

The feed cut to a recorded shot from early that morning. The chyron read 2:00 a.m. The shot had been filmed from the eastern bank of the Ashby River. In the background, Rachel could see four cops with Ashby PD jackets examining an illuminated area at the base of the bridge. The scene had a radius of about thirty feet. The body itself was blocked off by a yellow tent. The camera showed a dozen or so pedestrians gathered at the edge of the frozen river, watching the grim scene. The feed then cut to a taped report.

"Charles Willemore for Channel 8, here at the Albertson Bridge, just across from Woodbarren Glen. Ashby law enforcement responded to a 911 call just after 1:00 a.m. for what at first glance appears to be a suicide at the iconic structure. As you can see, the scene behind me is quite unusual, in that the investigation is taking place *atop* the frozen Ashby River, necessitating extra caution by police investigators."

Video showed a patrol boat cutting through the ice. A spotlight from the boat lit the crime scene with a harsh glow. The Channel 8 camera zoomed in to show a fortyish white male detective and a younger black female detective kneeling beside the tent covering the body.

Willemore added, "We were able to speak with one of the officers on scene."

The camera cut to a man identified by the chyron as Detective John Serrano of the Ashby PD. Serrano looked to be between forty-two and forty-four, with dark-brown hair and light-gray sideburns peeking out from under a wool trapper hat. He had green eyes the color of pine needles and a several-days-old beard with graying whiskers. He looked tired and annoyed.

"Detective, can you tell us whether you've identified the deceased?" Willemore asked.

"As of right now we're still performing preliminary forensics and have not made an official identification," Serrano said. "Once we do, we will notify next of kin prior to releasing any statements regarding the identity of the victim."

"You refer to the deceased as a 'victim.' Does that mean you believe this might have been something other than suicide?"

"People who take their own life are referred to as victims. Based on our initial findings we're not ready to make an official statement as to the cause of death."

"The Albertson Bridge has an unfortunate reputation for attracting those who wish to take their own life," Willemore added. "Is it possible this woman leapt to her death?"

As soon as Willemore said the word *woman*, Serrano's eyes widened in surprise.

*Willemore wasn't supposed to know it was a woman,* Rachel thought. *Somebody leaked that information to the media. Another cop, no doubt.*

"It is possible. We're not ruling anything out. Now, you'll need to wait for an official statement, which will come once we've completed our preliminary analysis."

Serrano left the interview. The camera followed him. Rachel could see that one of his fists was clenched.

The camera cut back to the tent. The female detective moved to the side. In that moment, Rachel saw the victim's hand. On her left index finger was a silver ring with a large topaz gemstone.

Rachel had seen that ring before. She remembered what the woman had said.

*This one is for family.*

It didn't make sense. She wouldn't have killed herself. Not now. Not after everything she'd been through.

*When you survive the fire, you don't let the winter kill you.*

Rachel rewound the livestream and took several screen grabs of the scene before pressing play.

"There you have it," Willemore continued. "Sad news in Ashby today as a woman seemingly took her own life in the early hours of this wintry day at one of our city's most beloved monuments. Back to you in the studio."

The female anchor said, "Our prayers are with her friends and family, whoever they may be. We here at Channel 8 know the holidays can be a difficult time, so please, use these resources. Help is waiting."

Several phone numbers appeared on the screen below the news desk: the National Suicide Prevention Hotline, Gamblers Anonymous, and RAINN.

"Now on to sports," the male anchor said, and they cut to a basketball game as if they hadn't been reporting on the gruesome end of someone's life just seconds prior.

Rachel sent the screen grabs to her email and opened the photos. Studied them. Made some mental notes. Opened the Calculator app on her phone. Within seconds, she knew that Constance Wright had been murdered.

◆◆◆

Rachel got into her car and checked the time. An hour before she needed to be at work. She'd be cutting it close. But it needed to be done. She didn't trust cops. And somebody inside the Ashby PD had clearly tipped off the media to the crime scene. But Serrano had seemed surprised, and the reaction felt genuine. Maybe he was on the up-and-up. But she needed to know for sure.

Rachel took a left down Merrybrook Lane and headed downtown. Southern Ashby consisted primarily of businesses and municipal buildings, all old brick and new steel. Despite the cold, the sun was bright in the sky, the glare off the snow blinding. Rachel slipped on her sunglasses.

She turned onto Isenberg Boulevard and headed west. Traffic toward the Albertson Bridge was a nightmare. Even though the bridge had reopened, the crime scene would still be taped off with rubberneckers backing up traffic for miles. But Rachel wasn't heading toward the bridge. She already knew everything she needed to.

She took a right on Branch Avenue, drove several miles south past the Westerby Mall, then took I-74 South toward Peoria. She drove twelve miles, then pulled off at a strip mall. She parked next to a silver Buick and got out of the car.

She approached a filthy pay phone nestled between a Chinese take-out restaurant and a check-cashing joint. A group of teens loitered outside, performing skateboard tricks. One of the kids filmed the stunts with his cell phone.

Rachel took a packet of disinfectant towelettes from her pocketbook and wiped down the phone and handset. She opened an app on her cell and tested it several times for clarity, pitch, and tone. Then she put on her gloves and dialed 911. Time to see if the Ashby Police Department was worth a damn.

When the dispatcher picked up, Rachel said, "This message is for Detective Serrano of the Ashby PD. It's regarding the body found at the Albertson Bridge last night. He needs to know this was not a suicide."

# CHAPTER 5

"Detectives Serrano and Tally, thanks for coming down. It's good to have some company. It's usually dead in here."

Hector Moreno smiled and waited for a laugh. Serrano and Tally simultaneously rolled their eyes.

"Good to see you too, Hector," Serrano said. "Thankfully for the Ashby PD your comedy career isn't in any danger of taking off."

Hector Moreno had been the chief medical examiner of Ashby County for sixteen years. He was a good-looking Hispanic man of about fifty, with warm brown eyes, sharp cheekbones, and a neat salt-and-pepper goatee. He wore a bolo tie with a silver cow skull inset with a turquoise stone over his scrubs.

"The less you see of us, the better," Tally said. "Means people aren't getting dead in suspicious ways. How are Camila and the kids?"

"Camila is wonderful. Just wonderful," Moreno said. "Two of her paintings are going on display at an art gallery in New York City. Can you believe that? She's flying out there in a few weeks for the grand opening. She could be the next Rembrandt for all I know."

"Good for her," Serrano said. "But it begs the question as to why she married you."

"I know, right? Ten years ago she tells me she wants to try painting, buys some acrylics and canvas, turns the garage into a rainbow-colored mess, and now she gets weekly calls from some guy who calls himself Gulliver and speaks with a British accent even though he's from Sheboygan. I looked him up. It's only a matter of time before she leaves me to shack up with some cornrowed bohemian poet she meets at a hookah bar in the East Village."

"Even so, I give her six months with the poet before she realizes how good she has it with you," Tally said. "Never date a writer. I made that mistake once."

Moreno laughed. "I'd pay to see the reaction she gets when all those hoity-toity artists ask what her spouse does for a living. 'My husband? Yeah, he spends his days covered in guts.' Hey, Serrano, you still reading those books about witches and magic beans? Learn any spells that can bring Mayor Wright here back from the dead? I'm not kidding. What happened to her a few years back was a travesty."

"I agree," Tally said.

Serrano remained silent.

Tally said, "So what have you got for us?"

Moreno snapped his fingers and beckoned for the detectives to follow him. He brought them into a well-lit gray chamber lined by sterile metal shelving containing forensic tools: scalpels, retractors, bone saws, rib spreader, enterotome, forceps, Hagedorn needles, and more. On a table in the center of the room was a body covered by a four-by-ten-foot white sheet. Serrano noticed a toe poking out from underneath the sheet. The nail was painted cherry red.

"Look there," Serrano said, pointing to the toe. Tally came over to inspect.

"Coat of polish looks fresh," Tally said. "She got a pedicure within the last week or two." Tally lifted the sheet higher and felt underneath. "And she shaved her legs recently."

"Means she was still grooming as of this week. Not exactly the behavior of someone getting ready to end it," Serrano added.

"Let's contact local nail salons, see if we can find the one Wright frequented," Tally said. She turned to Hector. "You ready?"

Moreno nodded. "Just to warn you, it isn't pretty."

"Death never is," Serrano replied.

"No, it is not. This woman deserved better." Moreno slowly peeled off the sheet to reveal the body of Constance Wright. Tally took a sharp breath but said nothing.

Serrano studied the woman laid out before them. Constance Wright's body was shattered. That was the first thought that came to his mind. She looked like a rag doll tossed haphazardly on the floor by a careless child, its limbs bent at horribly unnatural angles.

"Ice is an unforgiving bastard," Moreno said. "I'll walk you through it."

"Go ahead, Hector," Serrano said.

"The cause of death was blunt-force trauma to the head," Moreno said, slipping on latex gloves. Wright's entire face was caved in, from forehead to jaw, the bones dislocated. "Fortunately, she died immediately on impact. No pain."

"Thank goodness for small favors," Tally said.

Moreno nodded. "All twenty-four of her ribs are broken. Four pierced her heart and seven her lungs. Both her liver and spleen were punctured as well. Even if the head trauma hadn't killed her, those injuries would have almost instantaneously."

He moved on to her mangled limbs.

"Compound fractures of the left radius and right ulna, as well as both tibia and fibula in both legs. Her pelvis is basically dust."

"Toxicology?" Serrano said.

"Blood alcohol level of .43. No traces of any other narcotics in her system."

"BAC of .43? That's inordinately high," Tally said. "She must have really tied one on last night. Think she was numbing herself for the plunge?"

"Maybe. But there's one more thing." Moreno paused. "She was pregnant."

Serrano's jaw dropped.

"How far along?" Tally said.

"Her HCG levels suggest she was about nine weeks."

"Meaning she more than likely knew she was pregnant," Serrano said. "We'll check her apartment for pregnancy tests, prenatal vitamins, anything that could let us know her frame of mind."

Tally moved closer to Wright's body, put out her hand, let it hover over the woman's abdomen. She clenched her fist. Serrano put his hand over hers, gently brought it down to her side.

"I know," Serrano said. "I know."

Tally took a long breath. "Sorry. Just . . . the waste of life."

Serrano said, "Can we determine the identity of the father from the fetal tissue?"

Moreno shook his head. "At nine weeks the fetus only weighs about a tenth of an ounce. There's very little tissue to speak of. And a DNA test can't determine paternity unless you also have a sample from the partner to compare it to. The fetal tissue alone won't reveal paternity."

"It's also possible she did it on her own with a sperm donor," Serrano said.

"But why would she go through all that trouble to conceive and then jump off a bridge two months later?" Tally replied. Serrano didn't have an answer.

"First things first," Serrano finally said. "Both of Wright's parents are deceased. No children. No other living relatives. We'll need to bring in her ex-husband, Nicholas Drummond, to make the ID."

"Those were some ugly divorce proceedings, if I'm remembering correctly," Moreno said. "Drummond is not going to be happy to be dragged into this."

"Ugly doesn't begin to describe it," Serrano said. "I also want to check his DNA against the fetus."

"He can refuse to comply without a court order," Tally said.

"If he refuses, that answers our question."

"You think Constance Wright might have had one last roll in the hay with her ex and gotten knocked up?" Moreno said.

"It's not uncommon," Serrano said. "Drummond remarried soon after the divorce from Constance was finalized. Exes rekindle the spark, have an affair, get pregnant, and the husband tries to hide it from his new wife."

"That's why I made sure to hold on to some A-plus blackmail material in case Claire ever leaves me," Tally said. "We'd settle in arbitration in five minutes flat."

"Smart," Moreno said. "And cold blooded. Not sure cold blooded makes for a healthy marriage, but hey, I'm not judging."

"So, your initial thoughts?" Serrano asked.

Moreno replied, "Well, at this point, given the abnormally high blood alcohol content and the victim's messy personal life, it would be hard not to chalk this up as a suicide. If the pregnancy was unwanted, that may have been the last straw."

"Let's be thorough," Tally said. "The toenails bother me. And I want to talk to Nicholas Drummond."

"Nicholas Drummond walked away from that marriage with a heap of Constance Wright's money," Serrano said. "The man already got paid. Why kill her *now*?"

"The pregnancy . . . that gnaws at me," replied Tally. "Presumably Wright knew. But we'd have to get a court order to see her emails and texts. If Wright was already walking the razor's edge, and she *didn't* want the child, that could have been enough to push her over. Or perhaps she did want it, Drummond didn't, and that's your motive."

"If it was even Drummond," Serrano said.

"If it was even Drummond. Still, it shouldn't have come to this," Tally said. "Never cared much for that wackadoo family of Wright's—or for Nicholas Drummond himself. Always seemed like the kind of guy who hated being overshadowed by his wife. But damn, this woman had a good heart. She didn't deserve what all those people did to her."

Serrano nodded absently. Then the cell phone clipped to his waist began to ring.

"Don't tell me," Moreno said, rolling his eyes. "That's the theme from . . ."

"Lord of the Rings," Serrano replied. "One ringtone to rule them all."

"See? This is what I deal with on a daily basis," said Tally.

Serrano ignored them. He answered his cell and said, "This is Serrano."

"Detective Serrano, this is Wanda Bremmer from Ashby 911 dispatch. I have something you need to hear."

"Detectives don't respond to 911 calls," Serrano said brusquely. She must have been new.

"I understand that. But trust me, you need to listen to this," she said. "I'm patching you through. This person called 911 twenty-six minutes ago. I wouldn't normally forward along a 911 call, but . . . you need to hear it, Detective."

"All right," Serrano said, exasperated. "I'm listening."

Serrano heard a crackling sound as a recording began to play. Then a voice began speaking. It was a distorted male voice. Deep, husky, and robotic. The caller had clearly used some sort of voice modification tool.

"This message is for Detective Serrano of the Ashby PD. It's regarding the body found at the Albertson Bridge last night. He needs to know this was not a suicide. I know the victim's identity has not been released to the press, but it was Constance Wright. Constance Wright was murdered. And I can prove it. Keep listening and I'll explain. Please forward this entire recording to Detective Serrano."

Serrano listened to the rest of the message, his eyes growing wider with each word spoken. When the recording was over, Wanda Bremmer came back on the line.

"Detective? Still there?"

"Still here." Serrano's hands were trembling.

"You all right, John?" Tally said.

"Do you have a digital file of this call you can forward to my cell?" Serrano asked Bremmer. "Send it to this number."

He gave Bremmer his cell number. "Sending now," she said.

When Serrano received the file, he turned to Hector Moreno.

"You both need to hear this. Hector, I need to know if what this caller says is accurate from a medical standpoint."

Serrano pressed play and put the phone on speaker. The three of them listened in silence. Finally, Moreno said, "I'll need to confirm the calculations, but if they hold up, the caller is right. There's no way Constance Wright could have committed suicide."

# CHAPTER 6

"My ex-wife is a raging bitch."

*So that's how this evening is going to go,* Rachel thought.

The man sitting across the table from her was named Adam . . . something. She didn't remember his last name. Had he even given it to her? A coworker had asked if he could set Rachel up with a buddy, and against her better judgment she'd agreed. And so far the evening had been only slightly less painful than a root canal without anesthesia.

Adam was in his late forties, divorced, with three kids in high school and an ex who lived across the city in the Edgartown district with her new husband. His hair plugs were poorly done, resembling doll hair more than human, and the bloodshot eyes and the spider veins crossing his nose indicated a serious drinking problem. His lower lip seemed to be perpetually curled downward in an irritated manner, as though he'd just tasted unexpectedly cold soup.

Her coworker would need to atone for this setup sin.

For months, Rachel's friends had been pressuring her to "get back out there," as though she were a ballplayer nursing an injury. Yes, she was lonely. Eric and Megan were her life, but she'd be lying if she said there weren't nights she missed having a warm body to curl up next to, someone to watch movies with, to talk to about issues not related to state capitals and bedazzled toilet unicorns. Someone to touch her in a way that she missed desperately.

But seven words in, and Adam had already proven he wasn't going to be that guy.

So what now? They hadn't even ordered food yet. Rachel had booked the babysitter for another two hours. If she walked through her front door an hour and a half early from a date, she'd feel like the saddest person alive.

She'd grin and bear it, she decided. Not because there was a chance Adam might salvage the date but because the restaurant had a fantastic wine list and the best rack of lamb in Ashby, and damned if she was going to deprive herself of a good meal. She could tune him out and just enjoy dinner.

"Did you hear what I said?" Adam asked.

"Mm-hmm," Rachel responded. "This wine is delicious."

"You have great taste in wine. And you must have great taste in men, considering you're out with me." Rachel took a large gulp of her Bordeaux and offered a fake smile.

"Do you have any plans after this?" Adam said. He was beginning to slur his words. He must have pregamed before the date.

"Plans? Well, let's see, I have two children at home, a teenage babysitter, and three baskets of laundry that won't do themselves. So, no. Clubbing is not on my itinerary for the evening."

"But let's say you got home a little late. Your sitter wouldn't mind, right? You could throw her an extra few bucks."

"Define a little late."

"Say . . . tomorrow morning late?"

Adam snorted and laughed. Then he reached across the table and put his hand on hers. She immediately computed the force needed to pierce his metacarpal bone with her dinner fork.

Instead, she removed her hand from the table and placed it on her thigh. Adam snickered, as though laughing at her reaction.

"You know," she said, "I'm having second thoughts. I think I might go—"

"Rachel Marin?"

Rachel looked up. A tall man with dark-brown hair graying at the temples and a very serious look on his face was standing beside their table. She recognized him immediately. A black woman, about five six with braided hair and a look on her face that said *You think* he's *serious, don't get me started* stood next to him.

They both held Ashby PD badges.

"That would be me," she replied. "Or, she would be I? Can I help you?"

Adam looked at the cops and then at Rachel and then back again.

"Listen, Officers," Adam said, "I'm up on my child support this month. Ask Lisette, not that the bitch would ever admit she uses my money to pay off her asshole new husband's mortgage."

The cops ignored him.

"Ms. Marin, I'm Detective Serrano with the Ashby Police Department. This is my partner, Detective Tally. We'd like a few words with you."

"Can I ask what this is regarding?"

Tally said, "I don't think you want to have that conversation here."

"I'm sorry, did I miss something?" Adam said. *I'm betting you ask that a lot,* Rachel thought.

"Apologies, sir," Serrano said, "but we need to speak with Ms. Marin. Alone."

"You still haven't answered my question," Rachel said.

Adam was scowling at Serrano, peeved that his surefire score had been interrupted. Serrano scowled back. The detective's scowl was better. Adam looked down and stared at his shoes. That made her happy.

Serrano turned back to Rachel.

"We need to ask you about a strip mall outside of Peoria off of I-74."

Rachel's heart began to speed up. *That was quicker than I expected.*

"Listen, Magnum, P.I.," Adam said. "We're in the middle of dinner. You can't just walk in here and—"

Before he could finish his sentence, Rachel was out of her chair. She tossed a twenty-dollar bill on the table.

"For the wine," she said.

"Are you kidding me?" he said. "I paid for a hotel room!"

"And I paid for a babysitter," she replied. "Looks like neither of us got our money's worth."

When they stepped outside, Rachel said, "All right, Detectives. I get to ask the first question. How in the hell did you find me so fast?"

# CHAPTER 7

Rachel, Serrano, and Tally sat in a corner booth at the Starburst Diner off Wedgewood Lane. A cup of dark-roast coffee sat in front of Rachel, untouched. Tally was nibbling on an order of fries, and Serrano had already finished a bagel with scallion cream cheese.

"You realize you just ate breakfast," Rachel said, nodding at Serrano's plate. "That was breakfast food. It's 8:00 p.m. When do you eat dessert, seven in the morning?"

Serrano ignored the comment. He took out his cell phone and placed it on the table between them. He opened to a file marked "911 call—Albertson," put the phone on speaker, and pressed play. A robotic voice began talking.

*"This message is for Detective Serrano of the Ashby PD. It's regarding the body found at the Albertson Bridge last night. He needs to know this was not a suicide. I know the victim's identity has not been released to the press, but it was Constance Wright. Constance Wright was murdered. And I can prove it. Keep listening and I'll explain. Please forward this entire recording to Detective Serrano.*

*"Based on where Constance Wright's body was found at the base of the Albertson Bridge, it is a mathematical impossibility that her death was self-inflicted.*

*"The pedestrian walkway on the Albertson Bridge is 152 feet from the water based on current sea levels—or in this case, the iced-over river. From that height, in a free fall from the walkway, a body would reach the ground in somewhere between 5.5 and 5.6 seconds, increasing in velocity as it*

*descended and then hitting the surface of the ice at a speed of approximately 122.8 miles per hour.*

*"At the approximate time of death, which I cannot know with absolute certainty without a thorough medical examination, the wind was coming from the northeast at around 11 miles per hour. Not insignificant.*

*"Per video and photographs from the crime scene, Wright's body was found 18 feet from the bridge. If the height of the bridge is the y-axis and the distance of the body from the bridge the x-axis, then the total distance the body traveled was just over 153 feet.*

*"Given that the body was found on the western side of the bridge, 18 feet from the base of the bridge, and the wind was blowing northeast to southwest at 11 miles per hour, it is a mathematical impossibility that the body landed in its final resting spot of its own accord. To do so, the victim would have had to take a literal running start prior to jumping. The pedestrian walkway on the Albertson Bridge is uniformly 3 feet across, not nearly enough space to get any sort of momentum, which would be needed to reach a distance of 18 feet from the base and leaping into 11-mile-per-hour wind.*

*"There is only one way a body from that height could have reached that distance on the x-axis in that wind: momentum. And the only way that momentum could have been achieved is by force.*

*"In short, Constance Wright was thrown from the walkway on the Albertson Bridge. I am confident that your medical examiners will come to the same conclusion.*

*"Godspeed, Detective."*

The call ended. Serrano put the phone back in his pocket. Rachel sat there. Then she took a sip of coffee. Then another.

"Siri definitely doesn't do that on my phone," Rachel said.

"That's you on the tape, isn't it, Ms. Marin?" Serrano replied.

"I've been told I have a deep voice, but still—"

"Ms. Marin."

Rachel finished her coffee and pushed the mug aside. "Least you can do is buy me a beer. If I get home, and I'm not even slightly tipsy, my sitter will think the date was a bust. Which it was. But I digress. How did you find me?"

"We get to ask the questions," Serrano said. "Why did you say the victim was Constance Wright?"

"Because it is," Rachel replied. "Neither of you have refuted that. And looking at your faces, I know it's true."

"The victim's identity has not been released to the public."

"I'm not 'the public.'"

"Ms. Marin, the victim's family has not yet been notified. If anything was to leak—"

"Don't worry; I'm not saying a word to anyone. I could have called the press, but I called you. As for how I know it's Constance Wright, let's just say it was something of a personal nature."

"All right, Ms. Marin," Tally said, "911 traced the call to a pay phone outside a strip mall near Peoria. Obviously voice recognition was out due to your Mr. Roboto impression. So we took a ride out there."

"There were no usable fingerprints on the phone," Serrano said. "Not surprising. Middle of winter, people wear gloves. But we did find trace residue from a disinfectant cloth, as though someone had wiped the phone down before and after using it. We also found several fibers matted to the disinfectant. Wool, dyed beige. Can I see your gloves, Ms. Marin?"

Rachel didn't move.

"That call came in at 7:42 this morning," Serrano said. "Mr. Chow's restaurant next door to that pay phone was closed. No luck finding any witnesses there. But the Cash Money next door *was* open. The security camera inside the door, unfortunately, only had an obstructed view of the pay phone."

"But we did speak to the owner," Tally continued. "A Mr. Gunther Downs, who told us he shooed away a group of teenagers who were skateboarding outside right around the time the call came in to 911. Mr. Downs told us the kids were recording themselves doing stunts and that the same kids have been there every morning the last few weeks. In fact, they're there so often he knew their names."

Serrano said, "We cross-checked those names with addresses in the vicinity—these kids would be home for winter break, and they're all skateboarding or walking home, not driving—and found the amateur director who'd been videotaping the stunts. Lucky for us, he still had all the videos on his cell phone. Even luckier for us, for two whole seconds, the camera caught somebody using the pay phone. You can't see their face, but he or she is wearing thick beige gloves. The recording also picked up unobstructed views of several cars in the parking lot. We ran all the plates, and only one was registered to a resident of Ashby."

Serrano cocked his finger at Rachel and pulled an imaginary trigger.

"We went to your house," Tally said. "A young woman named Liesl Schilling said you were on a date and told us where we could find you."

"We can also subpoena the GPS tracking on your phone," Serrano said, "and place you at that strip mall at the time the call was made. But I don't think that's necessary. At least not right now."

Rachel offered a faint golf clap. "Solid police work, Detectives. Unfortunately now my sitter definitely knows tonight's date was a bust."

"Our apologies if we ruined your evening with Prince Charming," Tally said.

"More like Prince Charmin," Rachel said. "Get it?"

Neither detective laughed.

"Man, cops are a tough crowd. Anyway, you saved me two hours of my life I would never get back. Now, let's assume for a second that is me on the tape. Why am I here? Calling 911 isn't a crime."

"No, it's not," Serrano said. "And if you don't want to be here, we can bring you right back to Prince Charmin."

"No!" Rachel said, grabbing Serrano's wrist. He glared at her. She removed it. "I just want to help. I know Constance Wright's death wasn't a suicide. I *know* it. Like you know your own face. I'm positive."

"Based on this equation on the tape?" Tally said. "We'll let the medical examiner confirm whether or not you're correct."

"He already did," Rachel said. "Or you wouldn't be here."

Serrano and Tally remained silent.

"Let me ask you one question," Rachel said. "Was Constance wearing heels? Or flats?"

Serrano hesitated, then said, "Heels."

"And I'll bet she was found without her purse as well."

Serrano and Tally exchanged glances.

"Why do you say that?" said Tally.

"A woman leaves home without her purse, presumably planning to off herself. She figures she doesn't need her wallet, keys, or credit cards where she's going. Just her and fate. So if she thinks *that* far in advance—why on earth would she go out wearing heels in eight-inch snow and eleven-mile-an-hour winds? I'm willing to bet she'd also done some personal grooming recently. Shaved her legs. A mani-pedi, perhaps."

"Who *are* you?" Serrano asked.

"Rachel Marin," she responded. "Mother of two. Legal secretary. At your service."

"But how do you know all this? Why does a legal secretary know the velocity of a falling human body? Or that a victim wearing heels might point to homicide?"

"I watch a lot of *Law & Order.* Olivia Benson is my spirit animal."

"Cut the crap," Serrano said. "You could have walked into the station and asked to speak with me. You made us chase you for a reason."

Rachel looked into her coffee mug. "Somebody once told me I would have to make a choice," she said. "I could help people or just live my life. I made the wrong choice once. I swore I wouldn't do that again. Constance Wright was murdered. And her killer wanted us to believe she killed herself. Think about that. They took her life and wanted her buried in shame too. That's beyond cold. That's diabolical. I know about her ex. Her family. The lawsuits. But surely there were people who loved her."

Rachel's head jerked up.

"That," Rachel said, pointing at Serrano. "Your lip just twitched when I said there were people who loved her."

"It did not," Serrano said.

"When I said that people loved her . . . that struck a nerve. Tell me why."

"I think you're forgetting the fact that you're a civilian, Ms. Marin," Serrano said. "You have no legal authority. We have no obligation to answer any of your questions."

Rachel stared at Serrano.

"She was pregnant," Rachel said. "Wasn't she?"

"That's *enough*," Tally said. She stood up from the table. "Ms. Marin, you are not a part of this investigation. But if this ever goes to trial, you might be asked to testify. If your calculations are correct, it may help us prove the manner in which the victim died."

"Not *if* they're correct, Detective," Rachel said. "They're correct."

"And *if* this was a homicide," she continued, "*we'll* be the ones to bring the perpetrator to justice."

Detective Serrano stood up as well. He dropped thirty dollars on the table and said, "Finish your coffee. If you're still thirsty, buy yourself a beer. Apologies again for ruining your date. Thank you for your time, Ms. Marin."

The detectives left the diner. Rachel downed the rest of her coffee, grabbed her purse, and followed them. The parking lot was slick with ice. Rachel had to walk tentatively in her heels.

"Tell me one more thing," Rachel shouted. Serrano and Tally continued toward their brown Crown Victoria.

"Go home, Ms. Marin," Serrano said.

"Was she drunk?" Rachel shouted. She noticed a hitch in Serrano's step as he took out his car keys.

"Why?" Tally said.

"Call it a hunch. And I can tell from your hesitation that she was. What was her blood alcohol level?"

"Ms. Marin," Tally said, "that has not been releas—"

"Point four three," Serrano answered. Tally shot him a look.

"That's crazy high," Rachel said. "At a blood alcohol level of point three, her speech, balance, and coordination would have been severely impaired, and she may have lost consciousness. A woman her size, her motor skills would have been diminished, and her heart rate and breathing would have slowed to dangerous levels. At point four, there's no way she would have been able to even *get* to the bridge, let alone throw herself over it. I would check her teeth if I were you."

"Her teeth?" Tally said.

"See if any of her teeth are sheared, most likely front teeth, her incisors. They would look like an ice cube split by a pick. Any teeth broken from the fall would be pulverized, like a pretzel stomped on by a shoe. What I'm talking about would be a much cleaner cut."

"Why . . . ," Serrano began to say before catching himself.

"Because with a BAC at that level, plus a tooth with that sort of damage, it would indicate that she was force-fed alcohol shortly before her death. They may have even continued pouring it down her throat after she lost consciousness. Somebody wanted to make sure Wright was fully unconscious but didn't want any tranquilizers or drugs in her bloodstream that could raise questions on a tox screen. Plus the abundance of alcohol could bolster the suicide theory. But whoever killed her overdid it. This was deliberate. And it was planned."

The way Serrano looked at Tally, it confirmed to Rachel that they'd found such a chipped tooth during the medical examination.

The detectives got into the car. Rachel jogged up to the passenger side door, where Serrano was seated. She noticed a paperback copy of *The Fellowship of the Ring* on the dashboard. She pointed at it.

"My son loves those books," she said. "He practically speaks Orc."

Serrano offered a smile. It was genuine and wide and threw Rachel off.

"So does mine," he said. Tally looked at Serrano with a hint of confusion. Something passed between them that Rachel picked up on.

Then they drove off.

Her cell phone chirped with an incoming text. She took out her phone, looked at the message. It was from Adam.

Ur forgiven. Lucky 4 u I'll give u another chance, but only b/c ur

And then he added a fire emoji.

Rachel groaned, shoved the phone back in her purse, got in her car, and headed home. She had a sudden urge to hug her kids.

# CHAPTER 8

***Three Years Ago***

The knock at the door made Rachel's head swivel in the direction of the shotgun locked in her bedroom safe. In less than a second, her pulse went from its resting rate of fifty-eight beats per minute to nearly eighty.

She stood in the kitchen, a bag of groceries in her hand, waiting. The person knocked again. Rachel gently placed the bag down and immediately estimated how much time it would take to grab the kids, grab the shotgun, and flee.

She inched around the kitchen wall to get a view of the window overlooking the front door. Her visitor was a woman. She could not see her face, but Rachel's pulse returned to normal. None of *his* followers were women, as far as the FBI knew. Just a local busybody, most likely. A neighbor to welcome them to Ashby with a fruitcake and an invitation to the next PTA meeting.

*Just a visitor,* she told herself. Plus, it was only five o'clock. It was still light outside. This woman was not attempting to hide anything. But just in case, Rachel slipped a pair of scissors into the back pocket of her jeans.

"Mom?" Eric was in his room. His voice was nervous, scared. Rachel could count the number of people who'd knocked on their door since they'd arrived in Ashby on one hand. Maybe even one finger.

"It's all right, hon," she said, her voice calm and even. More for him than her. "I got it."

Rachel peered around the edge of the curtain and saw a woman standing alone on the front step. She was in her late thirties, trim, brown hair tied in a neat bun, her cheeks with a slight rouge tint. She wore a gray blazer over a white blouse with a black skirt. A classy string of pearls was looped around her neck, and her diamond earrings were small yet elegant. Her posture was impeccable, the look on her face patient and pleasant. Rachel figured she was either a Jehovah's Witness or selling Amway.

Rachel took a breath, placed her left hand on the handle of the scissors, and opened the door with her right. The woman's smile grew wider.

"Ms. Marin," she said, holding out her hand. "It's a pleasure to meet you. My name is Constance Wright. I'm the mayor of Ashby." She held out a bottle of wine wrapped in yellow paper. "Chardonnay from my father's vineyard."

Rachel took the wine and closed her jaw. She knew nothing about the woman's politics, policies, or background. In fact, she had no interest in anything other than surviving. But for some reason, the mayor was standing at Rachel's door.

"Rachel," she said. "Nice to meet you, Ms. Mayor. Or Mrs. Mayor. Or Ms. Wright. What do I call you?"

Wright laughed sincerely. "You can call me Constance. May I come in?"

Rachel hesitated for a moment, then motioned for Wright to enter. The mayor took off her shoes and placed them gently by the front door.

"New carpeting," she said, sniffing the air. "Don't want your rug to smell like the campaign trail."

"And what exactly does a campaign trail smell like?" Rachel asked.

"Money and insincerity," Wright replied with a wicked smile. She looked around. "You have a lovely home."

Rachel laughed. "If we ever finish unpacking, we will."

"Take your time. Although that chardonnay goes perfect with unpacking."

"So are you here to . . . ," Rachel said delicately, "campaign?"

"No, no. Though I do try to meet all my constituents, I know your family is new to Ashby, and, well, I just wanted to come by and see how you all were settling in."

Rachel heard soft footsteps approaching, and they both turned to the stairwell. Eric stood at the top, hand gripping the banister so hard his fingertips were white.

"Eric, am I right?"

Eric nodded.

*How did she know that?* Rachel's hand went back to the scissors.

"Well, Eric, my name is Constance, and I'm just here to see how your family is settling in. Are you liking it here so far?"

Eric nodded imperceptibly but did not take his eyes off Constance Wright.

"Constance is the mayor," Rachel said. Eric's eyes widened, but he remained silent. Then he went back to his room.

"And if I'm correct, you have a little one too. Megan, right?"

Rachel nodded.

"How old?"

"She's four," Rachel said. "Do you have any children, May . . . Constance?"

"Not just yet. But one day, if Nicholas and I are so lucky." Wright smiled, but Rachel could detect a twinge of sadness. Something told Rachel the question had hit a nerve. The mayor wanted children, but perhaps infertility, an unsupportive spouse, or another factor had prevented it.

"Can I offer you something? Coffee or tea?" Rachel prayed she would decline.

"No, thank you," Wright said with a smile. "Trying to cut back on my caffeine."

"Well then, we appreciate you stopping by, Constance," Rachel said. She eyed the door and hoped Wright would pick up on the gesture.

"Of course. Two kids, I can imagine how busy you are," Wright said, walking back toward the front door. "Like I said, it's very important for me to meet my constituents."

"Well, now we've met."

Wright nodded. "Yes, we have. Did you know we have a friend in common?"

"Is that so?"

"Jim Franklin. At Franklin and Rosato, in Darien."

Rachel's heart rate blasted to over a hundred beats a minute. She felt a cold shiver at the nape of her neck. Her body went rigid.

"Don't be alarmed," Constance said softly. "In fact, the opposite. The real reason I came by today is to let you know that you'll be safe here."

"I'm sorry?"

"Jim Franklin contacted the FBI field office in Springfield several months ago. That office oversees the western part of the state, which includes Ashby. The FBI briefed me as soon as you made an offer on this house."

"I . . . I don't know what to say."

"You don't need to say anything. But we protect our own in Ashby. I know what your family has been through. You have my office's resources at your disposal. And if you ever need anything . . . *anything* . . . call my personal cell phone."

Wright handed Rachel her card. Rachel took it, her hand trembling. A phone number was scrawled in black ink on the back.

Rachel's lip trembled. A tear formed in the corner of her eye.

Wright placed her hands on Rachel's shoulders and squeezed gently. "You'll like it here. And I'll tell you what. I have a fund-raiser coming up in a few weeks at Rhinebeck Hall. I don't want a penny from you. But this is a great way to meet people. To be a part of the community.

I have a feeling that it'll be good for you. Have a few drinks. A laugh or two. A reason to get dressed up. My office will send over the details."

"Th . . . thank you, Ms. Wright."

"Constance," she said, opening the door. "Give my best to Eric and Megan. They're lucky to have you as a mother."

"Thank you," Rachel said. She noticed Wright's hand. "That's a lovely ring."

Constance held up her left hand. Adorning her index finger was a silver ring with a large topaz gemstone in the center.

"My father gave this to me when I got married. He told me Nicholas's ring was for love, and this one was for family. I feel complete when I wear them both."

"It's gorgeous."

"Thank you. Take care, Ms. Marin."

"Call me Rachel."

Constance smiled warmly. "I hope to see you soon, Rachel."

Then she left.

As the door slammed shut, Rachel let out a massive sob and wiped her eyes.

She watched Constance Wright climb into a silver Mercedes C-Class. Wright lowered the window and waved back at Rachel, the brilliant topaz gemstone glistening in the spring sun.

# CHAPTER 9

***Today***

"How was the date?" Liesl asked with the wide-eyed naive smile of a high schooler who likely assumed every first date led to marriage.

"Very surprising," Rachel said.

Liesl giggled, rubbed her hands together, and made an *eeeee!* noise that could have shattered glass. Rachel thanked her babysitter, gave her an extra ten dollars, then marched straight into Eric's room. She wrapped her arms around her son, startling him. He tried to shake her off, but given that they both knew she was the stronger of the two, he simply let her finish.

"You done?" he said.

"Yes," Rachel replied. "Sometimes moms just need a hug."

"Well, you got one. Now let me study."

Rachel kissed him on the cheek before he could shoo her away and then went into Megan's room.

Her gorgeous daughter was asleep. A pile of pages lay scattered on the floor—more of her Sadie Scout story. Rachel moved a tangle of hair away from Megan's mouth and gently placed her hand on her daughter's chest, feeling it rise and fall with each breath.

When Eric was born, he'd spent sixty-four days in the NICU before the doctors permitted him to go home. For six weeks he required a gastronomy tube, which fed directly into his stomach through his abdominal wall until he was strong enough to feed. The scar was still visible on Eric's stomach. Faint, but a reminder to Rachel how delicate he once was. When they brought him home, Rachel sat by his crib every night for six months just to make sure he was breathing. She would place a small makeup mirror in front of his nose and hold her breath, waiting for it to fog.

Megan was easy. She was born two days past her due date, at a whopping nine pounds, seven ounces. She was the picture of health from day one.

A perfect daughter. A perfect son. A happy marriage. Their family was complete.

And just six months later, it all came crashing down. Four perfect lives shattered in a single unforgiving moment.

There were monsters out there. That lesson had been forced upon Rachel. It had also made her learn the hardest, most valuable lesson there was in life.

*You're on your own.*

And now, right here in Ashby, this sleepy little city, another monster had arisen. Constance Wright was dead. Rachel didn't know why. Not yet.

After Constance Wright had come to her home, Rachel had learned everything she could about the Wright family. They had been Ashby royalty, their names practically synonymous with the town. Once.

For years, the name *Wright* was plastered on schools, libraries, and hospital wings. But then those *respectable* establishments all washed their hands of the Wrights, scrubbed the name from their walls and plaques. They kept the money the family had donated, of course.

Constance's grandfather, Eugene Wright, was born in Ashby and founded the Wright Development Corp., which developed middle-class housing projects all across the Midwest. Constance's father, Cameron, leveraged the money Eugene made on Wall Street, buying him powerful connections in government and finance. They were on their way to becoming the Kennedys of the Midwest.

Constance graduated from Harvard with a degree in political science and then went to Yale Law before returning to her family's home in

Ashby and winning a seat on the city council at just twenty-nine. Four years later she was mayor, bolstered by a $4 million campaign funded in large part by her family's associates in construction. Louis Magursky of Magursky Construction spent half a million alone to blanket the airwaves with attack ads on the sitting mayor, poor Randall McGovern, a sixty-eight-year-old with thinning hair and the charisma of a comb, who was no match for Constance's work ethic, enthusiasm, humor, and deep pockets.

Constance was young. Smart. Attractive. Idealistic. Funny. Passionate. Genuine. And was poised for greatness.

Mayor Wright. Governor Wright. Senator Wright. And beyond. Ashby was the perfect place for Constance to cut her political teeth. After all, it wasn't long ago that the mayor of a small city in Alaska came within a hair of the White House.

But during Constance's second term in office and about a year before Constance's visit to Rachel's home, the ACLU sued Wright Development Corp. Six black employees claimed Eugene Wright had regularly used racist language in their presence, and soon after that seven women came forward with claims of sexual misconduct. There were tapes. And Eugene Wright was ruined.

The suit was settled out of court for millions, Eugene Wright suffered a stroke, and the company was sold for pennies on the dollar to a development firm that absorbed the company's assets and scrapped its name.

Soon after, Cameron Wright was arrested in the South Bronx in the bed of an underage prostitute. Constance's mother, Candice, went to clean him out in the divorce only to find that Wright Development Corp. was in debt eight figures to dozens of vendors. Magursky Construction was in the hole for $6 million alone. Zwinter Electric, $3 million. Creditors picked apart what was left like vultures on a fresh carcass.

Cameron Wright hanged himself in prison. Candice Wright died in a car accident a year later. Cable news hosts tossed around conspiracy theories about their deaths.

Before the scandals, Constance Wright's approval rating was floating in the high sixties. But the muck from her family's scandals began to spatter. And then it got worse.

Early in her second term, Wright's husband, Nicholas Drummond, accused her of infidelity. The *Ashby Bulletin* printed lewd texts, photos, and emails she'd apparently sent to a twenty-two-year-old staffer named Sam Wickersham. Wright furiously denied the affair but couldn't explain the abundance of communication. She claimed she was being framed. She had very few defenders. Rachel followed it in the news—from a distance.

Wickersham also claimed he witnessed Wright drunk during government meetings, and when a reporter from the *Bulletin* found an empty bottle of Jim Beam in her wastebasket, the picture of the offending bottle was splashed above the fold with the headline "Constance-ly Sauced?" Wright denied the drinking accusations, but by then it didn't matter.

Her political career came crashing down, and her marriage exploded in a matter of weeks.

Drummond cleaned Wright out in the divorce and soon after remarried a young woman named Isabelle Robles, who came with a trust fund that would have made Scrooge McDuck jealous. Constance Wright disappeared from public life. She was occasionally spotted pushing a shopping cart at the grocery store or sitting alone with a pack of Twizzlers at a movie. But the Constance Wright who was poised for greatness ceased to exist.

Constance was strong and smart, born with contacts and power and money, all the advantages she could ever need. She had everything. And none of it saved her reputation, or her life.

When Rachel moved to Ashby, Constance Wright had shown her kindness. And then her life was torn apart while Rachel sat back and watched. She'd believed Constance but had stayed quiet. But she was tired of monsters roaming the countryside unchecked.

She was going to make sure somebody paid for Constance's murder.

# CHAPTER 10

The news of Constance Wright's death hit Ashby like a bomb, and the aftershock rumbled far and wide.

The front page of the *Ashby Bulletin* ran the headline FAREWELL MS. MAYOR. The *Chicago Tribune*'s website read DEATH OF A DYNASTY. Notable cable channels sent crews to cover the police press conference. Rumors had begun to spread that Constance Wright's death was being treated as a homicide. Along with the winter wind came whispers of suspects and conspiracies. Constance Wright's previous transgressions were forgotten and forgiven while the city mourned. At least for one day.

Rachel sat riveted to the morning news. Her eyes fixated on the laptop's livestream. Her children could have been waving around samurai swords or painting the kitchen with Velveeta, and she wouldn't have turned her head.

Lt. Daryl George was scheduled to kick off the APD press conference that afternoon. Lieutenant George would be joined by Detectives John Serrano and Leslie Tally. They would brief the media on Constance Wright's death and the current investigation, take questions, and for the most part give the assembled reporters the runaround.

Rachel knew firsthand that killers often enjoyed surveying the aftermath of their handiwork. They liked to witness the destruction they'd wrought. There was a decent chance that whoever killed Constance Wright would be watching the press conference. In person. The FBI's *Crime Classification Manual* divided killers into three groups: organized, disorganized, and mixed. Organized killers planned their crimes. They were thoughtful yet remorseless. Disorganized killers often killed due to passion or an uncontrollable urge. This killer was organized. He or she would take pride in their work. Which meant Rachel needed to be at that presser.

For a prominent victim like Constance Wright, information would be kept close to the vest. Rachel couldn't rely on the morsels spoon-fed to the press, and even though Serrano and Tally seemed competent, she'd been fooled before and still had a distrust for law enforcement. She had to find the truth on her own.

"Mom!"

Rachel spun around, nearly spilling her coffee all over the laptop keyboard.

"What is it, hon?"

"Were you distracted?" said Megan, bounding down the stairs.

"Where did you learn that word?"

"Miss Wooster in homeroom told Alec Titus he was distracted because he was playing Candy Crush on his cell phone."

"Alec Titus has a cell phone? He's seven."

Megan nodded.

"So . . . can I have—"

"Absolutely not. Wouldn't want you to be *distracted*."

Megan left in a huff and got on the school bus.

Eric came downstairs wearing headphones. Rachel motioned for him to take them off. He rolled his eyes but did so.

She gave her son a once-over and said, "Nebraska."

"Lincoln."

"Nevada."

"Carson City."

"OK, smart guy. Japan."

Eric looked stymied. "We haven't done foreign countries yet."

"All right, Doogie Howser, we'll hold off on other countries."

"Who's Doogie Howser?"

"Never mind. Have a good day, kiddo."

She went to kiss him, but he ducked and sped out the front door.

Rachel watched Eric walk down the block, his shoulders hunched inward, hands in his pockets. When he was a boy, he'd been so carefree, confident, joyful. She hadn't seen that Eric in a long, long time. Nearly seven years. But at least he no longer woke up screaming.

Rachel walked in the door of the Ruggiero & Barnes law firm at 8:57 a.m. While she waited for Steve Ruggiero to arrive, Rachel devoured everything she could about Constance Wright's death and the life she'd led before she died at the foot of the Albertson Bridge.

Scouring old interviews and profiles of Constance Wright, Rachel learned she'd met Nicholas Harold Drummond at Harvard, where he'd run the 4 x 800. They'd split briefly after college, then reunited and married at twenty-eight before moving to Ashby. She'd won a seat on the Ashby City Council the following year.

Rachel clicked over to the *Ashby Bulletin* website. They'd run three pictures side by side on the home page:

1) Constance Wright graduating from Ashby High, beaming with a thousand-watt smile, golden tassels streaming from a red cap. Her curly reddish-brown hair gave her an even more youthful appearance.

2) Constance Wright and Nicholas Drummond standing outside the Apley Court dorm their freshman year at Harvard on a gorgeous, golden spring day. They had their hands stuffed in each other's back pockets. They were an insufferably cute couple.

3) Constance at city hall taking the oath of office after being sworn in as the seventy-ninth mayor of Ashby and the youngest in the city's history. Nicholas Drummond stood behind her, smiling. The caption read "The First Family of Ashby."

Rachel looked at Nicholas's smile. It seemed a little too wide, a little too forced. It seemed like the kind of smile worn by a man who didn't take kindly to being overshadowed by his wife.

Rachel's blood boiled as she read on. When Steve Ruggiero finally graced the office with his presence at 11:00 a.m., Rachel nearly snapped at him for breaking her concentration. He ripped off his boots and tossed them into the hallway, slush splashing onto Rachel's legs.

"Hold my calls; think you can handle that?" he said, slamming the door before Rachel could answer. She took a tissue and wiped the gunk from her clothes.

She heard him lock his door. Rachel had seen Steve in plenty of foul moods but never cared enough to ask why. As long as she had health insurance and a W-2, she didn't care if Steve Ruggiero came in with his hair on fire. She hated the job and certainly didn't need the money, but if she lived as an unemployed single mother, people would ask questions.

A moment later, she heard Steve shouting. Then, at 11:30 a.m., four of the partners entered his office. They shouted at each other for the next two and a half hours before the partners left. Men. Always thinking they could fix their problems by raising the volume of their voice.

Then Steve came out and said, "I'm going to lunch. I may or may not be back today. Just reschedule the rest of my calls. Think you can handle that?"

Rachel smiled sweetly and said, "I'll do my best."

If looks could kill, Steve's remains would have fit inside a can of tuna.

He nodded, then left with a quickness that suggested he was concerned the world might run out of Grey Goose.

Once Steve was gone, Rachel pulled up the Ashby PD website.

The presser was to be held at Bauman City Hall in downtown Ashby. Bauman Hall had been named after Philip Bauman, Ashby's fifty-sixth mayor, who had overseen the construction of the Albertson Bridge. To add insult to injury, following Constance Wright's resignation, Deputy Mayor Alan Caldwell had awarded a $15 million contract to Magursky Construction, already owed millions by the Wright family, to repair and refurbish the bridge as its supports began to rust.

It was scheduled to begin at 3:00 p.m. Rachel checked her watch. 2:03. She could make it. She grabbed her coat and left the office quickly and quietly.

◆◆◆

Detectives Serrano and Tally stood inside the foyer to Bauman Hall, preparing to face the mob. Bauman was a large red sandstone building four stories high with curved windows and brick steps that led to four two-story Ionic columns. The scaffolding had once been a pristine copper color but had deteriorated to green with rust over time. Waiting outside Bauman was a phalanx of reporters larger than any Serrano had ever seen in his tenure on the force. There were dozens of cameras and reporters and vans and satellite hookups, plus a horde of onlookers all cordoned off behind rope. In addition to the local crews, Serrano saw trucks from CNN, MSNBC, Fox News, and NBC. Constance Wright's death was a national story.

Lt. Daryl George would introduce the conference and briefly review the facts of the case and then turn it over to Serrano and Tally. Lieutenant George was fifty-nine but looked thirty-nine, which, since he was forty-three but looked fifty-three, made Serrano hate him. George woke up at 4:30 a.m. six days a week, swam fifty laps in the Olympic-sized pool at a local health club, didn't drink, and ate only foods that came directly from the ground or an animal. Serrano joked that Lieutenant George ate only meat from animals raised on special organic resorts where they played squash and got hot stone massages while drinking kombucha and coconut water.

Lieutenant George had invited Serrano to work out with him one morning a few years back. After a few years of hitting the bottle a little too hard, Serrano agreed, figuring it was about time to whip himself back into shape. He met the lieutenant at his health club and squeezed into a pair of old swim trunks that had fit better fifteen pounds prior. Ten laps in, Serrano was reasonably sure he was going to die. Twenty laps in, he wished he *had* died.

And in the locker room, Serrano got to see George in all his glory: he had muscle definition no fiftysomething should possess. He'd slipped on an undershirt and liberally doused himself in Yves Saint Laurent cologne.

Lieutenant George wore that cologne every single goddamn day, and Serrano could smell him coming from down the block. Everything about the man was by the book, but there was a kindness behind the resolve. He'd scored a big payday by working as a technical adviser on one of those cop shows where every detective had impeccable hair and makeup. Serrano regularly worked sixteen-hour shifts, and there wasn't enough hairspray and pancake makeup in the world to make him look TV ready. George drove a light-blue Chevy Camaro that other officers referred to behind his back as the Smurfmobile. But he was a good cop. Thirty-five years on the force. And Serrano would follow him into battle any day of the week.

Serrano walked up to the double-wide windows and peered out onto Tellyfair Green, a six-acre park outside Bauman Hall currently covered in a thick blanket of snow. Serrano could tell which TV crews were local based on how they dressed. Locals wore heavy knit gloves, thick, chunky scarves, and puffy jackets. The out-of-towners were decked out in Burberry coats and thin gloves that looked good on camera but had the insulation of toilet paper. They were the ones doing laps around their news vans to stay warm while the local reporters waited patiently for the presser to begin.

"This is already a madhouse," Lieutenant George said. "This investigation is going to be watched very closely. It's imperative that we keep things in-house. After today, I don't want anyone talking to the media without my say-so."

"We can't help leaks from within the department," Tally said. "Those news vans at the bridge the other night. Somebody in the department tipped them off."

George nodded, sighed. "I've been dealing with that for twenty years. That's why the flow of crucial information doesn't go beyond the three of us."

"You got it," Serrano said.

"Constance Wright was a good woman," Lieutenant George added. "She was a good mayor. The media loves a scandal. But beyond all that tabloid crap, she supported the department and gave us every resource we needed. She had friends on the force."

"Constance Wright's family had more enemies than Julius Caesar," Serrano said. "A lot of powerful people lost a lot of money when the Wright Corporation went belly up."

"And with Constance's family either dead or disgraced, the debts passed to her," Tally said. She looked at Lieutenant George. Her voice trembled with anger, remorse. "Why didn't we do more? If she had friends on the force, where *were* we?"

"Beg your pardon?" George said.

"You said it yourself," Tally replied. "She gave us everything we needed. Always had the department's back. Did we have hers? Did we ever send a squad car to check on her after the town turned on her? No. And so she slipped through the cracks. We could have caught her, Lieutenant."

Lieutenant George remained silent but bowed his head.

"Not everyone on the force was such a big fan of Constance Wright," Serrano said.

"If you can't keep your personal grudges out of this, Detective," George said bluntly, "I'm happy to reassign this investigation."

"You'll have my best, sir," Serrano replied. George nodded warily.

Serrano's phone vibrated. He took it out and checked his email.

"We got Wright's phone records from Verizon," he said. He opened up the file and skimmed quickly, looking for the last batch of calls and texts prior to her death.

"Holy crap," Serrano said.

"What is it?" George said.

"Guess the last two people Constance Wright called before she died."

They waited. Finally Tally said, "You're not actually going to make us guess, are you? OK, Brad Pitt and Jennifer Aniston."

"Close. Nicholas Drummond and Samuel J. Wickersham."

"Well, holy shit," Tally said. "Her ex-husband and the kid she had the affair with? That's better than my guess. Why in the hell would she be calling them? Drummond, maybe. Ex-husband, there are always issues to go over. Taxes and whatnot. But Wickersham? He ruined her."

"Guess we'll have to talk to Misters Drummond and Wickersham," Serrano said.

Serrano showed Tally the call logs. "Look: both calls were only a couple of seconds long. Which means she either hung up or didn't leave a message."

Lieutenant George thumbed his chin, thinking. "Keep this from the press until we know more."

"I would have believed this was a suicide in a heartbeat," Tally said. "Her life is ruined, she pulls a J. D. Salinger recluse deal. The pregnancy . . . I still can't wrap my head around that."

"If not for that Marin woman," Serrano said, "we just might have chalked this up to suicide."

Tally said, "I think that Marin woman just got lucky."

"Didn't sound like luck to me," Serrano replied. "The toenails, the tooth, those could all be chalked up as circumstantial. And she also knew it was Constance Wright before it was released to the public. Hector didn't pick up on the wind trajectory and rate-of-fall stuff. Neither did Montrose or Beene."

"She's a civilian," Tally said, curtly. "A nobody."

Lieutenant George interrupted them. "Done chatting? Ready?"

"I think I see Anderson Cooper out there," Tally said.

"Really?" Serrano said, perking up.

"No."

"You're a dick sometimes, Leslie."

She smiled and took a bow.

Lieutenant George said, "Let's get this circus started."

The harsh wind bit into their faces as they opened the doors to Bauman Hall. Lieutenant George walked to the podium, jaw clenched. The severity of the situation was etched on his face. Serrano and Tally flanked George on either side. It was a bright afternoon, no shade. The sun reflected off the snow, making it hard to see the crowd. Serrano held his hands together in front of his stomach. At his first press conference, twelve years ago, Serrano had clasped his hands behind his back. He'd figured it would make him look stoic. Afterward, Lieutenant George had told him he'd looked like he'd needed to take a piss.

So from that day forward: hands folded in front.

They waited as Lieutenant George adjusted the microphone. Serrano had given press conferences before. But not like this. And not for people with the notoriety of Constance Wright. He'd never seen the press corps so quiet. They didn't want to miss a word.

The wind blew east to west, meaning Serrano inhaled the lieutenant's pungent cologne with every breath. Even for this, he had to smell like a French brothel.

"Thank you all for coming," Lieutenant George began. "At 1:13 a.m. on the night of December eleventh, 911 dispatch received a call about the presence of a body at the base of the Albertson Bridge. Upon confirmation of the deceased, the Ashby PD forensics team, along with Detectives John Serrano and Leslie Tally, arrived at the scene to find the body of former mayor Constance Wright. According to early forensic analysis, Ms. Wright had been dead approximately two hours prior to the 911 call. Our hearts go out to the family and friends of Mayor Wright. She was a beloved member of our community, a true public servant, a woman who dedicated her life to Ashby. She loved this town with devotion and passion, and it saddens us to speak of her death at such an early age. At this point in time, we are treating Constance Wright's death as nonaccidental."

"Was she murdered? Or was it suicide?" shouted one of the reporters. Serrano stared daggers at him. He wasn't a local.

"At this point," George said, "I will cede the microphone to the detectives investigating Ms. Wright's death, John Serrano and Leslie Tally. They will answer any questions you have, but remember that this is an ongoing investigation. We will release further information at the appropriate times. Detectives, over to you."

Lieutenant George stepped back, and Serrano and Tally took the podium. Tally spoke first.

"Based on the location of the body, along with other mitigating factors, we were able to quickly determine that Ms. Wright's death was not self-inflicted. We are investigating under the presumption that Ms. Wright was the victim of a homicide."

Murmurs rippled through the crowd.

A reporter shouted, "Who killed her?"

"Was it her ex-husband?"

"Do you have any suspects?"

"Quiet down," Tally said sternly.

Serrano recognized Nancy Wiles, anchor for Channel 14. She was cute. Blonde. Serrano had harbored a crush on her for some time. About six months ago she'd interviewed him for a story about a rash of burglaries in the Wooten housing projects, and once the cameras had stopped rolling, he'd asked her for her phone number. She'd smiled and given him the office switchboard line. He'd gone home alone and drunk a six-pack alone.

"At the moment," Serrano said, "we are still gathering evidence."

"So you don't have any suspects," Wiles replied, fake impatience in her voice.

Serrano deflected the question. "We have not yet made any arrests."

"Bob Phillips, WPRD. What led you to the conclusion that Mayor Wright's death was a homicide?"

"The location at which the body was found is inconsistent with a natural—or unaided—fall from the height of the Albertson Bridge, given the weather conditions of that night."

"Is that the only reason?"

"No, it is not. There were other factors, but that's all we can discuss right now."

"Grace Meyerson, TNN. Do you believe Ms. Wright's death is connected to any of the Wright family scandals? As you know, Eugene and Cameron Wright had numerous legal, personal, and financial troubles."

"We have not ruled anything out and are examining all possibilities," Tally said. "Including people connected to the Wright family businesses."

Serrano continued to deflect questions with evasive or vague answers. Enough for salacious headlines, but little else. Over the next few days, the department switchboard would be inundated with calls from tipsters who claimed to either a) have witnessed Constance Wright's death, b) have information that could aid in the investigation, or c) have killed Constance Wright themselves (possibly aided by Bigfoot or Lee Harvey Oswald).

So the less information Serrano gave the press, the better. That made it easy to weed out the lunatics and rubberneckers. Not to mention the sociopaths who crank called cops with fake tips and posted the conversations on YouTube for kicks. It took an incredible amount of manpower to weed through those calls, hoping *one* might be worth more than cubic zirconia.

The truth was Serrano couldn't wait for the presser to be over. The media could be a useful ally when it came to tracking down criminals who were impetuous and/or stupid. The kind of criminal who might rob a gas station without a mask to hide their facial tattoo. Or mug an old lady in her apartment vestibule and get caught on camera doing it, then wander around the neighborhood like they were King Shit. In those cases, Ashby PD would get a police sketch out and canvass the neighborhoods, and more often than not, dispatch would get a legitimate hit on the tip line within hours.

Serrano didn't think that would be the case here. Constance Wright hadn't just happened to be on the Albertson Bridge that night. This wasn't a random attack. This was planned ahead of time. Serrano knew Constance Wright. She was in good shape, took kickboxing classes while in office. He never saw her drunk or without her wits. During her first mayoral primary, the press had given her the nickname "Cutthroat Constance." She could fight back. And fight dirty if need be.

Yet Hector Moreno's examination found no signs of struggle. No defensive wounds. No bruising other than from the fall from the bridge. But her toenails. Constance had rarely been seen in public since she'd resigned her office, but a fresh pedicure meant she'd wanted to look nice. Either for herself or someone else.

And the tooth.

Her jawline was shattered by the fall, and most of her teeth were jarred loose or knocked out. Four were not recovered and presumed to have slipped under the ice. But the third molar on her left side—it was chipped. Not shattered. Like a split ice cube. Just as Rachel Marin had presumed.

Constance Wright's blood alcohol content was staggeringly high. And Serrano was reasonably certain at least some of that alcohol intake had been against her will, likely while she was unconscious. Otherwise she would have struggled. There would have been defensive wounds.

No, Serrano believed Constance was force-fed the liquor. And with the sheared tooth, it meant the killer—or killers—weren't on stable ground while pouring. They might have been driving. A pothole causing the bottle, or Constance's head, to bounce around, the bottle cracking against her tooth hard enough to shear off a piece.

And he hadn't mentioned it to Rachel, but forensics had found a single Nature Made prenatal vitamin capsule that had fallen behind Constance Wright's bedroom dresser. Which meant not only did she intend to keep the baby, but somebody had emptied her apartment of all other signs of pregnancy and then wiped the place clean. The goal was to make it *look* like she had taken no steps to aid the pregnancy, giving credence to the suicide theory.

But still . . . there had been no signs of struggle in her house. No blood, hair, or fibers belonging to anyone but Constance. Which meant there was a very good chance that Constance Wright had known the person who'd killed her.

Serrano and Tally continued to field questions. As the glare grew brighter, Serrano put on his sunglasses. He surveyed the crowd.

Then he saw one face in the press pen he was *not* expecting to see.

Rachel Marin. She smiled sheepishly at him and waved.

◆◆◆

Rachel arrived at the press conference ten minutes before it began. It was a full-on cattle call, reporters and onlookers jockeying for position in the snow, a giant pulsating mass of custom suits, Spanx, and hair gel.

All the best vantage points were in the press box. One thing she'd learned a long time ago: act like you belong, and most people will assume you belong.

So Rachel simply ducked underneath the tape to the press pen and stood there, arms crossed so nobody could see she wasn't wearing an ID. The reporters and camera crews were too busy setting up and primping to notice. She checked her phone. It was nearly 3:00 p.m. No word from Steve Ruggiero. With any luck he'd never know she'd been gone.

Finally, Lt. Daryl George came out of Bauman Hall flanked by Detectives Serrano and Tally. Their faces were grim. Serrano looked uncomfortable, hands clasped in front of him, shifting weight from foot to foot. She'd met cops before. Too many. Most didn't like being on television or in the news. They preferred to stay anonymous, unless they had political aspirations or delusions of grandeur. Serrano and Tally didn't strike Rachel as that type.

Lieutenant George offered some kind words about Constance Wright, then ceded the podium to Serrano and Tally.

Rachel listened intently. They deflected most questions and remained vague on specifics. That was unsurprising. But Rachel wasn't there for their answers.

The real reason she was there was the crowd itself. Given Wright's fame and notoriety, Rachel knew the Wright presser would draw a crowd. And it had. There were at least a thousand people, in addition to several hundred in the press pen, hanging on every word and fighting for a better view.

Rachel had a gut feeling that somewhere among the crowd was a person who knew intimate details about Constance Wright's death.

As Detective Tally spoke, Rachel watched Serrano. He wasn't a bad-looking man. Seemed a little burned out, and he could lose ten pounds, but for some reason she was drawn to him. He had shaved his neck, made the beard stubble look a bit neater, but Rachel could make out an angry red line where he'd nicked himself just above the Adam's apple. A slight belly protruded over his belt—nothing a few months at the gym couldn't fix—and a strong, set jaw. Serrano had kind eyes, but something behind them looked haunted. Rachel wondered what it was. Eventually the detective put his sunglasses on, and Rachel listened.

Then Serrano looked up, and before Rachel could think to look away, he mouthed three words quite clearly: *What the hell?*

Rachel smiled and waved because, well, what else could she do?

Serrano looked away from her, clearly perturbed.

Rachel turned around, scanned the crowd. Looked from face to face to face, studying each set of eyes, waiting for a twitch, someone a little too happy to be there, some sort of giveaway. She studied each pair of lips, looking for the wrong kind of smile.

And then she saw something that made her stop scanning.

A man stood alone in the snow, about twenty feet behind the last row of spectators. He was gaunt, midtwenties, with dark hollows under his bloodshot eyes, a head of patchy black hair, and sallow skin that, to Rachel, suggested narcotics had sped up the aging process. He was nibbling on his right thumbnail like a squirrel on a nut.

The man was staring at Leslie Tally as she spoke. He looked concerned. *Very* concerned.

She had seen that man before.

Rachel took out her cell phone and found the email she'd sent herself containing the screen grabs from the original news report from the Albertson Bridge, before they'd identified the body as that of Constance Wright. She scrolled through the photos. The crime scene. The body. Detective Serrano. Charles Willemore. The crowd of onlookers gathered at the bank of the Ashby River.

And there he was. The same man she was looking at now. He was at the river the night of Constance Wright's death, standing among the crowd of onlookers. And now he was here at the press conference for her death.

Who the hell was this guy?

Rachel took out her cell phone, opened the Camera app, and zoomed in as far as it would go. Then she moved slowly to her left until she was hidden behind a portly reporter with apple-red cheeks and body odor like stinky cheese left to bake in the desert sun. She centered the camera on the man and took several pictures, both still and live shots.

When the presser ended, the man immediately began walking away. Fast.

Rachel hesitated, but only for a moment. She could easily send photos of the man to Serrano and Tally. Let *them* investigate. But a determination and anger burned inside her. Years ago, Rachel had watched one murderer walk free. She wasn't about to take a chance of that happening again. She needed to find out who this man was.

The man exited Tellyfair Green and headed north toward Dalkey Avenue. Rachel cursed herself for not changing into flats. He wore sneakers, which gave him little traction on the icy sidewalk. He slipped and fell twice, which allowed Rachel to keep pace.

He stopped at the M-38 bus station just across the street from the Kwik Park on Dalkey, where Rachel's car was parked. Rachel had already prepaid for two hours. She checked her phone. No word from Steve at the office. She had to follow this man.

An M-38 bus idled two blocks down on Dalkey. Rachel had maybe sixty to ninety seconds before the bus arrived. And if that happened, she'd lose him.

Rachel ran-stumbled to the Kwik Park—stupid heels—and started her car without taking her eyes off the man. She waited for the bus to pass the lot entrance, then pulled out so she was directly behind it. She angled the car to the right of the bus so she could still see the bus stop itself. Keep an eye on who got on and off. When she saw the man get on the M-38, Rachel followed it east on Dalkey.

She drove slowly, close enough to the bus to prevent other cars from sliding in front of her. The M-38 stopped every two blocks. Rachel waited at every stop, heart pounding, to see if the man got off. She knew the M-38 followed Dalkey Avenue all the way out to the suburbs in east Ashby. The longer he stayed on, the easier he'd be to follow. Less traffic, more residential. But if he got off in the middle of the city and started on foot or went into the subway, she'd be screwed. No way she'd be able to find a place to park fast enough to keep pace.

Stop after stop, he stayed on the bus. She could see him through the rear window, wearing a pair of wireless headphones. His head was bopping along to whatever he was listening to. She watched his movements. He didn't appear to be preparing to get off anytime soon, but he looked both unreliable and impetuous, so she stayed prepared.

The bus continued east until it crossed Lansdale Road, large office and public works buildings giving way to compact condos, which city ordinance prevented from being built over three stories high. Eventually they reached the suburbs. Split-level homes, kids pulling their siblings and pets on sleds down icy sidewalks, barren tree branches glistening with icicles.

The thin man was still grooving to his music. He hadn't picked up on the fact that the same car had been trailing the bus for miles.

Twenty minutes and six stops later, Rachel saw the thin man jerk up and look around. For a moment she panicked. Could he have missed his stop? If he doubled back, got on a bus going in the opposite direction, she could lose him.

He stood up and pressed the yellow tape to request a stop. Rachel would have to play the next few seconds carefully. On foot, the man would be more aware of his surroundings. Traffic was light, every vehicle more noticeable.

He got off the bus at the next stop, shivered, and waited on the sidewalk for a moment, as though getting his bearings. Then he put his headphones in his coat pocket and headed north up Van Brickle Way.

Traffic was light. If Rachel followed, driving slowly, he'd see her. So she pulled over at the nearest curb and watched him amble down the block. He barely got twenty feet before he tripped and fell, hard. Given his poor motor skills, Rachel surmised he was on some sort of drug—legal or otherwise—perhaps an opioid or even an SSRI, which affected the central nervous system and could slow down reaction time to poor footing.

Eventually he turned right off Van Brickle onto Valencia Lane. Rachel followed, driving cautiously. They were in a nice neighborhood. Not all that far from where Reginald Bartek lived. East Ashby was largely made up of single-family dwellings, and not cheap ones. Luxury SUVs parked in the snow-covered driveways, many homes looming behind wrought iron gates.

She noticed several homes had midsize sedans parked next to luxury vehicles. Given the time of year, Rachel figured the cheaper cars were gifts to college students currently home for Christmas break. This was the kind of neighborhood where parents gifted college freshmen a $22,000 Ford Fusion.

The man Rachel was following looked completely out of place among the stately colonials and Corinthian columns. She pulled over and parked at the curbside behind a silver Mercedes GLS. When the man was forty yards north of her on Valencia, Rachel got out of the car and zipped her coat. Her breath condensed into vapor in the cold. She'd have to follow him on foot from here.

The streets in the neighborhood were plowed, but icy patches made footing perilous. The roads where Rachel lived often went days without being plowed or salted during the winter. The Ashby government clearly prioritized the wealthier suburbs. Rachel walked carefully. If she slipped, he might notice, and then the game was up.

The sky was growing dark and gray, the color of brick mortar. Rachel was starting to think following him might have been a bad idea. But then she saw the man turn right into a driveway. She hung back across the street, watching.

The home he approached was a large Victorian, three stories high with twelve front-facing windows. It had a stone facade, wraparound veranda, and a white-columned portico. Three thousand to thirty-five hundred square feet, Rachel guessed. Probably ran a cool $4.2 million. Rachel doubted this was his home. He didn't look like he was capable of holding a job, let alone paying a pricey mortgage.

The man slowly climbed the stone front steps and knocked on the door. Rachel shifted from foot to foot. Her hands were cold, despite the thick wool gloves. She rubbed them together. The man went to knock again, but before he could, the front door swung open. A middle-aged man and younger woman stepped out onto the porch.

The woman wore a thick cardigan, black leggings, and hoop earrings. Her hair was done up in a bun. She was trim under the bulky sweater, with honey-colored skin and dark hair. Her skin was wrinkle-free, her legs toned. Rachel estimated her to be twenty-six or twenty-seven. The man with her was older—midforties by Rachel's guess—but she'd need a closer look to be sure. He was stooped slightly and winced with each step. He had a bad back, perhaps a slipped disc.

The woman threw her arms around the thin man and gathered him close. He responded by loosely hugging her back, as though ashamed. The older man had his back to Rachel, but she could tell from his reaction that he either disapproved of the embrace or disapproved of the man's presence altogether. Then the older man clapped the thin man on the back and said something Rachel couldn't hear.

She needed to get closer. She needed to see their faces, take pictures. She crossed the street calmly, like she lived in the area. At the foot of the driveway, Rachel took out her cell phone and opened the Camera app. This time she would take a video, then try to decipher what they said when she got home.

But just as she was about to press record, a car with APD plates pulled into the Victorian's driveway. Rachel recognized the car.

*Well, this just got interesting.*

All three people on the steps turned to look. For the first time, Rachel saw the older man's face. And her breath caught in her throat.

The man was Nicholas Drummond. Constance Wright's ex-husband. The woman must have been his new wife, Isabelle. So who the hell was the thin man?

Detectives John Serrano and Leslie Tally exited the car and began walking toward the house. Serrano said, "Mr. Drummond, Detective John Serrano with the APD. A few minutes of your time."

Then Serrano turned and saw Rachel standing at the foot of the driveway. His eyes grew wide. Rachel heard Tally say, "You've got to be kidding me." Serrano walked briskly toward Rachel, who stood there, rooted in place.

He leaned in and whispered acidly, "What in the *hell* are you doing here?"

# CHAPTER 11

Before Rachel could respond, Nicholas Drummond gingerly walked down the front steps to meet the detectives. He wasn't wearing a coat, just a lightweight red-and-black-checkered flannel over a gray T-shirt. He folded his arms tight across his chest for warmth. Breath misted in front of him. He seemed confused and pained and irritated. The thin man had gone inside. Isabelle was standing atop the steps, watching them, eyes narrow and suspicious.

Serrano waited for a response from Rachel. Clearly they'd come to question Drummond about Constance Wright. Was he a suspect? Or were they just getting background info?

"Mr. Drummond," Tally said, approaching him. Tally eyed Rachel like she would give anything to feed her to a school of piranhas. "My name is Detective Tally. This is my partner, Detective Serrano. May we have a word?"

Drummond said wearily, "This about Constance?"

"It is," Serrano said. "But just routine questions trying to piece together her life before this happened. Dot the t's, cross the i's, you know."

"Yeah, routine," Drummond said, nodding. He didn't seem to trust Serrano that this was routine. "Listen, my wife has had a long day. Her brother, Christopher, went missing, and, well, he's a handful. He's had *issues.*"

"Your wife?" Tally said. "Isabelle Robles, correct? That's her brother who just went inside?"

"She's Isabelle Drummond now, Detective. And yes. Chrissy, Isabelle calls him. Like he's a little girl."

"In-laws can be hell," Tally said with a laugh to put Drummond at ease. "Trust me, I married a woman with three kids who know how to push buttons like they're getting paid. We've been together a long time, and half the time I still worry about saying the wrong thing and getting kicked to the curb."

Drummond offered a weak smile, shivered.

"Listen, I know Chris has had a rough life," Drummond said. "Their dad was a pharmaceutical big shot, and when they got fed up with Chris's *extracurriculars*, they cut him off. So Isabelle has basically been the kid's surrogate parent since Chris was a teenager. She's his rock. Helped him get straightened out, tried to get him off the drugs. But it's hard on a marriage to have someone that volatile dependent on you, not to mention living with you. And Chris has friends . . . let's just say you wouldn't want to get on their bad side."

"How so?"

Drummond eyed the front door. "Listen, Detectives, it's cold out, and my sciatica is worse in the winter. You mind if I . . ."

"Do you mind if we ask you some more questions inside?" Tally said.

Drummond hesitated. Then he looked at Rachel. "Who's she?" he asked.

Serrano opened his mouth, but before he could respond, Rachel said, "Rachel Marin. Forensic consultant. I'm helping the Ashby PD on the Wright murder. Detectives Serrano and Tally have asked for my expertise on this case. It's official police business."

Both Serrano and Tally glared at her with barely contained anger. Rachel could tell it took every ounce of willpower for them not to rip her head clean off. But she knew starting a fight in front of Drummond could make him skittish, suspicious. And the cops needed him calm and, ideally, unlawyered. Rachel was happy to exploit that need.

"That's right," Serrano finally said, through gritted teeth. "Ms. Marin consistently surprises us."

"Yeah, like diarrhea," Tally muttered under her breath.

"All right," Drummond said. "But let's make it quick."

Drummond led them into the house. Rachel followed but felt Serrano's hand on her elbow, holding her back.

"We're going to have a *serious* talk when this is over," he said.

"I know, I know. Detention, right? Maybe take away my iPad for a month?"

"This is a *criminal* investigation, Ms. Marin," Tally said. "You are a citizen. And if Drummond realizes that, you're a lawsuit waiting to happen."

"I just want to know who killed Constance Wright," Rachel said. "If it wasn't for me, her death would have been labeled a suicide and forgotten about. She would be buried, and a killer would be walking *your* streets, Detective."

"I hate to say this," Serrano said softly, "but if we send her packing, it's going to make Drummond wary. That's not how we want to start this questioning."

"What, so she comes, then?" Tally said, exasperated.

Serrano nodded resignedly. "Lesser of two evils."

"God*damn* it," Tally said. She pinched the bridge of her nose. "All right, Ms. Marin. Come with us. But you're going to look, and you're going to listen. That's it. Anything else, and I'm sending you home in an Uber. In one piece *if* you're lucky."

"That's all I want."

Rachel entered the house. She could feel their eyes on her. The entryway of the Drummond home opened up into a large foyer, with clean black-and-white marble flooring, a curved wooden staircase with a wrought iron railing that led up to a second floor covered with taupe carpeting, recessed lighting dotting the cream-colored ceiling, and a crystal chandelier dripping with ornaments overhead. Every fixture looked custom built, every appliance renovated and upgraded. Given these furnishings, Rachel revised her estimate to $4.5 million. And she knew it hadn't been purchased with Drummond's money.

In his divorce filing from Constance Wright, Nicholas Drummond had claimed that, during their marriage, he had become accustomed to a certain luxurious style of living. And despite the Wright family's debts, much of which Constance was on the hook for as a minority owner, he was entitled to a substantial portion of her liquid assets. Drummond managed to negotiate a hefty spousal support, a decision many derided, given Constance's perilous financial situation and that Nicholas had developed a reputation as a freeloader early on. The press derogatorily referred to him as "Saint Nick," since he expected other people to bring *him* presents.

So he'd cleaned Constance out, married Isabelle Robles—a woman seventeen years his junior *and* wealthy—and consequently become the envy of most men in Ashby and a scoundrel to most women.

"Would you mind taking your shoes off?" Isabelle asked them. Rachel noticed the immaculate foyer was lined with a white Surya Milan carpet. The cost of cleaning it was probably more than a Fifth Avenue mortgage. They took off their shoes and assembled them neatly on a small maple bench next to the front door. Rachel placed one of her shoes six inches in front of the other, as a test. When she stepped away, Isabelle made sure to line them up precisely side by side. Rachel saw Tally notice it as well.

Drummond led them into a sitting room covered in fine Oushak rugs with gilded floral patterns. Rachel had seen them in magazines; they cost about four grand apiece. They sat on a pair of overstuffed white Haute House Smith sectional sofas. A quick Google search told Rachel that each one retailed for about $9,000. Large bay windows overlooked an expansive, fenced-in backyard with a pool, covered for the winter, and a large swing set, dappled with fresh snow. The slide looked like it had never been used. The swings and ladders were pristine, no rust on any of the metal. No scuff marks. Rachel noticed that the house had not been childproofed. The swing set was built on a wish, and for a moment she felt a pang of sympathy for Isabelle and Nicholas Drummond.

They all took seats on the Haute House couches: Isabelle and Nicholas on one, and Rachel, Serrano, and Tally on another. Rachel could feel Tally's gun against her hip. She guessed it was a Glock—those were the most popular law enforcement handguns—but couldn't tell whether it was a 19 or a 22.

Isabelle looked miserable. Rachel could understand. The young woman thought she'd married a man whose ugly past was behind him, yet now the police were sitting in her home preparing to question him about his dead ex-wife. Christopher had disappeared somewhere in the house. He seemed too disorganized, too erratic to have killed Constance without leaving an abundance of evidence. But she still didn't know why he was at both the press conference *and* the river the night of Constance's death. Even if he wasn't the killer, Christopher Robles knew something.

"Mr. Drummond," Tally began, "thank you for taking the time to speak with us. And let me say first off, we're sorry for your loss."

Drummond nodded slightly. He put his hand on his wife's knee.

"Connie and I had our troubles, we'd both moved on, but of course I was sad to hear about her death."

*You mean* you *moved on,* Rachel thought.

Isabelle spoke up and said, "Can we get this over with?"

"All right," Serrano said. "As you know, Nicholas, your ex-wife, Constance Wright, is recently deceased. We are investigating her death as a homicide. Can you tell us the last time you saw or spoke to your ex-wife?"

Isabelle spoke up. "First off, is my husband a suspect? Because if he is, I'm going to want our lawyer here before we say another word."

"Mrs. Drummond," Tally said, "right now all we're trying to do is understand the timeline of Ms. Wright's life prior to her passing. I'd prefer to keep this cordial. Whether or not it stays that way is wholly up to you two."

Isabelle said gruffly, "I saw her at the supermarket a few weeks ago. She definitely saw me too. Dropped a jar of almond butter on the floor. It shattered, and she walked out, fast." Isabelle paused, then said, as if to clarify, "We weren't exactly on speaking terms."

Serrano nodded. Tally said, "And you, Mr. Drummond?"

"Haven't seen Connie in a long time," he said. "Our split wasn't exactly the kind of thing where you sent each other Christmas cards."

"I have an ex-wife too," Serrano said. "I understand that. But can you tell us, specifically, the last time you spoke to her?"

Drummond thought. Too hard, in Rachel's opinion. He breathed in through his nose and tilted his head back like a man who knew the answer but had to pretend he didn't.

"I believe it was on the street, randomly," Drummond said. "I was leaving a doctor's appointment, and we just bumped into each other."

"When was this?" Tally asked.

"Maybe a few months ago? I don't remember the exact date."

"Did you say anything to each other?" Serrano asked.

"We exchanged pleasantries."

"What kind of pleasantries?" Tally said, leaning closer.

"Just this and that. Hello. Hope you're well. That was it."

"So it didn't last more than a few seconds."

"No. We both moved on with our lives several years ago, and I'm not much for small talk," Drummond said. Isabelle seemed pleased with this response.

"I think Ms. Wright may have had some trouble moving on," Serrano said. He took a folded printout from his pocket and handed it to Drummond. He underlined a number with his finger. "Is that your cell phone number?"

"It is," Drummond said warily. Rachel sensed hesitation in his voice. Drummond was nervous. Isabelle leaned over to see the paper.

"Because Constance Wright called that number—your cell phone number—the day she died."

Serrano let that sink in. Rachel looked at Isabelle. Her face showed no emotion. Either she knew about the call or wanted them to *think* she knew and simply didn't care.

Drummond snapped his fingers. "That's right. She did call my cell. But I'd deleted her number from my phone. So when it rang, I didn't recognize the number. And I don't tend to pick up calls from numbers I don't recognize. Nine times out of ten it's spam, you know?"

"Sure," Tally said. "Spam."

"So you didn't speak to her?"

"I told you, Detective, I didn't pick up the phone."

Serrano nodded. "If you say so." Drummond was getting defensive. If they kept pushing, Rachel thought, they'd lose him.

Serrano looked around, made a show of admiring the fabulous decor. Then he smiled and switched gears. "This is a gorgeous house. Which of you has the decorating touch?"

Drummond smiled. "That would be my wife." Isabelle rubbed her husband's hand.

"So when did you and Isabelle meet?" Tally said.

Drummond said, "Two years ago. I knew the second I laid eyes on her I wanted her to be my wife." Isabelle smiled again. His answer was warm but practiced.

Tally said, "And where did Cupid strike, might I ask?"

"The gym," Isabelle replied. "I was on the elliptical. He was using kettlebells—*and* with proper form. He was handsome. I don't normally talk to men at the gym. They tend to be creeps."

"That was two years ago?" Serrano said.

"Yep, two," Drummond replied. He removed his hand from Isabelle's and shifted in his seat. "Listen, I know my ex-wife had problems, and things didn't end well with us. Not all of the issues between us were her fault. But when a couple gets divorced, you can't blame the ex for what happens later."

"Depends on whether the ex had anything to do with it," Serrano said.

"Constance and I went our separate ways, and that was that," Drummond said firmly. "I never wished any harm on her. I had nothing to do with Connie's death, and I never had any ill will toward her. We broke up. *I* moved on. I have a wonderful wife. A great life. Now, if you'd like to ask more questions, I'll be happy to call my lawyer. I've talked to you today out of respect for Constance. She was a good woman, and she deserved better."

"Yes. She did," Rachel said. They all turned to look at her. Serrano's eyes grew wide. "I'm sorry, do you have a bathroom I can use?"

Isabelle stood up. She seemed more than happy to get away. "This way, Ms. . . ."

"Marin. Rachel Marin."

"This way, Ms. Marin."

Rachel followed Isabelle out of the sitting room. Rachel looked back at Serrano. He was biting his lip so hard she thought he might chew through it. He mouthed *Don't fuck us*.

The sitting room was off a long hallway lined with ornate brass sconces ending in a T-junction. They passed a gorgeous open kitchen with stainless steel Viking appliances and a beautiful wooden island inset with a second sink. Nonstick pots and pans hung from a hammered steel rack.

"Wow. Now that is something," Rachel said, stopping to marvel at the kitchen. She pointed at the island. "Look at the grain. What kind of wood is that?"

"Australian red ironbark timber," Isabelle said proudly. There was a lightness to her voice that hadn't been present in the sitting room. "It's maybe my favorite piece in the whole house. We had it shipped over from Queensland. The locals call it Mugga."

"It's simply stunning," Rachel said. "You have exquisite taste, Mrs. Drummond. Do you cook?"

Rachel already knew the answer, but she wanted to give Isabelle the satisfaction of answering. Let her feel confident and comfortable. Most of the pots and pans had scorched bases, a sign of frequent use, and Isabelle's fingers sported several miniscule, long-healed-over cuts, evidence of culinary training.

"I do," she said. "I try to cook at least five nights a week."

"Oh my God, you're my idol," Rachel said. "With two kids at home and no husband, it's all I can do to keep the house from burning down. I'm on a first-name basis with the delivery guy at Giuseppe's."

"I'm sure you do the best you can," Isabelle said. Her voice dripped with both sympathy and superiority. Rachel was happy to let her feel both.

"I try," Rachel said. "But it's so *hard.*"

"You must be quite skilled to work with the police department. What did you say you do again?"

"Forensic consulting," Rachel said. She actually liked the way it sounded. "Mainly, I'm just another set of eyes. But those two out there are pros. They don't really need me. I'd rather be learning how to cook like you."

Isabelle beamed. "Maybe one day I'll give you a few lessons. The washroom is at the end of the hall."

"Thank you," Rachel said. "I promise to leave it the way I find it!"

Rachel headed toward the bathroom but stopped before she got there. She waited for Isabelle's footsteps to confirm she was returning to the sitting room.

Rachel found the bathroom door and opened it. It was beautiful. Quartz countertops, a stone inlaid shower with a rainfall showerhead, and a deep soaking tub with massaging air jets. She might just have to befriend Isabelle in order to use her tub.

Without entering, Rachel closed the bathroom door. Loud enough to make a noise. Next to the bathroom was a small closet. She opened it. High thread count linens and soft towels. Artisan soaps and expensive cleaning supplies. Rachel scanned the shelves but didn't see anything particularly noteworthy.

She gently closed the closet door, then followed the T-junction. She opened another door and found a walk-in closet filled with coats, scarves, hats, and shoes. The closet itself was the size of Rachel's bedroom and far more organized. Rachel thumbed through the coats. More specifically, the small tab of cloth by the neck where each store had affixed its price tag.

She took out her cell phone and snapped pictures of as many items as she could, then flipped through the photos. One piece of clothing stood out. She looked up the SKU. Rachel whistled under her breath.

*Very* interesting. Serrano and Tally needed to see it.

Rachel had been gone four minutes. Any longer, and Isabelle would get suspicious—either that Rachel was snooping around or that she'd eaten a burrito for lunch.

She sneaked back to the bathroom, silently opened the door, and slipped in. She flushed the toilet, washed her hands, and then dried them on a hand towel. She refolded the towel perfectly and replaced it on the rack.

But when Rachel opened the door, she jumped back and nearly yelped. Christopher Robles was standing right outside the bathroom door, like he was waiting for her. The man said nothing. Just stared at Rachel. His eyes were sunken and red rimmed. His cheeks were the sallow grayish yellow of someone who'd ingested large quantities of illicit substances that the human body was not meant to process. But behind those sunken eyes was suspicion.

"Sorry about that," Rachel said, composing herself. "How do I get back to the sitting room?"

Robles did not respond. Rachel simply apologized again and slid by him. She could feel his eyes following her.

She rejoined the others, still thinking about Robles's face. She didn't like how he seemed to recognize her. That was the thing with junkies: they were all paranoid until they found someone who actually was out to get them.

Isabelle looked at Rachel, who mouthed the words *That bathroom is gorgeous*, accentuating it with an eye roll.

Isabelle smiled, blushed slightly, and mouthed, *Thank you.*

Rachel sat there, silent, as Serrano and Tally continued questioning Drummond. Routine stuff. He didn't have much of an alibi for the night Constance died—Isabelle was out to dinner with friends, and Drummond claimed he'd stayed home, ordered from Mr. Foo's, and binged season three of *Breaking Bad* on Netflix. Serrano told him they would check with Mr. Foo's to confirm. Rachel got the sense they simply wanted to gauge Drummond's reaction. See if he got nervous. Other than likely feeling the general discomfort of being questioned by police about his ex-wife's death, he didn't appear overly defensive.

When they finished, Serrano and Tally gave Isabelle and Drummond their cards and asked them to get in touch if they thought of anything else. Drummond looked at Rachel, expecting to be given a card as well. Rachel froze for a moment, then said, "Crap, left them in my other purse. But Serrano and Tally are leads on this. I'm just along for the ride."

Drummond got up to walk the detectives out. Isabelle stayed seated.

As he opened the heavy wooden front door, Drummond said, "I hope you find him."

"Sorry?" Tally said.

"Or her. Whoever did this to Connie. I know how it might look," Drummond continued. "Everyone looks at the ex-husband. But our marriage ended a long time ago. Even before the actual divorce, it had been over for a long time. I had no reason to want to hurt her after all this time. My wife and I have other things to worry about. We're trying to start a family."

"Thank you for your hospitality, Mr. and Mrs. Drummond," Serrano said. "If we need anything else, we'll be in touch."

"Good luck with the family," Tally said. "Things like that test a marriage."

"Don't I know it," Drummond replied. There was a weight to the comment that Rachel picked up on that the detectives did not.

Rachel looked over her shoulder as they walked to the Crown Vic. Drummond watched them depart. Then he turned around and went back inside.

When they reached the curb, Serrano put his hand on Rachel's arm and said, "We need to talk. *Now.*"

Rachel whipped around and said, "If you don't take your stubby little fingers off me right now, the next time you jerk off, it'll be with a prosthetic hand."

Serrano removed his hand and stepped back, surprised at the anger in Rachel's response. Tally's hand moved toward her sidearm.

"You are a civilian, Ms. Marin," Tally said coolly. "You threaten my partner again, and I'll have you in handcuffs before you take your next breath."

"I'm sorry," Rachel said. "That was an instinctual reaction. Lot of pent-up stress. It's been a while since I've been to yoga."

"Now let's talk about just what in the hell you think you're doing," Serrano said.

"They're lying," Rachel said. "Drummond and his wife. Both of them."

Serrano cocked his head, and Tally laughed.

"Is that so?" Tally said. "And what, pray tell, are they lying about, Nancy Drew?"

"Well, the timeline to start. Drummond and Isabelle started dating while he and Constance were still married. That 'two years' claim is crap."

"How do you figure?" Tally said.

Rachel took out her phone and opened the Photos app. She showed them the pictures she'd taken in Isabelle's coat closet.

"So you searched their home without a warrant. Fantastic," Tally said. She turned to Serrano. "You realize if Drummond *is* our guy and this case goes to trial, they could ram that down our throats and have this whole thing thrown out."

"Ms. Marin, before you start showing us inadmissible evidence of God knows what, just how the hell did you end up here anyway?" Serrano asked.

"Christopher Robles," she said. "Isabelle's brother. He was at the bridge the night you found Constance Wright's body." She showed Serrano and Tally the screen grab from Charles Willemore's broadcast. Christopher Robles's face was visible among the bystanders.

"And then he was at the press conference today," Rachel said. "So the brother-in-law of the victim's ex-husband is at the murder scene and then the press conference. No way that's a coincidence. Robles knows something."

"So you followed Robles home after the presser?" Tally asked.

"Hey, you *are* a detective!" Rachel said.

"My patience is wearing *real* thin with you, Ms. Marin," Tally replied.

"Try me," Rachel said with defiant ease.

"Stop it, the two of you," Serrano said, trying to defuse the situation.

"So, what," Tally said, "you think Robles killed Constance Wright?"

"Not sure. I don't know how Robles gets Wright to the bridge in the middle of the night," Rachel said. "But it's possible Drummond got her there and Robles knew about it somehow. Drummond said that

Isabelle has been Christopher's caretaker since their parents cut him off. And if Isabelle's husband gets put away for murder, it ruins her. If the one person who cared about you was about to have their life torn apart, wouldn't you be scared too? So maybe Robles knew something he wasn't supposed to."

Serrano walked up to Rachel and gently put his finger in the center of her chest. She looked at the digit like she wanted to rip it clean off. He saw her anger but didn't move. Neither did she.

"You need to hear this," Serrano said. "I don't know what the hell you think you're doing. This armchair Sherlock Holmes BS doesn't fly here. You want to sit at home, connect pushpins on a corkboard, solve the mystery of D. B. Cooper, find the Loch Ness Monster, or figure out who really killed JFK? Go right ahead. But you are a *civilian.* You have as much right to be at this house as my dog. Only difference is when my dog shits where he's not supposed to, at least it's confined to *my* house."

"Did you just call me a dog?" Rachel said.

"No, that's . . . it's a figure of speech."

"I'm not sure you know what *figure of speech* means."

"Just shut *up.* Go home, Ms. Marin."

"Just look," Rachel said. She turned the phone's screen to face Serrano and Tally. "That's the hanging tag on one of Isabelle Drummond's coats. This is a Lilly e Violetta Italian wool coat. Retails for about thirty-five hundred dollars. This particular coat was introduced in this year's line. It's brand new. *Everything* in that house is brand new and top of the line."

"So?" Serrano said. Rachel swiped to the next picture.

"This is a Mischa wool beanie. Retails for seven hundred and fifty dollars. Based on the SKU, this make was also introduced the current year. And you can tell from the slight fraying at the edges that it's been worn this winter."

"OK . . ."

Rachel swiped to the next photo. An unattractive, chunky gray winter hat. It looked out of place among the rest of Isabelle Drummond's pricey apparel.

"This hat was manufactured by a company called Freida. Based on the SKU, it retailed for about fifty dollars. And it's clearly never been worn. Every thread looks untouched." Rachel pinched the picture to zoom in on the tag. "See that?"

Serrano leaned in. He shook his head.

"Look at the hole. Where the plastic tag used to be. See how it's ripped? Like someone tore the plastic tag off instead of cutting it with scissors."

"Fine, I see what you're showing me," Serrano said. "But what does that matter?"

"Whoever took off the tag, they ripped it out with their fingers."

"So what?" Serrano said. "I do that."

"Exactly. Now look." Rachel swiped back to the previous picture and zoomed in. "This is the expensive Mischa beanie. The tag hole here is even. No pulling or stretching of the material. That means somebody trimmed it, delicately. Neat and tidy."

Rachel swiped through a number of photos. "Every one of these articles of clothing had a hole just like the coat. Isabelle clipped them all herself. A different person removed the tag from the hat. They just ripped it off. Which means . . ."

Tally said, "That Isabelle didn't buy the Freida hat for herself."

"Precisely," Rachel said. "And whoever bought it *for* her ripped the tag out."

"That hat," Serrano said. "When was it produced?"

Rachel smiled. He was catching on.

"Freida went out of business and was liquidated three years ago, right after this particular SKU was manufactured. Which means that hat was almost certainly purchased *prior* to Constance Wright's divorce from Nicholas Drummond."

"So Drummond bought it for her as a present," Serrano said. "No way Isabelle spends three grand on a coat and fifty bucks on a hat."

"So you think Drummond bought the Frieda hat for Isabelle?" Tally said.

"Absolutely," Rachel said. She swiped back to the hat photo. "Look at the wool on the Freida. No fraying. This hat has barely been worn, if ever. Isabelle doesn't keep it for practical reasons. It has sentimental value to her."

"Could be a gift from anyone," Tally said. "An ex."

Rachel shook her head. "If that fifty-dollar hat was a gift from an ex-boyfriend, no way it's sitting in the closet in plain sight. She's tossing that thing out as soon as she gets an engagement ring. And if she still holds a candle for an ex, she keeps it somewhere safe and hidden where her husband won't find it."

"If that's true," Serrano said, "it could mean Drummond started dating Isabelle Robles before he claims he did in his court filings."

"Why does that matter?" Tally said.

"Because in his divorce proceedings from Constance Wright," Serrano said, "Nicholas Drummond received spousal support to the tune of $100,000 a month. He only actually married Isabelle Robles two years ago. Which means there was a period where Drummond may have been dating Isabelle Robles while still raking in $100,000 a month from Constance. So if they were dating for a year, that adds up to . . ."

"One point two million dollars," Rachel said.

Tally whistled. "If a spouse engages in illicit sexual behavior prior to a legal separation, a court can bar postseparation alimony. If the court knew that Drummond was in a relationship with Isabelle Robles, who has her own money, there's no way they award Drummond that kind of spousal support. So he hid his relationship with Isabelle to make sure he got paid."

"If I was Constance," Rachel said, "and I found out that my ex-husband started dating his rich, practically teenage girlfriend while we were still legally married, and he then took me for a million two under false pretenses, I'd be pretty pissed off. I'd demand he give that money back. With interest. And maybe I'd murder him, too, just for kicks."

Tally said, "So if Constance did find out and demanded the money back, why wouldn't Drummond just get it from his new wife? Seems like she could afford it."

Rachel said, "Nicholas Drummond married a political star, then left her in ruins and married a rich heiress. He's been indebted to women his whole life. Asking his current wife for a million dollars to pay off his ex-wife would be tantamount to cutting off his dick and flushing it down the toilet."

"You're suggesting he'd kill someone before impugning his masculinity," Tally said, incredulously.

"You ever meet a man?" Rachel replied. "That's exactly what I'm saying."

Serrano looked at Tally and said, "A million two is a heck of a motive for Drummond to not want Constance Wright around anymore."

Tally replied, "Or it's possible Isabelle bought that hat herself, got drunk, pulled the tag out, and this is all speculative BS."

Rachel said, "Detective Tally, you saw how she straightened my shoes in the foyer. That house looks like Mary Poppins floats down from heaven and dusts everything twice a day."

"Still doesn't prove anything," Tally said.

"It might prove that Nicholas Drummond lied to save himself a million bucks," Rachel said.

"Isabelle Robles is loaded," Tally said. "Why risk so much for one point two mil?"

"Hedging his bets, perhaps," Serrano said. "He couldn't be sure he'd marry Isabelle. And even if he was, she probably has a prenup forged by the greatest lawyers money can buy. He'd need cash of his own if the marriage went south."

"Maybe Isabelle knew about the settlement money, maybe not," Rachel said. "She was probably happy to stick her head in the sand. But like your partner said, Detective Tally, bilking Constance for one point two million is a pretty good motive for Nicholas Drummond to want something bad to happen to her. Now *your* job is to prove it."

"You're right," Serrano said. "That's *our* job. Not yours."

"If you two did your job, you wouldn't need me," Rachel said. Tally stepped forward, fists clenched. Serrano gently took his partner's arm, held her back.

"You don't know the first thing about what we do," Tally said. "You snoop around some closets, and suddenly you think you know how to investigate a homicide? We've seen more in one night than you will in your lifetime."

"You don't know me," Rachel said.

"And I don't want to," Tally said. "Go home, Ms. Marin."

Rachel glared at Serrano. Then at Tally. She said, "A woman lost her life because no one cared enough to help her. I'm tired of seeing people slip through the cracks. A life was broken, and now you're just cleaning up the mess. Even if you do your jobs correctly, which is the mother of all *ifs*, you never should have let her break in the first place."

"What do you have against the police?" Tally said.

"The same thing I have against genital herpes."

"We'll say it once more," Serrano said, "Go *home*, Ms. Marin."

"Find whoever did this," Rachel said.

"You don't give us orders," Serrano said.

"It's not an order, Detective, it's a cry for help. I want to make sure *someone* is fighting for Constance Wright."

"We *are* fighting for her," Serrano replied.

"Easy to say that after the fact."

"You can't investigate a crime before it happens," Serrano said, "and you can't always prevent someone's pain."

"Pain is almost *always* preventable," Rachel said, her voice solemn. "I hope it doesn't take either of you losing someone you love to realize that, Detectives. Neither of you know the first thing about loss. Maybe one day you will."

When Rachel finished speaking, she saw Serrano's face turn ashen. The light left his eyes. His arms fell to his sides. Rachel knew she'd struck a nerve, crossed a line she didn't know was there. She immediately wished she could take the comment back.

Serrano turned around, walked to the car, and got in. Tally looked at Rachel with a mixture of disgust and disappointment on her face.

Tally said. "It's getting late. I'm sure your children would like to see their mother. Know that she's there for *them.*"

Tally got into the car, and the detectives drove off, leaving Rachel standing in the icy Drummond driveway alone. At that moment, Rachel realized how cold she was. She looked back at the house. Christopher Robles was staring at her from an open upstairs window. She wondered how much of the conversation he'd heard and why he was watching her. Even though she couldn't quite understand why, she felt tremendous guilt for what she'd said to Serrano.

For the first time, Rachel noticed that night had fallen over Ashby. Snowflakes gently drifted around her, beautiful in the evening glow. She checked her watch. Felt her heart clench. She was supposed to have been home an hour ago. She looked at her phone. There were four missed calls from Iris. Rachel felt frustration and rage well up in her chest as she ran to her car, the cold wind freezing a stream of tears on her cheeks.

◆◆◆

The car felt like a tomb. Serrano hadn't said a word since they'd left the Drummond residence. The silence unnerved Tally. Not the quiet itself. Lord knew she sometimes relished a respite from all of Serrano's talk about books full of goblins and magic. But the reason behind the quiet ate at her. As soon as the Marin woman had said those words—*Neither of you know the first thing about loss*—she had felt Serrano withdraw. Eight years since that night, and the wounds still hadn't healed. She knew they probably never would. The silence worried her. She'd seen the man's darkness. And she knew it had never fully lifted.

Tally would head home to her family and spend the night in bed, warm, next to her loving wife. Serrano would spend the night in a cold, empty house, alone.

Tally's wife, Claire Wallace, was ten years her senior. Claire had been married previously, to a man, and had given birth to three wonderful children. Claire and Tally met eighteen months after the divorce, on a blind date of all things, and they both fell hard. It was not an easy situation for Tally. Claire's children were struggling mightily with the split and their mother's coming-out. Their father was a good man—even Claire admitted that—and for a long time they struggled to forgive their mother. Detective Tally had the ignominy of being Claire Wallace's first girlfriend. At first, the children hated her. Refused to speak to her. But over time, the wounds from the divorce healed, and the children began to accept Claire's new life. And began to accept Leslie Tally.

It took time for the family to blend, but once they did, they blended like a fine Bordeaux. Tally watched over Claire's children like they were her own, and they allowed her into their own little worlds. She introduced them to her partner, John Serrano, and they loved hearing Serrano regale them with tales of demons and dragons. *At least some people appreciate my taste in literature,* he said. They had him over for dinner half a dozen times a year, and he always brought over a delicious bottle of Châteauneuf-du-Pape. Claire beamed every time Serrano helped himself to a second plate of her delicious osso buco.

One terrible night, Claire's youngest, Bobby, came down with meningitis. One moment the five of them were snuggled up watching a movie on the Disney channel, kettle corn peppering the sofa, and the next moment Bobby was on the floor, convulsing. They rushed him to the Mackenzie North pediatric unit, all the while Tally unsure of how large a part in this medical emergency she should play. She was Claire's girlfriend, not Bobby's mother, and the kids were still coming to terms with their relationship. So while Claire stayed at Mackenzie with Bobby, Tally remained at Claire's house and watched Penny and Elyse. The three of them sat by the phone with tear-streaked faces, hour after hour, praying Bobby would pull through.

Claire texted constant updates. Tally's heart stopped every time her phone chimed with a new text.

His fever hit 104 today

He can't hold down any food. They're feeding him through an IV. I can't cry in front of him.

And Tally would text back platitudes—Stay strong, we're praying for him—because she simply didn't know what else to say.

Bobby was in intensive care for two weeks. Two weeks straight, Tally was scared to death. Scared for the child. Scared for the future of her relationship. It had been a long time since she'd loved someone the way she loved Claire, and if something happened to Bobby, it would never be the same.

How was it possible to feel fear and selfishness at the same time?

Tally cried nonstop. Hid it at work. Hid it from Serrano. He knew something was up but knew enough not to ask. Cops cried, but not in front of each other.

During the two weeks where Bobby was touch and go, Tally cooked for Penny and Elyse every night. She did the laundry, cleaned the house when they went to bed, and said a prayer for Bobby before she closed her eyes. Tally figured it was the least she could do as her girlfriend sat by her son's bedside at the hospital, praying the virus wouldn't take his life. All the while, Tally was petrified both of doing too much and not enough and was never quite sure where the line was for either.

The night Claire brought Bobby home from the hospital, the family celebrated and cried until they had no tears left. Then, when they put the kids to bed, Leslie and Claire made love with a quiet intensity and urgency. And from that day forward, they had known they would never be apart again.

Driving now, with Serrano silent in the seat next to her, Leslie Tally thought about those haunting nights, waiting to hear from Claire, steeling her resolve if the dreaded call ever came that Bobby had passed away. Thank God it never had. But Tally remembered that fear, that sadness, that anxiety. And it hadn't even been for her own blood.

When John Serrano's life had cracked in half, Tally had been his partner less than a year. She hadn't known him well. She had given him the same platitudes.

*It'll get better.* Even though she had known it never really would.

She'd thought he would leave the force. Especially after his rift with Constance Wright. She'd even hoped, for a brief time, that she would be reassigned to a partner whose baggage didn't weigh them down. She regretted those feelings, because now Tally couldn't imagine working with anyone else. John Serrano felt like family the same way Bobby, Penny, Elyse, and Claire felt like family. Not her blood, but it didn't matter. And family took care of family.

"John," Tally said. "Talk to me."

Serrano offered a weak smile. "I don't remember the last time you called me John."

"I whip it out for special occasions. Hey, don't let what that Marin woman said get to you. She doesn't know anything, and she's clearly got a screw loose."

"I know. You're right," Serrano said. But it was lip service. Serrano was in pain.

As they crossed Parker Avenue, heading uptown toward the precinct, Serrano said, "Hey, pull over here."

"Why?" Tally said. Then it hit her. "John, come on. You're going to Voss Field, aren't you?"

"It's been too long since I visited. I need to see it."

"We need to write up our report on Nicholas Drummond. The lieutenant will be expecting it first thing tomorrow. I need you, partner. Going there tonight won't do you any good."

"It's not about good or bad. It's just something I need to do. Do me a solid, Leslie," Serrano said. "You write up the report tonight. I'll make it up to you."

"You sure?"

"I'm sure."

"All right. Don't stay out past curfew," she said.

Tally pulled over at the corner of Parker and Willoughby. Snow was dusting the windshield, collecting at the edges of her vision, where they were swept aside by the wipers. Serrano got out of the car, leaned in, and said, "Thanks." Then he shut the door and walked off.

Tally watched as Serrano walked to a bodega on the corner, his hair immediately carpeted with falling snow. Tally couldn't watch. She'd seen this story before. Alcohol and melancholy went hand in hand.

Tally put on her blinker and drove off. She let one tear slide down her cheek and quickly wiped it away. One tear in private. That's all she'd allow herself. She couldn't drown in other people's sorrows. John Serrano had an ocean of sadness he had to swim every single day. It wasn't her job to continually toss him a life raft when he drifted.

One of these days, Tally thought ruefully, Serrano would go under. She couldn't let him drag her down too.

# CHAPTER 12

By the time Rachel got home, she was cold, wet, shivering, exhausted, and scared. It was well after 8:00 p.m. She'd called Iris while running to the car from the Drummond house, praying she wouldn't slip and break her neck while doing so, pleading with her sitter not to leave her children home alone.

When Rachel opened the front door, she saw Iris standing in the foyer, her coat already on, purse slung over her shoulder. Rachel knew at that moment they'd never see each other again.

"I'm sorry," Rachel said. "I don't know what else to say."

"I love your children," Iris said, her voice full of regret. "But you need to find someone else to take care of them."

The comment cut through Rachel like a blade, searing her from stomach to eyes.

"Please," Rachel said, her voice trembling. "I'm begging you, Iris. We need you."

"You've always been kind to me, Ms. Marin. But we'll have this same conversation next week. And the week after that too. I already said goodbye to Eric and Megan. They don't understand. But that has to be on you to explain it to them, not me."

"I'll pay you more," Rachel said. "Just name your price."

Iris shook her head. "This job isn't always about the money."

She stepped forward and wrapped her arms around Rachel. Rachel hugged her back weakly, feeling like every last bit of energy had been siphoned from her body. She remembered how hard it had been to find

Iris. Demand for good, responsible nannies in Ashby far outpaced supply. With Iris's impeccable credentials and referrals, Rachel had agreed to pay her fifty dollars more per day than what other families were offering. Rachel couldn't have just anyone watching her children. Not after what they'd been through.

"I'm sorry," Rachel said.

"I am too." Then Iris picked up her umbrella and walked out of their lives.

Rachel took a deep breath and went upstairs to face her children. Her mind was racing. She'd need to find a stopgap solution. Another sitter. Eric wasn't old enough to watch Megan alone, and given his tempestuous attitude recently, she wasn't sure she'd even trust him.

Megan's door was cracked open. She was lying on the floor with a carton of markers and pages of colorful paper spilled out in front of her. One such page read *Sadie Scout and the Mystery of the Easter Egg Hunt*. Rachel smiled. She loved that her daughter's imagination was churning at such an early age. Both she and Eric had been bookworms, devouring every book they could get their hands on. It warmed Rachel's heart to see her making something of her own. For a moment, Rachel stood in the doorway, marveling at this small, gorgeous girl feeding her bottomless imagination.

"I hear you, Mom," Megan said, still scribbling. She didn't turn around, just grabbed another page and continued coloring. Then, dramatically, she flipped onto her back and craned her head up. "You try to be all sneaky, but I can hear you."

"You're like a little sonar machine," Rachel said, smiling warmly.

"Somar? What's that?"

"Sonar, not somar. It's a device that can pick up the smallest, tiniest sounds. Sounds nothing else can hear."

"So I'm like a radar."

"You are. My beautiful little radar."

Megan thought for a moment. She seemed to like the idea of being a radar.

"Iris said she isn't coming back," Megan said. "Is that true?"

Rachel's heart felt heavy. She sat down next to Megan and put her hand on her daughter's leg. Megan wasn't crying. That saddened Rachel. Megan was used to saying goodbye.

"Yes. I'm so sorry, sweetie."

"How come she's not coming back? I asked her, but she didn't really say much. She said you would tell us."

Rachel sighed.

"Mommy messed up. Mommy messed up big-time," Rachel said.

"How did you mess up?"

"Iris has her own family. Her own life. Not just you and Eric. And, well, Mommy made it hard for Iris."

"Why did you make it hard for her?"

"Mommy didn't do it on purpose . . . Mommy just lost track of time. She wants *so badly* to not just be a good mommy but also a good person. It wasn't Iris's fault at all. She loves you two."

"Then why did she leave? Why does everyone go away? Iris? Even our friends. And Dad."

There it was. The gut punch. Tears welled up in Rachel's eyes. She hugged Megan tight and stroked her hair.

"Oh, sweetie, your father didn't go away, you know that. He still loves you from up on high."

"But he's still gone. And now Iris is gone."

"You know that's not the same thing," Rachel said.

"How?" Megan said. She sat up, stared at her mother, defiance flaring in her eyes. "How is it different? I'm never going to see Iris again just like I'm never going to see my friends or Dad again. You *told* us that before we moved here."

"You'll always have memories of Iris," Rachel said softly, "just like we still have memories of your dad."

"*I* don't have memories of Dad," Megan said. "I was a baby. I don't really remember anything. Sometimes it feels like I never had a dad."

"Oh, baby, that couldn't be further from the truth. You had a wonderful dad, and he loved you with all his heart. He still loves you, just from somewhere else."

"I miss him so much. How can you miss someone you didn't really know?" Megan began to cry.

There was no agony greater than seeing your child in pain. Rachel gathered her daughter into her arms and held her close. Her face grew hot as her daughter's tears wet her blouse.

"You can miss your daddy. I miss him every single day."

"It's not fair," Megan said. "I hope that man who took Daddy is dead."

"Megan," Rachel said. "Don't say things like that."

"I do. I hope they caught him and killed him."

"Baby, you should never talk like that."

"It's not fair that he's out there and Dad's not."

Rachel stayed silent. There was nothing she could say to make the hurt go away.

*Besides, I agree with her.*

"Hold on to those memories," Rachel said. "And if they ever get fuzzy, come talk to me. I'll make them whole again. I remember every moment like it was yesterday."

Rachel kissed Megan on the cheek and stood up. "I'm going to see how your brother is doing. I hear there's a new Wimpy Kid book out. I'll bring you home a copy tomorrow."

"That's a bribe."

Rachel laughed. "How do you know what a bribe is?"

"Iris taught us. Eric told her he would do his homework if she let him play fifteen more minutes on his computer. She said he was bribing her."

"See. You really are a radar."

Megan smiled. Rachel kissed her cheek one more time and went to see Eric.

Her son's door was closed. She knocked—a habit that was hard to learn. One day he was her little man; the next day he wanted "privacy."

"Yeah?" he said. Not the warmest welcome, but she was used to it. Rachel entered his room.

Eric was sitting at his computer, playing a game with so much going on it made Rachel's eyes hurt. He was tapping away at the keyboard while a soldier with biceps the size of Buicks and a gun the size of a confectionary oven was massacring aliens that looked like giant gobs of purple-green phlegm with teeth.

"I didn't say you could come in," Eric said.

"You said 'yeah.' I took that as an acknowledgment of my presence."

Eric shrugged. He paused the game right as one of the phlegm creatures was being blasted into intergalactic space goop. He swiveled his chair around. "So I guess Iris is toast."

"She's not toast. We just decided it was time for her to move on."

"You're lying. She quit."

"Yes. She quit."

"So what are you going to do with Megan when she gets home from school?"

"I'm not quite sure yet."

"I can watch her when I get home."

Rachel laughed. "Not yet you won't."

"I bet I'm cheaper than Iris was," he said.

"And how exactly do you know how much Iris cost?"

"I saw you paying her one day. You were counting out twenties on the counter." Eric paused. "It was a lot of twenties."

"It costs a lot to convince someone to take care of two monsters like you and your sister."

"So what *are* you going to do?" he said.

"I'll think of something."

Eric didn't seem disturbed by Iris's departure. She knew it would hit Megan hard. But she supposed Eric was older, didn't need as much attention. He came home from school and went right to his room. But she knew he had also been pushing his emotions away, burying them. She worried his emotions had calcified. Megan had been younger when they'd left. Eric had friends. A life. And he had to say goodbye to all of it.

He was six when their lives were turned upside down. Young, but old enough to remember the way things used to be in a way that Megan did not. Losing Iris after everything he'd been through wouldn't shake him. He'd lived through worse.

But Rachel *wanted* him to be upset. She wanted him to be a normal kid. To be affected the way other kids would be. But after the horror he'd experienced, those "normal" wires had been frayed. Eric was a good kid. No, a *great* kid. But Rachel was waiting for him to exhibit all the erratic behaviors that *she* had as a child, the reckless and capricious behaviors of a growing boy. She *wanted* Eric to get in trouble. Throw a baseball through a window. Drink a beer. Moon a tour bus full of nuns. Eventually break a few hearts.

It was hard for Rachel to complain that her son came home, did his homework, played around on his computer, and went to bed. But she felt his youth had been stolen well before its time, leaving a thirteen-year-old shell of a boy in its wake.

Rachel looked at the computer screen. "What on earth are you playing?"

*"Galactic Warfare Brigade 11."*

"Eleven? Does that mean you already played the first ten? When do you have time for homework?"

"How are my grades?" Eric asked. "Because until my grades start to suck, you can't tell me to do anything. Plus number twelve will be out next month, and I intend to play that one too."

"How do you pay for these games?" she said.

"I don't. I belong to an online group, and they post pirated versions of games and movies and music where you can get it for free."

"Isn't that stealing?" Rachel said.

"They don't need the money," he replied.

"Imagine you made a game. Spent years of your life working on it. And then someone stole it. What would you say?"

"That I should have been more careful."

Rachel sighed and rubbed her temples. "I don't know where you learned this behavior."

"Can I unpause the game now? Or do you have more to say?"

Sometimes, at moments like these, she could visualize herself slapping her son. The casual cruelty was shocking. She took a breath. Eric was hurting. Lashing out.

"All right, Galactic Commander. Get back to shooting Play-Doh or whatever those purple things are."

Rachel went to leave but paused. There was a gentle thumping noise coming from outside his window. It sounded like someone rapping on a glass door. Not a gentle tap, though. Determined. Eric appeared to notice it too. He got up and looked out the window.

He leaned forward, a confused look on his face. Then the confusion turned quickly to alarm.

"What is it?" Rachel said. She joined him at the window and looked down. Her breath caught in her chest when she saw what he was looking at.

"Um, Mom?" Eric said. "Why is there a man with a gun standing outside our living room window? Is he . . . trying to get in?"

Before Rachel could answer, a gunshot rang out, and the window shattered. Eric screamed. Then a man with a gun climbed through the broken window and into their home.

# CHAPTER 13

Rachel heard three things simultaneously:

The sound of glass crunching on linoleum. Meaning the gunman was in the kitchen.

The sound of Eric screaming beside her.

The home alarm system blaring.

The alarm was hardwired to notify the local monitoring station. They would then call Rachel's cell phone and, if she didn't pick up, immediately dial out to 911. The gunshot had definitely come from a 9 mm handgun. But she didn't know if that was the intruder's only weapon.

"Stay right here!" Rachel shouted to Eric. She sprinted toward Megan's room just as her cell phone began to ring. She pressed accept.

"This is Rachel Marin. We have an armed intruder in our home. Dial 911 *immediately.*"

She hung up. Response time would be anywhere from three to six minutes, depending on the proximity of the nearest law enforcement officers. Rachel heard the sound of crunching glass on wood.

He was in the dining room.

Three minutes would be an eternity. Six might be too long.

Rachel flung open the door to Megan's room and found her daughter huddled under her desk, whimpering.

"What's happening?" she asked, eyes wide, terrified.

"Just come with me, baby." Rachel took Megan's hand and led her down the hall toward Eric's room.

"Mom?" Eric said. He was breathing fast, eyes wide with terror. Rachel brought Megan over to Eric. Megan took her brother's hand.

"You two stay together," she whispered. "Take your shoes off, Eric."

"But the broken glass downstairs . . ."

"You're not going downstairs. Follow me. And stay quiet."

Eric removed his shoes. Rachel took his hand, and they tiptoed down the hallway. Rachel could hear footsteps on the first floor and the sounds of someone mumbling imperceptibly. She'd bought the two story in part for this very reason. In case of an intruder, the perpetrator wouldn't be on the same floor as the children's bedrooms.

Rachel had only one option. They couldn't flee via the roof. They'd be sitting ducks, and she still didn't know what other weapons the gunman might have. There was one way to definitively keep her children safe. She'd have to answer a lot of questions after it was over. But at least they would be safe, and at least there would definitely *be* an after for them.

Rachel led Eric and Megan to a door at the end of the second floor hallway. It was locked by a keypad. Rachel typed in the numbers 824703. The red light turned green.

She'd paid a great deal of money to build a staircase that led to the basement from the second floor. She'd done it hoping a moment like this would never come.

"Go downstairs," Rachel said softly but urgently. "Stay there. Nobody will be able to hear you, and nobody will be able to get down there. The police will be here soon. There's a phone down there. It goes to an outside line. If for any reason I don't come down to get you in eight minutes, use that phone to dial 911. Tell them you're in the basement. Tell them the man inside our house is armed with a nine millimeter handgun and possibly more."

Eric looked confused. "I thought you said the basement was locked because of asbestos. That we couldn't go down there or we'd get sick."

"I lied," Rachel said. "I'll explain later. The code for the door at the bottom of the stairs is your father's birthday. It's six digits: year, then month, then day. Eric, do you remember his birthday?"

Eric nodded.

"Once I close the door behind you, the light will come on. Do *not* come back upstairs until either I come get you or the police arrive. Promise me. *Promise me.*"

"We promise," both children said in unison.

She opened the doorway, revealing a carpeted staircase. A single recessed overhead light flickered on. Eric and Megan hesitated. Rachel leaned down and kissed them both.

"It'll be OK. Now go!"

"Why aren't you coming with us?" Megan said, eyes wide. She was scared but trying to be strong. Eric was shaking, holding back a scream. She recognized the look of terror on his face. She'd seen it before, seven years ago, on their front porch.

"Because I don't want this one getting away."

"Like Harwood Greene," Eric said. Rachel kissed her son's forehead.

"Like Harwood Greene."

He nodded. "Go get him, Mom."

Rachel gathered them both together, hugged them quickly, and then pushed them toward the open door.

The children crept downstairs, the carpet muffling their steps.

She gently closed the door behind them.

Rachel was alone with whoever was inside her house.

She walked swiftly to her bedroom, opened the closet, and pushed aside several hanging dresses to reveal the metal safe. Rachel plugged in the code. The lock slid open. She opened the thick metal door, removed her Mossberg 500 shotgun, and poured half a dozen extra buckshot shells into her pocket.

Rachel then went to the hallway and opened the metal box containing the circuit breakers. She pulled each breaker switch up. Immediately, the house was shrouded in darkness. She'd cut the power. The basement circuits were separate from the main domicile, so Eric and Megan would still be able to see.

She switched on the gun's flashlight mount and moved to the bedroom door. She pressed her back against the wall and listened.

The house was pitch black except for the soda can–thick beam of light emanating from the shotgun. Rachel heard a crash downstairs and stopped moving. The gunman was muttering something indecipherable under his breath.

Bizarre. Whoever was inside their home was clearly an amateur. They weren't even trying to remain stealthy. But they'd have to know that the initial gunshot would have raised an alarm. Neighbors would call 911. His carelessness worried Rachel. The intruder was clearly not of sound mind, which made him unpredictable. Thieves were predictable. Get in, get out. This man wasn't a thief. The realization made her blood run cold. It meant he was there for her.

Rachel removed her shoes and slowly moved to the top of the stairs. She switched the gun light off, not wanting to give away her position. Then she listened. She heard footsteps.

Crouching, she eased down the stairs one step at a time, stopping on each one to listen. The noises stopped. Rachel waited.

Then she heard a voice. He was in the living room.

"I'm not gonna let you!" The man's voice was high pitched, unstable, and . . . scared?

*Not gonna let me what?*

When she reached the bottom of the stairs, Rachel turned the gun light back on. She knew the layout of the house in the dark. The intruder did not. The foyer off the stairs split off into two paths: the dining room to Rachel's left and the living room to the right. The living room flowed into the kitchen, which was connected to the laundry room, which then circled around back to the dining room. The man was somewhere in this circle. Rachel didn't hear any sirens. It had been, by her estimate, just under two minutes since the initial gunshot.

She turned right and crept into the living room. She looked at the TV, hoping to catch a reflection. Nothing.

She heard a crunching sound and wheeled around. Her right hand was tight on the shotgun's forearm, the stock nestled into her shoulder. She swept the gun light over the room. Nothing.

Rachel stayed low. She was sweating, blood pounding in her temples. She duck-walked into the kitchen. Empty. As was the laundry room.

Then she heard a creaking noise that was unmistakably the sound of someone going up a flight of stairs. He'd circled around behind her and was heading up toward the bedrooms.

Rachel turned the gun light off, inched back to the stairs, and raised the shotgun.

*"Freeze!"* she yelled, turning the gun light back on.

The light illuminated a man standing halfway up the staircase. His back was to her. He held a SIG Sauer P226 in his right hand. The hilt of a large hunting knife protruded from a leather sheath clipped to his waist. Rachel aimed the shotgun at the center of the man's back. She flicked the gun's safety button off. No way she'd miss.

*"Put the gun down!"* The man remained still. He was wearing a black sweatshirt. A balaclava was pulled over his head. She couldn't make out his face, hair, or features.

Rachel heard sirens. The man flinched. The gun remained at his side.

"Please," she said, her finger on the trigger. Her breathing was even. "Put it down. The police will be here in seconds. Nobody has to get hurt."

"I can't let you," the man said. She thought she heard him weeping.

"I promise you this can be worked out."

He shook his head. "It can't."

The man swung around and raised his gun. Rachel tilted her shotgun slightly up and to the left, breathed out, and squeezed the trigger.

The sound was deafening, a rocket blast that made Rachel's ears ring. The gun recoiled sharply into her right shoulder, pain shooting down her body. But she kept the gun in place and fed another shell.

The blast hit the man in the right shoulder and knocked him backward onto the steps. The SIG Sauer flew from his grasp as he let loose a howl of pain. Without a moment's hesitation, Rachel sprinted up the steps and grabbed his gun. She noticed that the hammer was back, and the safety mechanism was decocked. The gun was ready to fire. He was here to hurt someone. She released the hammer and tucked the gun into her waistband.

The man writhed on the staircase, hand on his wounded shoulder, blood oozing between his fingers. The sirens outside were growing louder as they neared. Rachel squatted over the man, knelt down, took the knife from his pants, and tossed it down the steps. She searched him quickly and couldn't find any other weapons.

"I told you it didn't have to go like this," she said. She pressed the shotgun barrel against his neck.

Rachel could see the man's eyes. They were hazel, bloodshot. His pupils were dilated. He was on something. She reached down, gripped the balaclava from underneath his neck, and slid it off.

"Oh bloody hell," Rachel said.

Staring up at her, bleeding all over her staircase, was Christopher Robles.

# CHAPTER 14

***Five Years Ago***

The sign on the door read "Slugfest Boxing" in faded red lettering painted on heavily rusted aluminum. The dot over the *i* in "Boxing" was a ring bell. She took the wadded-up napkin from her purse and double-checked the address in southwest Torrington. She was in the right place. She still didn't have the faintest idea what she was doing here . . . only knew that she needed to be.

Her son had woken up screaming again last night, a bloodcurdling howl that had had her running to his bedroom before the neighbors could call 911. She'd gathered him up in her arms, felt a sense of utter helplessness as his tears spilled onto her skin, his cries of terror tearing her heart to pieces.

*I saw it again.*

She'd rocked him and told him it would be all right. She would take care of him. Protect him. But she was barely holding on herself.

Her children could lean on her, but she had only herself. With no support, her only option was to strengthen her resolve, her mind, her body. She'd unpacked all the books, spent hours after the children went down, churning through them. For the first time in years, she'd felt invigorated, challenged. But God, what it had taken to get there . . .

They couldn't stay in Connecticut. The memories covered their lives like moss. Eventually they would have to move. Far away. Start over. Uprooting the children would cause even more chaos, but it was necessary to move on.

Jim Franklin had told her about the secret classes at Slugfest. A client had gone there after leaving her abusive husband. It was a haven for those hurting, he'd said. A dojo for the damned.

The front door took two hands and a grunt to budge. The scent of perspiration and chemical cleanser wafted out.

She slid inside, her heels sinking deep into the rolled rubber floor. *Poor choice of footwear,* she thought. She looked around. Heavy bags were chained to the ceiling, speed bags mounted to wooden beams. The walls were covered in posters and illustrations of boxers, none of whom she recognized save Muhammad Ali and Rocky Balboa, the latter of whom, to the best of her recollection, was not a real person.

"Hey, Blondie! Over here!"

She turned around. A group of twenty or so people of varying ages, shapes, and sizes sat on rows of bleachers facing an empty boxing ring. A woman stood in front of the bleachers, looking at her impatiently.

The woman—the instructor, she presumed—was about five ten, with long red hair tied back in a ponytail. She looked to be in her early thirties, wearing a tight gray tank top and black leggings. She was pure muscle from the thighs to the shoulders and looked like she could pick the bleachers up and carry them around without breaking a sweat.

"Over here," the instructor shouted. She walked over to the group. She was nervous, and it showed. A gym bag was slung over her shoulder, filled with a change of clothes, a water bottle, baby wipes, feminine hygiene products, lipstick, ChapStick, deodorant, and a protein bar. She climbed into the stands and sat down next to a timid-looking man in his midforties with a terrible comb-over and an awful case of halitosis.

The instructor pulled a cell phone from her bra and then looked from the phone to the stands, counting.

"Looks like that's everyone," she said. "So let's get started. My name is Myra. That's not my real name, but that's what you're going to call me. We don't use real names here because even though I'm going to kick your ass into the next century, I want you all to feel safe. Protected. You're all here because you've been through some shit. Bad shit. Shit that would make weaker people lie down and die. But not you, right? You're here because you've already been through the worst of it. You're here to make sure it doesn't happen again. Right?"

The bleacher crowd murmured.

*"Right?"*

The murmuring grew louder.

"All right. Better. We'll get there. My classes are free. Your effort is not. When I point to you, give me a name. Not your real name. *A* name. This is the name we're going to call you here from now on. Pick a stupid name like Carrie Bradshaw, and I will boot your ass out the door before you can say *Cosmo*."

A heavyset woman wearing too much foundation and too little clothing raised her hand. Myra rolled her eyes.

"You have a question."

The heavyset woman stood up. "I didn't know we had to pick names. I'm not ready."

"I'm going to throw a *whooooole* bunch of things at you that you won't be ready for. This is an easy one. If you can't handle this one, then you're screwed right out of the gate. Everyone ready? Then let's go."

Myra pointed at the short bald man at the end.

"Um, Pedro," he said.

"Fine. Next."

"Audrey."

"Nice to meet you, Audrey. Next."

Myra went down the line. The heavyset woman became Starla. Comb-over guy became Earl.

"Earl. Next."

Myra pointed at her. Without thinking, she blurted out, "Rachel."

"Rachel. In the future, leave your stripper heels at home, Rachel. Next."

"Rachel" slipped her shoes off, her face having turned a bright shade of red, and put on a pair of ASICS.

When they were finished, Myra climbed into the boxing ring.

"All right. Everyone, take your jewelry and watches off. Next time, you're better off leaving it at home." She pointed and said, "Earl. Get your ass out here."

Earl stood up and looked around, perhaps expecting one of the others to go up in his place.

"Don't make me come get you." She said it in such a way that had Earl clambering down the bleachers and sliding into the ring. Earl stood ten feet away from Myra, body tucked in concavely, hands folded across his abdomen in an X. He reminded Rachel of a snail.

"Come closer."

Earl took a step forward.

"Closer. Until I can smell your breath," Myra said. Earl did so. "Christ, why didn't you warn me about your breath?"

Earl breathed into his hand, smelled it, and recoiled.

"Go ahead, Earl. Hit me."

Earl looked back to the bleachers, as though awaiting further instruction or clarification. He turned back to Myra.

"Sorry?"

"I said hit me."

"Hit you?"

"Good. We've confirmed that you speak English. Now, hit me."

"Um . . . where?"

"Anywhere. Face. Stomach. Arm. Tit. Just make contact."

"You're going to sue me if I hit you."

Myra let out a full-bellied laugh.

"If I cross my heart and hope to die, Earl, will you believe me that I won't sue you?"

Earl turned back to the bleachers. "You all heard her. She asked me to hit her and promised not to sue me if I did."

Rachel nodded, along with the others. She watched intently, curious to see if Earl would actually hit Myra and even more curious to see what would happen if he did.

Finally, after thirty seconds of gathering up his courage, Earl reared back and brought his palm forward in a wide, looping arc, whereupon Myra swatted it out of the air like a bothersome gnat.

"Ow!" Earl said, grabbing his hand.

"Openhanded? Really, Earl? You were going to hit me openhanded?"

"I . . . I've never hit anybody before."

"Try again."

This time Earl swung a closed fist at Myra. She brought up her arm in an L shape and blocked the blow.

"Try again. *Hit* me."

Earl swung again, and once again Myra blocked it. One more time, and Myra caught his bicep, twisted his arm behind his back, and pushed him away like she might a pesky younger brother.

"Get out of here, Earl, before you hurt yourself."

Earl slunk back to the bleachers, rubbing his arm, hair askew.

Myra pointed to the bleachers.

"You."

She was pointing at Rachel.

Rachel looked around.

"Yes, you, Blondie. Let's go."

Rachel stood up hesitantly, grabbed her bag, and walked toward the ring.

"Leave your bag," Myra said. Rachel sheepishly walked back into the stands, put her bag on the seat, and asked Earl to watch it for her.

"Let's go, Rachel, my hair is going gray waiting for you."

Rachel climbed into the ring and stood before Myra. They were nearly the same height, but Myra's quadriceps were about as thick as Rachel's waist.

"Now. Hit me."

Rachel looked at Myra. She knew how this would play out. She would go to punch or slap her, and Myra would block or dodge or do something to make Rachel look silly.

"What are you waiting for, Miss Prissy? Hit me!"

Rachel brought her fist back, balled up her fingers, and saw the subtlest movement in Myra's lower body as she prepared to counter.

*She's expecting this,* Rachel thought.

So when Rachel brought her hand forward, instead of following through with the punch, she jabbed out her left foot and kicked Myra in the shin.

The blow landed softly, but Myra stumbled back, startled.

Then she began to laugh.

"I think I like you, Blondie."

◆◆◆

Once Myra repeated the "drill" with everyone in the bleachers, she began the real lesson: self-defense. Everyone partnered off and mimicked Myra's movements. Rachel paired up with Earl. After his embarrassment at Myra's hands, Earl was doubly tentative, even though they were going at half speed.

"I don't need any broken noses or dislocated elbows on our first day," Myra said. "This is not Fight Club. There's no pride in getting injured. This is about *defense.*"

Three people dropped out. One, a Spanish woman calling herself Giselle who came sporting freshly manicured nails and a pleather tube top, left after a not-terribly-coordinated hairdresser named Diane clocked her across the cheek, drawing blood. Two men vomited during their first sparring session and never returned.

They practiced blocks and counters, positioning and striking. Footwork and poise. Balance and breathing. Slowly, methodically. Soon enough Rachel was coated in a thick layer of sweat, and her muscles ached. But she felt terrific.

After the session ended, Myra led the class to a janitor's closet that held the cleaning supplies. Rachel recognized the smells. Myra had them wipe down the ring canvas, rubber mats, and bleachers. They got to use the facility for free, she said, with the caveat that they didn't leave their stink.

Rachel felt bruised, battered, sore, sweaty, and alive. The group paraded past Myra to the parking lot, giving her small nods and thank-yous. They would then go home to their wives, husbands, children, or whatever normalcy waited for them.

Rachel grabbed her bag and checked her cell phone. No missed calls but one text from her nanny, Esmerelda—or Essie, as they called her—containing an adorable video of her two-year-old singing a Taylor Swift song.

They had lived in their current house just a few months, and Rachel still hadn't gotten used to it. There were so many boxes still unpacked, drawers still empty, and she still didn't have the faintest idea how to work the remote control for the TV. Her eight-year-old son had been begging her to get them an Apple TV, but when Rachel learned you needed to hook it up to a credit card account, she nixed that suggestion, to her son's lament.

Rachel limped through the front door like someone had taken a golf club to every bone in her body. They had moved to a nine-hundred-square-foot single-level ranch-style home in Torrington, an hour north of Darien. It had two small bedrooms, a narrow living room, a galley kitchen with off-white laminate countertops and old appliances, and a small backyard where Eric could kick a soccer ball and not much else.

They ate breakfast and dinner at a coffee table. The kids were growing. They could not last here long.

The backyard was fenced in. It hadn't been when they'd moved in, but Rachel had had the cedar pickets built and painted within the week. She didn't need people staring at her kids. Nobody in Torrington knew who they were, and Rachel aimed to keep it that way.

Rachel paid Essie and thanked her. She got a glass of water from the kitchen and sank into the brown polyester sofa. She downed the entire glass in a single gulp, caught her breath, and went to check on the kids.

Her daughter was fast asleep in her daybed. She slept on her side, curled into a little C shape. She clutched her Baby Stella doll, with its removable pacifier stuffed in its mouth. They looked like little pink twins. It took every ounce of willpower not to wake her daughter up, hold her to her chest, and cry for hours.

Her son was on his bed, buried in yet another thick paperback. The cover featured a young man sitting in the gnarled branches of a tree with a human face. She knew it wasn't easy for him, sharing a room with his sister, but none of what had happened was fair. This was a small inconvenience compared to everything else. Besides, they'd move soon enough.

"What are you reading?" she whispered. She was amazed that he could finish such a doorstop. He held his page with his finger and turned the book so the cover faced Rachel. "*The Two Towers*. Any good?"

He nodded his approval.

"What did you have for dinner?"

"Essie ordered in pizza. Meatball. There are a few slices left."

"Thanks, sweetie."

A hot shower, clean pajamas, and a few slices of pizza sounded heavenly.

"Hey, Mom?" he said.

She looked back at her son. "Yes, hon?"

"Are we going to stay here?"

Rachel smiled at him and said, "For a little while. But then we'll get a house where you and your sister can each have your own room."

He nodded, placated. Then he said, "Will things ever be back to normal?"

This question took her by surprise. Without thinking, she said, "Yes. Yes, they will."

Her son turned back to his book. "No they won't."

She sighed. *No,* she thought. *They won't.*

# CHAPTER 15

***Today***

Before Rachel's brain had time to process the fact that she'd just fired a buckshot shell into Nicholas Drummond's brother-in-law, she heard a pounding at the front door.

"Ashby PD!"

Rachel moved away from Christopher Robles. He didn't seem to be going anywhere. She kept the shotgun trained on him and moved to the front door.

"My name is Rachel Marin," she shouted. "I'm the owner of this house. An armed man trespassed on my property and forced his way inside. I am a licensed gun owner, and I shot him in self-defense. His name is Christopher Robles. He is alive and has been disarmed and is currently incapacitated, but he needs immediate medical attention."

"Ms. Marin," a man's voice replied from the other side of the door. "Please put your weapon down on the ground, let us into the house, then stand back with your hands raised above your head."

"All right. When you enter, there's a staircase right in front of you in the foyer. The man is on the steps. He was carrying a SIG Sauer P226 and a tactical hunting knife. I've disarmed him of both. I'm placing both of his weapons, and mine, a Mossberg 500 shotgun, on the floor next to the door. I will then open the door."

"We've called paramedics. Let us inside."

"OK."

Rachel placed the Mossberg, the SIG Sauer, and the knife off to the side of the front door. She opened the door, then stepped back and placed her hands up so the officers could see she was unarmed. A gust of cold wind blew inside, and Rachel shivered. The streetlights cast a pale glow into the darkened home.

Four Ashby PD officers entered. Two of them immediately went over to the steps to check on Robles. One of the officers, a bald black man with a neat goatee in his midthirties, took out a notepad. The other, a fortysomething Asian man with his hair tied in a short ponytail, stepped outside and went to fill in the EMTs. Rachel knew that following a shooting, the house would be crawling with police and medical personnel.

*Why in the hell did Christopher Robles break into my house?*

The black officer spoke in an even, sympathetic voice. "Ms. Marin, I'm Officer Lowe. Tell me what happened, in detail."

"I was upstairs with my children when we heard a gunshot and a window break downstairs. I told my children to hide in our basement. When my security system administrators called due to the broken window, I told them to contact 911 immediately."

She told him that Robles had been armed and made an aggressive move toward her with the gun, leaving her no choice but to shoot him.

"You have experience handling shotguns?" Lowe asked, somewhat incredulously.

"I do. And I am fully trained and licensed. I purposefully aimed for his shoulder."

"You wanted to incapacitate him. Not kill him."

"That's right."

"Gun like that has a lot of stopping power."

"That's why I use it. Someone breaks into your house with a gun and a knife and intent to use them, you don't want to have to worry about getting off multiple shots to bring them down."

Lowe shook his head, amused. "Glad I'm not on your bad side, Ms. Marin."

An ambulance pulled into the driveway. Three EMTs entered with a stretcher. Robles screamed bloody murder as they placed him on the board and strapped him down. One of the EMTs handcuffed his non-injured wrist to the stretcher.

"My kids," Rachel said to Officer Lowe. "They're in the basement, hiding. I need to let them know they're safe."

"All right, go ahead. But we'll need to take you down to the station to make an official statement. Do you have an attorney?"

"Yes . . . do you think I need one?"

"Can't hurt. If this went down the way you said it did . . ."

"It did," Rachel said.

"All right. Go get your kids. An officer will accompany you while we secure the house and make sure there are no more intruders."

"Thanks, Officer. Just need to go upstairs to switch on the breakers so you have light to work with."

The other cops had already begun taping off the staircase, waiting for forensics and ballistics to arrive.

Rachel slid past them and turned the breaker switches back on. Then she went to the basement door, entered the security code, and opened it. She went downstairs and came to the metal security door. Through a ten-by-ten-inch window in the door, she could see Eric and Megan seated. When they saw her, they leaped up and ran over. Rachel opened the security door and gathered her children into her.

"It's over," she said. "Everything's fine."

Megan was weeping. Eric was strangely limp in her arms.

"The police are here," she said. "We need to go upstairs and then just answer a few questions at the station so they can do their job."

"Where's the bad man?" Megan said.

"The police have him. He can't hurt anyone now."

"Are you sure?" Eric said.

"I'm sure."

He nodded. "You got him."

She nodded. "I did."

They walked up the stairs to the ground floor. Rachel made sure both the security door and the main door closed behind her. As they passed by the staircase, still slick with Robles's blood, Rachel covered Megan's eyes.

Eric took it all in. He walked slowly, observing the carnage. Just feet away from where he slept. Rachel prayed this was the last horror the boy had to endure.

They gathered their coats from the front closet. The police had let the front door remain open. Cold winter air was blowing through the house. Within minutes, their home was freezing and overrun with police officers and technicians.

Officer Lowe knelt down slightly so he was closer to the kids' eye level.

"I'm Officer Derek Lowe, and this is my partner, Officer Chen. Officer Chen is going to take you all to the station. It's warm there. And we have a pretty great vending machine with a lot of snacks."

Eric and Megan nodded. Rachel mouthed the words *Thank you* to Officer Lowe. Officer Chen loaded them into a squad car and drove away. Rachel watched their house disappear in the side mirror, cops surrounding it like ants.

Rachel sat in the middle of the squad car: Megan to her left, Eric to her right. They were both silent. In shock, she supposed. A man had been shot in their home by their mother just minutes earlier.

Not to mention what they'd seen in the basement.

"Mom," Eric finally said, "why did you lie to us? About the basement?"

Rachel took a deep breath. She knew this conversation would have to take place at some point.

"I'll explain everything later," she said. "I promise."

◆◆◆

The Ashby North PD precinct was a two-story brick building with a triangular green roof and blue awning. Officer Chen parked in front and led the Marin family inside the double sliding doors. The officer spoke to a woman behind a glass-paned partition, who then buzzed them inside.

Rachel held Megan's hand as they followed Officer Chen. Eric's face was a mixture of awe and caution. She could understand that. Nobody *wanted* to be in a police station. But to a young boy, it was still kind of cool. She felt his fingers curl around hers.

"We're not in trouble," Rachel said, trying to reassure Eric. She remembered the last time they had been in a police station. Obviously so did he.

"I know," he said unconvincingly. Chen led them to a bare white break room with a small rectangular wooden table with four metal chairs. The furniture was all bolted to the ground. There was a microwave, refrigerator, water dispenser, and single-brew coffee maker. Rachel was dying for a cup.

"Thanks, Officer. I'll take Ms. Marin's statement."

Rachel turned around and was surprised to see Detective Serrano standing there. She was partly relieved to see a familiar face, partly worried since she wasn't exactly on his good side. He was dressed in jeans and a Cubs sweatshirt. They looked clean. Rachel could see crease lines. He'd clearly just arrived and changed clothes at the station.

"You sure, Detective?" Chen said.

"I got it, Officer; thanks for your help." Serrano then spoke to the children. "Kids, Officer Chen is going to take you into that room right over there and get you some hot chocolate and a snack."

"I don't like hot chocolate," Megan said.

"What kid doesn't like hot chocolate?" Serrano said in mock surprise.

"Mine, apparently," Rachel said.

"That's OK. He'll get you whatever you want. Nonalcoholic, so don't get any ideas." Serrano winked at Eric, who smiled. Megan looked at Rachel, concerned.

"It's OK, sweetie. I'll be right here. This is the safest place on earth. When we get home, Megan, you can go back to your stories, and Eric, you can play all the *Galaxy Star Trek Goop Fighter* you want."

*"Galactic Warfare Brigade 11,"* Eric corrected.

"Well, what do you know," Serrano said. "I'm a big fan of those games."

"No way," Eric said.

"Yes way. Haven't played the last couple *Galactic Warfare Brigade* games—job gets in the way sometimes—but number nine, the ending, when the giant mutated snake creature eats your entire platoon and then regurgitates them all into a humongous soup bowl? I couldn't sleep that was so awesome."

Eric smiled. "That was pretty cool."

"It *was* pretty cool. Listen, we'll chat about the games later. Go have a snack. Let your mom and I talk for a bit."

Megan took Eric's hand, and Officer Chen led them away.

"Thank you for that," Rachel said to Serrano.

"Don't sweat it," he said. "You know, you can set your watch by the snowfall in Ashby. Every year, the first week in December it hits like clockwork. The town, I'll tell you, it transforms into something magical. Bright lights looping around every home, snowballs flying everywhere. When I was a beat cop, I introduced myself to everyone on my route. Best part of the job. I wanted police work to feel like it did when I was a kid, where you knew the names of the people sworn to protect you."

"Why are you telling me this?" Rachel asked.

"Because I want you to know I have your back. Despite what happened at the Drummond house. That's why I came tonight. Sit with me," Serrano said, motioning to the table. Rachel sat down. Serrano took the seat across from her. "I'm going to record this. Do you wish to have an attorney present?"

Rachel shook her head. "Why are you here, Detective?"

"I went for a walk after leaving the Drummond place. Thought a lot. And happened to catch what happened at your house over the radio. Figured we have a little history, and you wouldn't mind seeing a friendlyish face tonight. Or at least a recognizable one."

"I didn't realize you were that friendlyish."

"Friend or not, an armed man broke into your home, and it's my job to find out why and to make sure you and your kids are safe."

Rachel looked down. "Thank you."

"All right. Take me through what happened tonight. Start from the beginning. Don't leave any details out, no matter how small."

Rachel told him everything. And every word was true. The break-in, the fact that Robles had been armed, that she was licensed to own and wield the Mossberg, and that she had only wounded him in self-defense.

When it was over, Rachel said, "What now?"

Serrano said, "What now is we have forensics and ballistics going over the scene and running tests on both Robles's gun and yours. If the analysis matches up with the official story you've provided, it'll likely be written up as a clean self-defense shoot."

"Can the kids and I go home soon?"

"Not just yet," Serrano said. "It'll take a day or two to bag and tag the scene. We'll put you up in a hotel for a few nights. First I'll take you all home, and you can pack bags for yourself and the kids."

"Thank you," Rachel said.

Serrano leaned forward in his chair.

"Let me ask you a question, Ms. Marin," he said. "Do you go *looking* for trouble on a daily basis?"

"Listen, Detective. Robles came to *my* house, armed with a gun and a knife big enough to cut the Rock in half."

"And do you think there's any chance he does all that if you don't follow him home after the press conference?"

Rachel didn't respond.

"I don't know what your deal is. But tonight you just shot the brother-in-law of a murder victim's ex-husband."

"I feel like there's a joke in there somewhere," Rachel said. "You know, like a priest, a rabbi, and a shaman walk into a bar."

"Laugh all you want, but this is serious."

"I shot a man tonight, Detective. I know how serious it is. So why would Robles come after me?" Rachel asked. "And what he said. 'I'm not gonna let you.' I still don't know what he meant."

"Step back for a moment," Serrano said. "You said your children went down to the basement. You told them they'd be safe there, that it was locked from the inside. Now if it was so safe, why didn't you go with them?"

"Pardon?"

"If the intruder couldn't get into the basement, why wouldn't you wait down there with the kids until the police arrived?"

"Response time for our security system is up to six minutes. We both know that's on a good day. I wasn't willing to take a chance that whoever was in my house could leave and then come back for us another time. He was there to hurt someone. Maybe next time he comes to my office. Or the kids' school. I had to make sure he'd be taken into custody. For that to happen, he couldn't get away."

Serrano nodded, but it was clear Rachel's answer didn't sit well with him.

"I'll drive you all home; you can pack up; then I'll take you over to the hotel."

"Four star? Maybe somewhere with a spa where I can get a seaweed wrap?"

"Best Western," Serrano said. "And even that's stretching our budget. Let me ask you something, Ms. Marin."

"Shoot."

"Funny you should say that. The Mossberg you shot Robles with. That's not a small gun. Most people I know keep a handgun for self-defense. The Mossberg has a hell of a recoil."

"Don't I know it. My shoulder feels like it got kicked by a mule. And I don't think that was a question."

"Where'd you learn to handle a shotgun?"

Rachel shrugged. "Spent some time on gun ranges. Wanted something for home defense. Something that would put somebody down quickly, if need be. The nine millimeter Robles carried would only put someone down if you hit them here or here." Rachel pointed to her heart and then her head.

"Did someone get you into shooting? You were married, right? Husband teach you?"

Rachel glared at Serrano and said curtly, "Number one, I don't need a man to teach me how to shoot. Number two, my personal life is none of your business."

"Fair enough."

Rachel knew Serrano wasn't "just asking." But she couldn't answer that question. Still, something gnawed at her gut. A fear that this night had opened up a Pandora's box she wouldn't be able to close.

"Listen, Detective, I'd really like to try and get my kids settled the best I can right now. We've all had a hell of a night. If you want to talk about my romantic past, let's do it another time."

"Fair enough. Let's go."

Rachel gathered her belongings, and Serrano led her into an office where the kids were watching a rerun of *Modern Family* on a small TV. Eric was sipping a hot chocolate, and Megan was devouring a bag of cheddar-flavored Goldfish.

Serrano drove them home in his brown Crown Victoria. Rachel sat in the front with the kids in the back. Snow was coming down heavy. The roads would need to be plowed in the morning.

"How long have you been a cop?" Eric asked from the back seat.

"About eighteen years," Serrano replied.

"Wow. Ever shoot anyone?"

"Eric!" Rachel scolded.

Serrano laughed. "It's OK. But yes. I have. It's not cool like you probably think. And you never want to hurt anyone unless you have to. There's usually an alternative."

"My mom shot a guy tonight. I guess there was no alternative."

Serrano nodded. "No, doesn't seem like there was. She did a good job protecting you two."

As they approached their house, Rachel could spot the police vehicles from several blocks away. Red and blue lights bouncing off the snow-covered streets. By this time, the neighbors had left their houses and were congregating on their front steps to watch the scene unfold. Rachel did not look forward to having to deal with all the questions from local busybodies.

Serrano led them inside. Forensic techs were still doing blood-spatter analysis. There were several yellow tags stuck to the stairwell where some of the buckshot from the shotgun shells had embedded in the wall and stairs.

They laid a plastic tarp over the stairs so Rachel and the kids could get upstairs to pack. She grabbed a suitcase from her closet and packed several outfits for work and evening and toiletries, then went to each kid's room and helped them do the same.

"Don't forget your schoolbooks," she said. "Take anything you might need for a few days."

"Ugh," Eric said. "I'm going to have to pack, like, eight books. They weigh a hundred pounds each."

"Then pack eight books, and pretend you're strength training."

"I'll help you carry them to the hotel," Serrano said. He looked around Eric's room. There was a wistful smile on his face. He went over to Eric's bookshelf.

"Do you mind?" he asked. Eric shook his head. Serrano took out a tattered copy of each of the Lord of the Rings books and held them gently, delicately, like they were the Dead Sea Scrolls.

"How many times did you read this?" he asked, holding a dog-eared copy of *The Fellowship of the Ring*.

"Ten? Maybe eleven times?"

"Wonderful books."

"You read them?"

"I have," Serrano said. "My son . . . he loved them when he was your age."

"Cool. How old is he now?"

Serrano ignored the question. "It's late. Let's get you settled."

Serrano carried the luggage to the Crown Vic and drove to a Best Western off Lakeland Drive. Another officer followed in Rachel's car, parked, and gave Rachel the keys. Serrano talked to the pimply clerk at the front desk and handed Rachel two keys.

"Officers Lowe and Chen are going to check on you from time to time. We may need you to answer some more questions about the shooting, so don't leave the state without letting me know."

"I have two children in school, Detective. I barely leave the house."

Serrano laughed. "Get some rest, all of you. I'm glad you're safe."

"How is he?" Rachel asked. "Robles."

"You shattered his collarbone into a jigsaw puzzle. He'll live, but he'll never do a full jumping jack again."

Rachel nodded, taking no joy in the news. "So you think Robles might have killed Constance Wright?"

Serrano didn't respond.

"Me either," Rachel said. "That kind of murder took planning. Precision. Getting Wright to the bridge, incapacitating her. What happened tonight was sloppy and spur of the moment."

"I'll call to check on you tomorrow," Serrano said, ignoring her comment. "If anything comes up, or you remember anything else, you have my card. Robles is in the hospital. You know who his sister is. She has money, and Chris has some friends in low places. Be careful."

"Christ, you think Isabelle will come after me for shooting her brother?"

"Just play it safe. No more stunts like you pulled at their house," Serrano said. "Lay low. Now I have to head to the hospital to check on the guy you unloaded a shotgun into."

Serrano headed to his car.

"Detective?"

Serrano turned around.

"Thank you," Rachel said. "And I'm sorry about what I said before. At the Drummond house. I believe you're a good cop. That you look out for people."

Serrano said nothing. Just smiled thinly and walked back out into the cold.

Rachel brought the children to the second floor. The hotel room was sparse. Two single beds, a small desk, an empty minifridge, and a combination shower and bathtub. Tomorrow she'd pick up some groceries and cleaning supplies. She didn't want to frighten the kids, but laboratory petri dishes tended to have less bacteria than the average hotel room.

Megan read a *Fancy Nancy* book while Eric put on his headphones and got lost in an iPad game. Once Megan was asleep, Rachel tapped Eric on the shoulder. "Your turn."

Eric nodded, switched off his game, put on shorts and a T-shirt, and climbed into bed next to his sister.

When they were finally down, Rachel changed into sweatpants and a fleece. Her brown hair was a bedraggled mess, and she could see blonde roots poking through her scalp. There was a massive red welt in the meat of her shoulder where the Mossberg had kicked after she'd shot Christopher Robles.

She was bone tired. She'd call out sick from work tomorrow. She couldn't fathom dealing with Steve Ruggiero after a night like this. Plus, her sitter had just quit. She'd have to fill in until she could find a suitable solution. Someone trustworthy.

Someone who wouldn't ask too many questions.

Rachel turned the light off, plugged her phone in, and closed her eyes.

Just as she began to doze, Rachel heard Eric's voice.

"Mom?" he whispered.

"Yes, hon?"

"I'm glad you didn't let him get away."

Soon enough Rachel heard the twin rhythmic sounds of both her children sleeping. Rachel lay awake in bed in the darkness for a long, long time.

# CHAPTER 16

Serrano was already at his desk when Leslie Tally walked into the precinct. She was pleasantly surprised to see him.

"I figured you'd wake up beside the train tracks somewhere without your pants and with a hangover that would pain the devil," she said. Tally sat down and sipped a cup of coffee.

"No way; I've had a busy night. Heard about the Marin shooting over the radio," Serrano said. He was freshly shaven, had on a clean suit, and smelled like cologne rather than liquor and stale coffee like she'd expected. "I came in, took Rachel Marin's statement. Set her and her kids up in a hotel while forensics goes over the house. Stopped by the hospital to see if Chris Robles was lucid enough postsurgery to answer any questions."

"Surprised you did that for the Marin woman after what happened at the Drummond place."

"Yeah, well, I surprise myself sometimes."

"So you didn't go to Voss Field?" Tally asked.

Serrano nodded. "I was going to but decided against it. It's a battle. Every day. I just happened to win this one."

"Proud of you," she said. "I know it still hurts."

Serrano nodded. "Thanks, partner."

"So what's the word from the Marin home?" Tally asked.

"It appears to be a clean shoot. Woman knows how to handle a shotgun. Montrose found footprints in the dirt outside that matched the boots Christopher Robles was wearing when he was brought to the hospital. GSR test came back positive. Ballistics found a slug embedded in the wall in the kitchen that matched Robles's SIG Sauer. Marin's gun permit checks out. Everything appears to have happened just the way she said it did."

Tally tapped her lower lip. "So Marin BSes her way into Isabelle and Nicholas Drummond's house. Then later that night, Isabelle's brother goes to Marin's home and tries to kill her. Why?"

"Maybe he saw her snooping around," Serrano said. "Those photos she took in Isabelle's closet. Possible Robles spotted her, assumed the worst."

"Which was what, exactly? Even if Drummond and his wife are lying about the timeline, why would her brother go after Rachel?"

"I ran background on Chris Robles," Serrano said. He dug around in the pile of mess on his desk and pulled out a brown manila folder. "He has quite a record. Did two stints in his early twenties at Baskerville penitentiary. First one for possession of heroin with intent to sell. The second for prostitution."

"Prostitution?"

"Yep. Seems after his first stint in the joint, the Robles family cut him off. They were worth millions but didn't appear to want the black sheep getting any of it. So he started turning tricks off Dewey Circle, solicited a cop, and did three months upstate. And while Chris is locked up, their parents, Arturo and Yvette, are killed in a plane crash. They leave every cent to Isabelle."

"So she goes back on her parents' wishes, takes Chris in."

Serrano nodded. "Sibling love. He moves in with her. She enters him into a 20K-a-month rehab program. Didn't seem to fully take, because three years later Robles is arrested again for trying to buy crystal off an undercover. This time, Isabelle hires him a fancy-pants lawyer who convinces the judge that Robles is bipolar and gets him committed for a year. He got out and has a clean record since."

"So Chris owes sis," Tally said. "Big time. But there's still nothing on his record that suggests violent tendencies, let alone homicide."

"Everyone starts somewhere," Serrano said. "But if you're Chris Robles, in and out of prison and psych wards your whole life, the odds of you being dead by thirty are fairly high. Then his sister swoops in like an angel of mercy and saves him. Uses her family's resources to get him help. Keeps Chris out of jail, where, by the looks of him, he'd easily be worth a Twix bar and a pack of cigarettes. He owes his life to Isabelle."

"And you think he'd do anything to repay that," Tally said. "So you think Chris going to Rachel Marin's home was his messed-up way of trying to protect his sister? Maybe because he knows Drummond killed Constance and doesn't want people digging?"

"Possibly," Serrano said. "But here's what I don't get. Constance Wright and Nicholas Drummond divorced several years ago. He remarried right away. Isabelle Robles is rich. I don't see a motive in Drummond wanting her dead *now.*"

"Unless the Marin woman is right," Tally said, "and Wright found out she'd been swindled out of one point two million and was planning to come after it."

"So you think Robles finds out and offs Constance to protect Nicholas?" Serrano said. "You'd have to presume Isabelle didn't find out about Chris's bad intentions—which, given his history and their closeness, I don't buy. I think if Wright decided to go after Drummond's money, Isabelle Robles finds a way to keep her quiet."

Tally chewed a fingernail. Then stopped. "Claire hates when I do that."

"She should. It's a disgusting habit."

"Let's not go there. I remember the days when I used to find you passed out in the dugout at Voss Field regularly, smelling like you'd been fermented in a distillery."

"Point taken. But I'm having a hard time seeing how this plays out with Drummond as the killer. Even if Constance goes after him for the money, I think he tells his wife, and they pay her off. Isabelle has the money. Maybe they have to liquidate some stock holdings, sell a property or two, but that seems like a safer plan than killing her."

"But it still begs the question: Why was Chris Robles so scared for his sister that he felt compelled to try to murder a woman who was snooping around?"

"Robles isn't right in the head," Serrano said. "Let's not immediately assume his actions were based in logic."

"I think we should talk to the Robles black sheep," Tally said. "See what Chris has to say."

"No doubt Isabelle will have one of Sauron's minions representing her little Chrissy. We'll be lucky to get a sneeze out of him before her lawyers shut us down."

"Doesn't Sauron work for the Zackowitz & Keenan law firm? Dale Sauron, am I right?"

Serrano stood up, closed his eyes, and shook his head in shame. "One of these days we're going to have to get you to watch some real movies."

"One of these days we're going to need to get you a psych eval."

"Fair trade. Robles is at Mackenzie North, Maitland ward. You drive."

As they got up to leave, Lt. Daryl George rounded the corner and headed for their desks.

"Perfect timing," George said. His posture was straighter than a two-by-four, his gray hair close cropped at the sides and receding ever so slightly on top. "Detectives, what's the latest on the Marin shooting?"

"Checked her in to a hotel myself," Serrano said. "Was just telling Detective Tally that the shooting looks clean. Forensics and ballistics seem to confirm her story. Robles shot out a window; she took him down in self-defense."

"And the Wright investigation?"

Tally said, "I spoke to Annette Zhang, who owns the Fancy Nails salon on Mutterman Way. Credit card receipts show that Constance Wright came in for a pedicure the day before she died. Ms. Zhang recognized Constance but said she only came in sporadically. Maybe two or three times a year."

"My hunch is that she was seeing someone romantically," Serrano said. "She was prepping for date night."

"So you think her paramour may have had something to do with this?" George replied. "Any leads on the guy?"

"Not yet," Serrano said. "But the theory would explain why there were no defensive wounds and confirm that she knew her assailant. But there's nothing that stands out in her phone records. If she was seeing someone, both parties were keeping it heavily under wraps. So we're still working the Nicholas Drummond angle as well."

"Good work. Now, your report also says Rachel Marin was with you when you questioned Nicholas Drummond yesterday. Care to explain why a civilian tagged along during your homicide investigation?"

Tally looked at Serrano, annoyance on her face. Serrano sighed.

"She saw Robles on the news. He was at the bridge the night Constance Wright died, standing among the onlookers. Then she saw Robles at the presser, too, got suspicious, and followed him. We all happened to arrive at the Drummond residence simultaneously. She made up a story on the spot in front of Drummond about being an Ashby PD 'forensic consultant.' Had we blown up her story and sent her home, Drummond would have immediately been suspicious and lawyered up. It might have been our only good crack at him. We made a judgment call."

"Your judgment call nearly got her killed last night. And she put a bullet in a suspect's brother-in-law."

"To be fair, Lieutenant," Tally said, "Robles has a long rap sheet. He didn't need any pushing to do something stupid."

"Maybe so. But this investigation is operating under a microscope. Cable news is dredging up all the old Wright family scandals; we've had more press requests in the last twenty-four hours than I've seen in my career. We need to keep this ship tight. If Marin doesn't back off, arrest her for interfering with the investigation. The last thing we need is some loose cannon thinking she's the star of a police TV show showing up at crime scenes and badgering witnesses or suspects. She does it again, lock her up."

"Sir, with all due respect, someone tried to kill Rachel Marin last night. She has two young children. We throw a single mom in prison right after an armed gunman broke into her home, the press is going to eat us alive."

George considered this. "Fine. But it's on you two to make sure she stays away from this case and away from the press."

"Done and done," Tally said.

"We were just on our way over to Mackenzie North to question Christopher Robles," Serrano said.

"Then you'd better bring a priest with you," George said. "Mackenzie North just called over. Christopher Robles died this morning."

# CHAPTER 17

The hospital morgue was located in the basement of Mackenzie North, a gorgeous four-wing medical center with one of the best cardiology and NICU centers in the country. After Christopher Robles had been shot, Isabelle Drummond had been notified of his injuries by the Ashby PD watch commander. She'd insisted her brother be operated on at Mackenzie North, despite the Lovett-Hewes Hospital being fifteen minutes closer to the Marin residence. Given that the Robles family had donated over $100,000 to hospital charities over the years, they'd been more than happy to acquiesce to her demands.

Serrano couldn't say he blamed Isabelle. Mackenzie North had the best trauma unit within a hundred miles. If he was wounded on duty, he'd want to be taken there.

So the question was, How did a man admitted to such a renowned medical center without a life-threatening injury wind up dead twelve hours later?

Serrano and Tally drove to the hospital in silence. Strong gusts from the northeast had brought the windchill factor down to four degrees. Ashby looked frostbitten, moving in slow motion. Puffy coats and thick gloves, scarves and hats covering ears and mouths and noses. The city looked anonymous and bleak.

Upon arriving at the hospital, the detectives took the elevator down to the morgue level and were met by two attendants. One ME, Stevens, was thirtyish and pale and suffered from a bad case of rosacea; another,

Krish, was a fiftysomething Indian man with a firm handshake and kind eyes. Krish offered the detectives masks and gloves, which they put on.

"Thank you for coming, Detectives," Krish said. "He's this way."

Krish led them to an examining room with three metal tables side by side. Robles lay naked on the middle table. The air was thick with the sickly-sweet scent of antiseptic and death. Every surface gleamed. Harsh overhead lights gave the dead man's body a grotesquely illuminated sheen.

Robles was even thinner than Serrano remembered, his body all angles. His rib cage looked like twigs covered by tissue paper. His collarbones protruded from his torso like the ends of a coat hanger. And Serrano could have fit a golf ball into the hollows of his cheeks. His skin was covered in thin scars and cheap tattoos that had already begun to fade despite his young age.

Serrano circled the body. He noted track marks on Robles's arms and between his toes. A large putrid abscess had formed in the crook of Robles's right elbow. Serrano leaned in, took a whiff, and recoiled.

"Sepsis," he said, stepping back. "A few more months without treatment, and Robles would have needed his arm amputated."

"His record might have been clean recently," Tally added, "but Chris knew how to keep his extracurricular activities under wraps."

"Or his sister did," Serrano said.

"Mortuary van is on the way," Krish said. "Cause of death was a pulmonary embolism. You need to know there was nothing in Christopher Robles's medical history regarding the extent of his recent drug use. But as you can plainly see, his usage had been long, and it had been frequent, and it was ongoing."

"You think there were complications postsurgery due to the long-term effects?" Serrano said.

"No doubt," Stevens said. "I'm sure the autopsy will confirm it. Sepsis had already set in. See that abscess?" Stevens pointed to the green-and-black wound on Robles's arm. "No doubt blood poisoning had already begun to develop. We pumped him full of antibiotics, but this infection should have been treated a long time ago."

"Look at the scars," Stevens said, pointing to the marks on Robles's arms. "Those are years old. That kind of long-term usage, you develop thrombosis, tuberculosis, bacterial infections, you name it."

"I'll request his full medical records," Serrano said. "We can get HIPAA waived given that Robles was the suspect in a crime."

"I still don't understand. Why in the hell wouldn't all this be in his charts?" Krish said.

Tally looked at Serrano. They both knew Robles had spent time in rehab. No doubt his stints in prison had come with trips to the medical wing.

Tally said, "Pretty sure I can guess."

◆◆◆

Tally parked the Crown Vic at the curb in front of the Drummond residence. Snow fell into trenches where the streets had been recently plowed. The lawn outside the Drummond house looked lovely covered in a blanket of fresh powder. It brought back difficult memories for Serrano: sledding and snowmen and hot chocolate. Memories that, no matter how hard he tried, he was unable to suppress.

They began to trudge up the driveway when Nicholas Drummond came barreling out the front door, waving his arms like he was signaling a plane on a runway.

"No, Detectives," he said. "Turn around. Not today."

"We need to speak to your wife," Serrano said. "I know emotions are running high, and our hearts go out to you both. But we need her to come to the hospital, and then we need to ask her a few questions."

Tally added, "Christopher's medical records were wiped clean of his recent substance issues. Meaning someone had them expunged."

"And you think it was Isabelle," Drummond said, his voice laced with anger and confusion, as though he hadn't considered the possibility but was now forced to. Drummond came down the steps and lowered his voice. "Listen, this isn't a good time. Chris was . . . I can't say I ever knew the kid all that well. But to my wife, he was the most precious thing on earth. She doesn't need this right now."

"I'm sympathetic to that, Mr. Drummond," Serrano said. "But Christopher was in police custody after breaking into someone's home while armed and with intent to harm. This isn't a courtesy call. We need to talk to your wife about her brother."

Then a voice rang out: "*You* did this to him."

Serrano and Tally both looked up. Isabelle Drummond was standing in the doorway, her eyes streaked with red. Her face was not marked with anger but hate. Pure *hate*.

"Mrs. Drummond," Tally said. "We are so sorry for your loss. If we can just take a minute of your time—"

"You already took some of my time, and now my brother is dead. Maybe if you take more time, you can kill my husband too. Maybe me? You goddamn murderers."

"Mrs. Drummond," Serrano said. He took a step forward.

"Take one more step, I'll consider you trespassing, and I'll get my gun," Isabelle said. Serrano couldn't tell if she was serious.

"Please don't threaten us, Mrs. Drummond," Tally said. "We understand this is a difficult time. It doesn't need to come to this."

"You came here to talk to my husband about that bitch ex-wife of his. And you bring, who, that strange woman with you? And then I find out that she's not even a real cop? What was it, some sort of fun ride along? Did you feel sorry for her and her two sad, fatherless children?"

*Fatherless children?* Serrano's eyes narrowed. Clearly Isabelle had done some digging into Rachel Marin. Which made him wonder whether Christopher really had acted of his own accord.

"The sooner we talk to you," Tally said, "the sooner we can find out why your brother is dead."

"My brother is dead because of you and that woman. You're lucky you're police. You have all your buddies to protect you. I know how it works. You take in a suspect, he dies in your custody, you wipe your hands of it."

"That's not the case," Serrano pleaded. "We want to know the truth."

"The truth is that I'm not saying another word to you without my lawyer present. And that Marin bitch had better keep her loved ones closer than I did. You never know what could happen to someone when you think they're safe."

Isabelle went back into the house, leaving the door open. A signal that she expected her husband to join her. Nicholas sighed and said, "I'm sorry, Detectives. Our lawyer will be in touch."

He turned around to join his wife.

"Please, just one question, Mr. Drummond," Serrano said. Drummond turned around. "When did you *really* begin dating Isabelle Robles?"

Drummond said nothing, hesitated a moment, and then went inside and slammed the door. A shelf of snow loosened from the roof and tumbled to the ground.

# CHAPTER 18

Tally pulled the Crown Vic into the parking lot of the Best Western as Serrano finished the last dregs of his now-cold coffee. Serrano saw the unmarked police car parked at the other end of the lot. They walked over and rapped on the driver's side window. Officer Lowe rolled it down and offered a tired smile. Lowe and Chen appeared to be sleepy but lucid.

"Detectives," Lowe said.

"Any action last night?" Serrano asked. Lowe shook his head.

"Nothing. Lights went out at 11:36, came on just a few minutes ago."

"Getting the kids ready for school," Serrano said. "Any sign of Isabelle or Nicholas Drummond?"

"Nothing," Chen added. Serrano leaned over, saw half a dozen coffee cups, three Red Bulls, an empty bag of Twizzlers, two hamburger wrappers, and a box of Nerds littered beneath Chen's seat. Serrano smiled. He remembered the joys of pulling all-nighters.

"I didn't even know they still made Nerds," Serrano said. "Aren't they basically just flavored sugar lumps?"

"And they're delicious," Chen said. "Only downside is that my tongue feels like the underside of a carpet. I've never needed to brush my teeth so badly."

"Go home; get some rest," Serrano said. "I'm going to check on them. The kids have school, and I'll keep an eye on Ms. Marin if need be."

"You sure?" Lowe said.

"Please, for our sake, go shower," Tally added, holding her nose. "And throw all this crap away. You're gonna start attracting fruit flies."

Lowe nodded. They pulled out of the lot and headed south on Lakeland.

"Give me a minute with Rachel," Serrano said to Tally. She nodded, content to stay in the heated Crown Vic.

Serrano showed the desk clerk his badge and went up to Rachel Marin's room.

He thought about what Isabelle Drummond had said. It unnerved Serrano. Not just her words, but the emotion behind them. The anger. Nothing in this world was more dangerous than someone with means and a grudge.

He still couldn't figure out why Rachel hadn't hid in the basement with her children. Police were on the way. Ninety-nine out of a hundred people would have headed for safety. But Rachel confronted Robles with a shotgun. She was smart. She knew there was a strong chance the confrontation would end in blood. He recalled what Rachel had said at the station, and it gave him chills.

*I had to put him down to make sure he'd be put away.*

He knocked on the door and said, "Ms. Marin? It's Detective Serrano."

"Hold on!"

He heard a commotion from behind the door and a young girl shrieking.

"Eric, what did I tell you about pulling your sister's hair?" Serrano smiled. "And Megan, your dirty clothes do *not* belong in Eric's backpack."

"But *Moooooom*," came a young girl's voice, "Eric said he *wanted* my underwear and socks in his backpack."

"I did not, you little monster!"

"You, Megan, finish getting dressed. Eric, you . . . go play a warfare brigade game or something."

"My computer is at home, and the Wi-Fi here sucks."

"I know. We'll be home soon. Just grin and bear it for now. *Please*."

"What does grin and bear it mean?" Megan said. "Is there really a bear in here?"

"No, sweetie," Rachel said. "It's a figure of speech."

"What's a speech figure?"

"It's . . . ugh. I'll explain later. Just finish getting ready."

Finally Rachel opened the door. She wore a shiny blue work shirt tucked into a gray skirt. Her brown hair was tied in a slightly unkempt ponytail. Her makeup was uneven, and there were small clumps of mascara caked on her lashes. She looked frazzled, harried, overwhelmed, and weirdly enough, kind of cute. Serrano coughed and pointed to her collar, where only one button was fastened. Rachel fixed it.

"Thanks, Detective."

He could see Megan in the background twirling around a pair of what appeared to be boys' athletic socks, which she then threw at her brother's head as he sat in a chair tapping on an iPad. Rachel looked back into the room and let out an exasperated sigh.

"It's hard enough when we're in our own home and I have a handle on things," Rachel said. "Living out of a suitcase and sharing a bathroom with two quarrelsome devils? Forget it."

"Need me to throw them into solitary confinement for a little while?" Serrano asked.

"Actually, that sounds wonderful. Maybe for a year or two."

Serrano said, "I could just keep them in the holding cells for a few days. Bet the drunks and hookers would scare them straight."

"I may take you up on that," she said. "So what can I do for you, Detective?"

"Just came to check on you and the kids. Last night could have gone another way. I'm glad it didn't."

"Me too," Rachel said.

"So how are you all holding up?"

Rachel shrugged. "Kids are acting out. Hopefully we can get home soon and get them back into the routine where my son barely speaks to me and my daughter works on becoming the next Sue Grafton."

"We're moving as fast as we can. So far your story checks out. That will speed things up."

"It will check out," Rachel said. "It was clean and justified."

Serrano nodded. He toed the floor.

"There's one more thing," Serrano said. "Christopher Robles is dead."

Rachel's eyes grew wide, and her mouth opened slightly. She looked back inside the hotel room.

"Hey, kids, give me a minute. Try not to set anything on fire."

She stepped out of the hotel room and closed the door. Serrano motioned for her to follow him. They walked to a small alcove down the hall with a pair of vending machines.

"How did he die?" Rachel said. "I shot him in the shoulder. It was a nonlethal wound. I *could* have cut his spinal cord in half, but I didn't because I *wanted* him to live."

"I know," Serrano said quietly. "It wasn't you."

"So, what? Complications during surgery? Did a doctor screw up?"

"We don't know for sure," Serrano said. "But he suffered a pulmonary embolism postsurgery. It's not uncommon in intravenous drug users, since their veins are often shot to hell to begin with."

Rachel pinched the bridge of her nose. "Isabelle. She's going to blame me." She looked at Serrano. His facial expression didn't change. "She already said something, didn't she?"

"We've made it clear to Mrs. Drummond that her brother was about to be booked on charges of breaking and entering, trespassing, and attempted murder. Whatever happened to him, he brought on himself."

"Look at me, Detective," Rachel said. "Do you think *she* believes that?"

Serrano hesitated, then said, "No, I don't."

"Shit shit *shit*," Rachel said. "My children . . . Robles was at the bridge the night Constance died," Rachel said. "And he was at the press conference. Somebody else knows that besides me. Somebody wanted him dead."

"We don't know Robles's death was a homicide," Serrano said.

"Yes you do," Rachel said. "You just can't say it yet."

"You'll have protection twenty-four seven until we can establish there are no threats," Serrano said. "We had two officers in the parking lot all night last night watching the hotel. You're safe."

"Thank you," she said. "He was there for a reason. Robles. At the press conference. He was scared of something he saw that night at the bridge."

"If you were right about the money Drummond swindled from Constance Wright, and Robles knew about it, he might have thought he was protecting his sister and her husband. Not the most logical thing to do, but Robles had a mother of a rap sheet. He didn't really have a tendency to do the smart thing."

Rachel paced back and forth. Serrano could sense her mind was racing. She was scared. And based on his somewhat limited knowledge of Rachel Marin, Serrano couldn't be confident that she would do the smart thing either.

"I need to get back to my children," she said. "They have school."

"We'll have eyes on them throughout the day," Serrano said. "You don't need to worry."

Rachel laughed nervously. "Let me ask you a question, Detective. How did those news vans get to the scene of Constance Wright's murder so quickly the other night?"

"I don't follow."

"That night, you gave a statement to the media at two in the morning. A bunch of news trucks were already on-scene. Weird, right?"

Serrano could see where she was going with this.

"So how'd they know a woman had died? How'd they get to the scene so fast? It wasn't dumb luck. My guess is their producers got tips from people in *your* department. Look at me and tell me I'm wrong."

Serrano's silence answered the question.

"So . . . let's say there's a cop or two in your precinct," Rachel continued. "A deputy a little down on his luck. A watch commander getting cleaned out by her husband's divorce attorneys. Isabelle Robles offers them some money. *Real* money, for information about the woman who put buckshot in her brother. Can you promise me they'll say no?"

"It's not your fault Robles is dead," Serrano said.

"It's my fault he was in the hospital to begin with."

"Robles was a candle. Only a matter of time before he burned out."

Rachel nodded. "Thanks, Detective. For apparently being one of the good ones."

She walked back toward her room. Serrano followed her.

"These cops are good people," Serrano said.

"Not all of them," Rachel said. She opened the hotel room door. Eric was upside down on the bed, holding an iPad above him. Megan was crab-walking toward him, holding a pair of scissors, a mischievous grin on her face.

"Kids! Let's go!"

They both popped up. Had Rachel waited thirty more seconds, Eric would have likely left for school missing either a lock of hair or an ear.

They grabbed their backpacks, jackets, hats, and gloves and trundled outside. Rachel grabbed her coat as well.

"Ms. Marin," Serrano said. She held back a moment while her kids walked ahead. She turned toward Serrano.

"Find out who killed Constance Wright," she said. "And Christopher Robles. Put them in jail or in the ground. That's the only way I'll know my kids are safe."

The Marin family got in their car and drove off. Serrano took out his cell phone and dialed.

"This is Lowe."

"Derek, it's Serrano."

"What's up, Detective?"

"Who else knows where we're keeping Rachel Marin?"

"Just you, me, Tally, Chen, Lieutenant George, and the watch commander."

Serrano nodded. All people he could trust.

"Keep it that way."

"Everything OK?"

"Yeah. Just don't have a great feeling about all of this. Keep all information on the Marin family close to the vest. I don't want anything happening to her or her kids."

"You got it, Detective."

Serrano hung up. He went back to the Crown Vic and climbed into the passenger seat.

"Let's go talk to Sam Wickersham," Tally said. "Find out why Constance Wright called the guy who helped break up her marriage and ruined her life."

Serrano replied, "I spoke to the leasing office for the management company he rents from. Let's just say Mr. Wickersham is living slightly above his means."

Tally smiled as they turned onto the freeway.

But as they prepared to question Constance Wright's alleged former lover, two things gnawed at Serrano.

First: he felt deep down that there was a connection between Christopher Robles's death and Constance Wright's murder. Second: he wasn't entirely convinced that Rachel Marin wasn't somehow involved in both.

# CHAPTER 19

Samuel J. Wickersham lived in a condo complex on East Oakland Avenue in an upscale neighborhood just a ten-minute walk from Velos Strategies, the political consulting company where he had been employed since testifying to a prior affair with Constance Wright. Wickersham was twenty-seven years old, with shoulder-length black hair tied in a ratty ponytail, a thin face with high cheekbones, and skin so smooth and pale that Serrano wondered whether he'd ever shaved a day in his life.

He was skinny but not in shape and wore a white T-shirt just tight enough that a small belly protruded over his gray pajama bottoms. His three-bedroom apartment was modern and well furnished with a glass-topped round dining room table with four wooden upholstered chairs, a brown leather sofa, and several pieces of ornately framed artwork hanging on the walls.

A pair of walnut bookshelves bracketed a sixty-inch LCD television, packed end to end with books. Serrano, always drawn to bookshelves, went to check them out. A cursory look told him that none of the books had had so much as their spines cracked. And curiously, Wickersham seemed to own only copies of canonical titles. Nothing contemporary. They could have been the bookshelves of an English lit major who'd never been to class.

*Middlemarch*, *Anna Karenina*, *Ulysses*, *Lolita*, *The Tin Drum*, *The Sound and the Fury*, *Brideshead Revisited*.

In fact, Serrano was reasonably sure that Wickersham had simply printed out the Modern Library Top 100 and ordered a copy of each title. This wasn't a bookshelf owned by someone who liked to read but someone who wanted people to *think* he liked to read. To Serrano, there were few greater sins. Maybe homicide. But that was debatable.

Two years ago, Samuel J. Wickersham, at the time a volunteer canvasser, had testified in open court that he'd carried on a ten-month sexual relationship with then mayor Constance Wright. He produced text messages, emails, and explicit photographs traded between them. Wright denied every word of it but couldn't explain the dozens of outgoing calls and messages sent from her phone to his. Wright had left office in disgrace, a punch line. Wickersham had trundled off and taken a cushy job with Velos.

Serrano had to mask his contempt as he and Tally stood in Wickersham's apartment.

Wickersham went into the kitchen and scooped coffee into a drip machine. "Can I make you guys a cup?" he said.

"No," replied Serrano.

"Sure," said Tally.

Tally's response seemed to surprise Wickersham, but he tossed an extra two scoops into the filter. He took a gallon of Poland Spring from the fridge and used it to fill the tank, pressed "On," and turned back to the detectives.

"I don't have any doughnuts," Wickersham said. He was met with silence. "You know. Coffee and doughnuts. Isn't that a cop thing?"

"I prefer croissants," Tally said.

"Danishes," said Serrano.

"Right," Wickersham said. "So what can I do for you, Detectives?"

"Obviously you know that Constance Wright died the other night," Tally said.

"I heard," Wickersham said. He didn't appear to be too beat up about it. "She was killed, right?"

"Appears so," Serrano said. Wickersham pulled a metal stool from under the granite countertop and sat down. "Obviously you two had a history."

"That's one way of putting it." Wickersham looked at the coffee maker as though hoping it had miraculously brewed in the thirty seconds since he'd turned it on. "That's exactly what it is. History. I've moved on. I didn't do anything wrong."

"Nobody said you did," Serrano said. "By the way, this is a nice place. What do you pay in rent?"

"Scuse me?" Wickersham said.

"Rent. What do you pay?"

"I don't know. Three grand a month. Why does that matter?"

"Try fifty-one hundred a month," Tally said. Wickersham looked up from the coffee maker.

"What's your point?"

"Point is," Serrano said. "We checked the FEC records for your time at the mayor's office. Lucky for us you were a government employee, so your salary is a matter of public record. You were making thirty-seven grand a year. Before taxes."

Wickersham turned back to the coffee maker, seemingly trying to will it to finish brewing. "Stupid thing takes forever," he said. He looked at Serrano. "Did you say you did or didn't want a cup?"

"I prefer iced," he said.

"It's twenty degrees outside," replied Wickersham.

"Coffee tastes better when it's frosty."

"We spoke to other employees at Velos," Tally said. "Do you know a woman named Adeline Bowers? She's your age. Been there five years. Started a month before you. Do you know her?"

"Of course," Wickersham said. "Adeline works in the office next to mine. Boyfriend is always coming by to take her to lunch. Sends her flowers, like, every other week. I mean, some people just don't act professional."

"You really have it out for her," Serrano said.

"It's nothing personal," Wickersham said, in a tone of voice that made it sound *very* personal. "I mean, don't you hate when people can't keep their personal and professional lives separate? It's gross. Like, this is a place of work, right?"

"Sure," Serrano said.

"And I don't need my desk smelling like whatever hooker scent she decided to wear that day."

Tally's eyes widened. "Hooker scent?"

"Just, it's overpowering is all I meant. I have sensitive nostrils."

"Sensitive nostrils," Tally said. "That's a first."

Serrano said, "Ms. Bowers told us she makes sixty-four grand a year. She seems like a smart and ambitious woman. She even wants to open up her own consulting firm down the road."

"And?"

"And if she's making sixty-four grand a year and seems to have far better people skills than you, I have to ask: What do you pull down a year, Sam?"

"None of your business," he said.

Tally said, "No way you're clearing more than sixty, sixty-five grand a year."

Serrano added, "I can tell from your reaction that's on the high end."

"So what?" Wickersham said.

"So you're on the hook for over sixty grand a year in rent alone. So, after taxes, you must be running at quite a loss."

"I have money," Wickersham said. "In savings."

"That right?" Serrano said. "Where'd that money come from?"

"An inheritance," he said, with just enough of a pause between the two words so that all three of them knew he was lying.

"Oh yeah? Who died?"

"My . . . aunt."

"On which side?"

"Mom's," he said quickly.

"When did she die?"

"Last year." Again, too quickly.

"Last year," Tally said. "So how did you afford the apartment when you first moved in?"

"I meant she died five years ago," Wickersham said. The coffee maker beeped. Wickersham poured himself half a cup, filled the rest with half-and-half, and then added two Splendas. He sipped it and grimaced.

"Too hot?" Serrano said. Wickersham shook his head and took another sip.

"What was your aunt's name?" Tally asked.

"Why do you want to know?"

"I'm making a collage of the Wickersham family tree for a class project," Serrano said. "Now what. Was. Her. Name."

Wickersham opened his mouth, but nothing came out. He looked from Serrano to Tally and back. His eyes were despondent, his confidence evaporated.

"What do you want from me?" Wickersham asked. His voice had changed. Fear dripped from it.

"Constance Wright called you the day she died," Serrano said. "We cross-checked her phone records against yours. In fact, she had called you eight times over the past three weeks."

"We want to know why," Tally said.

"I never spoke to her," Wickersham said. He put his coffee on the counter, placed his palms on the granite, and took a deep breath. "She kept calling and calling, but I never picked up."

Tally said. "Why didn't you want to speak to her? You two had a thing, right? You're single, she's single . . ."

"How do you know I'm single?" Wickersham said.

"There's a condom in your change dish by the door, Romeo," Tally said. "You show me a girlfriend who isn't suspicious of that, and I'll show you an imaginary girlfriend. So why didn't you want to speak to Constance?"

"I had nothing to say to Ms. Wright," Wickersham said. Serrano noted the respectful way he addressed her. *Ms. Wright.*

"She obviously had something to say to you. And we think we know what it was," Serrano said.

Wickersham looked up at Serrano. Even he was curious.

"I think she wanted her money back," Serrano said. "I think you were paid, and paid well, to lie about having an affair with Constance Wright. You brand her an adulterer, a drunk, maybe plant a bottle of booze where a photographer can get a shot of it, and she subsequently gets annihilated in her divorce settlement and ends up resigning from office. Everybody wins."

"Except the dead woman," Tally said, "and her child."

Wickersham's jaw dropped. He studied Serrano's and Tally's faces to see if they were serious. Serrano nodded.

"That's right. She was pregnant when she died."

He stammered, "I . . . I didn't know. It's not mine, I swear to God."

Serrano looked at the kid. Nobody was that good of an actor. He believed him.

"Maybe it wasn't your kid," Serrano said, "maybe it was. We'll need you to submit a DNA sample to confirm paternity or lack thereof. Will you submit to one?"

"Yes, in a second, yes," Wickersham said. "What do I need to do?"

Serrano eyed Tally. They were thinking the same thing. If Wickersham thought there was any chance he was the father of Constance Wright's unborn child, there's no way he'd offer to submit to a DNA test without a fight.

Tally took a red plastic bag labeled "Buccal Swab Kit" and tore open the top. She removed a pair of latex gloves, two swabs, and a small plastic tube. She slipped the gloves on, opened the tube, and told Wickersham, "Say aah."

He opened his mouth, and Tally collected the sample. Then she put the swab in the plastic tube, screwed the top back on, and placed it in the plastic bag.

Both she and Serrano knew it would come back negative.

"We're going to subpoena your bank account statements," Tally said. "I'm going to personally review every single penny that's come in and out of your accounts for the last ten years. And by that look on your face, we both know there's going to be money you can't account for legally. So let's stop pretending. You didn't bring down Constance Wright by yourself. So who helped you? If you'll be a good boy and talk to us, you might not spend the next twenty years of your life making license plates."

"Let's start with the text messages," Serrano said. His voice was soft, nonjudgmental. Now he wanted Wickersham to feel comfortable. "In court, there were texts between you and Constance."

"They cloned her cell phone," Wickersham said resignedly. He'd placed his hands behind his head, interlaced his fingers, and started to pace around the room. "They wrote up a script. Almost like a movie. They would send me texts from the cloned phone, and I responded on mine."

"There were records of you paying for hotel rooms around Ashby," Tally said.

"I'd rent a room out every now and then, just so they'd have a credit card receipt of me being there. And the desk clerks could testify that they'd seen me." Wickersham looked up. "Everyone figured, Why the hell would this kid rent a hotel room for no reason? They just assumed I was telling the truth because—"

"It was a great story," Tally said. "The mayor and the coffee boy."

"Screw you, man; I wasn't a coffee boy," Wickersham shouted. "I was good at my job. It was just . . . I was making thirty-seven grand a year. My parents have lived in the same crummy house for forty years. I don't have a 'rich aunt.' You know what thirty-seven grand buys you in Ashby? Three roommates and ramen for dinner."

"It's called paying your dues," Serrano said. "I made fifteen five my first year on the force."

"Well, *good for you,*" Wickersham said, dripping sarcasm. "I wanted a *life.*"

"So you stole someone else's," Tally said.

"That's not true. Besides, after what her family did? They're all crooks." Then Wickersham grew concerned. "Wait, are you going to tell my boss about all this?"

"Your boss?" Tally said, laughing. "You're worried about your *job*? Kid, you might spend the next few years of your life in prison."

"No . . . ," Wickersham said. "I . . . I can't do that."

"So tell us. Who paid you to be their patsy?" Serrano said. "Somebody wanted Constance Wright cleaned out and embarrassed. Who?"

Wickersham shook his head. "I feel like I need a lawyer."

"If you're guilty," Tally said, "then sure. Call your lawyer. We want to know who killed Constance Wright. Where were you the night she died?"

"I was here," he said, eyes level, deadly serious. "But I'll swear on a Bible that I had nothing to do with it."

"I'm not sure if God would be the best character witness for you. If you didn't kill her, help us find who did. Make this right. You owe her."

Wickersham went around the counter and removed his cell phone from a charging pad. He spent several minutes scrolling, then returned to the detectives. "Here you go."

Serrano leaned in and looked at the screen, where Wickersham's Contacts list was visible.

"Mr. X?" Serrano looked up, incredulous. "Seriously?"

"I never got a name," Wickersham said. "So I called him Mr. X. He contacted me about a year before it all went down. From this number. Whoever it was knew everything about me. *Everything.* Knew my parents' names, where they lived. That my dad had his hip replaced. That my mom likes pistachio ice cream. Hell, they knew I had a cocker spaniel named Titus growing up. It scared me half to death. They made it clear that if I didn't cooperate, something bad would happen to me or my family."

"All right," Tally said. "Tell us everything."

Wickersham nodded hesitantly. "I think I'm going to need to call a lawyer."

"I think that's a good idea."

"Am I under arrest?"

"Not yet," Serrano said. "But that could change very quickly. So if you plan on going anywhere, and I mean *anywhere*, if you cross the street to get a bagel or go see a movie, you need to let us know. Terrible things happen in those holding cells."

"Horrible things," Tally added.

"Trust me," Serrano said, "you don't want to give us a reason to put you in one."

"Things happen I wouldn't wish upon my worst enemy," Tally said.

At this point, Wickersham's face had turned a shade paler than the half-and-half he'd poured into his coffee. But Serrano knew that if they arrested Wickersham, whoever had paid the kid would find out and circle the wagons. It was better to keep Wickersham out of prison—and scared.

"So now that we know you helped destroy an innocent woman for money," Tally said, "this is your chance to make amends. We want to find out who paid you and why. Somebody wanted to ruin Constance Wright's life."

"I didn't want that," Wickersham said softly. "I just . . . I was in love. I wanted to be able to support her."

"Aw, you were in love," Serrano said in a mocking tone. "I'm sure whatever sorority girl caught your fancy appreciated your committing multiple felonies for her."

"She wasn't some *sorority girl*," Wickersham said angrily. "She was special. And I was broke. I had no right to even *be* with her. We wanted to start a family, but I couldn't support a kid on what I made. Then someone offered me more money than I'd make in twenty years. What was I supposed to do?"

"Well, definitely not what you *did* do," Tally said. Wickersham was silent. He looked ashamed.

"Does this sweetheart of yours have any information about the payments from this Mr. X?"

"No," Wickersham said. A little too quickly.

Tally said, "One more question, for now. Do you know anyone named Rachel Marin?"

Wickersham looked confused. "No. Why?"

"No reason," Tally replied. "Let's go, lover boy. We're not done with you by a long shot."

# CHAPTER 20

Before calling Steve Ruggiero, Rachel perfected her grossest, bubonic plague–esque hacking, phlegmy cough. By the end of the conversation, Steve made her swear on her children not to set foot in the office until she had a clean bill of health. Rachel figured she had two weeks before he started getting suspicious.

Once she dropped Megan and Eric off at school, Rachel went back to the hotel and booted up her laptop. The Wi-Fi took ten minutes to connect. She could have cooked a Thanksgiving turkey in the amount of time it took each page to load. This wouldn't work. She threw the laptop in her purse and found a coffee shop a few miles down Lakeland where the Yelp reviews praised the speed of their free Wi-Fi and the strength of their espresso.

When Rachel went downstairs, she noticed an Ashby PD patrol car idling in the parking lot. Its wipers were on, brushing back the light dusting of snow gathering on the windshield. A thirtyish female cop with red hair and freckles sat in the driver's seat sipping a Coke. An overweight, balding cop sat next to her. He was chewing on an overstuffed breakfast sandwich and staring at it like it contained the mysteries of the universe. The female cop noticed Rachel crossing the parking lot and gave her a subtle nod. Rachel cinched up her coat and offered a thin smile. She found an unfortunate irony in the fact that she now had two sitters watching her family.

She drove to the coffee shop, parked, ordered a double espresso, and found a seat at a communal table. She noticed the patrol car pull into the lot. She could see the redhead behind the wheel. Their eyes met again. This time Rachel didn't bother to smile.

*Ignore it,* Rachel thought. *You have work to do.*

The Wi-Fi information was printed on her receipt.

Network: BeansNBrew

Password: x6G$d6J0*DNM(c15M'C72#0S!

It took her four tries just to correctly enter the mishmash of letters, numbers, and symbols. She took a quick look around the cafe. It was late morning, so the only patrons were stay-at-home moms and their zeppelin-size baby carriages, unshaven aspiring writers, and a few retirees with nothing to do but enjoy a hot cup on a cold day. Rachel envied their serenity.

Once she was connected, Rachel was relieved to find that the Wi-Fi speed was fast and reliable. She created a folder on her desktop and labeled it "CR." Then she spent the next two hours digging up everything she could on Isabelle Drummond, née Robles, and her brother, Christopher.

Isabelle was, from what Rachel could tell, a model citizen. On paper. She paid $49.95 to run a full background check on Isabelle, which came up clean. No arrests or convictions, no marriage or divorce decrees outside of Nicholas. She had purchased the house she currently lived in with Nicholas Drummond just under two years ago for $4.15 million. The mortgage was in Isabelle's name. Rachel was moderately pleased that her initial estimate on the property value was so close.

Isabelle previously owned a three-bedroom, two-bathroom condo on East Stallworth Boulevard, purchased seven years ago for $2.05 million. She sold it right before moving in with Drummond, for $3.14 million, a cool $1,090,000 profit, before taxes and Realtor fees.

She graduated from George Washington University in 2012 (current tuition with expenses: $70,443 per year) with a BA in art history, then spent several years working in public relations for a tech firm that had created a suite of social networking apps. Isabelle's name was attached as a contact to a number of press releases. It was during that time that her parents, Arturo and Yvette, died.

Arturo had emigrated from Ecuador in 1971, having graduated from Escuela Superior Politécnica del Litoral with a degree in marketing, communications, and sales engineering. He took a job as a sales rep with Carton-Phipps, a small pharmaceutical company, but rose through the ranks and was made CMO by 1980. Carton-Phipps, or C-P, had a market cap of $37 billion as of 2014.

And when Arturo and Yvette were killed when their Cessna CJ3 jet crashed after takeoff at Toncontín airport in Honduras, Isabelle Robles was the sole inheritor of her family's multimillion-dollar holdings.

Isabelle Robles had cash in the bank, millions in stock, and no oversight. She had both the time and the means to repay a grudge.

Christopher's history was more checkered than a flannel shirt. Arrests for possession, possession with intent to sell, possession with intent to distribute, resisting arrest, loitering, and multiple counts of disturbing the peace. He'd spent six months at the Whitecaps treatment facility outside of Vail, Colorado. He had never owned property, which didn't surprise Rachel. She couldn't imagine banks were tripping over themselves to lend him money, and even if Isabelle was willing to be a guarantor, Isabelle surely knew Christopher living on his own was a disaster waiting to happen. Which was how he had ended up living with the newly married Drummond couple.

Rachel opened up Facebook. She had no legitimate social media profiles but had created a pseudonymous one several years ago solely for the purpose of spying on her children and, occasionally, doing exactly what she needed to do now. She searched for and found Christopher Robles's account. She couldn't see the bulk of his profile—it was restricted to friends—but there were a dozen public photos he was tagged in that she could view.

One photo caught her eye: Christopher Robles standing with two other people in front of a gray-brick, graffiti-covered wall holding the very same SIG Sauer he'd been armed with when he broke into her house. Robles held the gun in front of his crotch, an angry sneer on his face. The caption read, "They're both locked and loaded."

Subtle.

But what concerned Rachel more were the two people on either side of Robles. To Robles's left stood a behemoth of a man. He was Hispanic, at least six feet four, and closer to four hundred pounds than three hundred. And not all of it was fat. His forearms, heavily tattooed, had ripples of muscle mass. And the single blue teardrop tattooed just below his left eye, ink commonly received in prison, suggested he did not live a life of pacifism.

His right arm was draped around Robles's shoulders. In his left hand he held a Desert Eagle .50 Mark XIX. One of the most powerful handguns in the world.

In fact, because the Desert Eagle used gas-operated action as opposed to the blowback or recoil action of most handguns, it actually had more in common with AK-47 rifles than most pistols. It was also hugely popular in films because, well, it looked cool. But that cool gun could stop a rhino in its tracks.

On Robles's right was a woman about five feet six who looked like a living canvas. Her entire body was covered in tattoos. She had a metal stud in her lip, a hoop through her septum, and a chain linking that hoop to one of the ten piercings in her ear. She had green hair styled in a pixie cut and wore cutoff jean shorts and a washed-out purple tank top with an image of bloody knuckles printed on it.

But her look was not what caught Rachel's eye—even Rachel had gone through a punk phase when she was younger—it was the Ruger AR-556 semiautomatic rifle hanging at her side.

The caption on the photo read *Friendz 4 Life. Friendz 2 Death. Bulletz N Blood.*

Just the kind of pals you'd want to bring home to meet your parents.

Robles's "pals" were tagged in the photo. The Hispanic Hulk was Nestor Aguillar, and the girl with the nuclear waste hairdo was Stefanie Steinman.

Rachel clicked on both of their profiles, and her heart sank. They had each posted the same photo that very morning. The photo was of Christopher Robles, and he was wearing a tuxedo. His hair was cut and parted. He was clean shaven, and the smile on his face was bright and genuine. A far cry from the washed-out, strung-out man in her home. There was a time stamp on the lower right hand of the photo. Rachel cross-checked that date with a search for Isabelle Robles and confirmed that the photo had been taken two years prior at Isabelle's wedding to Nicholas Drummond.

Nestor's caption read *RIP Crazy Chris. Never B 4Gotten.*

Stefanie's read *Will Never 4Get U.*

Underneath Stefanie's message was a link out to YouTube. Rachel clicked on it. It took her to a clip of the famous scene from *Pulp Fiction* where Samuel L. Jackson recited a verse from Ezekiel 25:17 to some poor schlub before filling him with enough lead to start a pencil factory. Rachel turned the volume down on her computer and watched the scene in full.

*And I will strike down upon thee with great vengeance and furious anger, those who attempt to poison and destroy my brothers. And you will know my name is the Lord, when I lay my vengeance upon thee.*

She closed the browser page and thought about what Nicholas Drummond had said about Chris's friends.

*Let's just say you wouldn't want to get on their bad side.*

Then she muttered two words.

"Fuck. Me."

# CHAPTER 21

Serrano and Tally were driving on I-84 West in the Crown Vic out toward Rosenwood Township, ten miles west of Ashby. Rosenwood was a small, mainly pastoral principality with a population of less than twenty thousand. It bordered the Ashby River on the north and was made up predominantly of midsize office buildings filled with family medical and insurance practices and ranch-style, single-family dwellings. If Ashby was the budget Chicago, then Rosenwood was the budget Ashby. The housing and commercial real estate markets in Rosenwood were cheap, and because of that it was attractive to companies with employees based out of and serving Ashby, Peoria, and Chicago.

Rosenwood's biggest claim to fame was that it was the birthplace of the esteemed, noted, *respected* inventor Victor Maloriano. Maloriano was a botanist who, one day, after growing tired of the constant red marks on the side of his nose made by his glasses, glued two small silicone pads onto the frames to protect his skin. Two years later he patented the Nose Pad, then sold the patent for $20 million to an eyeglass manufacturer in 1981. Soon after that Maloriano went mad and began abducting local dogs from their homes. When the Rosenwood PD received a noise complaint of incessant barking by a neighbor, they found Maloriano stark naked in his easy chair, with no fewer than twenty dogs of different breeds roaming his spacious Craftsman home. The dogs were returned to their owners. Maloriano was committed to a sanatorium. People preferred to focus on the Nose Pads when remembering Maloriano.

Serrano was about to make a crack about Maloriano to Tally when his cell phone rang. The call was coming from Rachel Marin. Tally saw the caller ID and rolled her eyes.

Serrano pressed answer and put the call on speaker.

"Ms. Marin," he said. "How's the Best Western treating you?"

"Listen, Detective," she said, ignoring the question. "I need you to keep an eye on two people for me. Names are Nestor Aguillar and Stefanie Steinman."

"You need us to keep an eye on two people for you?" Tally said, irritated. "Ms. Marin, we're employees of the state, not you personally."

"I could go the 'I pay your salary' route, but that's too clichéd, and I'm not an asshole. Anyway, this isn't a favor. You warned me about what Isabelle Drummond might be capable of, right?"

"That's right," Serrano said.

"Well, I was doing a little digging into Christopher Robles, and he has two good friends, Nestor Aguillar and Stefanie Steinman. They posted videos today that lead me to think they're looking for some payback for Robles, and let's just say they also like taking pictures with weaponry strong enough to take out the Avengers." She gave Serrano the correct spellings for both names.

*Nestor Aguillar.* The name sounded familiar to Serrano. Which meant he'd probably done some very bad things.

"Anyway, I know the hotel is being watched by your people. But during the day, my kids are in school. My son's school is fifteen minutes from my daughter's grade school. I can't possibly watch them both at the same time. And if, God forbid, something was to happen . . ."

"I hear you," Serrano said. "Let me call the station and see if I can get a uni to check in on them during the day. In the meantime, we'll look into Steinman and Aguillar and see if there's anything to be concerned about."

"Thank you, Detective."

"Not a problem. Be safe. Call if you need anything."

"I will."

Marin hung up. Serrano put the phone back in his pocket.

"I think you're sweet on her," Tally said, grinning. Serrano tapped his finger against his chin.

"Nestor Aguillar," he said. "That name rings a bell. Which probably means it's not a good thing for Rachel. Who's on watch commander duty today?"

"Pat Connelly," Tally said.

He dialed the station. "Hey, Pat, it's Serrano. Listen, I need you to run full background checks on two Ashby residents: Nestor Aguillar and Stefanie Steinman. Criminal records, known associates, arrest reports, anything you can dig up. Send it over to my cell as soon as you have it."

Serrano hung up.

"You're worried about her," Tally said. "Rachel Marin seems like she knows how to take care of herself pretty well. I wish Claire could handle a shotgun like that. I would have proposed sooner."

"It's not Rachel I'm worried about," Serrano said.

"You think Isabelle would go after her kids?" Tally said.

"Isabelle blames Rachel for her brother's death. Fair or not. And they were tight. Chris was basically her child, the way she took care of him. I'd like to think she could understand that her brother dug his own grave, but grieving family members are not always rational. Better to be safe."

Tally nodded. "She's cute, you know. The Marin woman."

Serrano laughed. "Cute? Come on, Leslie. You aren't allowed to call a woman 'cute' past the age of twenty-two."

"Trust me, Casanova, I've been with way more women than you have, and yes, you can. But it's all about how you say it. You should work on your game. Maybe convince a woman who's not your partner to spend some time with you."

"I don't need dating advice."

"Sure about that?"

"Concentrate on what we're here for, Tally. We're almost there."

J&J Accounting was located in a midsize steel-and-glass office building off I-84. Serrano pulled into the parking lot. According to property records, J&J owned the entire building but only occupied the third floor, leasing out unoccupied office space to other companies.

The number Sam Wickersham had corresponded with to set up Constance Wright was registered to a company called Albatross LLC. Albatross had leased office space from J&J three years ago, right around the time Wickersham said the calls had started coming in. There was only one problem: Albatross was registered in the name of a Walter Mackey, an eighty-four-year-old retired florist who lived in Ashby with his eighty-eight-year-old wife, Beattie, in a house they'd bought in 1974 for $8,000.

Walter Mackey had a grand total of $12,474 in his savings account. This was a man who spent his Saturdays cutting coupons, not coordinating secret payments to take down a sitting mayor. Somebody had used Mackey's social security number to fraudulently register Albatross as an LLC, most likely to transfer money to Sam Wickersham without it being under the name of a real individual or legitimate company.

Albatross had no employees and no tax records and was not registered with the Better Business Bureau. It appeared to be a company that had literally been set up to facilitate money transfers to Sam Wickersham and nothing more.

Wickersham claimed to have no knowledge of the identity of Albatross, that he did not know who he'd spoken with, and that he'd never met anyone in person. Yet he'd received three wire transfers during that period of time totaling $480,000. Which explained why a guy with limited means and ethics could afford a high-end bachelor pad stocked with unread books to use as romantic bait.

They needed to know who, exactly, was behind Albatross. Because whoever set up the fake company was willing to spend a whole lot of money to ruin Constance Wright's life. And if they were willing to ruin her life, Serrano bet they'd be inclined to go a step further and take it as well. He was hoping J&J Accounting would have more information on Albatross. Leasing records. Signatures.

Follow the money. Between the nearly half a million dollars Sam Wickersham had received and the $1.2 million Nicholas Drummond had received in spousal support, it had taken less than $2 million to utterly destroy Constance Wright. Or the annual salary of a mediocre baseball relief pitcher.

Tally buzzed J&J from an intercom in the lobby vestibule. A woman answered.

"J&J, how can I help you?"

"Detectives John Serrano and Leslie Tally of the Ashby PD."

"Yes, Detectives, Mrs. Givens is expecting you."

She buzzed them in, and they took the elevator to the third floor. A rather plump woman with waist-length blonde hair wearing an unflattering floral print frock and too much rouge was waiting for them when the doors opened.

"Detectives, I'm Anne Weems. Please have a seat. Mrs. Givens will be right with you. Can I get you water? Coffee? Orange juice?"

They declined and took seats in two overstuffed brown leather chairs in the reception area. Tally picked up a J&J brochure and thumbed through it. Serrano checked his phone. It was a secure connection and encrypted through the department. He had two emails from Pat Connelly: background reports on Nestor Aguillar and Stefanie Steinman. He opened the Aguillar file first and cursed under his breath as he read.

Nestor Aguillar had been arrested four times: drunk and disorderly in '09; harassment and public urination in '11; assault with a deadly weapon in '12, for which he'd served three years in Pickneyville; and unlicensed possession of a firearm in '15, which had sent him back to Pickneyville for another year.

Stefanie Steinman was another matter entirely. She had no criminal record whatsoever, her most egregious offense being a string of unpaid parking tickets back in '14. She had a concealed carry license and had not racked up a single firearm infraction. She was an eight-year, card-carrying member of the Lock & Stock Riflery Club on Greenwood Avenue in Ashby.

She had also graduated from Ashby High with honors, then spent three years at Northwestern before dropping out for unknown reasons. This was a smart young woman with seemingly no history of illegal activity beyond parking tickets as well as access to excellent schooling. Her parents were Saul and Lexi Steinman, owners of several car dealerships in Ashby, Galesburg, and Bloomington. They lived in a large Victorian in east Ashby, which they'd purchased in 2001 for $2.4 million.

So how in the hell had she befriended Christopher Robles and Nestor Aguillar?

Serrano leaned over and shared the information with Tally.

"What do you make of it?" he asked.

"Strange," Tally said. "Aguillar and Steinman are from two completely different walks of life."

"Her parents live in east Ashby," Serrano said. "Not too far from where Isabelle and Nicholas Drummond live and where Isabelle grew up. Stefanie and Isabelle are of similar ages, grew up in the same neighborhood, and went to the same high school. My guess? Isabelle and Stefanie were friends. Chris and Nestor were friends. And they cross-pollinated."

"It would make Steinman and Aguillar loyal to the whole family," Tally said.

"Yeah . . . there's something off with this girl, though."

"For some reason, she scares me more than Aguillar. And *he's* the one with the record."

Serrano shrugged. "The smart ones know how to stay under the radar. But when they decide to make their presence known . . ."

He let the sentence trail off.

A tall, slim Asian woman in her early forties came into the reception area wearing a thousand-watt smile. She had straight shoulder-length jet-black hair and wore a smart gray blouse with heels that had probably cost a week's pay. She walked toward them with long graceful strides, her right hand outstretched for the last five steps. Serrano and Tally stood up and shook her hand.

"Detectives, I'm Dorothy Givens, CFO of J&J Accounting. Thank you for waiting."

"Not at all, Mrs. Givens," Tally said. "We know you're busy. Thanks for making the time."

"Of course. Here, let's talk in my office."

Givens led them down a long hallway with light-blue wallpaper and recessed lighting. Givens had a spacious corner office overlooking a small park with a handball court, a merry-go-round, and an empty kiddie pool. During the summer it must have been a joy to watch children playing, but in the faint light of a cold, bleak December, the park looked empty and sad.

Givens closed the door behind them and took a seat in an ergonomic desk chair. She motioned for Serrano and Tally to sit.

"So what can I do for you, Detectives?"

Serrano began. "To cut to the chase, J&J owns this entire building, is that correct?"

"We do," Givens said. She sat back, folded her hands across her lap.

"But the firm itself only occupies the third floor. You lease out the rest of the office space to other companies."

"That's right."

"How much square footage is that, and how many separate offices are there?"

"In total, we own about four thousand square feet. It can be broken up into various different layouts, depending on the needs of the tenant. Sometimes companies will lease an entire floor, and sometimes they'll lease a single office."

"How much of that space is currently occupied?" Serrano asked.

"Let me check." Givens woke her iMac computer from sleep, clicked a few times, and said, "We're currently leasing space to seven different companies, for a total of twenty-five hundred twenty-five square feet. We have another company whose lease starts next month, but they're just taking up a single, small, four-hundred-square-foot office."

"Presumably you have records of every leasing agreement with your tenants."

"We do," Givens said.

"We'd like to see records of every tenant agreement from the last seven years, then," Tally said.

Givens narrowed her eyes. "May I ask why?"

"You may," Tally said. "But suffice it to say we need it as part of an ongoing criminal investigation."

"A criminal investigation," Givens said. "Do I need to bring in our counsel?"

"That depends," Serrano said. "As of this moment, we're only interested in the tenants that may have leased space from you during a specific time frame. If we find any of your tenants were involved in criminal activity, and your firm either leased it to them knowingly or aided and abetted them after the fact, then you might want to lawyer up."

"We have nothing to hide," Givens said. "We file everything with the SEC, and we've never been cited for any improper practices. I've worked here for eleven years, and I've overseen leasing agreements of at least fifty companies in that time. I can assure you that at no point were we aware of any criminal activity. And if any took place without our knowledge, we'll happily cooperate with law enforcement."

"Now you see?" Serrano said, smiling at Tally. "Who says accountants are always pains in the ass?"

"Actually, I think you're the one who always says that," Tally replied.

"Well, I'm going to make an exception for Mrs. Givens. Or is it Dorothy?"

"It's Mrs. Givens."

"Right. Mrs. Givens. Let me ask you this: Do you remember a company called Albatross LLC?"

She tapped her lip with a red manicured nail. "I don't recall the name and don't recall ever meeting anyone from the firm."

"They were one of your tenants," Serrano said. "They leased space here about three years ago."

"That's odd," Givens said. "In that time we've only had about ten or so new lessees. I don't recall ever meeting someone from Albatross. And I make it my business to get to know our tenants."

"Does anyone else sign the lease agreements besides you?"

"No. Although after my son was born, other people at the firm handled leasing arrangements while I was out on maternity leave."

Tally said, "We'll need the names of any J&J employees who had the authority to sign leases for the firm at any point in time."

"Absolutely. I know them offhand; there aren't many. Esther Warren, our vice president. Alphonse Russoti, our managing director. And Caroline Drummond, in management services."

Serrano's eyes went wide. "Caroline . . . Drummond."

"That's right," she said. "You probably recognize the name because of her brother and the whole mess with his ex-wife, Constance. Say, she died recently, didn't she? Does this have anything to do with that?"

Serrano looked at Tally, then said to Givens, "We need to see every leasing agreement signed off on by Caroline Drummond. *Now*."

◆◆◆

As they were leaving J&J Accounting, Serrano called Lieutenant George on his cell phone.

"This is George."

"Lieutenant, it's Serrano."

"Detective. What do you have for me?"

"Get this. Earlier today, we spoke with Sam Wickersham, Constance Wright's alleged lover, who testified to an affair and helped blow up her marriage and career. Well, turns out Mr. Wickersham may not have been fully forthcoming in his sworn testimony."

"How so?"

"He was paid nearly half a million dollars to create a false affair. Bank records show three payments of a hundred and sixty grand apiece deposited into Wickersham's Bank of America account. He also claims Wright's phone was cloned, which is where all those dirty texts on her end came from."

"Jesus. Who paid Wickersham off?"

"That's where it gets interesting," Serrano said. "Wickersham never met anybody in person but still has records from the phone calls he received to help him fabricate the allegations. The phone number is registered to an Albatross LLC. There's just one problem: there *is no* Albatross LLC. It's a shell company whose only purpose, it seems, was to provide cover for those payments. Now, we traced the payments to Wickersham from an account in the Cayman Islands. And with their banking laws, it'll be near impossible to trace those accounts back to anyone."

"OK. Tell me you have some good news."

"Good and bad. The good news is that Albatross leased an office in a building owned by an accounting firm called J&J. J&J confirms they leased out the space . . . and you'll never guess who signed off on the paperwork."

"Don't tease me."

"Caroline Drummond."

"Caroline Drummond . . . is that any relation to . . ."

"Nicholas Drummond's sister."

"So you're telling me Nicholas Drummond's sister leased space to a shell company whose sole purpose was to help destroy the life of her brother's wife."

"And I thought I had issues with *my* in-laws. Now, the name on the lease for Albatross is a Walter Mackey, but Walter Mackey is a retired octogenarian. His identity was stolen to create the LLC."

"Where is Caroline Drummond now?"

"That's where this gets tricky," Serrano said. "Turns out Ms. Drummond took a somewhat unexpected sabbatical, which happened to begin one month before Constance Wright was killed. According to the J&J CFO, Dorothy Givens, she's somewhere in Italy with no return date."

"Doesn't sound like you think Ms. Drummond's travel timeline is a coincidence."

"I do not. I think somebody had a feeling this was all going south, and Albatross is trying to tie up loose ends. Caroline Drummond getting out of the country is part of that."

"Can we extradite her?"

"Not yet. We have enough to charge Sam Wickersham with fraud and perjury, but that's about it right now. Wickersham said he doesn't know who's behind Albatross, so we wouldn't be able to get much by offering him a deal in exchange for turning state's evidence. But somebody wanted Constance Wright's life to go up in flames in the worst way. And it appears her ex-husband and his sister were in on it."

"Are you going after Nicholas Drummond?"

"Not just yet. He can claim plausible deniability, that his sister was acting independently, unless we have something concrete to tie him to Albatross or Wickersham. I'd rather find that link before bringing him in."

"Keep at it, Detective. Find the link. And keep me posted. Nice work."

"Will do, sir."

Serrano ended the call.

"It's possible Isabelle is connected to Albatross," Tally said. "Would make sense. Gets Constance out of Nicholas's life, frees them up to marry. And she has the money and connections to make it happen."

Serrano thought as they got in the car. "I don't know. Doesn't feel right. No doubt Isabelle made out well, got the man she wanted, but seems like a *whole* lot of trouble to go through just to break up a marriage. Why wouldn't Nicholas just divorce Constance and remarry? This Albatross situation feels personal. Like a vendetta of some sort."

"So what now?"

"Let's head back. I want to come up with names of people who may have had motive to want Constance Wright ruined."

Tally slid into the driver's seat. Serrano hooked his cell phone up to the stereo through a USB port.

"What do you think you're doing?"

"Clearing my head."

He opened the Audiobooks app and pressed play. A man's voice came over the speakers. British and slightly nasal, but jovial.

*This book is largely concerned with hobbits, and from its pages a reader may discover much of their character.*

Tally looked at Serrano and said, "Speaking of suffering, I can't listen to this again. Listen to the radio like a normal person."

"This helps me think," Serrano said. "Just ignore it. Or better yet, pay attention. You might learn something."

"Not a chance. No more hearing about hobbits or their hairy feet while I drive." She unplugged the USB.

"Come on, Tally."

"God, you're whiny sometimes." Tally sighed. "I didn't mean that, John. But this can't be healthy. You need to speak to someone."

Serrano's voice lowered and he said, "Just because I want to listen to *The Lord of the Rings* on audiobook?"

"You know it's not the book. It's why you're listening to it. You can't carry this around with you, this . . . weight. It's crushing you."

"Sometimes I *want* the weight, Leslie. When I feel it, it helps me remember." Serrano turned to her. "Sometimes . . . I have trouble picturing his face. It takes a minute to remember. Isn't that terrible?"

"No. Memory is fickle. What you feel in here," Tally said, tapping her chest, "that, you'll never forget."

Serrano smiled. "When we first got paired together, did you ever think you'd have to be my part-time shrink?"

"Hell, I keep doing this, you'd better *pay* me like a shrink. Let's head back to Ashby. We're close on this. I can feel it."

Tally pulled out of the J&J parking lot and merged back onto I-84. They hadn't gotten far before Serrano's cell phone rang again.

"Serrano."

"Detective, it's Connelly at watch command."

"Hey, Pat, what's up?"

"Anonymous tip just came in. Said Nestor Aguillar and Stefanie Steinman have been casing the hotel where Rachel Marin is staying. And that they may try to make a move on Marin's family."

"Christ. How did they find out where we put her?"

"I don't know, Detective, but somebody was thankfully keeping an eye on these two. Tipster said they left the hotel and were heading south."

"Where are Aguillar and Steinman now?" Serrano listened. His eyes widened. A look of fear spread over his face.

"Where are they?" Tally said. "John?"

He turned to his partner. "Aguillar and Steinman are going to try to kill Megan Marin. *Floor it.*"

# CHAPTER 22

The silver 2014 Dodge Avenger idled at the corner outside of Bennington Elementary. Behind it was a blue Mercedes-Benz E-Class wagon. In front of it was a red Volvo V90. The block was littered with station wagons. Parents milled about outside waiting to take their children home. Nobody paid attention to a well-kept Dodge Avenger with two people sitting inside because, frankly, there was no reason to. At pickup time, cars came and went constantly. It was cold out, and everyone was far more concerned with grabbing their kid and getting home. Nobody gave them a second look.

Stefanie Steinman figured this was serendipitous.

"It's serendipitous," she said.

"Seren . . . what?"

"Fortunate," she clarified.

Nestor Aguillar nodded. Stefanie was wearing a black Eddie Bauer coat with a fur trim and a blue wool cap to hide her green hair. People would notice the hair. Nestor had on a gray Old Navy sweater fleece. He hadn't dressed warmly enough and had forgotten to bring mittens. Their clothes didn't matter; they'd burn them after it was done. They each had a pair of unopened leather Isotoner gloves. They would be used and then discarded immediately.

The Dodge Avenger would never be seen again. The plates had been taken off a Subaru at a rest stop off Grissom Parkway. And the car itself was registered to a Mr. Donald Kovacs. Mr. Kovacs would be mighty pissed when he came back from the restroom to find his parking spot empty.

Both the car and the plates would be burned in the abandoned quarry southwest of Peoria. And by this time tomorrow, Stefanie and Nestor would be on their way to Bermuda for three weeks of R and R at the Elbow Beach resort, courtesy of Isabelle Drummond. Isabelle had promised them that fifty grand would be waiting for them in a Cayman Islands bank account by the following morning. Two more payments would then follow six months apart.

In fact, the only thing bothering Stefanie at the moment was not knowing if she'd packed enough reading material. She would need something to occupy her time at the pool while Nestor binged episodes of *Chopped* on his Surface Pro.

Nestor looked agitated. Nervous. He was biting his lower lip hard enough that, if he wasn't careful, he could draw blood. And if he wasn't careful and a drop fell while they were taking care of business, they might not even make it to Bermuda.

Stefanie reached over and put her hand on top of his. The trembling stopped. Nestor's skin was rough, palms calloused. She knew his time in prison had hardened his skin but softened his heart. He was a troubled boy. Had been ever since Stefanie first met him—at a party at Isabelle's house, of all places. This was back when Isabelle was still a Robles, while her parents were still alive. They were humorless assholes and never gave Chris a dime, but they sure could throw a party.

Nestor came with Chris. The boys sat by themselves, drinking rum and Cokes and smoking menthols. But when Stefanie locked eyes with Nestor . . . that was it.

She waited for him while he was in prison. She never dreamed of touching another man. And she made him swear on the Holy Bible—literally—that he would never lay a finger on another woman. He did so without hesitation. And she, perhaps jokingly, had given him permission to kill anyone in prison who tried to make him his bitch.

She remembered the look on his face. Half smiling because he knew it was a joke, half terrified because he knew that he might just be obligated to murder someone for her. And he would. She knew it. And she would for him. And they *both* would for Chris.

Which was why they were sitting in the Dodge Avenger in the first place, a Desert Eagle and a Ruger hidden inside a cargo duffel bag in the back seat, along with a canister of bleach, a bottle of lighter fluid, and several boxes of waterproof matches.

Stefanie looked at Nestor. He continued to chew his lip. His eyes flitted back and forth, watching the unsuspecting parents gab and laugh. Stefanie reached over and gently placed her hand on the back of his head. His black hair was short and buzzed all over. She loved the prickly feeling on her palms. Loved the way it felt when his head was between her legs. It electrified her. She'd made him swear never to grow it out.

She gently caressed his head, kneading the flesh below the stubble, and instantly felt him calm down. Nestor turned toward Stefanie and smiled, then leaned over and kissed her, deep and loving.

"For Chris," he said.

"For Chris," she replied.

They heard a bell ring, and the school doors opened. Soon enough they would see a horde of children come barreling out, rug rats in pastel backpacks covered with illustrations of unicorns and dogs and superheroes. Stefanie checked her phone again and found the picture of Rachel Marin that Isabelle had sent her. They didn't know what her daughter, Megan, looked like, so they had to wait for Rachel in order to make their move.

But no children came out. No parents ran up to hug their children, swaddled in mittens and hats, cheeks turning a ruddy red in the cold. Nestor and Stefanie waited. *Where are all the kids?*

She could feel beads of cold sweat trickling down her spine. Could they have missed Rachel Marin? Was there another entrance?

"There," Nestor said, tapping Stefanie on the shoulder and pointing at the school entrance. "Coming out."

And there she was, Rachel Marin, exiting the school carrying her daughter, the young girl's face buried in her shoulder, arms and legs dangling. She must have gone in to get Megan while they hadn't been looking. She was the only parent crossing the schoolyard. Easy prey.

Stefanie had stayed up all night wondering if she would really be able to go through with it. Kill not just the Marin woman but her daughter too.

And now, seeing them both, Stefanie felt no hesitation. Once the first shot shattered the air, everyone would scatter. They would have time to put another round or two in the Marin woman to be thorough. She'd never have a chance.

Then they would burn the car and be in Bermuda before the cops even knew what had happened. And who knew? Maybe they would stay abroad. Start a family. Change their names. Forget the past. The world was their oyster. With $150,000, they could do just about anything.

Stefanie and Nestor slipped on the leather gloves and brought the duffel bag into the front seat. Nestor unzipped it and took out the Desert Eagle. She removed the Ruger and slid it down by the footwell.

"Ready?" she said to Nestor.

"Ready."

As Rachel Marin crossed the yard holding her daughter, no more than twenty feet from the Dodge, Nestor and Stefanie exited the car. Nestor held the gun by his hip. Stefanie had the Ruger upright. She didn't care if anyone saw them. Screams would be good. Screams would get everyone out of there. Panicked witnesses gave terrible testimony.

They walked toward Rachel Marin. She was whispering something to the girl in her arms. The girl seemed light. Almost floppy. Stefanie figured a bitch like that probably underfed her own children to save money.

She and Nestor exchanged a glance. Time to dance.

But as Marin got closer, a feeling of dread started in the pit of Steinman's stomach. Something wasn't right. The girl's hair looked . . . off. Then it hit her: Marin wasn't carrying her daughter. In her arms was a child-size doll. Stefanie looked at the doll, with its large button eyes and stitched-on smile, and wondered what in the hell was going on.

But before she even had a chance to look up, Stefanie felt the prongs embed themselves in her chest, and suddenly fifty thousand volts were coursing through her like lightning. Stefanie screamed, dropped the Ruger, and fell to the ground.

Nestor looked down at her in shock, and before Stefanie could warn him, three men wearing APD windbreakers knocked Nestor sideways. The Desert Eagle flew into the air and clattered on the stone sidewalk. Stefanie had never felt so much pain in her life. She couldn't move. Couldn't speak. One of the men had his knee in Nestor's back, pinning him to the ground. Another held his legs, while the third handcuffed him behind his back. Stefanie saw a cut on Nestor's chin from where his face had hit the pavement. That would have been enough for her to kill someone.

*They hurt my baby,* she thought as she felt a knee drive into her back as well.

Stefanie managed to look up. She saw an Ashby PD officer holding a Taser. She also saw the Marin woman, her face oddly blank. Marin walked over to Steinman's Dodge. Stefanie watched, helpless, as Marin reached into the wheel well of the right front tire, felt around, and removed a small metal box.

*The bitch tracked us. She set us up.*

Marin pocketed the item, then turned to look at Stefanie. A look of satisfaction on her face.

And then Marin waved at Stefanie and mouthed the word *Bye.*

# CHAPTER 23

***Four Years Ago***

To "Rachel," the only thing better than a cup of hot, freshly brewed arabica on a cool September morning was the rhythm of a speed bag being beaten to a pulp. She stood perfectly balanced in front of the bag and pummeled it endlessly, shoulders burning, sweat pouring down her face and pooling on the rubber mat at her feet.

It had taken her a long time to get the hang of the speed bag. Sure, she'd seen *Rocky*. Who hadn't? The first time Myra set her up in front of the bag, she punched it as hard as she could and mistakenly led with her first row of knuckles like an amateur. The bag barely moved, and her hand ached for a week.

Myra taught her the correct positioning and striking form.

"The speed bag isn't about strength," Myra said. "Too many people try to beat the crap out of it like it's a driver who rear-ended you. The bag is all about endurance and hand-eye coordination."

Myra taught her to lead with the flat underside of her fist and to keep her hand slightly open. One of the biggest mistakes newbies made with the speed bag was using an open fist. Amateur hour.

"Keep your shoulders relaxed. Hit the bag *before* it reaches its center point. If you hit the bag while it's coming forward, you'll just drive it straight up into the platform. And always try to hit the bag in the same exact spot. If you hit it every which way, you'll never be able to control it. So find a stitch, or lettering, and aim for that spot every single time. Repetition. Muscle memory. Don't think. Just do."

Rachel soaked in every word, not just hearing Myra, but *listening.* She evolved. Got better. She learned the difference between bad pain, which hurt, and good pain, which disappeared in a haze of adrenaline and pride.

She was working the red speed bag like a demon when she heard the front door open.

"Tell me you went home last night, Blondie, you crazy bitch," Myra said. "Tell me you didn't sneak back in after I locked up and spent the night beating that bag like it was a shitty ex-husband."

Rachel laughed and stopped working the bag. She caught her breath and took a long pull from a water bottle.

"Hey, Myra," she said. "Just needed to get some work in."

"Apollo Creed is quaking in his star-spangled booties," Myra said. "Just remember, elbows up. Almost perpendicular with the floor."

"Got it. Thanks."

She was getting used to being called Rachel. It took some time at first. Myra had to call her by the new name several times before she responded. It felt silly. Like she was playacting. But Myra had been clear.

No real names. No sharing details about your life. *Everyone here needs to feel comfortable. These classes are a sanctuary, and the walls around us are real. We do not breach these walls. If you feel unsafe, let Myra know, and the offender will be gone.*

At the conclusion of a recent class, one of the students, a thirtysomething man calling himself Abe, had asked another student, "Tabitha," out for drinks. Tabitha had come back the next session. Abe had not. Rachel had quickly realized that not everybody understood just how serious Myra was about the group being a sanctuary.

Every day she would drive her son to school, drop her daughter at day care, and spend the rest of her hours toiling at the gym or ensconced in a book. Since meeting Myra she had transformed her body and her mind. And it wasn't about getting back to her prepregnancy weight. She didn't care about that. Her stomach would never look the same. But that didn't matter. The C-section scar was the only scar on her body, but she considered it a badge of honor.

Her fingertips and palms had all developed hard calluses, courtesy of throwing around free weights, but finding the right lifting gloves had cut down on those. Every night she put her young daughter to bed, forced her son to do his homework, and then soaked her hands in Epsom salts and shaved off the dead skin layers with a pumice stone. And once both were in bed, Rachel spent an hour doing plyometrics in the living room.

She could see her body changing before her eyes. She had tried to stay in shape through her two pregnancies, always back at a barre or spin class within six weeks of delivering. But this was different. She could see the definition forming in her shoulders, the ropy muscles on her back. She almost looked like a different woman.

Myra's training had given her a feeling of power she had never imagined. Unleashed something inside her that had been dormant. And just as important, it had given her a place to direct her anger. She *wanted* to pound the speed bag into oblivion. To put every ounce of her strength into every single punch during sparring sessions. But one thing Myra had taught her was that strength only mattered when controlled. Anger uncontrolled was useless. A bull let loose on a raft would drown.

"Think of anger like a bottle of seltzer that's been shaken up," Myra had said to the class early on. "You twist the cap, the liquid spurts everywhere, and you end up a soaking mess. Each of you is that liquid inside the bottle right now. *Dying* to get out. *Pushing* to get out. But you're only at your best when *controlled.* Open the cap slowly. Let some out—but not all. And then close it before it overwhelms you. Learn to control your anger, and you'll be capable of great things."

And Rachel could feel it. The anger welled up inside her almost constantly. She liked Myra's seltzer analogy, but there was just one problem.

Eventually, the carbonation in the seltzer would subside. Eventually, it would be safe to open and pour. But Rachel could spend hours at the gym working the bags, practicing self-defense and attack techniques, hauling kettlebells until she couldn't raise her arms above her head. She would go home, exhausted, barely able to lift a pan to cook dinner. And yet she would wake up the next morning with the anger still there. The bottle shaken up all over again.

What did you do when the anger never went away?

The truth was, when Rachel left class at night, she was at a loss. Everything felt unfamiliar. The world as she knew it had ceased to exist, and she didn't know how to live in the new one. Her children were her dock. When she was home, she fed them and clothed them and bathed them and nurtured them. When she was home with them, she had a purpose. But when she was away from them, she felt unmoored.

She presumed that was why she spent hours on end battering speed bags and heavy bags, lifting weights that, several years ago, would have seemed too heavy to even consider. It was why when, after her children went to bed, she read every book she could find to understand the world and how it worked. She was soaking up knowledge: physical and mental. At first, because she wanted to understand what had happened to her husband. To understand the system. But now, it was beyond that. She wanted to understand *everything.*

About *him.*

Harwood Greene.

The man who'd torn their life to pieces and walked away with his own intact.

She searched the books, threw the weights around, looking for an answer that even she knew she would probably never find.

Each training class with Myra was three hours long, broken up by a fifteen-minute water break. After the first session, Myra had bestowed upon Rachel the moniker of "shin-kicker." Rachel had smiled and then retched into a bucket. By the end of the third hour, she'd felt like her insides were liquefying. Now that fifteen-minute break was simply an annoyance. Breaks were for soft people. And she was granite.

Sometimes Myra would stay after class to work out on her own. One night, Rachel had gathered up the courage to ask Myra if she could stay late and work out alongside her. Myra obliged. They pounded the heavy bag until their arms were numb, did burpees until their legs wobbled. Rachel felt only a modicum of guilt arriving home half an hour late to relieve her sitter.

And as fulfilling as it was to toughen her body after two children and years of neglect, she also stayed because she wanted—*needed*—to know more about Myra. Why this woman spent three nights a week teaching a free self-defense class to a group of strangers. But Rachel had no idea how to broach the subject. Myra had made it clear the students' privacy was tantamount. And Rachel didn't want to risk crossing that line.

They worked out together but rarely spoke. Rachel would hold the heavy bag while Myra pounded away. Myra would hold Rachel's ankles as she did sit-up after sit-up, tightening up the muscles that had helped grow two glorious children.

At the end of that crisp fall day, Rachel and Myra both finished their workouts, cleaned up the equipment, and left the gym at the same time. There was a cool breeze in the air. It felt wonderful on Rachel's tired muscles. Myra walked fast, and Rachel had to make an effort to keep up.

The gym was not in a particularly good neighborhood, but class usually ended early enough that the sun was still out, and the trainees could feel safe going to their cars or waiting for a taxi. But since they'd stayed an extra hour after class, the sun had faded to burnt umber on the horizon. Darkness was descending like a soft blanket.

They walked in silence. Myra seemed fine with this arrangement. Rachel did not. She wasn't sure how to cross the silent divide, so she just barreled ahead.

"So . . . where do you go when class is over?" she said, immediately regretting it.

Myra turned to Rachel and laughed. "How long have you been waiting to ask me something about myself, Blondie?"

"A while. A long while."

"Yeah. I figured. I'm heading home. Got a son and a husband, and if I'm lucky, I'll catch some TV before I pass out."

They continued to walk, Rachel speechless. This was already more information than Rachel had ever gotten in the year she'd been training with Myra. A husband? Son? She watched television?

Rachel searched for a follow-up question but came up blank.

"What, you didn't think I had a life? I might be boring, but I'm not *that* boring."

"I don't think you're boring," Rachel said.

"Well, thank you, Blondie," Myra said.

"How old is your son?" Rachel asked. Had she gone too far?

"Fourteen," Myra said. "I know, I know. Had him young. Met my ex our freshman year of college. Was knocked up by my senior year. And that waste of carbon was gone two years after that. Thankfully he left me the best part of him. Other than his sperm, he wasn't worth a damn."

"Can I see a picture of your boy?" Rachel said. Every question felt like a massive intrusion, breaking the class omertà. But without hesitation, Myra took her cell phone from her gym bag and opened the Photos app. She held it up for Rachel to see.

In the photo, Myra had her arms wrapped around the neck of an adorable young boy. He had sandy-brown hair, blue eyes, and the happy, toothy grin of someone who'd just had his braces removed. Myra's eyes sparkled with joy.

"His name is Ben," Myra said. "And he's the love of my life. Even my husband knows that."

"He's beautiful," Rachel said. "I'm happy for you."

"Took my husband a little getting used to," she said. "We married when we were both thirty. Most dudes aren't looking to marry into a family at that age. They're happy to play the field, lay pipe for a while, or looking to start their own family fresh. Not easy dating as a single mom in your twenties. But when Javier met my Ben . . . I swear, he might love that kid more than I do by now. So, what about you, Blondie?"

Rachel was taken aback by the question. She'd been so curious about Myra's life that it hadn't occurred to her someone would want to know about hers.

"I . . . I'm not sure what there is to say."

"Really? That's it? Come on, shin-kicker. Kids?"

"Two kids," Rachel said. "Eight and three."

"Smart?"

"Sharp as a knife. My son, he's the older one, he memorizes things on the spot. Reads like there's no tomorrow. Loves fantasy books. If it has a dragon or wizard in it, he'll read it. And my daughter, story time could last for weeks. She just sits there, rapt. Even makes up her stories. I picture her writing books of her own one day."

Myra smiled. "That's lovely. Do you have . . . someone in your life? Someone whose shins you kick instead of mine?"

Rachel looked at the ground. Guilt and fear and shame and anger welled up inside of her. "I did," she said. "And he was taken from me."

"He was sick?"

"Not exactly."

"Left you?"

"No."

"Oh," Myra said. "Oh, I'm sorry, Rachel."

"I don't remember you ever calling me Rachel."

"Rachel, shin-kicker, Blondie. It's all protection. Armor. It's important that a lot of the students in class *wear* that armor so they *feel* protected. When you're wounded, like we all were, you need time to heal.

But once you're strong enough, you don't need it anymore. You haven't needed it for a long time, Rachel."

"My name's not Rachel. But you know that."

"And mine's not Myra. But you know that too."

They continued down the street in silence. Rachel wanted to ask the question so badly it was tearing a hole in her throat. But she'd already crossed a boundary, told Myra about her life. And as far as she knew, she was the only one in class Myra had confided in. It made Rachel feel special, important. Hearing Myra tell Rachel she was strong—the compliment gave her wings. It made her think that after all the horrors, everything that had come *so close* to breaking her and her children, she was finally mending. And perhaps even coming out stronger than ever.

"You can tell me," Myra said. "Your name. If you think you're ready."

"I'm not sure if I should."

"Suit yourself. I'm Evie."

Rachel looked at Myra—Evie—and felt her breath catch in her throat.

*Evie.*

Such a nice, pretty, simple name. The kind of name Rachel could have named her own daughter. The kind of name that might belong to a girl she could see her son bringing home before prom.

*Evie.*

"Well?" Evie said. "You are?"

Then, just as she was going to speak the word, without any warning, a man came up from behind Evie, looped his right arm around her throat, and held a penknife against her neck.

Rachel recoiled in horror. Evie froze and gritted her teeth but remained calm. He dug the tip of the knife into the soft flesh of Evie's neck. Rachel looked around for help, but the streets were empty. There were no lampposts on this stretch of town. The night covered the crime.

The man had a goatee that looked like a messy black O and a jagged scar running down his right cheek that looked like a poorly stitched-up knife wound. He smelled like shoe polish, and his deep-blue windbreaker was two sizes too big. A bracelet made from brownish-yellow Tiger Eye beads looped around the wrist of the hand that held the knife. The beads clinked together gently. Rachel could not take her eyes off them. They looked oddly pretty, soothing and spiritual in a way their owner was not.

"See my pocket?" the man said. He nodded to the open pocket on the left side of his windbreaker. He looked at Rachel. "Money, jewelry, and cell phones. You, put them in there."

Rachel nodded and unzipped her gym bag. Her hand shook as she removed her wallet. She cursed her luck; she'd just gone to the ATM before class, and a wad of twenties jutted out. The man's eyes widened when he saw it. His lucky day.

"Please, sir," Evie said. She began to sob. She raised her hands as if in surrender. "I have a family. I don't have any money. Please, let me go."

Rachel was shocked; she'd never heard Evie so much as whimper or complain, let alone cry. It was like she'd morphed into a completely different person.

"Shut up," he said. "You, Blondie, get her money and put it in my pocket. Waste my time, and I'll give this cunt a new mouth below her old one."

"Please, Mister," Evie bawled. Her hands continued to rise. "I have a sick daughter. She has epilepsy. My husband has a bad heart. Please."

There was less than a second between Rachel thinking *That isn't true* and Evie grabbing the man's knife hand and pulling it against her chest, holding it in place. The whole time she'd been babbling, she'd been slowly raising her hands until she could get into the right position.

The man bucked and struggled, trying to free his knife hand, but Rachel could tell that Evie was stronger, angrier, and more in control.

Finally, when the man gave her an inch of room, Evie slid her head underneath his armpit and, still holding the wrist of his knife hand, wrenched herself free and pulled his arm behind his body. The Tiger Eye beads rattled against each other. Then, without hesitation, Evie wrenched his arm in a counterclockwise direction until Rachel heard a gruesome snap.

The man howled and dropped the knife. Then Evie kneed him in the groin, and he fell to the ground, sobbing, clutching his broken arm.

Evie picked up the knife and kicked the man onto his back. His head smacked off the pavement. Tears streamed down his face. Rachel watched, frozen, unsure of what to do. And suddenly terrified of Evie.

Evie straddled the man, pinning his shoulders to the ground with her knees. She placed the blade against the man's throat.

"This is what it feels like," she said, her voice calm. Even. "How do you like it?"

"Please," the man sobbed. "Please, just let me go."

"Not a chance," Evie said. There was a spark of insanity and determination in her eyes that frightened Rachel.

"Evie . . . ," Rachel said. "What are you doing?"

"Making sure he never does this again."

"We can call the police," Rachel said, plaintively.

"If you think we're the first ones he's done this to, you're insane," Evie said. "And if you think we'll be the last, you're naive."

Evie moved the knife to the man's groin. Point facing downward. His eyes widened. Tears and mucus poured down his face. Rachel looked at his maimed arm. The sound of the Tiger Eye beads rattling on his wrist echoed in her ears.

"There has to be another way," Rachel said.

"One day you'll be faced with a choice like this," Evie said. "And you'll sleep well at night knowing you prevented something terrible from happening to someone who *couldn't* defend themselves."

"Please," the man said. "I'm sorry. I'm sorry. I need a doctor. I need help."

"You'll need two different types of doctors now," Evie said. She switched her grip on the knife and raised the blade until it was hovering a foot from the man's crotch.

"Evie," Rachel said. "Please stop."

Evie looked at Rachel, confused. "Stop what? This man would have slit my throat without hesitating. Wouldn't you, you sick freak?"

The man shook his head and whimpered, "*Nuh—no.* I just wanted money. I got nothing. I was hungry."

"Spare me the sob story. Something tells me you'll think twice next time you see a woman walking down the street."

Evie raised the knife again, but as she went to plunge it into the man's skin, Rachel tackled her, sending her flying to the ground. The knife skittered away. The man saw his chance, got up, and ran off like a wounded dog.

Evie sat up and watched him flee. Then she looked at Rachel.

"You dumb bitch," she said.

"I couldn't let you do it," Rachel said, panting. Her shoulder hurt where she'd driven it into Evie. The woman was *solid* muscle.

"Couldn't let me? You know what that bastard is going to do, right? You think this is going to stop him? No. He's going to lick his wounds and get back in the hunt. And next time, he might go after someone who can't take care of herself." Evie jabbed Rachel in the chest with her finger. "And *that's* on you."

"So killing him is the answer."

"Can't say whether I would have killed him. Depends how fast EMTs got here. But it sure as shit would have put a hitch in his future pursuits."

"He would have gone to the cops. You'd be in prison."

Evie laughed. "The cops? You think he would have gone to the *cops*? And said what? 'Hey, Officers, I tried to cut this girl's throat, but she stabbed me in my tiny dick; can you please arrest her?' Besides, guy like that probably has a rap sheet a mile long. He wants to spend time in a police station like I want to spend time in a piranha tank."

"That doesn't give you the right to maim him."

"And nobody ever gave him the right to hold a knife to my neck. Here's your last lesson, Blondie. Nobody *gives* you the right to protect yourself. People take things from you. Nobody gives them permission to do it. They just *take.* But if I take that man's pride and joy, he'll never hold another knife to a woman's throat again. But instead, he's out there. And who knows who's next. You protect one, or you protect none."

The words hit Rachel like a punch to the stomach, her memories flooding back.

*You protect one, or you protect none.*

She thought of her husband. She could hear her son's screams, could feel how helpless she had been that night and so many nights following. And how so many people who had promised to protect her family had merely let her down.

Evie stood up. She kicked the knife into the gutter.

"Don't come to class tomorrow. I don't want to see you back at that gym. There are things you need to learn that I can't teach you."

Evie walked away, leaving Rachel panting on the sidewalk. One thought ran through her mind as she watched Evie round the corner and disappear.

*I never told her my name.*

# CHAPTER 24

***Today***

"I'm a little tired of hanging out around here," Rachel said. "Don't get me wrong. The food choices are impeccable. And I love the smell of bad coffee, cheap cologne, and stale cigarette smoke. But I think after this I'd be OK not setting foot in the Ashby police station for the rest of my life."

Rachel sat across the table from Detectives John Serrano and Leslie Tally at the same table as the night she'd shot Christopher Robles. Lieutenant George himself had offered to watch the children in his office.

"And as much as we love your company," Tally said, "I think you've been involved in enough police business over the last week to last you a lifetime."

Rachel laughed. A fake laugh. "Oh, Detectives," she said. "If you only knew."

"So let's go over this one last time," Serrano said. "You say you did *not* make an anonymous phone call to the PD switchboard about Nestor Aguillar and Stefanie Steinman."

"No, I did not," Rachel said. Serrano nodded. He knew she was probably lying, but whoever had made the call had run the number through half a dozen masking sites, so the call appeared to have come in from Vladivostok, Russia.

"All right. Fine. And just so it's on the record: after receiving that tip, Detective Tally and I contacted you to warn you about the potential criminal intentions of Steinman and Aguillar. We removed your daughter, Megan, from class prior to the end of the school day. Officers Lowe and Chen watched Megan at the station. When we confirmed the presence of Steinman and Aguillar, we had you exit Bennington Elementary School carrying the lifelike CPR doll, which doubled for your daughter."

"Correct."

Tally continued. "Body cams confirm all of this and that both suspects were armed with loaded weaponry. Aguillar and Steinman are currently being held and charged under Illinois state law, section 65, graph 2, which states that the law prohibits carrying a firearm into a building, onto property, or in a parking area under the control of a preschool or childcare facility, including any room or portion of a building under the control of a preschool or childcare facility.

"Wally Shaw, our computer forensics examiner, is just starting to go through Aguillar and Steinman's emails, texts, phone records, and social media posts. My guess is that by the time he's done, we'll have them on quite a few more charges, including premeditated attempted murder. The only light of day they'll see in the immediate future is the prison yard."

"Do you think that's it?" Rachel said. "I know they were friends of Isabelle and Christopher Robles. I imagine they might have more friends."

"We're going to have twenty-four seven surveillance on both you and your children for a good while," Serrano said. "Detective Tally and I are overseeing it personally. And without going into too much detail, we're also going to be paying very close attention to Isabelle Robles and everyone she speaks to over the next few weeks. With Aguillar and Steinman locked up and the police on high alert, she'd have to be pretty stupid to try something."

"With all due respect to the deceased," Rachel said, "Christopher Robles didn't seem like he swam in the deepest end of the smarts ocean."

Tally replied, "And we have some dedicated officers going through all of Robles's associates. We'll have eyes on every one of them."

Rachel nodded. More out of acceptance than satisfaction. She could only do so much.

"Can I ask you something?" Serrano said.

"Sure."

"All this," he said, "didn't have to happen."

"What do you mean?" Rachel asked.

"You first contacted us with the information about Constance Wright's death. It was very clear that you wanted to be found but wanted us to jump through some hoops to find you. You have a gift for misdirection. Now, to be frank, without that information, I don't know where the investigation might have led. You helped us."

"Is that a thank-you?" Rachel said.

"I'm not finished," Serrano said firmly. "But after that. Going to the press conference. Following Robles home, conniving your way into their living room. All of that led to Robles breaking into your house. Where your children sleep. And that led to this, two people showing up at your daughter's school armed to the teeth."

"I'm not sure what the question is, Detective," Rachel said.

"I'd like you to come with me somewhere. I have something I want to show you."

Rachel narrowed her eyes. "What about my kids . . ."

"They can come too. It's nothing dangerous, I promise. Actually, I think they'll have fun. But there's something you need to see. Trust me."

"All right . . . ," Rachel said.

Serrano led her to the lieutenant's office and knocked on the door.

"Come in."

He opened the door. Rachel breathed in and smiled. Megan was sitting on the floor licking her fingers, which were covered in dust from a shredded bag of Funyuns. Eric was in a plush chair playing on an iPad, beeps and boops coming from whatever game he was engrossed in.

"I hope you don't mind the Funyuns," Lieutenant George said. "I wasn't sure if the little one had any dietary restrictions."

"She's unfortunately not restricted from junk food," Rachel said. "Thank you, Lieutenant."

"Please, don't mention it. Your daughter is quite the conversationalist. Your son, well, let's just say I've had better conversations with my shoe."

"Eric, did you hear that?" Rachel said. Eric did not look up. She sighed. "OK, kids, playtime's over. Let's go."

They got up and marched out of the office. The lieutenant tousled Megan's hair as she walked past, and she giggled.

"Be good, young man," he said to Eric. Eric nodded and slunk past.

Rachel extended her hand.

"Lieutenant, I . . ."

Lieutenant George shook her hand and waved her off. "Please. Don't mention it. They can tell their friends they were in protective custody. They'll be the coolest kids in their class for a day or two."

"Thank you," Rachel said. Lieutenant George smiled, and Serrano closed the office door behind them.

The kids put on their coats, and they followed Serrano out to the parking lot.

"Where are we going?" Eric asked.

"I'm not sure," Rachel said.

"I'm scared," Megan said. "I want to go back to the loonant's office."

"Lieutenant," Rachel corrected.

"Whatever," Megan replied. "It was warm in there."

"I promise you that in a few minutes, you won't even think about the cold," Serrano said, turning around. He knelt down to speak to Megan at eye level. "As a matter of fact, I'm taking you to the place where you can make the absolute *best* snow angels in Ashby."

Megan's face lit up.

"Mommy, can we?" she said, her face glowing with excitement. Rachel laughed.

"I guess so, sweetie."

"I bet mine are better than Eric's," she said.

"Snow angels are stupid," Eric said glumly.

"*You're* stupid."

"Let's settle this: best snow angel gets to be an Ashby PD deputy for a day," Serrano said.

That got Eric excited.

Serrano unlocked the Crown Vic, and the kids slid into the back seat. He motioned for Rachel to get in the passenger side.

"Can you tell me where we're going?" she said.

"To see the angels," Serrano replied. "Just trust me."

Rachel hesitated, then got into the front seat. Serrano turned on the car, and a voice piped in over the stereo.

*Home is behind, the world ahead,*

*and there are many paths to tread*

"That's from *The Fellowship of the Ring*," Eric said, proud at recognizing the lines.

"That it is," Serrano replied. "I think you and I have a lot in common."

Serrano drove off. Rachel stared at the side-view mirror, watching the police station disappear into the white night, wondering where Serrano was taking them. But for some reason, she trusted him.

Rachel thought about the last time she'd trusted a cop, and it terrified her.

# CHAPTER 25

Serrano pulled into the empty parking lot and turned off the ignition. He sat there, unspeaking, unmoving, for a full minute while Rachel and the children waited for an explanation.

"Look at this," Serrano said finally, his voice full of awe and reverence. "Isn't it just about the most beautiful thing you've ever seen?"

"A baseball field?" Rachel said, confused. "You took us to a baseball field? In December? Have you been drinking?"

Serrano laughed. "This isn't *just* a baseball field. This is *Voss* Field, where the Ashby Angels play every spring. This field is where local legends are made. Did you know that six players from Ashby High have gone on to play in the major leagues?"

"No way," Eric said.

"Yes way," Serrano said. "Two of them actually had pretty good careers. Bobby Callahan made an All-Star team twice, and Ricardo Dominguez hit a walk-off homer for the Astros in the 2004 ALCS."

"Whoa," Eric said. "What about the other four?"

"Eh, let's just say it's a good thing they had backup plans. Let's go."

"Do we really get to go on the field?" Eric said. Serrano nodded.

"Let's just say I know people."

Serrano got out of the car, and the Marin family followed.

Voss Field was covered in a layer of glistening snow. Tall spotlights ringed the small stadium, dark in the winter, but they could still see snowflakes falling around the tall structures, reflected in the glass. The grass was long and unkempt, poking through the powder in spots, and the dugouts were covered with tarps to shield the wood from moisture.

"This is where I played in high school," Serrano said to Eric. "Left field. I wanted to play shortstop or third but always had problems making that long throw off a hot grounder in the hole."

"I played first base for a little while in peewee," Eric said, his voice downbeat. There was sadness underneath. Serrano picked up on it.

"What happened?" Serrano asked. Eric remained silent. Rachel cast her son a look that Serrano noticed as well.

"Just stopped playing," he said.

"Mom Mom Mom Mom Mom," Megan said, rapid fire. "Can I go make snow angels?"

She pointed toward the infield, covered in mounds of undisturbed white. Rachel smiled.

"Go ahead, hon," she said, "but make sure you're wearing your hat and gloves. Eric, go with her. And *no* eating the snow. You don't know what kind of presents animals might have left in it."

"I'm too old to make snow angels," Eric said as Megan made a dash for the field.

"Well, that's just about the saddest and most untrue thing I've ever heard," Serrano said. "In fact, snow angels get *more* fun the older you get. 'Cause at some point you get so busy with life that you forget how much fun it is. One day you'll wake up an adult and wish you'd spent more time being a kid. Go ahead. Let's see what you got."

Eric smiled and gave a *Sure, why not?* look and trundled off after Megan.

"I haven't seen him smile like that in a long, long time," she said softly.

The children bounded toward the infield. Megan collapsed next to the pitcher's mound and flung powder into the air. She hopped to her feet, packed a heap of fresh snow into a round mass, and threw it at her brother. It sailed wide of Eric, who made a larger snowball and drilled his sister in the leg.

As they laughed, Serrano led Rachel to the empty bleachers lining the infield. Serrano wiped the frost off two seats along the first base line, and they sat down. They watched in silence as Eric and Megan played in the snow. Rachel had a look of pure bliss on her face as her children frolicked.

"They're great kids," he said.

Rachel nodded, wistful. "They are. I'm very lucky."

"So are they," he said.

"Sometimes I wonder. If they might have had it easier some other way. They've been through so much. Seeing them like this . . . it kills me that they don't get to just be kids more often. Sometimes it feels like my son was forced to stop being a kid too soon."

"In what way?"

Rachel shook her head. She'd come close to telling him something, Serrano could feel it. But she'd pulled back.

"Why did you bring us here?" she asked. Snowflakes were melting on her eyelashes, the water droplets glistening. Her eyes were a gorgeous green, and Serrano felt his heart pick up the pace.

Serrano said, "I came here that night after we questioned Nicholas Drummond. What you said to me, it made me want to come here. For the first time in a long time."

"I don't understand," Rachel said. "I apologized. But I'm not really sure what for, now."

Serrano breathed in. He pointed at the pitcher's mound, just a few feet from where Eric and Megan were playing in the snow.

"My son, Evan, died on this field," he said. "Right there."

He heard Rachel take a sharp breath.

"Oh my . . . God. I'm so sorry. I . . . I didn't know."

"On the pitcher's mound. Evan was a lefty. A southpaw fireballer. He was throwing heat in the eighties at fourteen years old. He was a prodigy. You know how rare good southpaws are at that age?"

Rachel shook her head. Her breath misted in front of her, tears welling in her eyes.

"But he wasn't just an athlete," Serrano continued. "He was *smart*. Smarter than I ever was. Read every book he could get his hands on. His favorites were big, epic fantasy novels. Books about wizards and warriors and dragons and magic. Books I never would have touched when I was his age. He'd sit in his room for hours at a time, just churning through those pages like he was running out of time, like he was worried he wouldn't get to finish all the books he wanted to in his life. As it would happen, he didn't."

Serrano grew silent, watching Eric and Megan playing beneath the dark moonlit sky.

"I tried to go to every game he pitched. Couldn't make them all with the job, but my wife, Deirdre, went whenever I couldn't. Evan always had a parent there to cheer him on. It was important to us, for him to know we supported him. Deirdre once brought a big orange sign to a game that read EVAN SERRANO BRINGS THE HEAT! Evan was mortified, but I think deep down he kinda liked it. You know how kids are at that age."

Rachel nodded. "I do," she said softly.

"You always hear about kids getting hurt in other sports. Concussions and head injuries in football and soccer. Sure, there are all these studies about aluminum bats, how fast the ball ricochets off the barrel, but you think about it in terms of hot grounders to third. Long fly balls. Not . . ."

Serrano trailed off. Rachel put her hand on his, gently.

"He had a no-hitter going through five innings. He was *untouchable*. Then this twig of a kid steps to the plate. Billy Wootens. In the nine spot. Couldn't have been a hair over four feet tall, couldn't have weighed over seventy pounds. Kid looked like a red-haired noodle. The bat was thicker than he was. The kind of kid who closes his eyes and just prays to make contact. So Billy Wootens . . . he swings and misses at

Evan's first two pitches, and I swear, you could have driven a truck into the space between the bat and the ball. But the third pitch . . . somehow Billy Wootens got the meat of the bat dead center on the ball. Luckiest swing ever. As soon as you heard the ping of the aluminum bat, you knew he'd gotten all of it."

Serrano turned his hand over, squeezed Rachel's, his voice full of memory and pain.

"There were two sounds," Serrano said. "The first was the ping as the bat hit the ball. Now, that's all you're supposed to hear. Just one sound. But a microsecond after that, there was another sound. A *thunk*. Hard and loud and solid. It happened so fast it didn't even register, at first. But I knew something was wrong when Billy Wootens stopped running toward first base and just collapsed to his knees and put his hands to his mouth. Then everyone else on the infield, catcher, first baseman, second baseman, shortstop, third baseman, all started running toward the pitcher's mound. Like the fingers of a hand closing. And then the coaches ran out. And all I can see among all those people are a pair of legs, flat on the ground. Unmoving. And then it hits me. *Those are Evan's legs.*

"I don't remember getting off the bleachers. I don't know if I pushed anyone out of the way, but all of a sudden I'm on the field. And I'm trying to get into the scrum at the pitcher's mound. And Evan is splayed out. Flat. Arms and legs extended. Like he's making a snow angel."

Rachel felt tears slip from her eyes. Serrano bit his lip, took a breath, continued.

"The doctors said he never felt a thing," Serrano said. "He was in a coma for three weeks and . . . just never woke up. You know, when you become a parent, there are a million books that teach you how to do everything for your kid. How to feed them. How to wash them and change them. How to raise them. How to keep them safe when they're too small to fend for themselves. But there's nothing that teaches you what to do when you lose them."

"I'm so sorry, John," Rachel said. "I don't know what to say."

"Deirdre and I, we didn't last after that. We used to say we had an unbreakable bond. Well, that broke it. I heard she remarried. Every now and then we have to deal with old tax issues. But the life we had . . . it's almost like it was another life."

He continued. "You know, I used to tease my son about the books he read. Fantasy. Magic and nonsense. As a cop, you deal in reality. Hard truths. I didn't think there were any truths in those books. I'd tease him. A little too much, sometimes. But when Evan died, and it came time to clean out his room, I kept his bookshelf the way he did. All the well-worn paperbacks. Books he'd loved and worlds he wanted to visit over and over again. And I decided that it was time to understand more about who my son was. Why these books spoke to him. So I started to read them. I used to come home, back when we were still a family, pop open a beer, turn on the TV, and fart away the night. But when Evan was gone, I'd stay up until 4:00 a.m. reading about all those things that I used to tease him about. And finally, I started to understand. Sometimes there are truths in fiction. In fantasy. Sometimes made-up stories tell us more about who we are than reality. That was how I kept Evan alive, in my mind. When I read those books, I could *hear* him telling me, *See, Dad, I told you.*"

"Evan sounds like he was a special kid," Rachel said. Serrano nodded.

"About six months after Evan died, I applied to take the sergeant's exam," Serrano said. "I'd been studying for a year. My life was falling apart, I was drinking too much, but I felt like this promotion would help me get back on track, in some way. I passed the exam, but Lieutenant George told me they were still holding me back. The decision was made by Constance Wright herself, if you can believe it. She met with Lieutenant George and after reviewing my file said she didn't think I was in the right frame of mind to take on more responsibility. She was probably right. But I didn't know it at the time. And so it pushed me even further down into the dark. I spent a long time hating Constance Wright, thinking she pushed me into that hole. When you're messed up, you blame everyone but yourself."

They both looked down. Their fingers were intertwined. Kind of a silly sight, given that they were both wearing heavy gloves. Serrano removed his fingers from hers. He pointed out to the field, where Megan was dumping armfuls of snow onto a prone and giggling Eric.

"Those kids out there, they're special. I don't quite know who you are, Rachel, or who you were before you came to Ashby. I don't know who the father of those children is or why you seem like you're ready to do battle every day of your life. But Eric and Megan aren't part of your fight. I never got a say in what happened to my son. You have a say in what happens to Megan and Eric. You've put yourself in situations where they've been in harm's way. And thank God they didn't get hurt. But if you do battle every day, there's bound to be collateral damage. Don't let it be those beautiful kids."

Rachel looked down. She opened her palm. Snowflakes began to collect on her fingers.

"I made a promise once," Rachel said. "I'm just trying to keep it."

"A promise to who?" Serrano asked.

Rachel closed her fist. And when she opened it, the snowflakes were small droplets that slipped through her fingers.

"Someone I loved," Rachel said. She looked at Serrano. "My children and I have been through more than you could ever possibly imagine."

"Then protect them," Serrano said. "Keep them away from evil."

"The person who killed Constance Wright is still out there, Detective," Rachel said. "Tossed her off a bridge like she was a piece of garbage. *That's* evil, Detective. I want to find them. Prevent anyone else from being hurt."

"Why is that on you?"

Rachel looked down again. Snow was gathering on her shoes. "I've seen what happens when evil goes free."

"I never had a chance to help build a future for Evan," Serrano said. "Your kids are your purpose, like Evan was mine. I'll do whatever I can to help protect Eric and Megan. But it starts with you. Do you really think they'd understand everything you've done?"

"Strangely enough," she said, "I think they would."

"Tell me what happened," he said. "Before you came here."

"I can't," she whispered.

"You know," Serrano said. "I wish you'd met Evan. He would have liked you. And I have a feeling he and Eric would have been good friends."

"I think they would have too."

They watched Eric and Megan playing in the snow, their laughter echoing throughout the empty stadium. Rachel put her head onto Serrano's shoulder. He flinched, briefly, but settled down. Let her head stay there, on him. They sat in silence, listening to the joyful shouts from Rachel's children, both hoping the night would take longer than usual to end.

Serrano turned his head to face Rachel. Her hair blew gently in the cold. She smiled. His heart was beating madly, so loud he was sure she could hear it.

He turned back to the field, watched Rachel's children playing blissfully in the night, all the while unaware of the man watching them from a distance.

# CHAPTER 26

***Three and a Half Years Ago***

The apartment was in shambles. Her daughter's toys were strewed across the hardwood floor, which was chipped to the point where Rachel doubted she would get her security deposit back. The kitchen looked like someone had opened up a *Chopped* mystery basket, thrown it into a blender, and then thrown the contents of that blender into an industrial fan.

Her son had left for school. And like every morning, she had gathered him into her arms and held him close, praying he would return home safe. She noticed that her boy didn't hug her quite as tight as he used to. Something had been taken out of him. A spark. A boyishness. He had been forced to grow up far faster than a nine-year-old should, forced to endure the cruelty life could inflict long before he was ready to deal with it. Her daughter was still too young to fully understand. At some point, she would, but for the time being, Rachel enjoyed the moments where she played and fussed and ate and sang and yelled and bopped around like any toddler.

But occasionally she would say, "Where's Dada?" and it would break Rachel's heart to once again tell her that Dada was watching them from the sky and that he still loved her with all his heart.

Her son knew enough not to ask. And that hurt even more.

Once the kids were off, Rachel brewed a pot of coffee and turned on the news.

She plunked down on the sofa, hard backed and uncomfortable, and sipped her coffee.

Rachel stretched her legs. She was still sore from yesterday's workout. Though she hadn't set foot in Slugfest Boxing since the night she and Myra—Evie—had been accosted, she had doubled her efforts, spending nearly the entire day at the gym, in spin classes and following online training videos. She soaked everything up. When she saw herself in the mirror, her body was nearly unrecognizable. Taut and muscled, lean and vascular.

Her daughter loved to swing from her biceps, yelling, "Mommy, you're like a tree!" But despite how strong she'd become on the surface, her insides still felt like oatmeal stirred in too much water.

As she took another sip, the landline rang. She muted the television, picked it up, and said, "This is Rachel."

"I'm sorry, did I dial the wrong number? This is Jim Franklin from Franklin and Rosato."

She mentally slapped herself. She'd been spending so much time thinking about Myra—Evie—and that adopted name that she'd begun to refer to herself as Rachel.

"Sorry, Jim, I was watching a *Friends* rerun, and Rachel was in this scene with Chandler, and, you know what? Never mind."

"No problem; it happens. My father once called me Frasier for a whole year."

"How are things in Darien?" she said.

"The town is trying to move on. Folks ask about you. Where you are. Reverend Elias still prays for you and the kids."

"He told you that?"

"He did."

"Please thank him for me," Rachel said.

"I don't think that's a good idea. If I do that, it could be used against me in a court of law to confirm that I know where you're currently residing. And I don't want anything to even have the remotest chance of getting back to *him.*"

"God forbid," Rachel said.

"Anyway, on a better note, it looks like the money is going to come through."

Rachel sat up, nearly spilling the coffee all over herself. "You're serious."

"I am. They know if the civil suit goes to trial, they could end up paying multiples of what we proposed in the settlement, not to mention the public relations catastrophe and media coverage of a trial. The lawsuit has been snaking its way through Connecticut Superior Court, but I just got a call from Ariel Nesbit at the Darien Law Department saying they wanted to talk."

Rachel sat back, closed her eyes. "Tell me you're not kidding."

"You know I wouldn't do that to you. Not after what you and those kids have been through."

Rachel felt tears spring to her eyes. "How much, then?"

"Six."

Rachel's jaw dropped. Her fingers felt tingly. "Did you say . . . *six*?"

"Six point two, to be precise."

"Oh my God. Oh my God."

"Now, if it goes to trial, there's a chance the jury sympathizes with you, sees those kids, knows the full extent of what the police did—and didn't do—and awards you more than we're asking. But that's not a given. And the amount of time and, frankly, money it would cost you to go through with that isn't worth it, in my opinion. This gives you a chance to move on with your life. Start fresh. Find a new home, get out of that furnished rental you're in right now. Get your life back."

"Money won't give us our life back," she said.

"You're right. I'm sorry. It was a poor choice of words. But this will give you a chance to move forward without worrying about groceries, clothes. You won't have to worry about any of that for a long, long time."

"Is this before or after taxes?"

"After."

Rachel paused, let it sink in. "It'll pay for their college."

"And then some."

Rachel felt tears welling up. "Now I just have to worry about raising them."

"I think you'll do splendidly," Franklin said. "If I can make a suggestion, with the money you have coming, I would recommend starting up a 529 account for both children. I can send over the paperwork as soon as the money clears."

"Thank you, Jim. I'm sorry for snapping. As you can imagine, I'm still not dealing with all of this very well. Strange to think about money, given everything."

"Who *would* deal with this kind of situation well?" Franklin said. "I can't speak about the emotional side, but I know you'll take care of those kids. And the money will allow you to go back to work on your own terms."

"I will, eventually. Something without a lot of responsibility where I don't have to take my work home with me at the end of the day."

"I think that's a good idea. Just make sure that when you do go back, you get health insurance. Six point two seems like a lot, but if something happens, there's nothing more expensive than a lengthy illness."

"I'll make sure of that," Rachel said. "Also, I've been thinking. I think it's time to leave the East Coast. Start all over somewhere else."

"I can help with that," Franklin said. "I know some Realtors."

"Fine. But it would have to be someone we can trust. I don't want a trail *he* can follow."

"I may know someone here in Darien," Jim said. "Whenever you're ready, we can talk about getting you settled elsewhere. Do you have a place in mind?"

"Maybe somewhere in the Midwest. Someplace quiet. I'll think about it."

"I'll await word."

"Thank you, Jim. I'll be in touch. And send over the paperwork for the kids' accounts. They need to be taken care of first."

"You got it. Be well, Olivia."

"Jim?" she said.

"Yes, Olivia?"

"Just one more question. Do they . . . know where he is?"

She heard a long, drawn-out breath on the other end.

"The official word is that the police and FBI are currently unaware of the location of Harwood Greene. And given the circumstances surrounding his arrest and trial, they are not looking for him and *will* not look for him unless he becomes a person of interest in any further criminal activity."

"And the unofficial word?"

"They don't want to go near this guy. Having to let him go was an embarrassment not just for the department but for the FBI and mayor's office too. It's not just you: half a dozen other widows want answers. And they probably won't get them. A contact of mine in the district attorney's office tells me they have it on good authority that Harwood Greene left the country following the trial and is currently laying low somewhere in eastern Europe."

"Do you think that's where he really is?"

"I couldn't say. I pray to God he's a million miles away or, better yet, rotting in a ditch somewhere being eaten by maggots. But the truth is I don't know. But I also don't think he'd come within a thousand yards of you or any of the other women. He's one of the most recognizable men in the country, and there are probably a fair number of people who'd want to off him. If he's smart, he's working on a farm somewhere in Moldova."

"God help the Moldovan women, then. Thank you, Jim. Take care."

"I'll be in touch, Olivia. We'll talk soon and put together a plan for the money."

She hung up the phone.

*Olivia.* For some reason, the name didn't seem to fit anymore.

Her head was swimming. She hated allowing that monster Harwood Greene to occupy a molecule of space in her head any longer. But Eric still woke up at night screaming. If her child was in pain, she was in agony. She prayed Franklin was right, that Greene was decomposing somewhere. That would be better than all the money in the world.

But that kind of money—millions—it could change their lives. Following Brad's death and his meager life insurance payout, she had become their children's sole provider. Being a widow to two young kids hadn't been a cakewalk to begin with. And to have to do it while also coming to terms with her husband being torn away like a page from a magazine? But now that hill was not insurmountable. Money could not bring her husband back. But it could alleviate a great deal.

Maybe moving would give them a chance to start anew. Get the kids into a school where they wouldn't be subjected to daily taunts of *Hey, are worms eating your dad's face?* or *At Halloween does your dad's ghost haunt your house?*

The cruelty of children could be shocking.

A fresh start. That's what they needed. And now they would have the money to do it. Once the payment cleared, she would take Jim Franklin up on his offer. Find somewhere else to live. Buy a house. Begin a new life.

*Rachel.*

She'd gotten used to the name.

She turned the volume on the news back on and finished her coffee. An electrical fire had claimed two lives in a brownstone downtown. Police were searching for a man who'd mugged an elderly woman in the vestibule of her apartment building. A group of schoolchildren put on a talent show at an old folks' home, cheering up the residents. And if she stayed tuned, she would learn how not flossing regularly *just might kill you*.

She poured another cup of coffee, then heard the anchor say, "In a stunning development, the Torrington PD was forced to relinquish custody of Stanford Royce, the man suspected of several rapes and numerous armed robberies throughout the city."

When she turned around and saw the photo of Stanford Royce on the television screen, Rachel dropped her coffee mug. It shattered on the white linoleum floor, scalding brown liquid spattering everywhere.

She knew that man. She recognized the oily goatee, the scar that cut across his right cheek like a cut from a drunken surgeon. Royce was the man who had pulled a knife on Rachel and Evie as they were leaving Slugfest Boxing—the last time she'd seen Evie. That name. *Evie.*

The news feed cut to video of Royce leaving the TPD precinct. Royce still wore the same Tiger Eye bead bracelet he'd had on that night. His arm was in a sling, still recovering from the injury Evie had dealt him.

Those brownish-yellow Tiger Eye beads. For some reason, that damn bracelet made anger burn in Rachel like wildfire.

Evie had wanted to maim him, possibly even kill him. She could still picture Evie holding that knife, blade down, ready to plunge it into the man's flesh. But Rachel had stopped her.

And for what? Because she didn't think the response to violence should be more violence. But armed robberies? Suspected rapes? She remembered what Evie had said that night.

*One day you'll be faced with a choice like this. And you'll sleep well at night knowing you prevented this from happening to someone who couldn't defend herself.*

Rachel felt nauseous. She ran to her computer and googled *Stanford Royce*. The results made her ill.

There were accounts from nearly twenty people claiming Royce had robbed them at either gun- or knifepoint. And five women identifying Royce as their rapist. The man was a monster.

When Royce had accosted Rachel and Evie that night, he'd already had a slew of victims under his belt. But some of the claims were more recent. An elderly man claimed Royce put a knife to his throat and stole his wallet. A fifty-year-old mother of three claimed Royce followed her home, forced his way into her apartment, and sexually assaulted her.

Royce had been arrested several weeks ago near the Harwinton Senior Center after robbing a seventy-eight-year-old man in his apartment, then fleeing out the fire escape. A patrol officer stopped Royce's car for a busted taillight and, on a whim, opened the trunk to find items stolen from nearly a dozen different robberies. Watches, jewelry, antique coins.

Royce's lawyer claimed the arresting officer had no probable cause to search the trunk. A routine traffic stop should have ended with a ticket and a fine. Royce followed the officer's instructions to a *T*—the dashboard cam backed it up. Everything the officer found in Royce's trunk was deemed inadmissible. The judge had reluctantly sided with the defendant. Which meant Stanford Royce was a free man.

Rachel remembered knocking Evie off Royce. She'd believed she was doing the right thing. But now, she wasn't so sure. If she'd let Evie plunge that knife into Stanford Royce, maybe no more people would have gotten robbed. Maybe nobody else would have been assaulted.

She thought about Stanford Royce. And she thought about Harwood Greene.

Rachel needed to learn everything she could about Stanford Royce.

*Somebody could have stopped Stanford Royce,* she thought. *Just like somebody could have stopped Harwood Greene.*

Rachel had made the wrong choice once. She wouldn't a second time.

# CHAPTER 27

***Today***

Rachel opened the door to her house for the first time since an armed gunman had entered it with the intent to kill her. Now that man was dead, and two of his friends were in police custody for trying to finish the job.

The back window had been replaced. The alarm system rebooted. Officers Lowe and Chen sat in an unmarked police car just across the street. The 24-7 security would be in place until Aguillar and Steinman were arraigned.

Eric and Megan ran upstairs. Rachel heard the familiar thump as Megan jumped on her bed. No doubt a book would soon be splayed in her hands. Moments later Rachel heard the irritating *bleep blorp kapow!* as Eric booted up *Alien Commando Pilot Shooter Brigade Face Splattertime 18* or whatever it was.

As for Rachel herself, she stood in the hallway, the lights in the foyer still dim, listening to make sure the house was empty. She felt unsettled. As though Christopher Robles shattering that window had destroyed the protective barrier that she'd carefully constructed around her family.

As her children played upstairs, Rachel thought about what Detective Serrano had said. She couldn't imagine the devastation of losing a child, how your entire world would simply cave in. She'd already lost one person she'd loved, and it nearly broke her. But to lose a child, a life you'd created, a child you protected, fed, clothed, whose heart was connected to yours in the most intimate way imaginable—that was a loss that Rachel could not imagine ever recovering from.

She thought about what she'd said to Serrano that day at the Drummond house.

*Neither of you know the first thing about loss. Maybe one day you will.*

She felt so ashamed she could cry. She knew, in that moment, the way he'd looked at her, that she may as well have plunged a knife into the man's heart.

Those two heartbeats upstairs were her whole life. Serrano wanted her to back off. Stay uninvolved. But if not for her, Constance Wright would be cold in the ground, people assuming she had been just another sad woman who couldn't deal with life.

Somebody had to speak for the Constance Wrights.

Rachel cooked dinner: roast chicken with glazed carrots and *labneh* mashed potatoes. She even let the kids have dessert: two scoops of ice cream each, with sprinkles. She read some of Megan's latest Sadie Scout story, then made sure Eric put the digitized blasters away to finish his homework.

Then, when Eric went to bed, Rachel went downstairs. She spent two hours working her body, then another sharpening her mind. When she came back up at 2:00 a.m., she was wired.

Still coated in dried sweat, Rachel pulled out her laptop, poured herself a glass of water, and got back to work.

She scoured the internet for everything she could find on Nestor Aguillar and Stefanie Steinman. Now that they were both in custody, it was only a matter of time before their social media accounts were taken down. So Rachel saved every photograph, took a screenshot of every post, and wrote down the names of everyone who liked and commented. She did this on all their feeds: they both had Facebook, which was semiprivate. Nestor had Twitter but had not posted since June 2016, and most of his posts seemed to be innocuous. Comments about favorite musicians, rappers, TV shows, and liquor. He also loved *Downton Abbey.* Go figure.

Neither of them had Instagram, Pinterest, Tumblr, or YouTube accounts, at least to the best of her knowledge. She found several old email addresses but could not link them to any other accounts.

She compiled a list of seventeen people who were regular commenters or posters and also lived within driving distance of Ashby. Most of them appeared to be ordinary citizens. No criminal records. Gainfully employed. Many were married and/or had children. Rachel would send the list over to Serrano, just to be sure. Rachel was confident she was more thorough than the cops, but they had more resources.

She didn't recognize any of the names. Except one.

Samuel J. Wickersham.

Wickersham had liked nearly every photo of Stefanie Steinman, and he'd made sure to post "Happy Birthday!" on her Facebook page every year.

Sam Wickersham was the staffer whose affair with Constance Wright had, in part, led to her divorce and disgrace. *How on earth does he know Stefanie Steinman?*

A more thorough examination of Wickersham's and Steinman's social media feeds didn't offer any illumination. Their Facebook feeds were private, so Rachel could only see posts they'd been tagged in by other people. She didn't find anything useful.

Wickersham's Instagram feed was public, but he'd posted only three times, all several years ago and nothing noteworthy. But then Rachel clicked on the "tagged in" button on his profile—and found half a dozen more photos of Wickersham.

One photo in particular piqued her interest.

It was taken at Rhinebeck Hall, a social club in downtown Ashby often used for high-end parties and events. Three people were tagged in the photo, all primped and nattily dressed in cocktail attire: Sam Wickersham, in a gray suit; Stefanie Steinman, wearing a deep V-neck sleeveless purple crepe gown that showed off her tattoos; and a tall, attractive blonde woman wearing an ombré Badgley Mischka dress. The woman was tagged in the photo. Her name was Caroline Drummond.

Drummond.

A quick Google Image search confirmed that the Caroline Drummond in the photo was Nicholas Drummond's sister. There were photos of Caroline Drummond from parties, photos with her brother and then mayor Constance Wright, and professional photos on the website of a firm called J&J Accounting.

Caroline was a few years younger than Nicholas, thirty-seven or thirty-eight based on her college graduation year, with shoulder-length blonde hair and the kind of posture, shoulders, and toned arms that said that the yoga mat was her second home. She was an attractive woman: poised, with deep hazel eyes and full lips. There was a spark in her eyes, a sharpness. Rachel could tell Caroline Drummond was a smart woman.

Then Rachel looked at the date the photo was posted and gasped.

She'd been there that night.

The photo had been taken at the fund-raiser Constance Wright had invited Rachel to after visiting her home. Rachel wore a gorgeous oxblood dress from Rent the Runway and was summarily hit on by a drunken (married) state senator whose cock she threatened to bend sideways if he snapped her bra strap one more goddamn time. She was not exaggerating. And even though Constance had made it clear she didn't want Rachel's money, she'd donated $1,000 anyway.

The photo was from the feed of a professional photographer named Tyrone Wheatley, of Wheatley Photography. It was captioned "All out to support Mayor Constance Wright." He'd used several hashtags: #OurMayor #ConstanceWright #PowertothePeople #NoMorePoliticsAsUsual.

Rachel's head was spinning. How the hell did Nicholas Drummond's sister know Stefanie Steinman and Sam Wickersham? It was entirely possible that the photo was simply a candid. Event photographers were notorious for approaching random people and having them pose for photographs.

But Rachel studied the photo. Sam Wickersham had his arm around Caroline Drummond's waist. And his fingers were slightly clenched, not loose, like he was taking a photo with a stranger. There was a familiarity between the two. They *knew* each other.

Rachel enlarged the image. Looked at Wickersham's fingers. They were low on Caroline Drummond's waist, resting against the curve of her backside. And though it was certainly possible that, as soon as Tyrone Wheatley was done shooting, Caroline turned around and smacked Sam Wickersham across the face, she didn't appear to mind his touch.

Rachel had been in enough situations where men had taken liberties with their hands during "friendly" photographs. She'd felt hands on her buttocks, fingers gripping the hem of her skirt. And she'd had no problem informing them that if they didn't remove the offending digits, she would open another hole in their urethra with a salad fork.

But the photo of Wickersham and Caroline Drummond felt different. The touch was not unwanted.

Rachel clicked on the website listed on Tyrone Wheatley's feed. There were dozens of photo albums taken at weddings, engagement shoots, gender reveals, and more. Rachel clicked on one album and was prompted to enter a login and password. Crap.

She clicked the "Contact" tab. A phone number was listed for Wheatley Photography. Under the photograph, it read "Call 24-7!" Rachel checked her watch. She wondered if anyone had ever tested that offer.

She dialed the number and waited. On the third ring, a deep, sleepy voice answered.

"Huh-lo?"

"Mr. Wheatley? Of Wheatley Photography?"

"Speaking."

"Hi, my name is Rachel Marin. I do some freelance design work for the *Ashby Bulletin*, and we're doing a story on the late mayor, Constance Wright. I see on your website that you photographed a fund-raiser for the mayor a few years back. I'd like to view your album with the possibility of using one or more of the photographs for our article. I'm sorry for the late call, but we need to get this layout finished immediately, and, well, you know, deadlines."

"Yeah, no problem. One sec."

Rachel could hear shuffling and muttering in the background as Tyrone pulled himself out of bed.

"Who is it, hon?" came a female voice.

"Work call," Tyrone answered.

"At this hour?"

"Yep."

"Are they crazy? It's the middle of the night."

"Go back to sleep, babe. I'll take it in the other room."

She felt bad waking Tyrone Wheatley and lying about her motives, but somehow she had a feeling Tyrone would forgive her if he knew the truth. She heard a humming noise as a computer booted up. About thirty seconds later, Tyrone said, "So which album are you asking about?"

"From an event at Rhinebeck Hall for Constance Wright." She gave him the date.

"Yeah, I remember that event," Tyrone said. "She was a good woman, Ms. Wright. Damn shame what happened to her."

"Yes, it is," Rachel said.

"OK, got the album. So what can I help you with?"

"Well, I'd like to view the full album so I can run it by our design chief and see what photos work with the current layout."

"All right," Tyrone said. "Go to my website. Click on the album. When you're prompted, use the login *wheatleyphotography* with the password *guest74249*. You'll have access to view and enlarge the photos, but you can't save them without a watermark. Once you know which photos you want to use, email me with the file numbers, and we can negotiate a usage fee."

"You got it. One sec." Rachel clicked the link, entered the login information, and was granted access to the album.

"You get in?"

"Yep. All set. Thank you, Mr. Wheatley. I'll be in touch."

She hung up. Rachel had no idea what common usage fees were for event photographs, but she would send Tyrone Wheatley $500 in cash in an unmarked envelope as an apology.

There were nearly four hundred photographs in the album. She sighed. It was nearing 3:00 a.m. Rachel poured herself a cup of green tea to help her stay awake.

Photo by photo, Rachel browsed the album. Most of the photos were typical event snaps. Attendees in snazzy dresses and crisp suits pretending to act candid. She even found herself in several photos, mainly in the background, standing alone. She remembered feeling out of place, lonely.

Constance Wright was featured in many of the photographs. Seeing her gave Rachel chills. She was so animated, full of life. Nicholas Drummond looked tired. Irritated. By this point, he'd been sleeping with Isabelle Robles and was likely counting the days until he could formalize his split.

Rachel created a folder on her desktop and saved every photo featuring either Sam Wickersham or Caroline Drummond. Three hundred photos in, and that Instagram photo was still the only one where they'd been photographed together.

Rachel's eyes were bleary. She downed two more cups of green tea, then turned the thermostat in the living room down to sixty-two degrees to keep her chilly and awake. The photographs were blurring together. Fancy people in fancy clothing eating fancy food in a fancy hall.

The first ray of sunlight shocked her. It slipped underneath the drawn curtains and cast a faint yellow glow across the living room. She had lost all track of time. The tea was ineffective. Rachel put on a pot of coffee, then went back to the computer.

She rubbed her eyes, knowing her time was limited. The kids would be awake soon. She had fewer than fifty photographs to go. And it dawned on Rachel that she might come up empty.

Then, with twenty photos to go, she found what she was looking for.

The photograph was of two couples, each in their midfifties. The men decked out in tuxedos, the women clothed in gorgeous, shimmering dresses, jewelry dripping from their necks and ears. They were all grinning from ear to ear and wearing large red, white, and blue pins that read "The Wright Way."

But Rachel didn't care about the partygoers, their attire, or the pins. What she cared about was going on in the background. Slightly out of focus, but unmistakable.

In the corner stood Sam Wickersham and Caroline Drummond. His hand was placed gently on her stomach, a touch that appeared light but incredibly intimate. Her hand grasped his tie. Rachel zoomed in. The striations in the blue fabric on his tie said to Rachel that Caroline was pulling on his tie, gently. Pulling him toward her.

Her palm lay flat on his chest, half pushing him away. Being coy.

*Come closer, but not too close.*

Rachel had no doubt that Sam Wickersham and Caroline Drummond had been sleeping together. Rachel went back through all the Google Image photos of Caroline. In none of them did she appear to be wearing a wedding ring, and there was no indent or tan line that would indicate a previous marriage.

Caroline was ten years older than Sam. But they both appeared smitten.

Rachel rubbed her eyes, pinched her arm until it hurt, willed herself to stay awake.

The young man who'd come forward about having an affair with Constance Wright had also been sleeping with Wright's sister-in-law? Sam Wickersham may have been kind of cute, in a shaggy-dog kind of way, but he didn't seem to Rachel to be the kind of heartbreaker who could seduce two older, successful women.

Had Caroline Drummond been using him? If so, for what?

Just as Rachel was about to start searching for those answers, she heard the door to Megan's room open. She listened as her daughter shuffled out of her room and down the stairs. She wore her Wonder Woman pj's, and her hair was a glorious bed-headed mess. Megan rubbed her eyes and smiled.

"Morning, sweetheart," Rachel said. "How'd you sleep?"

"I had a dream I was a famous author," Megan said. "Everyone loved my Sadie Scout books."

"Aw, that's so wonderful, sweetheart. I bet one day it'll come true."

"You think so? You think people will like Sadie?"

Rachel nodded. "I do."

Then Megan's smile changed. She looked confused. "Mom?"

"Yes, hon?"

"Weren't you wearing those clothes when we got home last night?"

Rachel looked down and realized to her embarrassment she'd never changed.

"I guess I was, sweetie."

"Did you sleep in your clothes?"

"Not really. Mommy had some work to do, and, well, I didn't really go to bed."

"That's weird," Megan said. "I don't know why you wouldn't go to bed."

Then another door opened, and Eric sauntered downstairs. He was wearing mesh basketball shorts and a Stephen Curry jersey.

"Morning," Rachel said.

Eric stood at the bottom of the stairs and cocked his head.

"Mom," he said, "did you go to bed last night?"

"No, unfortunately I had work to do."

Eric nodded, a disapproving scowl on his face; then he turned around and went back upstairs. Megan shuddered as his door slammed shut.

"What's wrong with him?" Megan said.

"Nothing," Rachel replied. Her daughter came over, and Rachel gathered her into her arms. "There's nothing wrong with him at all."

Rachel wondered if Megan knew she was lying.

# CHAPTER 28

Rachel had four strong cups of coffee pumping through her veins by the time she arrived at the offices of Velos Strategies, a political consulting firm that also happened to employ one Samuel J. Wickersham. She parked on the second floor of a public garage and entered through the walkway into the office building where Velos was housed. She wore a gray pantsuit over a white blouse, large quantities of concealer hiding the dark circles under her eyes.

She walked up to the curved glass-topped security desk. The guard eyed her, knowing she didn't work there, and said, "Photo ID, name of company, and person visiting."

Rachel handed over her driver's license and said, "I'm here to see Sam Wickersham at Velos."

The man nodded and scanned her ID. Then he tapped a few buttons on his computer.

"I don't see you registered as a guest. Do you have an appointment with Mr. Wickersham?"

"He must have forgotten to add it in the system. Call Mr. Wickersham and tell him Caroline Drummond is here to see him. He'll clear it up."

"Your identification says Rachel Marin."

"Sam and I are old friends. Trust me, he'll know what I'm talking about."

The guard eyed her suspiciously, then nodded and picked up the phone. He dialed, waited, and then said, "Mr. Wickersham, there's a Caroline Drummond here to see you. Um, yes, that's what she said. Ms. Drummond. Caroline Drummond. All right, thank you, Mr. Wickersham."

The guard tapped a few buttons, then handed Rachel a sticker that read GUEST. "Take the second elevator bank to the sixth floor, Miss . . . whatever your name is."

Rachel thanked him and followed the instructions. The receptionist at Velos was a young blonde woman who appeared to be barely a day out of college. She seemed both bored and angry about her boredom. She didn't look up when Rachel approached.

"Help you?" she said.

"Here to see Sam Wickersham."

"Name?"

"Caroline Drummond. He's expecting me."

She picked up the phone, pressed a button, and said, "Mr. Sam, there's a Caroline something here to see you. OK, hots, you got it."

Rachel wondered if calling Sam "hots" meant they were hooking up or if that was just how millennials greeted each other these days.

"Give him a minute," the girl said. "He comes quickly."

"I'll bet," Rachel replied.

"Huh?"

"Nothing. I'll wait."

Rachel barely had time to sit before a young man with a haphazardly tied ponytail and a crinkled suit entered the reception area. He looked at Rachel, his eyes full of utter confusion. But behind them was a trace of fear. He couldn't have actually been expecting to see Caroline Drummond but knew that her name was being used as some sort of leverage. *I know your secrets.*

"Mr. Wickersham," Rachel said, offering her hand. He took it, waited for Rachel to give her name. She didn't.

"Um, please, come with me," he said. Wickersham's face was covered in five-day-old scruff, and his cheeks looked ashen, eyes bloodshot.

He was wearing an unfortunate amount of cologne, and his suit jacket was wrinkled. He looked like he hadn't showered—or slept—in several days.

Rachel followed Wickersham into a small office. She heard the handle rattle slightly as he closed the door behind them. His hands were shaking.

Wickersham's desk was glossy, polished oak, covered with just enough papers to make him look busy, but each page had a freshly printed look, which said to Rachel that they were just for show. There were no photographs anywhere around the office, no pieces of memorabilia, nothing that gave the space a personal touch. It said to Rachel that he was either a bad decorator or was waiting to be fired.

Wickersham stood behind his desk. He was already sweating. Surely hearing the name Caroline Drummond would have upset him, but Wickersham was acting like something had already gone terribly, terribly wrong.

"Are you going to sit down?" Rachel asked. "Or should we talk standing?"

"P . . . please have a seat," he stuttered. Wickersham sat down but leaned forward. He was as relaxed as a guy who'd just been pulled over by a SWAT team. Rachel took a seat on the other side of the desk.

"Nice place you got here."

Wickersham didn't respond.

"I guess you figured out by now that I'm not Caroline Drummond," she said. Wickersham still didn't speak. He was either trying to figure out what this lady was trying to pull—or he was petrified. Rachel guessed a little of both. But she wasn't quite sure why. Something else besides her ruse had spooked him.

*Serrano and Tally,* she thought. *Do they know about Sam and Caroline Drummond?*

If so, she had to give the detectives some credit.

"I'm here for Constance Wright," Rachel said.

"She's dead," Sam said matter-of-factly.

"Did you facilitate that?"

"Did I what?"

"Did you have anything to do with her death?"

Sam's eyes widened. "Who are you?"

"An interested party," Rachel said. "I know about you and Caroline Drummond. Not many guys have the kind of game to carry on an affair with a mayor while also sleeping with her sister-in-law. And I'm guessing you're not one of them."

The blood drained from Sam Wickersham's face, leaving his cheeks the color of printer paper.

"I . . . we . . ."

"Save it," Rachel said. "I don't think you killed Constance Wright. But I think you know who did."

"I swear to God I had nothing to do with it," Wickersham said. "Just leave me alone. It was a long time ago, and I already talked to the cops. Wait, are you a cop?"

*He already talked to the cops,* Rachel thought. Which explained why he had been on edge from the moment she'd arrived. But the fact that they hadn't arrested him meant either he hadn't committed a crime—or they were using him to hook a bigger fish.

"Tell me about Constance Wright," Rachel said. "Your affair. The truth."

"I already told the cops, the black lady and the white guy. Albatross paid me to make up the affair with Ms. Wright. I just went along with it."

*So there was no affair.*

Rachel's brain started whirring. *Albatross. Paid him. Went along with it.*

"So how was Caroline Drummond involved?" Rachel said.

Wickersham hesitated.

She slammed her fist down on Wickersham's table and shouted, *"How?"*

A petite brunette in a sharp yellow blazer knocked softly and opened the door.

"Mr. Wickersham?" she said. "Is everything all right?"

Rachel glared at him.

"It's fine," he said. "Go back to your desk, Edith."

Edith nodded, skeptical, and disappeared. She closed the door behind her.

"Caroline was playing you," Rachel said. "Sleeping with you to get you to do what she wanted."

"She wasn't *playing* me," Wickersham pleaded. "We were in love."

"Oh come on," Rachel said dismissively. "Successful woman, sister-in-law of the mayor, a hotshot politico on the rise? She suddenly decides to start doing the devil's dance with some pissant twenty-year-old? No way. She was diddling you to convince you to go ahead and testify against Constance Wright. She was worried—*they* were worried—that the money wouldn't be enough."

"Stop it," Wickersham said. Tears had begun to spring up in his eyes. Rachel felt a modicum of sympathy for this poor young sap. But then she remembered that Constance Wright had been thrown off a bridge like an empty soda can, and this little asshole knew something about it.

"How did you two meet?" Rachel said. "You and Caroline."

"A fund-raiser when Ms. Wright was first running for office. I had just graduated high school, and her campaign held a rally in our gym. My folks were big supporters of Ms. Wright. At one point I wandered off and saw Caroline standing alone. She'd finished her drink. I offered to get her another. She laughed, asked how old I was. When I told her, she said to get her a cranberry vodka. I did, and she seemed impressed. I told her I loved politics and would love to work for someone like Ms. Wright. She gave me her email address and said to get in touch. I did. We emailed every now and then, no big deal, just friendly. But when I graduated college, she hooked me up with a job in Ms. Wright's office."

"When did you start sleeping with her?"

Wickersham looked at his lap.

"About a year into the job, there was a cocktail party. Just for staff and family. Caroline was there. She wore this little black dress, and . . . we hit it off, and . . ."

"Was she the one who approached you to lie about the affair?"

Wickersham nodded. "She told me that Ms. Wright had made some people angry. Her family had lost them a lot of money. She wasn't trustworthy. She said for the good of the people of Ashby, they needed to get her out of office. I figured if the mayor's husband's sister was saying this, it had to be true."

"You were already sleeping together by this point."

"Yes," he said softly.

*She was grooming him.* And she got the sense from the anguish in Sam Wickersham's eyes that he'd just realized it.

"Caroline told me someone would be in touch. To handle all the details. She said there would be a lot of money in it for me. That I wouldn't have to worry about anything."

"That 'someone'—was this the Albatross you mentioned?"

Sam nodded. "Albatross offered me the money. I still don't know who was behind Albatross. I told that to the cops."

"But Caroline was the facilitator."

"She was my girlfriend," Wickersham said.

"Right. Where is she now?"

"I don't know. She stopped returning my emails and texts. I ran into Christopher Robles a few weeks ago, and he said he thought she was in Europe or something. A sabbatical."

*Interesting timing,* Rachel thought. Caroline disappearing right before Constance was killed.

"So Caroline sets you up as a patsy and has you fake an affair with Constance Wright to help ruin her career and get her brother paid,"

Rachel said. "And you go right on with your career. How much did Albatross pay you?"

"Four eighty."

"Four hundred and eighty thousand?" Rachel said with a whistle. "So that's what a life is worth."

"I didn't kill her," he said.

"But you know who did."

"No, I don't. I swear to God."

Rachel eyed Wickersham. Either he was telling the truth, or Meryl Streep had ceded the title of world's greatest living actor to Samuel J. Wickersham. It still didn't quite jibe. Albatross and the Drummonds had gotten what they wanted. Constance left office in disgrace. Nicholas remarried Isabelle and made a mint from the divorce. Wickersham moved on to a cushy new job and pocketed close to a half million dollars. Everything had gone according to plan.

So why would they want to kill Constance Wright now, years later?

It was possible Wright had found out about the plan and had been looking to clear her name, get even, or get her money back from Nicholas. And between the Drummonds and whoever this "Albatross" was, there were enough folks with serious money on the line who probably felt taking Constance out was quicker and cheaper than a lawsuit. But why wouldn't Constance have gone to the press? If she *had* found out the truth, she'd kept quiet. Not something politicians were wont to do.

Something about the scenario didn't quite sit right with Rachel.

"I need everything you know about Caroline Drummond, Albatross, and Constance Wright," Rachel said. "I'm not a cop, but I've been working with them."

A lie—but a white one, she figured.

"And what then?" Sam said.

"Then we find out who's behind Albatross, what Caroline Drummond knows, and hopefully that will get us closer to getting justice for Constance Wright."

Sam nodded.

"And what about me?" he said.

"You," Rachel said, as though she hadn't given it any consideration. Because, well, she hadn't. "You'll do some time. Perjury. Maybe accessory to murder. Fraud. But that's not within my jurisdiction."

Sam nodded again. He opened his desk drawer. Stared at it. Rachel leaned forward, but she couldn't see what he was looking at. Then he reached into the drawer and came out holding a Ruger .22-caliber LCR pistol.

Rachel froze. The gun itself was not large. Less than seven inches long and five inches high. It weighed a hair under fifteen ounces. The snub nose made the Ruger LCR a poor choice for long-range targets. But at this distance, just three feet across the desk from Rachel, Wickersham couldn't miss.

"Sam," Rachel said, her heart pounding against her rib cage. "Put the gun down."

Sweat began to trickle down her back. And suddenly Rachel realized that her coming here to confront Sam Wickersham had been a terrible, terrible mistake.

Sam held the gun listlessly, aiming it somewhere slightly to the left of Rachel's head.

"It's over," he said. "If I go to prison or cut a deal, I'll never work again. This . . . *thing* . . . will be the first item that comes up when anyone looks for me online."

"You're young," Rachel said. "You made a mistake, and you have your whole life to atone. You have a chance to make it right. Caroline loves you . . ."

"No she doesn't," Sam said. "You said so yourself. She was using me to help take down Mayor Wright."

"You're going to listen to *me*?" Rachel said. "I don't know what I'm talking about. I'm a fool. Ask my kids. They'll say, 'Mom's a fool.'"

She looked down at her purse. She could see her cell phone. If she could keep Sam distracted, perhaps she could dial 911. But even if she did, they would take minutes. Sam could end her life in less than a second.

She considered her options. She couldn't reach him from where she sat. And she couldn't grab the gun without lunging across the desk. And that would give him more than enough time to pull the trigger. Too much time. Too many variables.

If he wanted her dead, she was dead.

"I wake up every day wishing I could take back what we did to Ms. Wright," Wickersham said. His gun hand was shaking. Rachel didn't take her eyes off it, hoping an opportunity would present itself.

"You can't take it back," Rachel said. "But you can help us find who killed her."

"I don't *know* who killed her!" he wailed. At that moment, the door opened, and Edith appeared once again.

"Mr. Wickersham . . . oh my God!" When she saw the gun, Edith's hand went to her mouth. Almost instinctively, Sam's gun hand moved toward the sound, until the barrel was pointed directly at Edith's heart.

"No!" Rachel shouted. Edith began to cry. "Point it at me!"

Sam looked at Rachel, his gun hand moving left until it was pointed at Rachel's midsection. Edith didn't move. "Edith," Rachel said evenly, "go back to your desk."

"Should I . . . should I call the police?"

"No!" Rachel said. She didn't want Wickersham any more agitated. "Just sit down."

Sobbing, Edith disappeared from view.

Sam looked down at the gun. Then he looked at Rachel. He seemed almost surprised by the weapon in his hand.

"There's no coming back from this," Sam said. "I never thought it through. I just wish I could tell Ms. Wright I'm sorry. I wish she still had her old job. She was good at it. And I messed it all up. I'm so, so sorry."

In that moment, Rachel realized the gun wasn't meant for her.

Just as Sam Wickersham brought the gun to rest in the soft flesh underneath his chin, Rachel dove across the oak desk. She wrapped her hands around his gun hand just as he pulled the trigger, redirecting his aim ever so slightly. The gun went off, the explosion shattering the air. She and Sam both toppled to the floor.

Instead of bursting through the bottom of his jaw and exiting through his brain, the bullet tore through the flesh on the side of Sam Wickersham's neck. As they hit the floor, Rachel saw a river of red spreading on the tasteful gray carpeting. Blood was pumping out of a gash in Sam's neck. She immediately knew the bullet had nicked his right external jugular vein.

The gunshot still ringing in her ears, Rachel pulled off her jacket, balled it up, and pressed it hard against Wickersham's neck. Blood immediately soaked through it. His eyes were bulging and terrified.

*"Edith!"* Rachel screamed, hoping the girl hadn't left the office in fear. *"Dial 911!"*

"Are you sure?"

*"Yes!"*

A moment later, Rachel heard Edith's quivering voice from the hallway, explaining the situation to the emergency dispatcher. Blood was pooling around Rachel's knees as she held the jacket firmly against Sam's neck.

A red bubble formed on Wickersham's lips and then burst, leaving a foamy red coating on his chin.

"Stay with me," Rachel said. The blood was coming out fast—too fast. *"Edith!"*

*"What?"*

"Tell the dispatcher that the victim has severe trauma from a gunshot wound to the neck, with a likely arterial severing. Tell them they'll need clamps, a catheter, and blood for a transfusion. Edith, are you with me?"

*"Yes!"*

"When they confirm an ambulance is on the way, keep the dispatcher on the line. Find Sam's employment file. It'll list his primary physician. Tell the dispatcher what you're doing, put them on hold, and call his physician. Tell them it's a life-and-death emergency and you need Sam's blood type. Then give that to the dispatcher. *Edith, did you get all that?*"

*"Yes!"*

Now there was nothing for Rachel to do other than try to keep Sam Wickersham alive. As she held her blood-soaked jacket against his neck, she felt something weak and sticky wrap around her wrist. Sam's hand. He was staring into her eyes and holding her wrist. For a moment, Rachel thought he was clinging to her as he clung to life, his eyes wide and pleading.

But then she felt his hand pulling at her wrist. Trying to pull her hand away.

He wanted her to let him die.

Rachel fought back tears and gently removed his hand from her wrist. He was too weak to resist.

"Please," she said, "stay with me."

Sam's eyes closed. For a moment, she thought he was dead. But she could see his chest rising and falling with the breath of life. She could feel a weak pulse. He was still alive. For now.

A single tear slid down Rachel's cheek and fell noiselessly into the pool of Samuel J. Wickersham's blood.

# CHAPTER 29

Rachel sat on the back bumper of an ambulance outside the Velos offices. She shivered in the frigid winter air, her bloodstained suit jacket having been taken away and bagged as evidence. She watched as EMTs loaded Sam Wickersham into the back of another ambulance, blood seeping through the towels held to his neck. He was strapped to a gurney, an IV already inserted into his vein, just enough blood left in his body to keep his heart pumping. Rachel asked the EMTs if they thought Sam would live, but they ignored her questions and focused on the wounded man.

Rachel was still shaken, her nerves jangling. If she'd been a split second slower, Sam would be dead.

She'd given a statement to the first officer on scene. She didn't go into much detail or say why she'd been there in the first place, just that Sam took a gun from his desk and tried to kill himself. She left out the part about Caroline Drummond.

Even though Sam contributed to Constance Wright's downfall, lied about their affair, and then helped cover it up, she believed him when he said he didn't know who'd killed her. She'd sensed genuine remorse in his voice. He was a tormented young man who'd done something terrible. But he didn't deserve to die.

She rubbed her eyes, forgetting for a moment that her hands were still coated in someone else's blood.

"You all right, Ms. Marin?" the EMT asked.

"Yes. Long, very bad day."

Then Rachel saw a familiar brown Crown Victoria pull up in front of the Velos entrance.

"Guess the day can only get worse," she said to nobody.

Detectives John Serrano and Leslie Tally exited the vehicle. Serrano had a look of disappointment on his face that made Rachel feel sick and ashamed. But Tally had a look of pure anger, glaring at Rachel with eyes that could light a match. An EMT was checking Rachel's vitals, to her embarrassment. Sam Wickersham was headed to the hospital near death, and some guy was checking *her* blood pressure.

Rachel had nearly forgotten that she hadn't slept in over twenty-four hours, but it was all starting to hit her. Serrano and Tally went over to a young officer writing in a notepad outside the Velos lobby. Rachel eavesdropped.

"How is he?" Serrano said.

"Partially severed jugular vein," the cop replied. "Lost a ton of blood."

"He gonna make it?" Tally asked.

The cop shrugged. Then he pointed at Rachel. "That woman there saved his life. Kept pressure on the wound, had Wickersham's secretary give the 911 dispatcher the trauma details so the EMTs knew what they would be looking at. Even had the foresight to get his blood type to the hospital to prep for a transfusion."

Serrano nodded but looked at Rachel gravely. She couldn't meet his eyes.

"Is it true," Tally said, nodding at Rachel, "that she gave a false name to the security guard to get into the building to talk to Wickersham?"

The cop nodded. "Guard said she gave her name as Caroline Drummond. Security tapes confirm it. Now why would she do that?"

Tally marched over to Rachel with a purpose. Rachel shooed away the EMT.

"I'm fine," she said, then turned to Tally. "Detective, I can explain—"

Before she knew what was happening, Tally had spun Rachel around, bent her over the bumper, pulled her hands behind her back, and clapped a pair of handcuffs on her.

"Rachel Marin," Tally said. "You are under arrest for interfering in a criminal investigation. You have the right to remain silent. Anything you say can and will be used against you in a court of law. You have the right to an attorney. If you cannot afford an attorney, one will be provided for you. Do you understand the rights I have just read to you?"

"Detective Serrano?" Rachel said. She caught a look of surprise on Serrano's face, which said that he didn't know Tally had been planning to arrest her. But the look quickly faded. He had to back up his partner. Anger and panic and adrenaline flooded Rachel's body. *"Detective?"*

"I'm sorry, Ms. Marin," Serrano said. "We have to take you in."

If looks could kill, Rachel was reasonably sure her glare would have killed not only John Serrano but all his ancestors as well.

Tally brought her around to the back of the Crown Vic, opened the door, and held Rachel's head down as she pushed her inside. Then Tally slammed the door and threw Serrano a look that Rachel caught but that was clearly not meant to be seen by her.

It said, *We have to clean up this crazy bitch's goddamn mess* again.

Thing was, Rachel couldn't really blame Tally. *She* was the one who'd gone to Wickersham's office and posed as Caroline Drummond. She'd *wanted* to get under his skin. In fact, Rachel felt a little lucky that she hadn't been arrested before this.

"My children," Rachel said, as Tally got behind the wheel. "My kids are in school. Detective, please."

"We'll have a blue and white pick them up and bring them to the station," Tally said.

"You're going to have a strange police officer go pick up my children from school after what happened with Aguillar and Steinman? Are you kidding me?"

"I'll get them myself," Serrano said. "Tally will book you, and I'll get Eric and Megan."

Rachel wasn't sure whether to thank him or spit in his face. She said nothing. She knew fighting would get her nowhere. But her heart hammered.

"You can't let my children see me like this. In handcuffs," Rachel said.

"You should have thought about that before you faked your identity to question a witness in a murder investigation," Tally said.

"I didn't know Wickersham was involved in the investigation. I was just following a hunch. Please, Detective Tally," Rachel said. "You don't know what my kids have been through."

"Let's get one thing clear, Ms. Marin," Tally said, pulling onto the highway. Snowflakes dusted the windshield. Rachel was cold, and she could feel the handcuffs sticking to the blood still caked to her hands and wrists. "*You're* the reason you're in this situation right now. Not us."

"I'm just trying to do the right thing," Rachel said.

"And a boy is on his way to the hospital, and he might not make it," she said. "Did you do the right thing with him?"

"That boy helped ruin a woman's life," Rachel said. "You know it. You obviously spoke to him and know about Albatross. The only innocent person in this equation is Constance Wright. And it took a long, *long* time for someone to finally fight for her."

"We're fighting for her," Serrano said.

"A little too late for her," Rachel replied coldly.

Then there was silence. Tally drove them to the station. Rachel rubbed her wrists together to keep circulation flowing, but her fingers were growing numb. The ride was pure agony.

Finally they pulled into the Ashby police station. Tally came around back and dragged Rachel out of the car.

"Take her inside, book her, and put her in holding," Serrano said. "I'll go get the kids and bring them back here."

"Eric is in class," Rachel said. "Social studies right now, then history next period. Please be discreet. He's been through enough."

"What exactly *has* he been through?" Tally said.

Rachel merely said, "I'm asking you, Detective, to look out for my son and daughter. They did nothing wrong."

Serrano could tell she was holding back, hiding something. He nodded and said, "I will."

Then Serrano got back in the Crown Vic and drove off.

"Guess it's just me and you," Rachel said, smiling politely. Tally did not return the warm gesture.

"Let's go." Tally led Rachel into the station, her hands still cuffed behind her back. Suddenly Rachel felt nervous. She'd spent time with these people. They'd been kind to her after the Robles break-in and Aguillar-Steinman incident. And now she was being hauled into the station like a common perp.

As Tally led her inside, Rachel saw Lieutenant George. He gave Serrano a look that said, *She's back again?*

"Is this necessary?" Rachel said to Tally. "The handcuffs."

"Oh, so you expect special treatment now?"

"No, it's just . . ."

"Just what?"

Lieutenant George walked over to them. "Back again, Ms. Marin?" he said.

"Misunderstanding," she said, but her voice let him know it wasn't.

"Fine example you're setting for Eric and Megan," he said, shaking his head. She opened her mouth to curse him out but stopped. She felt ashamed. The lieutenant had shown her children such kindness. And he wasn't wrong.

Tally led Rachel to the booking desk, where the clerk wrote down her name and address, took her fingerprints, and confiscated her purse and other belongings. They removed her bloody clothing and gave her a pair of sweatpants and a sweatshirt that looked like they'd been passed down among various incarcerated women since the 1920s. They also gave her a pair of socks. She desperately wanted to refuse them—Lord knew how many grungy feet had worn them—but she was still frigid from the ride over. So she turned the socks inside out and promised to bathe herself in Clorox the moment she got home.

Then Tally walked Rachel to a pair of holding cells at the far end of the station. She opened the door to one sepulchral chamber and gestured for Rachel to enter.

Rachel balked.

Three other people occupied the small cell, which Rachel estimated to be about eight by twelve, with metal benches bracketing each gray stone wall. The floor was an off-green, pea soup–ish color, made from an epoxy coating that adhered directly to the concrete underneath, preventing inmates from picking or peeling at the material, which could then be used as a makeshift weapon.

"Detective," Rachel said. "You know I'm just trying to do the right thing. I never wanted that to happen to Sam. You and I are on the same side."

"You say another word without getting your ass in that cell, I'll add resisting arrest to your docket. You're totally unhinged, Ms. Marin."

"I never claimed to be fully hinged."

Tally glared at her. Rachel sighed and entered the cell. Tally closed the door. The lock clicked into place.

Rachel looked around. She'd been arrested once, as a teenager. Three of her friends had closed down a bar on a road trip to New York and were stupid enough to smoke a joint outside. A cop happened to walk by, and the next thing Rachel knew, she was high as a kite and in the back of a police car. They released her the following morning and dropped the charges—a night in a holding cell was enough time served to pay for a public joint—but it was the last time Rachel smoked anything other than meat.

Still, that night had stuck with her. She never thought she'd be arrested again. Deep down, though, she knew she'd been playing with fire. The Drummond ruse. Going to Wickersham's office. At some point, she'd have to answer for all of it.

Rachel observed her fellow cellmates. A fortysomething scraggly-looking white woman paced back and forth, scratching at the back of her hand. She was either a hooker or a meth addict or was just having a *really* bad hair day. A young black man with scraped, bleeding knuckles stood in the corner, looking anxious. And an older gentleman sat silent and contented on one of the metal benches, as though this was his usual spot to drink a cup of coffee and feed the pigeons.

She detected a faint whiff of perfume on the black man. No wedding ring. And other than his knuckles, there were no other scrapes or bruises. She immediately knew he'd punched a guy who'd insulted his girlfriend. His eyes darted around the station. He was expecting someone to come for him. But nobody had. The girlfriend was cheating on him. Poor guy. His day would only get worse.

The woman wore a lime-green halter top under a leopard-print jacket. Her stomach bore old cigarette burn scars. Her pale, blotchy legs were covered in sores. The cigarette burns weren't deep, so it was more likely she had developed a habit of falling asleep with a lit cigarette in her hand and dropping them on herself than actually being burned by someone else.

The older man confused Rachel. He was in his seventies and wore brown corduroy pants, a chunky cable-knit sweater, and polished Cole Haan shoes. His hair was neat and parted. He wore thin wire-frame glasses. He looked like somebody's kind grandfather or maybe a small-town pharmacist. Not someone who looked comfortable in a holding cell.

"What are you in for?" Rachel asked him, unsure of whether she'd broken some sort of unspoken jailhouse code of conduct.

"Attempted shoplifting," he said.

"Attempted shoplifting," Rachel said. "What does that mean?"

"I didn't actually shoplift anything," he said. "Just tried to."

"Right," Rachel said. "*Attempted* shoplifting. Did you, like, stuff too many Kit Kats in your pocket at the drugstore counter?"

"No," the man replied. He paused. "You know, ATM machines are heavier than they look."

Rachel laughed. "Can't say I've ever tried to carry one."

She took a seat on the metal bench next to the would-be ATM thief and waited. She knew how this went. Tomorrow, she would be arraigned. Which meant she would need a lawyer. But with no prior record (she'd paid a lot of money to ensure that Rachel Marin had no arrest record) and the recent threats against her family, Rachel was reasonably sure she could agree to a fine with no prison time and be released quickly.

She'd messed up. Pushed too hard. But it felt like the threads were weaving together. Sam Wickersham. Albatross. Caroline Drummond. She was pleasantly surprised to find out that Serrano and Tally had already spoken to Wickersham—even if they hadn't come across the Caroline Drummond angle yet. The detectives were growing on her. They were competent, and they cared.

If only they'd been the ones investigating Harwood Greene . . .

"Mom?"

Rachel's eyes widened and her head snapped up.

*No. No. I'm not ready. I don't know what to say to my children yet.*

Standing in front of the holding cell was Detective Serrano.

Eric and Megan stood on either side of him.

Megan looked confused. She couldn't figure out the look on Eric's face—revulsion?—but seeing her children broke her heart.

"Kids," Rachel said, standing up against the cell bars. "Everything is going to be fine. This is just a big misunderstanding."

The same thing she'd said to the lieutenant. He hadn't believed her, and Rachel could tell her children didn't either.

Megan stayed silent, then went over and hugged Eric. Rachel's son just stared at his mother. He had his father's eyes. God, were they striking.

"Mom?" Eric said.

"Hon, I swear this is going to be over very soon. Just stay with the detective for a bit while we figure this out."

"Is this about the basement?" Eric said.

"What?" Rachel said.

"The basement. Is this about the stuff in the basement?"

Serrano looked at Eric. Rachel cursed silently.

"No, sweetheart, this has nothing to do with the house or you or anything else. Mom made a mistake, but it's getting sorted out. I promise."

Serrano knelt down so he could talk to the kids. "Listen. Eric. Megan. I'm going to take you to get a snack; then I'm going to talk to your mom."

"People get killed in prison," Eric said.

Serrano smiled. "This isn't prison. And I promise, anyone who wants to hurt your mom is going to have to go through me. Nothing is going to happen to her."

"How can you be sure?" Eric said. Serrano stood up and mimicked holding a staff in his right hand.

"Because I am a servant of the secret fire," Serrano said dramatically, banging his invisible staff against the ground. "And *you shall not pass*!"

"In the books, it's 'you *cannot* pass,'" Eric said. "I never understood why in the movie he says *shall not*. And you're a giant dork."

But Eric was smiling.

"Guilty," Serrano said. "Come on. Your mom will be fine." As they left, Serrano looked back at Rachel, still clutching the bars of the cell. A few minutes later, the detective returned.

"Where are the kids?" she said.

"The lieutenant will watch Eric and Megan until we can figure out a longer-term solution. I'll bring them some drinks and snacks."

Rachel leaned against the cold metal. "Thank you," she said. "And please thank the lieutenant."

"I will. Now, one question."

"Yes?"

"Just what the hell is wrong with you?" Serrano said. She lifted her head, shocked by Serrano's sudden change in tone.

"Excuse me?"

"I thought I got through to you last night," Serrano said.

"Oh, you did," Rachel said coldly. "You got through loud and clear. You pretend to care for us, to care for my *children*. And then you do this?"

"You're the reason you're in here," Serrano said. "Not me."

"How many other single mothers have you told your sob story to?" she said. "How many other kids have you taken to that field?"

Serrano's eyes narrowed.

"The world isn't against you, Rachel."

"You haven't seen the world the way I have," she said.

Serrano paused. "What do you mean by that?"

"Nothing," she said.

"What was Eric talking about? Your basement."

"None of your goddamn business."

"Ms. Marin, you're the only reason you're in this cell. Not me. Not Tally. Not Sam Wickersham. *You.* You want to be angry, be angry at yourself."

After the intimacy of the other night, hearing Serrano call her *Ms. Marin* felt cold, impersonal.

"I've spent a long time being angry at myself."

"Tell me why," Serrano said. He gripped the bars, his finger brushing hers. "All these comments. Insinuations. I have no idea who you are. So *tell* me."

"Detective, you're trying *way* too hard to get laid."

Serrano removed his hands from the bars.

"Call a lawyer," he said. "Your arraignment is tomorrow morning."

"What about my kids?" she said.

"They can't stay in the lieutenant's office overnight. There's a room upstairs we call the Bunk. It's where officers can catch some sleep after a long night or between shifts. There are a few beds. They're not that comfortable, but they're clean. They can share one. I have some paperwork, and after that I'll take another bed up there to keep an eye on them. Nobody enters that room who isn't law enforcement. They'll be safe. Just be careful."

She looked over her shoulder at her cellmates.

"Be careful?" she asked. "Am I not safe in here?"

"I'm not worried about what these people might do to you, Ms. Marin," Serrano said. "I'm worried about what you might do to them."

# CHAPTER 30

Serrano collected Eric and Megan from Lieutenant George's office and brought them up to the Bunk. There was a library with a few tattered paperbacks, a bunch of magazines of varying ages, a deck of playing cards, a few board games, and a television. Eric took a Michael Connelly novel from the shelf, and Megan grabbed a six-month-old copy of *Field & Stream*.

Sgt. Inez Fortunado, a twenty-year vet, occupied one of the other beds. Serrano explained the situation, and Sergeant Fortunado offered to stay awake an extra hour and watch them while Serrano finished his paperwork. He thanked her and said a bottle of Maker's Mark would be waiting on her desk.

Serrano gave each of the kids one of his cards and told them to call him anytime, day or night. No matter what.

Serrano went back downstairs and found Tally at her desk. He took a seat.

"You know we had to take her in," she said.

"I know."

"I'm running background on Rachel Marin," Tally said, "and it's very, very strange."

Serrano rolled his desk chair over to Tally's cubicle and leaned in. "Strange how?"

"Look at this," Tally said. She shifted to her right to allow Serrano access to her computer screen. "I ran Marin's property records. She bought the house her family currently lives in just over two and a half years ago for 800 grand."

"All right, so what's strange?"

"She paid cash. In full. There's no mortgage attached to it whatsoever."

"Really . . ."

"Yep. Ms. Marin currently works as an executive assistant to a lawyer named Steve Ruggiero. Glassdoor states that the average exec assistant at that firm gets paid about 55 grand a year."

"Factor in childcare, and . . ."

"There's no way 55 grand a year buys you a house for 800K."

"She might have had money before she moved. She was married before. Alimony? Child support?"

"See, that's where it gets weirder," Tally said. "There are no marriage—or divorce—records listed for Rachel Marin. There's a marriage record for a Rachel Marin who lives in Sioux Falls, South Dakota, but the wedding took place in 1972. She's currently eighty-four years old. And black. And that's just the beginning."

"Go on," Serrano said.

"The NCIC lists no prior arrests. A few parking tickets, but nothing more serious than that, and nothing prior to her relocation to Ashby. But here's where it gets *really* weird. I checked out the birth records for Eric and Megan Marin. Neither record lists their father. The birth certificates are both blank."

"It's possible she had them both on her own," Serrano said. "IUI or IVF via donor. And just lied about having a husband because she didn't want to get into it."

"I thought about that," Tally said. "Here's the thing: Rachel Marin made enough money to buy an $800,000 house in cash. She could have had a good job prior, saved up a lot, right? But if she was smart and talented enough to have the kind of job *before* moving to Ashby that allowed her to buy a house for that amount of money, why would she then take a job as an assistant barely making enough to make ends meet?"

"Job market isn't great," Serrano said.

"True," Tally said, "but I called Steve Ruggiero. Her boss. He said when Rachel applied for the job, she was the most overqualified candidate he'd ever interviewed. Said she was smarter than most of the partners at the firm. In fact, he said he was reluctant to hire her because someone with her skills would leave for another job within months. Plus, if she paid cash for the house, and then took a job barely making ends meet, I'm thinking she had a lot more money than that 800 grand stashed away. Enough to make taking a job below her market value manageable. Even preferable. To me, this all sounds like a woman who wanted to stay under the radar."

"And yet here she is in our holding cell," Serrano said. "Not quite what I'd call staying under the radar."

"Yeah," Tally said, rubbing her cheek. "Still haven't figured that out yet. But you've seen how far she's been willing to go. The Drummond house escapade. Showing up at Wickersham's office. Something primal in that woman is overriding her need to lay low. And I'm betting it's related to money and this missing husband of hers."

Serrano rubbed the bridge of his nose and exhaled.

"You feel something for her," Tally said sympathetically.

He replied, "Something terrible happened to that family. She won't tell me what it is, but there's this awful cloud hanging over them. You see it in her son. A sadness. An anger. And somehow what happened to that family is connected to everything Marin has done."

Tally listened.

"I told her about Evan," he said. Tally sighed.

"Oh, John. Why?"

"After Robles, Aguillar, and Steinman, I wanted her to see that her children were being brought along for this insane ride, whatever it is, against their will. That whatever crusade she was on, she wasn't on it alone. That I lost a child and it nearly broke me. That there's a responsibility to protect people who depend on you. Because you can lose them just like that." He snapped his fingers to accentuate the last word.

"She'll go free tomorrow," Tally said. "More than likely they'll let her off with a fine. But I want Caroline Drummond. I want Albatross. And now I want to know who the hell Rachel Marin is."

"I'm with you, Leslie."

"On all of it? Marin included?"

Serrano hesitated, then said, "Yes."

"Good. Because I have a call in to the broker she used to buy that house. I want to see her application package."

"If she paid cash, there won't be bank records since there's no mortgage."

"No, but I'll bet she had a lawyer review the contract. We can start there."

Serrano nodded. "In the meantime, I have a subpoena in for Caroline Drummond's phone records for the last five years."

Lieutenant George approached Serrano and Tally and stopped by their desks. He looked bone tired, no doubt from fielding questions about the Wickersham shooting. His normally clean-and-steamed suit was rumpled, with a soy sauce stain on the tie. On an ordinary day, the fifty-nine-year-old lieutenant looked forty. Today, for the first time Serrano could recall, he looked his age.

"The Marin kids in the Bunk?" he said.

Serrano nodded. "Sergeant Fortunado is keeping an eye on them."

"Lord, what a clusterfuck," George said, rubbing his eyes. "Let me ask you both a question. What do you make of this Marin woman? She seems to either have a vendetta or a death wish."

"Maybe both," Tally said.

"Something bad is going to happen if she doesn't get a grip. She's lucky that Wickersham kid didn't blow her head off. If she was smart, she'd either stay home or in our holding cell. At least there she can't endanger herself or those kids."

"I'll give her that choice, Lieutenant," Serrano said.

"Don't be shocked if she becomes a regular in that cell," Tally said. "Moths who circle flames always get burned."

"Hopefully a night in holding will wake her up before someone gets killed," George said. "Speaking of which, that Wickersham boy is damned lucky to be alive."

"They think he'll make it?" Tally said.

"Bullet nearly severed his vocal cords, so he'll never sing opera, but he'll live."

"And probably spend the rest of the decade in prison," Serrano said. "We have him cold on conspiracy and fraud for the fake Constance Wright affair."

"So what are you waiting for?" the lieutenant said.

"We still don't have all the pieces. Wickersham was in a sexual relationship with Caroline Drummond, Nicholas Drummond's sister. She works for an accounting firm that set up a lease with a shell company called Albatross, which paid Wickersham for his role in the setup. But we still don't know who was behind Albatross, or which of them may have actually killed Constance Wright."

"Get Albatross," George said. "Once we have Wickersham, the Drummond sister, and this money man, one of them will cop to the killing. Or we charge them all with conspiracy to commit murder and see which one sings first."

"I like the way you think, Lieutenant," Tally said.

"My wife said that to me the other day," George said wistfully. "But I think she was being sarcastic. Anyway, get on it. Bring these bastards down."

Serrano said, "With pleasure, sir."

George walked away, and Tally's cell phone chimed. She clicked it open and smiled.

"Phone and text records for one Caroline Drummond from our friends at Verizon," she said. "Let's get to work."

◆ ◆ ◆

Serrano and Tally were able to electronically eliminate over 97 percent of Caroline Drummond's incoming and outgoing phone calls for the five-year duration of the records they received. Calls to and from her work, various restaurants for reservations and deliveries, and friends and family they were able to confirm as legitimate and unconnected to Wickersham or Albatross.

The other 3 percent consisted of hundreds of calls and texts to and from Samuel Wickersham, many of which contained graphic sexual content. The communication started slow, increased in volume and duration over the next two years—which coincided with Constance Wright's troubles and her divorce from Nicholas Drummond—and then tapered off once the legal troubles ended.

"What is a purple-headed warrior?" Tally said, reviewing the text messages.

"Sounds like something you get diagnosed with after a bachelor party in Las Vegas," Serrano replied.

"And why would anybody want one of those in their"—Tally squinted—"spicy love muffin? Is this how people sext these days? Hell, when I want a romantic night with Claire, I just come home with a bottle of rioja and put on some Coltrane. I feel so old fashioned."

"I just open Tinder and start swiping right," Serrano said.

"You are *not* on Tinder." Serrano stayed silent. "Oh God, you are. Wait, have you matched with anyone on the job?"

"I plead the Fifth so as not to incriminate myself," Serrano said.

"Ugh," Tally said, mock shivering. "I don't want to know."

After removing the Wickersham correspondence from the list, there were still seventeen phone numbers they could not confirm.

One by one, they cross-referenced those numbers with Sam Wickersham, Nicholas Drummond, Isabelle Robles, Christopher Robles, Nestor Aguillar, Stefanie Steinman, and anyone at J&J Accounting. They were able to eliminate thirteen of the seventeen numbers as incidental. They then called the remaining four.

The first number went to a man named Ricardo Jimenez, currently living outside of Denver. Jimenez admitted to having had a sporadic consensual sexual relationship with Caroline Drummond during the period in question, which had ended after he'd accepted the job he presently occupied. Jimenez had married last year and now had a daughter on the way. Nothing about the situation seemed extraordinary, other than the fact that it would have broken Sam Wickersham's heart to know he hadn't been the only one sharing Caroline Drummond's bed during that time.

Tally asked Jimenez if he'd ever heard Caroline discuss the name Albatross or any of the other people on the list. Jimenez said he couldn't recall for certain but didn't think so. Tally thanked Jimenez for his time. He seemed on the up-and-up.

The second number was out of service. Serrano checked the phone company's records. The number had once belonged to a psychic / tarot reader named Diane Loderbaum. Serrano found Loderbaum's now-defunct website, featuring a banner that read: "Your Future Is in the Cards."

Based on the enormity of outgoing calls to that number, it seemed that Caroline Drummond had a regular Tuesday-night call with Ms. Loderbaum. Every call lasted between fifty-eight and sixty-two minutes, and it had been consistent for the better part of three years. Tally estimated Caroline Drummond must have spent around $10,000 to $20,000 getting psychic advice from Diane Loderbaum.

They were able to track down Ms. Loderbaum, now working as a professional matchmaker in Saint Louis. She acknowledged regular communication with Ms. Drummond.

"Why did she call you so often?" Tally asked.

"Same reason anyone called me," she said. "She wanted to understand where her life was going. She seemed fairly unhappy, unsure of her direction, and thought I could help her untangle the threads of her life."

"Did you?" Serrano asked.

Loderbaum sighed. "To be frank, I got the feeling that Caroline Drummond was the kind of woman who liked to talk about doing the right thing, without actually doing it. Making the effort made her feel good. Absolved. Like she cared."

"How so?"

"Well, she kept talking about her guilt over stringing some young kid along. She was sleeping with him but didn't have any real feelings. But boy howdy, he fell for her harder than a ton of bricks."

"Does the name Sam Wickersham mean anything to you?" Tally said.

"She never used real names," Loderbaum said. "But she mentioned a man she was seeing, a Hispanic man, whom she saw a real future with. Then he moved away for work, and they broke up, and it seemed to hit her hard. After that, we didn't speak much. And then we stopped."

"So why did you get out of the psychic business?" Serrano asked.

Loderbaum laughed. "No room in today's marketplace for psychic phone lines. People get all that stuff for free now on the internet."

They thanked Ms. Loderbaum for her time.

The third number was for an Italian restaurant called Mutz & Friends. When Serrano reached the store, the proprietor, a man named Vincent Biancamano, told him that Caroline Drummond had ordered the same meal every Thursday for as long as he could remember: a *soppressata* and mozzarella sandwich with oil, vinegar, lettuce, tomato, roast peppers, and onions on an eight-inch Italian roll with a side salad.

Serrano asked Biancamano if he remembered Drummond ever coming into the shop with anybody. Biancamano said she always seemed like a bit of a loner, never came in with anyone, never seemed up for small talk, left the store like she was always in a hurry, but always tipped.

He did note that Drummond hadn't called in any orders in several months—they weren't listed on Seamless—and wanted to make sure she was OK. Serrano said she was, not to worry, but if he could remember anything out of the ordinary to let him know.

"I feel bad for Sam Wickersham if he ever kissed Caroline Drummond after she ate one of those oniony sandwiches," Serrano said.

"Reminds me of the time Lieutenant George's wife started wearing that perfume—what was it called?"

"Oh God, I remember that," Serrano said.

"He came in every day smelling like a lilac that had thrown up on a sugar cane. And I thought that Yves Saint Laurent he wears was bad. That couple needs to get their olfactory senses checked."

"I didn't want to shake his hand because I was worried I could contaminate crime scenes with whatever perfume molecules landed on me."

"On that note," Tally said, "it wouldn't kill you to wear a scent *occasionally*. Not saying you need to drench yourself in Hugo Boss, but smelling like something other than whatever clothes you picked up off your floor that morning wouldn't be so bad every once in a while."

"So you'll come to Sephora with me then?"

Tally laughed. "Only if I can invite Claire to witness this."

"Deal's off. On to the last number."

The area code was 917. And the calls were only incoming, no outgoing.

"A New York City number," Serrano said.

"And most likely a burner phone," Tally said. "Look. The calls are frequent for the year leading up to Wickersham's testimony, then cease completely once the proceedings finished."

Tally called the number. It didn't surprise them when the number came back no longer in service.

"We can get a warrant on this line," Serrano said. "Most burners these days have built-in GPS. If the caller made enough calls from a single location, it could provide a lead as to where they live or work."

Based on Wickersham's admission of fraud and perjury, the payments from Albatross, and his relationship with Caroline Drummond, Serrano had no doubt they had sufficient probable cause to get a warrant on the cell phone number.

"Judge Watson is probably up," Tally said. "Send him the affidavit."

Serrano called the judge, then sent over the warrant request. It was approved in less than two hours.

As soon as he had the warrant, Serrano submitted it to all the major burner cell phone manufacturers and suppliers. He got a call back half an hour later from a company called CodeTek. They confirmed the phone was one of theirs, a Samsung model using Verizon's network, and their distribution center had packed it in a shipment that had gone out to electronics and convenience stores in Manhattan. Serrano confirmed that the model in question had GPS built in.

Serrano then contacted the Data Forensics Unit of the NYPD and asked them for GPS tracking on the number for the one-year period in question. He hoped they would find enough similar data points to narrow down the location of the person who'd used it. And he was willing to bet that whoever had been using that phone had been coordinating with Caroline Drummond about Albatross.

While they waited for the records to come in, Serrano went upstairs to the Bunk to check on the Marin children. They were curled up next to each other, lying facedown, elbows touching. Eric was playing some sort of shoot-'em-up game on his phone, while Megan was flipping through a copy of *Vanity Fair*. They looked content enough. But the frequency with which Rachel's children spent time in the station upset Serrano. It had gotten to the point where they didn't even seem inconvenienced by it. Just another bed in a string of beds.

Serrano wondered what circumstances had forced them to get used to such consistent turmoil in their lives.

Then he went to check on Rachel.

She was lying on her back on one of the metal benches in the holding cell, staring at the ceiling. Her eyes were open. Her mouth was moving.

"Rachel, how are you—"

"Shh . . . ," she said. "I'm trying to figure out how many people have been in this cell."

Serrano laughed. "I'm not even sure I know the answer to that."

"Let's see," she said. "Currently, there are four occupants. In any given day, a day like today, I estimate between four and six guests. But that rises in the summer—people tend to have shorter fuses in hot weather—and around the holidays. People get depressed, drink more, take things out on loved ones or former loved ones. And in the winter, when days get shorter and it gets dark earlier, people start drinking earlier. Which leads to an increase in bar brawls and DWIs. So for the two weeks before and after Christmas and Thanksgiving, I'm estimating it goes up to between seven and nine. From Memorial Day to Labor Day, six to eight. With a spike on July Fourth. Morons who don't know how to properly light fireworks or drive speedboats. So in a calendar year, I'm estimating the number of guests in the Ashby PD holding cells to be one thousand, eight hundred and eighty-three."

Serrano stood there, dumbfounded.

"This police station itself was constructed in 1967. Certainly crime rates were higher back then—the civil rights era, Vietnam protests—and precincts weren't monitored nearly as closely as they are now. Can you imagine how quickly water fountains would have been desegregated if social media existed in the sixties to mobilize protests? Or how many cops would have been arrested, charged, and, let's be honest, executed? It's a well-known fact that a number of cops were actively involved in the Ku Klux Klan—"

"You were telling me how many people have been in this cell," Serrano said, losing his patience.

"Oh, right. One hundred and four thousand, three hundred sixty-eight people."

"I'll check with the lieutenant and get back to you," Serrano said. "And if you're right, you get a free sandwich."

"Please thank Lieutenant George for me," Rachel said. "He's been good to Eric and Megan."

"I will."

"I wonder how many of those people you personally put in here," Rachel said. "I bet I could estimate."

"Don't you have anything better to do with your time?" Serrano said.

"Not at the moment, no. Instead of a sandwich, how about the leniency of the court?"

Serrano shook his head. "The judge's bench is above my pay grade. You know, I was wondering. Whatever happened to that guy you were out with? You didn't seem all that upset when we showed up."

"Adam," Rachel said. "The next day he texted me an emoji of an eggplant and a doughnut, which I'm pretty sure means he wanted to have sex with me. Or have sex with a doughnut, maybe a threesome with an eggplant involved somehow. So I sent him an emoji of an eggplant and a knife to let him know that if he ever came near me, I'd chop his dick off. Then I blocked him."

"Reminder: never text emojis to Rachel Marin."

"Now if only you can educate the men of Ashby."

"I'll do my best," Serrano said.

"I spoke to my lawyer," Rachel said. "He thinks I'm going to get off without even a fine."

"Is that so?"

"When I went to the Velos offices, I had no idea that Sam Wickersham was part of an ongoing criminal investigation. That's the honest truth. So therefore I couldn't have knowingly impeded one."

Serrano mulled it over. Then he shrugged. "I'm not a judge."

"No. That's above your pay grade," she said with a wicked grin. Then it dissipated. "How are Eric and Megan?"

"They're fine. Eric is gaming. Megan is reading."

"Just another day."

"They seem a little too comfortable. Like they're used to having their lives turned upside down."

Rachel looked away.

"Tell me what happened to you," he said.

"Thanks for taking care of them," she said, ignoring the comment. "Hopefully I'll be out of here tomorrow."

"But for how long?" Rachel said nothing. Serrano nodded. "Think about what I said to you the other night."

Then he left and went back to his partner.

"How's the Marin family doing?" Tally said.

"Fine. Which is bizarre in and of itself."

"Well, guess who I just got a call back from. Man named Aleksy Bacik. He's a senior Realtor with Irongate Properties. He sold Rachel Marin her house."

"No shit. What did Mr. Bacik say?"

"Well, he wouldn't give me her application package without a warrant," Tally said. "And since the charge we're holding Rachel Marin on is unrelated to her financial situation, I don't think a judge would grant us one."

"It was worth a shot."

*"But,"* Tally said, "he seemed a little spooked that he was getting a call from the police to begin with regarding Rachel Marin. So he gave me the name of the lawyer she used to negotiate the contract. Bacik said this guy could give us more information. He *strenuously* implied that he wanted no part of anything Marin related. Then he hung up."

"Who's the lawyer?"

"His name is James R. Franklin, of Franklin and Rosato, a law firm in Darien, Connecticut. They specialize in personal injury, medical malpractice, and sexual assault. And they're not ambulance chasers. These guys are heavy hitters. Franklin is a civil litigation attorney who's settled suits in the millions."

Serrano said, "Why the hell would a litigation attorney in Darien, Connecticut, be involved in a real estate transaction in Ashby, Illinois?"

# CHAPTER 31

Rachel had been right. Because her lawyer could legitimately argue that she had no knowledge of Sam Wickersham's involvement in an ongoing police investigation, the charge of interfering with a criminal investigation didn't stick. She was released in the morning having paid no fine, with an extra crick in her back from the metal bench in the holding cell, while having been up all night worrying about her children.

She thought about everything Serrano had said. Rachel was at war with herself. Everything she did to try to expose Constance Wright's killer pushed her children further away. Further away from her. Further away from a normal life. Their grasp on normalcy was already a thread, already tenuous. Now it seemed like Rachel was standing over that thread with a chainsaw, revving it with glee.

She drove the kids to school. Megan sat in the back, reading a *Vanity Fair*. Eric stared out the window. Silent.

"Where did you get that magazine?" Rachel asked, peering at Megan in the rearview mirror.

"From the Bunk," she replied.

"The Bunk?"

"It's where we slept. Mr. Serrano said we could play with anything in there."

"Did he say you could take that?"

"No," she said, concerned. "Are you going to tell him?"

Rachel smiled. "No. But if you get to any bad words, you have to promise me you'll put it down."

"OK. Hey, Mom?"

"Yes, hon?"

"What's . . . lin-ger-ee?"

*"Lingerie,"* Rachel said. "Put it down now. That's the last copy of *Vanity Fair* you get to read until you go to college."

"That's fine. Everyone in this magazine is in their underwear. It's weird."

Rachel laughed. Then looked at Eric. He didn't move. Said nothing.

"Eric, are you OK?"

He didn't reply.

"Eric?"

Nothing.

"Are you ignoring me?"

Still nothing.

"Please, talk to me, hon."

Silence.

She took a deep breath and said, "Sean!"

Eric's head sprang up. His eyes were wide. Megan's mouth fell open.

"You told me we needed to forget about those names," he said quietly.

"I needed to do something to get your attention," she said. "Answer me, please. *Are you OK?*"

"Why do you care?" he said. "We had to sleep in a crappy bed in a police station because you got arrested. And just a few days ago, we had to stay in a hotel after someone broke into our home. People with *guns* came to Megan's *school.*"

"Am I still Megan?" her daughter asked. "Or am I Chloe again?"

Rachel felt her heart ascend into her throat. Tears welled up, but she fought them back.

"You are Megan, and you are Eric," she said. "But you are my children first and foremost."

"You told us these names were for our own protection," Eric said. "So we'd be safe. You made us *swear* not to use the old ones ever again. That we could be in trouble if we did."

"You're right. I said that."

"How are we safe now? How do you protect us by getting arrested?"

The dam burst. Rachel began to weep.

"Mommy?" Megan said. She, too, began to cry. "Mommy, are you OK?"

Rachel pulled the car into a strip mall. She put her hand to her forehead and squeezed her eyes shut. How had it come to this?

"Mommy, please stop crying," Megan said.

"I'm sorry," Rachel said. She got out of the car and went around to the back seat. She opened the door and motioned Megan to move over. She did. Then Rachel got into the car, leaned over, and threw her arms around both her children.

It was uncomfortable and awkward, and Eric was *not* the kind of son who appreciated sudden hugs from his mother, but within seconds the three of them were embracing and sobbing.

"I love you both with all my heart, with everything I am," Rachel said. "Something in me changed after your father died."

"I know it did," Eric said. "That's why when I saw the basement, for the first time it actually kind of made sense."

"What do you mean?" Rachel said.

"Where you go every night. You don't think we know you go down there every night, but we do."

Rachel looked at Megan. "You knew too?"

Megan nodded. "Sadie Scout has a supercool basement. Like ours."

This caught Rachel by surprise. "You're both much more clever than I gave you credit for."

"Come on, Mom," Eric said. "I mean you could crush soda cans with your biceps. You could kick my gym teacher's ass. And he played football."

Rachel laughed and wiped her eyes. "Don't use the a-word in front of Megan."

"What a-word?" Megan said. "Asses?"

Rachel was laughing too hard to be angry. When the laughter subsided, she said, "I couldn't do anything to save your father. And it eats at me every day of my life. So when that woman, Constance Wright, died, it felt like nobody did anything to save her either. I thought I needed to do something, even if it was too late to save her."

"You're, like, a superhero," Megan said. "Trying to bring the bad guys to justice."

"I'm nothing like a superhero," Rachel said. "Superheroes don't let their children sleep in police stations."

"It wasn't that bad," Megan said. "I got to read about fishing lures. And this nice sir-gant named Inez talked to us. But the room smelled like feet."

"Sergeant," Rachel corrected. "Not sir-gant."

"I don't want you to go to jail again," Megan said, those gorgeous blue eyes melting Rachel's heart. They had their father's eyes. His sense of humor too. He lived on through them, and it both pained Rachel and warmed her heart, because with every blink she was reminded of what she had—and what she'd lost.

"I'm not going back to jail, sweetheart," Rachel said.

"Maybe not today," Eric said. "But what about tomorrow?"

"I don't plan on going tomorrow either," Rachel said. "But I understand what you're saying. I promise you both, right now, that you will *always* come first."

Eric nodded. She knew he believed her, but he had grown accustomed to the world breaking promises.

Rachel gave Megan a kiss and squeezed Eric's hand and went back to the front seat. She started the car and eased back onto the freeway. As she neared Megan's school, her cell phone chirped from her purse. She ignored it for the time being. Kids first.

She got out of the car, gave Megan a big hug, and watched her daughter meet up with two other girls and jog inside, three small humans in cute puffy coats.

"You're next," Rachel said. "Sure you won't be embarrassed having your mom drop you off at school?"

"Actually," Eric said, "would you mind dropping me a couple blocks away so I can walk there without anyone seeing you?"

Rachel opened her mouth to protest, but Eric added, "Just kidding."

"You're a little jerk," she said lovingly. He smiled, that easy, lazy grin. His father's grin.

Rachel's phone beeped again. When she stopped at a red light, she took her phone from her purse and checked the call log.

When she saw the caller ID, her heart began to hammer in her chest.

*Oh no,* she thought. *Oh God.*

Jim Franklin had called. Twice. He had not left a message. Jim Franklin had not called Rachel in over two years, and not since she had closed on the house.

There was only one reason why Jim Franklin would call her.

Something was very, very wrong.

# CHAPTER 32

***Three Years Ago***

She stood on the northwest corner of East Main Street and Harwinton Avenue in Torrington wearing a long black raincoat.

It was not raining.

A gray backpack, filled to capacity, weighed on her shoulders. It would leave a mark the next day. The coat covered her from her neck to her ankles, and that was necessary.

Soon they would be leaving Torrington, and the East Coast, for good. They would start over. Begin their new lives. Jim Franklin had already set them up with a "No Questions Asked" broker in some nowhere midwestern city called Ashby. But before that, she had unfinished business with one Stanford Royce.

She had spent the last three months learning everything she could about Royce. Since the charges against him were dropped, he had been a model citizen. He knew the cops were looking for an excuse to either put him in irons or the hospital. So for once in his miserable life, Stanford Royce was obeying the law. At least as far as Rachel could tell.

He had shaved the goatee and dyed his black hair a brownish red, the color of cedar mulch. Stanford Royce could try to change his appearance. But Rachel knew his eyes. He could never change what lay behind those.

Royce had taken a job working as a car service and limousine dispatcher for a company called Door2Door, arriving at their office every morning at 8:00 a.m. sharp and getting out the door at precisely 4:00 p.m., when his shift ended. Most days after work he went to happy hour at a pub called Herlihy's two blocks south of the Door2Door offices. He always ordered between three and five pints of Yuengling and alternated between a plate of nachos or a cheddar burger with sweet potato fries.

He never got drunk, never picked a fight, and never talked to anyone except when ordering another round. Royce seemed desperate for companionship. When an unaccompanied woman approached the bar, he would eye her, *pleading* with her to start a conversation. If a woman took the stool next to him, he would stare into his drink. It amazed Rachel how confident he'd been assaulting her and Evie and how lost he was when trying to make actual human contact.

It was easy for her to observe him. The bar had floor-to-ceiling windows, and it was never crowded to the point where Royce got lost in the bustle.

After drinking his fill, Royce went home to a small bungalow off Litchfield Turnpike with a dirty-white frame and dark-red roof that was on the verge of collapse. The one-bedroom house had a small covered porch and dirt-smeared windows. An old Buick gathered rust in a dirt driveway. Royce never opened his window shades. Other than the mailman and gas meter reader, Rachel never saw a single person visit Royce.

That would change tonight.

Her neighbor, a nice older widow named Claudette, was watching Sean and Chloe. Rachel had told Claudette she might be home late. Order in a pizza, let them watch some extra TV, anything to keep them happy and occupied. Claudette just seemed happy to be around children. She'd told Rachel to take her time. Probably assumed she was going out on a date.

Rachel watched Stanford Royce drain the last of his fourth beer. He raised his hand, like he was about to order a fifth, and Rachel cursed under her breath. Each beer took Royce approximately twenty-four minutes to finish. Another beer meant another half hour wandering the street, trying not to look suspicious.

But rather than ask for another beer, Royce clearly mouthed the word *check*.

Now came the hard part.

Royce paid his tab in cash and left the bar. When he stepped outside, he lit a cigarette with a matchbook and walked to the corner to wait for the M-94 bus. At this point, keeping an eye on Royce wasn't quite as necessary. He never went anywhere but home after the bar.

After he got on the bus, Rachel walked to the same corner and waited. Twenty minutes later, another M-94 bus arrived. She got on and took a seat.

Soon the downtown district full of bars, restaurants, and office buildings fell away to low-slung, poorly made houses surrounded by weed-infested lawns and cars with rusted-out hubcap wheels. She got off the bus, still wearing the raincoat, and walked toward 2926 Willow Tree Lane.

As if to justify her own attire, a sprinkle of rain had begun to fall. A pang of fear rose in Rachel's chest. She was wearing a synthetic blonde wig that covered her own brown hair but had not considered whether raindrops on synthetic material would look realistic. Would he get suspicious that her hair wasn't frizzy due to the inclement weather? She shook the thought from her mind. It was too late, but now she was wishing she'd gone the extra mile and bought a wig made from human hair.

When she arrived at the house on Willow Tree Lane, Rachel quickly surveyed the area. The homes had been built close together, no more than thirty feet between neighbors. This meant silence would be imperative. Thankfully Royce kept his windows drawn. She could see light behind the shades. He was home, as expected.

She took her backpack off, laid it on the sidewalk, opened it, and took out a pair of plastic shoe covers. She had purposefully worn flats three sizes too large, stuffed with pantyhose to make them snug enough to walk in. The shoe coverings would prevent tracks, and even if she miscalculated, the larger size would still throw off forensics.

Prior to slipping the plastic covers on, she placed a perfectly cut strip of cardboard underneath the shoe sole to avoid leaving any markings. Then she secured the plastic with masking tape.

The rain was beginning to fall steadier, each droplet loud as a shotgun blast to Rachel. She'd have to be careful. She checked her wig, then took a large plastic bag from the backpack and stuffed the raincoat inside. Underneath the jacket she had been wearing a too-tight leather jacket, which she unzipped down to her breastbone. The top of a Lily of France leopard-print bra was visible beneath the jacket, the push-up bra doing wonders. It was almost too bad she'd have to incinerate it.

She took out a small makeup mirror and applied a large amount of blush and purple eye shadow and stuck on false eyelashes. Then she slid in blue-colored contact lenses. They irritated her eyes slightly, so she put a few drops of Systane Ultra in each eye then dabbed them with a tissue. She put two sticks of Carefree mint gum in her mouth and chewed until her breath was good and minty.

She looked at herself in the mirror. She was unrecognizable.

Everything else went into the same plastic bag as the raincoat. Before zipping the backpack up, she placed a small device into her pocket.

It was time.

Rachel walked quickly across the street. The weather worked to her advantage; none of Royce's neighbors were outside. Her heart jackhammered as she climbed the three wood steps to his front door. They creaked, and she paused. A deep breath calmed her nerves.

Then she rang the doorbell.

Rachel took two steps back. She wanted Royce to see her in full. Cleavage, tight jacket, runny makeup, the works.

She waited. Nothing happened. *Where was he?*

She rang the doorbell again and unzipped her jacket just a little bit more.

Still nothing.

She couldn't panic. But she could look desperate. It could even work to her advantage.

"Hello?" Rachel said, rapping on the door. She spoke in a voice an octave higher than her own and added a slight southern accent. "Sorry to bother you, sir, but I need to use your phone somethin' bad. It's an emergency."

A crusty voice came from inside.

"So what the hell do you want from me?"

It was Royce. Rachel thought fast.

"Sorry to bother you, Mister. I was seeing a man friend down the street, and, well, he don't treat me too good. Pulled my hair and pushed me and kicked me out the house. My cell phone is still at his place, so I can't get it cuz I don't know what he'd do to me. Why do men have to be so mean? Are you mean, Mister?"

There was a pause, and then Royce replied, "I'm not mean."

"Oh thank God," Rachel said. And she meant it. She had him.

Rachel heard footsteps. She placed her hand in her pocket. The eyehole went dark. Rachel pushed her bust forward, pouted her lip.

She heard the door being unlocked. There were several locks. Royce was cautious. When you were as despised as Stanford Royce, you had to be.

The door opened with a gentle creak, revealing the apprehensive man inside. Royce's eyes went wide when he saw Rachel's body in full. She could see his tongue flick around inside his mouth.

"I promise I'll be quick," Rachel said. "Just need to call a cab."

Royce nodded. Then he looked down at her feet.

"Why you wearing bags on your—"

Before he could finish the sentence, Rachel jabbed the Taser into his sternum.

Royce's teeth chattered, and he made a hacking sound as he toppled backward onto the dirty green area rug inside his house. Rachel quickly stepped inside and closed the door behind her. She dropped the backpack on the floor and got out a roll of heavy-duty electrical tape. She had four more rolls just in case. She tore off a nine-inch strip of tape, which she used to cover Royce's mouth. Then she pulled a strip loose and bent down over him. She picked up his right hand, wound the tape around it, and then went for his left to secure them together.

She didn't see the knife.

He must have had it tucked into his jeans. Her first thought was *That was stupid of me not to check for a weapon.* Her second was *That stings.*

Instinctively, Rachel's hand went to her chest. There was a clean slice through her coat. She felt inside the jacket; her fingers came away coated with red.

Adrenaline began to course through her. He'd cut her. Deep.

Before she tended to herself, she needed to make sure he was no longer a threat. As Royce tried to sit up, Rachel jolted him again with the Taser. The knife fell from his grasp, and she picked it up. As he lay twitching, she wound the electrical tape around both his wrists, then did the same with his ankles. She wound several strips between his ankles and wrists, creating makeshift prison manacles.

She took another large plastic bag from the backpack and took off her jacket, leaving just a tank top and the bra. Blood was soaking through her top. She pulled off her tank top. The knife had opened a large red gash just below her rib cage. Blood streamed from it. Rachel wound the tape around her midsection several times, tightly, praying the wound would clot. It would require stitches.

*Shit. How could she be so stupid?*

She tossed her bloody garments into the plastic bag.

Royce was staring at her. His eyes were wide open, terrified. Rachel removed the wig from her head and placed it into the bag as well. He was trying to scream. The Tiger Eye bracelet clinked against the floor as he shivered.

"I don't know if you remember me," she said.

Royce shook his head from side to side.

"It doesn't matter."

Rachel looked down at the man whimpering at her feet. When she had begun preparing for this task, she'd worried that when it got to this point, she might hesitate. That she would be unable to go through with it. But at that moment, she felt no indecision.

"Now, Mr. Royce, I have a lot of work to do. You have about two minutes to make peace with whatever you've done in your life."

She could see the glimmer from the steel reflected in Royce's bulging eyes as she brought the blade to his chest.

# CHAPTER 33

Louis Magursky refused to wear suits to the office. He had started working on construction sites when he was just fourteen, hauling copper piping and pushing wheelbarrows full of concrete mix onto jobs alongside men eighty pounds heavier than him with twenty more years' experience. Louis had never considered himself a "suit," one of those fat cats who sat in trailers puffing on cigars while everyone else did the grunt work. No, Louis was one of the boys.

So even when he took out a $28,000 loan against his row house in the Bronx to start Magursky Construction thirty years ago, which meant spending more time in boardrooms than on construction hoists, Louis had still shown up in loose stonewashed jeans and a flannel shirt, usually red, over a brand-new undershirt. Over the years, that outfit became his calling card. He came to loathe fancy black-tie dinners where he had to squeeze his stout form into a tuxedo, his wife constantly checking his clean white shirt to make sure it hadn't been sullied by droplets of red wine and cocktail sauce.

Louis Magursky was a short, stocky man, five feet six inches tall and nearly the same width. His shoulders and arms had grown thick and strong due to years of hauling concrete. He had smooth, shiny cheeks and short black hair that was just beginning to recede. Louis walked into every room like he owned the building. And Louis Magursky took every slight personally, swore to carry grudges to the grave, which is why few people crossed him. He had the money and the means to make people's lives very, very difficult.

Today, Magursky Construction was worth upward of $50 million. It was his only child. He'd done things to both build and maintain his business and his fortune that he wasn't necessarily proud of, but he had long ago learned to live without regret. And when you looked all around the island of Manhattan, enough buildings bore Magursky exoskeletons that he could legitimately say his fingerprints were visible all over one of the greatest cities in the world. Over the last few years he'd spread those fingers into the Midwest. The Albertson Bridge in Ashby and now contracts for three commercial buildings in Chicago. That $50 million value would double in the next five years.

So when Louis Magursky walked into his office, adorned with plaques and honors and photos of him with mayors and governors, and saw a man in a suit—a suit!—sitting behind *his* desk in *his* chair, he had to refrain from ripping the man's spine out through his back. To add insult, the man had his elbows—his *elbows!*—on Louis's desk. The man looked calm. He was tall, trim, with neatly parted blond hair. And he didn't appear to understand—or care about—the consequences of sitting in Louis's chair.

Louis approached the desk with murder in his eyes. But then the man took his elbows off the desk and removed a leather-bound case from his suit jacket pocket. He flipped it open to reveal a gold badge with a bald eagle at the center of a five-pointed star.

It bore three words that Louis could read from across the room.

US Marshal.

"Bet you thought you were a smart guy, using those burner cell phones to talk to Sam Wickersham and Caroline Drummond," he said. "Unfortunately you weren't smart enough to buy them at different stores. Thankfully A-Plus Electronics around the corner uses digital surveillance and keeps their files. Just like Mayor Alan Caldwell, in Ashby. You knew him back when he was deputy mayor under Constance Wright. We have your email and phone records, and soon we'll have

Caldwell's too. No, you're not a smart guy, Louis. Or should I call you Albatross?"

Louis didn't need to hear another word.

He turned and bolted out the door. For a short man with short legs carrying a fair amount of both fat and muscle, Louis could move. He rounded the hallway corner and sped into the reception area. He pulled out his cell phone. His lawyer kept Louis a "Go" bag, which he could have delivered anywhere in the five boroughs in twenty minutes. Louis could disappear overnight and start over with half a million in cash and a passport with a new name. He'd been dreading this day for a long time, but he was prepared.

Louis bounded down the stairs, not stopping for a moment to catch his breath, taking three steps at a time. Sweat was pouring down his body. He could smell his own wretched odor.

Then Louis burst through the stairwell door and into the lobby atrium. He could see the sun shining outside. He would be a ghost in seconds.

He didn't notice the older man with gray hair and a handlebar moustache leaning against the wall, reading a copy of *Fortune.* As Louis ran past, the man stepped out, grabbed Louis by his stocky arm, and used his own momentum to fling him onto the marble floor. Before Louis could even comprehend what was happening, his thick wrists had been pulled behind him and handcuffs clicked into place. Louis yelped as the metal bit into his skin.

"Louis Magursky," the man said. He had a deep voice with a southern accent. "You're under arrest for data fraud, cellular fraud, conspiracy to commit perjury, bribery, and being a general shitheel."

Magursky's cheek was pressed against the floor. He managed to spit out, "Do you know who I am? I'm gonna have your badge, you southern-fried asshole."

Then he heard a *ding*, and the elevator door opened. Out stepped the blond marshal from his office.

"Tortoise and the hare, my friend," the marshal said. "It's time for you to answer for Constance Wright."

◆◆◆

Nicholas Drummond did not try to run. When he saw the brown Crown Victoria pull up outside his home, flanked by three other police cars, he stood up and smoothed out his shirt and regretted not having had more for lunch.

He had always loved the bay windows in the foyer, how he could see the whole neighborhood splayed out in front of him like a private movie theater. Even right now, as the police lights swirled and reflected off the downy snow, there was something poetic about it. Truthfully, he was surprised it had taken this long. But as soon as Serrano and Tally had arrived at their home that day with that odd Marin woman, he'd known it was only a matter of time.

Isabelle came running downstairs in a panic. She was wearing a tight white Rag & Bone T-shirt and Moussy distressed jeans, gold bracelets jangling on her wrists. She always wore good jewelry and the best labels at home. That was one thing about Isabelle: she never phoned things in. When they had begun seeing each other—Nicholas couldn't really call it dating, more like monogamous screwing—Isabelle had worn gorgeous outfits every time they'd met up. Sometimes she hid them under bulky, shapeless coats so as to not turn heads. It was imperative they saw each other in secret. Nicholas had too much to lose—namely close to a million dollars if Constance could prove he had been getting laid on the side before they legally separated.

"Getting laid" was such a crass term, though. To Nicholas, that was what it was at first. Once the marriage went sour, he and Constance stopped having sex. And at his age, simply giving up intimacy was not an option. He needed a release. He'd met Isabelle at one of Constance's myriad fund-raisers. At first, Nicholas enjoyed the galas. It was a chance to dress up, mingle with Ashby's elite, be something he never thought he would be: a star.

But he wasn't really a star. He was the arm candy to a star. A garnish. Sprinkles on ice cream. It might add a little flavor, but nobody would *really* notice if it wasn't there.

Isabelle was young. Gorgeous. Wealthy. She had no political aspirations. Her only baggage was her idiot brother, Chris. Chrissy, she called him. Nicholas felt that once you could buy alcohol legally, you had to stop answering to the name Chrissy.

They ran into each other again at a cheese shop. And Nicholas knew his cheeses. He helped her pick out a sumptuous imported Camembert and recommended a tasty Napa red to pair with it. She thanked him for saving her dinner party and invited him to a future soiree. He declined, said it was hard for Constance to get out these days with reelection coming up.

"Who invited Constance?" she replied with a mischievous smile. They slept together three days later on her luxurious Egyptian cotton sheets.

He knew he would marry her after a month.

Getting free from Constance was another matter. He told Caroline about it; they shared everything. Caroline hated Constance, felt she was always upstaging Nicholas. So when Caroline told Nicholas that there might just be a way to get him out of the marriage *with* hefty spousal support, Nicholas was all ears. Isabelle had money, but this would be *his* money. All he had to do was be willing to let Constance burn.

It didn't sit particularly well with him. Caroline knew a guy who knew a construction guy in New York who would spearhead the effort. Some guy named Louis with an eastern European last name who'd lost millions when the Wright family business had gone belly up.

Nicholas Drummond knew Constance would fall. He didn't anticipate how hard.

He had a hard time stomaching the Sam Wickersham testimony, hearing this young man lie about screwing his wife when the truth was

Nicholas was the one screwing around. But Isabelle watched it with glee. She bought half a dozen copies of the *Ashby Bulletin* with the forty-eight-point-font headline "Mayor Cradle Robber."

Caroline told him to stop seeing Isabelle while the trial was ongoing. Nothing made a man look more unsympathetic than screwing a gorgeous woman fifteen years younger than his ex while simultaneously trying to empty her bank account. Caroline didn't know how long he and Isabelle had been sleeping together. That was for the best. She might not have gone along with it if she'd known.

When the divorce was finalized, Nicholas Drummond breathed a sigh of relief. Not because he was finally a free man. Well, not only that. But he'd grown weary of seeing Constance dragged through the mud every day. He'd wanted to be rid of her, yes. But the marriage hadn't been *all* bad.

When she pulled a J. D. Salinger and became a semirecluse, Nicholas felt it was for the best. Not for her necessarily, but for him. She could live however she wanted, and he could start his life fresh with Isabelle. If only he'd known about her fertility issues. She was in her twenties with the ovaries of a woman in her forties. *Raisins,* she'd called them. *They're shriveled like raisins.*

Not that he would have changed his mind about marrying her. Well, *probably* wouldn't have changed his mind.

And then life went on. But somewhere in the back of his mind, Nicholas knew there would be a reckoning. Somebody would find out. Maybe Constance. She called him right before her death. He ignored her calls but always had a feeling Christopher was listening to his voice mails before he could delete them.

He shared some of the blame for Constance's death. No, he didn't throw her from the bridge and hadn't even seen Constance in months. But he helped destroy her career and kill her spirit. And if those hadn't died, she would still be alive today. He knew it.

So when Detectives Serrano and Tally marched up to the front door, boots crunching on the snow-covered gravel, he didn't plan to run or fight or resist. He would tell them everything.

Except who murdered his ex-wife. That one small detail he did not know.

"Nicholas!" Isabelle yelled. "Baby? What's going on?"

Her eyes were wide, panicky. He was calm, which probably upset her even more. She could enter a room as graceful as a swan, then turn into a wolf in a moment's notice. In the bedroom, it was the biggest turn-on ever. She could go from caressing his back with fingernails like feathers to digging furrows in his flesh in a heartbeat.

"I'm going to prison," he said. Like he was going to the store for milk.

"Like *hell* you are," Isabelle replied.

He took her hand in his, caressed her thumb. "You knew this day would come eventually," he said.

*"Like hell I did,"* she said, angrily ripping her hand away from his. "I'm calling Chester Barnes. He'll meet you at the police station. Don't say a *goddamn word* until he gets there."

Nicholas nodded, though he wasn't sure he'd follow through. Barnes was the Robles family's longtime lawyer. He'd stuck around even after Isabelle's parents died because, well, they still had gobs of money, and he had a hefty retainer. If not for Barnes, Chris Robles might still be in prison. Of course if that were the case, ironically he might also still be alive.

The doorbell rang.

"Don't answer it," Isabelle pleaded. The anger had vanished, replaced by fear. "I can't lose my brother *and* you."

Nicholas took her face in his palms and kissed her passionately. Her fingers burrowed into the small of his back. They reminded him of the bolts of a prison cell door locking into place. It made him shiver.

"You'll be fine," he said. He tried to pull away, but her nails were dug in. Deep. Gently, he reached around and removed her hands. "You're the strongest woman I've ever met."

Then he walked toward the door. Toward the inevitable.

"No I'm not," he heard Isabelle say. Nicholas opened the front door. The detectives stood there placidly, wearing long overcoats and thick gloves. Chilly air blew in from the outside, but Drummond didn't shiver.

"You know why we're here," Tally said.

"Nicholas K. Drummond," Serrano said. "You are under arrest for criminal conspiracy to commit fraud, perjury, accomplice to data and cell phone fraud, and giving false statements to the police."

Tally held up a piece of paper. "We have a warrant to search your property. Any and all items removed will be cataloged and returned to you upon completion of our investigation. Mrs. Drummond, if you'll come with me, please."

Serrano read Drummond his Miranda rights, and then they handcuffed him and led him to the car as half a dozen officers marched into their house. Halfway to the car, Nicholas realized he'd forgotten his jacket. Too late now.

As Tally held his head and slid him into the back seat of the Crown Victoria, one more realization dawned on Nicholas Drummond.

They hadn't charged him with anything related to Constance's murder.

*Maybe they caught the guy,* he thought as the door slammed shut.

# CHAPTER 34

After Nicholas Drummond had been booked and processed, Serrano and Tally prepped for their briefing with Lieutenant George. It had been a good day.

Drummond was in custody. US Marshals had picked up Louis Magursky in Manhattan, where he would be arraigned. Andy Burke from the Marshals service told Serrano that Magursky had tried to run, bounding out of his office and into the lobby looking like Willem Dafoe running from the Vietcong in *Platoon*. They were more than happy to tack on resisting arrest to Magursky's litany of charges.

Sam Wickersham was still hospitalized. He had been read his rights as an IV bag dripped antibiotics into his veins. The officer said Wickersham had cried and, still unable to speak due to his neck wound, written on a pad of paper, *Is Caroline OK?*

Italian authorities and Interpol had been alerted to a warrant out for the arrest of Caroline Drummond. Phone records from Magursky Construction showed dozens of calls to and from Ashby Mayor Alan Caldwell, all prior to Constance Wright's resignation. When the Wright family had gone under, Magursky had been left millions in the hole. Emails showed Wright had rebuffed Magursky's bid to restore the Albertson Bridge, a contract worth millions that would also firmly establish Magursky Construction in the Midwest. So Magursky killed two birds with one stone. He ruined Constance and got Deputy Mayor Alan Caldwell to approve the Albertson contract. Magursky made millions and got revenge on the Wright family in one fell swoop. Thankfully he had eager participants in the Drummond siblings and a lovesick puppy in Sam Wickersham—all willing to pick Constance apart with him.

It was a massive multistate conspiracy whose outcome ruined Constance Wright's life. And it had worked, nearly to perfection. But as Serrano and Tally entered Lieutenant George's office, Serrano couldn't shake the one piece of the puzzle still unresolved.

Constance Wright's murder itself.

They had enough on Drummond, Wickersham, and Magursky to relocate them all to cozy eight-by-ten concrete studios in Pickneyville. But they didn't have enough to link any of them to her actual murder. Which was why, despite the day's victories, Serrano felt apprehensive entering Daryl George's office.

The lieutenant's office was immaculate: shiny mahogany desk, papers and pens all arranged in their proper holders. The walls were covered with commendations and citations, the frames and glass sparkling clean. A photo of George's pretty wife, Tabitha, and their daughter, Mia, faced outward, ensuring visitors would see that Lieutenant George was a dedicated family man. There were rumors in the department that Lieutenant George was thinking about making a run for city council. If he did decide to run, Daryl George would be a shoo-in. Hell, given that Mayor Caldwell would likely be forced to resign for awarding Louis Magursky the construction contracts Constance Wright had denied him, Lieutenant George could be in line for mayor.

Daryl George sat behind his desk sipping a cup of organic black coffee. Next to it was a thermos containing something green that smelled like seaweed and sadness. It made Serrano crave a cheeseburger.

Serrano and Tally sat down. George downed the rest of the coffee and folded his hands. He didn't touch the green gunk. Serrano was thankful for that. Some of Lieutenant George's health concoctions reeked like Satan's armpits.

The lieutenant was in a good mood.

"Congrats, Detectives," he said. "This was really fine work."

"Thank you, sir," Tally said.

"Sir," Serrano said. "Wickersham refused a lawyer. Said he wants to plead guilty to all charges. Now, we've already heard from Chester Barnes. He'll be representing Nicholas Drummond. My guess is Barnes will dig his claws into Wickersham, too, because if the kid sings, he incriminates both Nicholas and Caroline."

"And Isabelle won't have that," Tally said. "She'll spend every dime she has to poke holes in this case."

"I've dealt with Barnes," George said. "He's a television hound. He'll be on the news every night trashing our case. But he's a mediocre trial attorney. Once this case gets past the court of public opinion, it's all about how airtight the evidence is. So tell me, Detectives, how airtight is it?"

"Pretty airtight, sir," Tally said. "We have Wickersham's uncoerced confession. We have phone records for Wickersham and both Drummonds, the burner cell data and GPS coordinates from the phones Magursky used, plus surveillance footage from the electronics store where they were purchased. We have a subpoena for Magursky's bank records, personal *and* business, and we expect to find $480,000 in transfers to Albatross LLC, which then paid off Wickersham. Plus we have the Albatross leasing documents from J&J Accounting, signed by Caroline Drummond."

"And where is Ms. Drummond at this time?"

"We don't know for certain," Tally said. "J&J says she's somewhere in Italy, but they can't confirm. She's not responding to calls, emails, or texts. She took a, quote, unquote, 'sabbatical' right before this exploded. We've contacted Interpol, but it's possible she was able to procure fake identification before she came onto their radar."

"You don't think her sabbatical timing is a coincidence, am I right?" George said.

"Not a chance," Serrano replied. "But the timing is strange. According to J&J, she left for the sabbatical a *month* before this investigation even started."

"Is it possible it was a legitimate sabbatical, and she just decided to stay once everything blew up?" George said.

"Unlikely," Tally replied. "Three weeks before Constance Wright's death, Caroline called both Sam Wickersham and Louis Magursky. Phone records confirm she hadn't had any contact with either Wickersham or Magursky in two years. Caroline Drummond's 'vacation' came right on the heels of those calls."

"But therein lies the major loose end," Serrano said. "Right now we don't have enough to pin Wright's actual murder on any of these people. The fraud and conspiracy, yes. But that's it right now."

George sat back, trying to mask the disappointment on his face.

"You said Wickersham cracked," George said. "And these people aren't the Mafia. There's no omertà. Once they know what kind of prison terms they're looking at, they'll be tripping over each other to cut a deal."

"That may be so," Serrano said, "but right now we haven't charged anybody with homicide. Chester Barnes knows this. Which means he knows we don't have enough on Drummond and likely not enough on Magursky or Wickersham. And even though she's likely guilty of half a dozen various felonies, Caroline Drummond was out of the country when Constance Wright was killed."

"These jokers all know that they're on the hook for conspiracy to commit murder charges—or at the very least accessory after the fact," George said. "If we haven't charged them on those counts yet, Chester Barnes might convince them to keep their mouths shut to try and prevent murder charges. So it's on you two to make this stick."

"How so?" Serrano said.

"Wright's killer came from the Drummond, Wickersham, or Magursky camps. Not to mention Christopher Robles trying to kill that Marin woman, and then his degenerate friends tried to finish the job. My take? Constance Wright got wind of the conspiracy to ruin her. That's why she called Drummond and Wickersham, to let them know she was onto them and was going to go after the money. Which gives Wickersham and *both* Nicholas Drummond and his wife motive to shut her up."

Tally nodded, but it was clear she wasn't sold.

"Here's one consideration," George said. "The Marin woman. Strikes me as a little more than a coincidence that she's been at the center of so many of these incidents. Maybe she's involved. Maybe not. But something tells me it's a little more than criminal rubbernecking."

"I've considered that, sir," Tally said. Serrano shot Tally a look.

"Chester Barnes will be talking to District Attorney Katz imminently, if he hasn't already. If we can't charge Drummond or one of the others with Wright's death before Barnes cuts a deal, we're going to eat shit from the media for letting the killer slide. I see a circus of dirtbags in our jail for ruining Constance Wright's life and Rachel Marin circling like a vulture on roadkill. Constance Wright was a *good* woman. It's our duty to make sure these scumbags pay the price for Constance; otherwise we're going to get eaten alive by the media. Am I clear?"

Serrano and Tally both nodded.

"Now go get them," he said. The detectives left.

"What do you think?" Serrano said once they were out of earshot of the lieutenant's office.

"Part of me thinks he's right. That if this group of assholes was willing to go so far as to bury Constance Wright that of course they'd go a step further. And if you work backward on the time frame, it matches up. Wright somehow gets wind of the conspiracy. Contacts her ex-husband and the patsy who helped set her up. They then send Caroline Drummond to Europe to get her away from everything, give her plausible deniability."

Serrano nodded.

"But . . . ," Tally said.

"But if Wright found out about the setup, why call Drummond and Wickersham *before* going to the cops? Why give them a chance to get to her?"

"She might not have had enough proof to come to us," Tally said.

"So she calls them just to scare them? Let them know she's onto them? Constance Wright was a smart woman. She knew how to play the game. She wouldn't have contacted either of them unless she had evidence of something."

"What if," Tally said, "and this is a big if. What if Drummond *was* the father?"

"Of Wright's unborn child? I don't see it."

"Hear me out," Tally said. "There's always a spark between exes. I *know* you and your ex went at it a few times after the divorce."

"What the hell are you talking about?"

"Please," Tally said. "You came into the station wearing her perfume every Wednesday morning for six months."

Serrano pled guilty through silence.

"And I *know* the first few months I was with Claire, I was terrified she'd go back to her ex-husband. So Wright and Drummond relapse. She gets knocked up. Isabelle finds out. Probably because Drummond told her, because he's a doofus."

"And they decide to kill her rather than let her give birth to Drummond's kid?"

"Think about how much money they took from her," Tally said. "If he has to pay child support to her after all that, it's insult to injury."

"Isabelle Drummond doesn't strike me as the kind of woman who would divorce her husband for cheating," Serrano said. "More like the kind of woman who would kill the girl he cheated on her with."

Tally nodded. "But still . . ."

"Why would Wright call Sam Wickersham too?"

"Yeah. Why call Sam Wickersham too?"

Serrano thought for a moment. "What if," he said, "we've all been looking at this wrong? You, me, the lieutenant. We've always assumed the killer was part of the Albatross crew, the people who ruined Wright's life. But what if they're totally separate crimes?"

"Pretty elaborate crimes," Tally said. "Trying to make her death look like a suicide—that means it was preplanned."

Serrano said. "And if not for Rachel Marin, it might just have gone down as a suicide."

"There you go with that Marin woman again," Tally said. "The lieutenant and I are on the same page about her. There's something not quite right."

"What exactly do you mean by that?"

"I don't trust her. She calls us right after Wright's murder, comes to the presser, and then shows up at Drummond's house? And Wickersham—I mean, John, you have to see this too. You and I both know the kind of people that buzz around crimes like this."

"Don't even go there," Serrano said.

"Tell me you haven't considered it."

"Considered it and dismissed it."

"She's a criminal rubbernecker," Tally said. "You've been around long enough to know civilians who hang around crime scenes and get involved with witnesses aren't fully right in the head."

"Maybe, but she's not a killer," Serrano said. "But her kids . . ."

"John Wayne Gacy had kids."

"Come on, Leslie."

"We've both investigated thrill-seeker killers. People who commit murder, then call the tip line. And this lawyer of hers, Jim Franklin? A civil litigation attorney negotiates a routine home purchase? I *called* Franklin. He claimed attorney-client privilege, refused to answer questions about Rachel Marin, and threatened to sue the department for harassment. Something's up with this chick."

"You won't be able to subpoena Jim Franklin," Serrano said. "Marin isn't being investigated for any current criminal acts. You can't prosecute based on curiosity or theories, and if we push harder, we open ourselves up to a harassment charge."

"But you know there's a reason Rachel Marin used this guy Franklin for her home purchase," Tally said. "There's something she doesn't want to get out. Something she wants to keep hidden. How much you want to bet there's a crime in her past that would connect her to this?"

"I know there's more to Rachel Marin than she lets on," Serrano said. "Knew it from the moment she left that message about Constance Wright's death."

"See?" Tally said. "You know I'm not totally out of my mind on this."

He shook his head. But for someone who wanted to keep her past in the shadows, Rachel Marin was not doing a particularly good job of staying hidden in the present. It felt like she wanted to step into the light but was holding back. At this point, Serrano didn't know what Rachel's intentions were. And Tally was making him worry he'd made a terrible mistake confiding in her. Something had happened that had tilted the Marin family on its axis. Those children had experienced trauma. And Serrano knew better than anyone that trauma often begot trauma. People who'd experienced evil often committed evil. Was it enough to push Rachel to do something terrible?

Sometimes the most terrifying crimes were the ones with no meaning. No warning. No motive.

"All right," Serrano said. "We look at Rachel Marin. But if it doesn't look like it's going anywhere, we move on. Those kids have been through enough."

"Works for me," Tally said. "Let's go see Aleksy Bacik at Irongate Properties. He put together the Marin home purchase with Jim Franklin. He knows something."

"He won't show us the closing documents unless we have a warrant," Serrano said. "And no way we're getting one without an actual crime or probable cause."

"I don't need a warrant," Tally said as she led Serrano to the car. "I'll simply tell Mr. Bacik that someone *might* leak to the press that he was meeting with the police, and he can watch as his client list dries up faster than a puddle in the desert. He'll talk."

*He will,* Serrano thought. And it scared him to think what Mr. Bacik might say.

# CHAPTER 35

The first thing Serrano noticed when they entered the offices of Irongate Properties was that they smelled like cookies. Not real cookies, though, not the kind his mother used to make fresh, loaded with more chocolate chips and walnuts than dough. This office smelled like cookies that had been sprayed with air freshener and left inside a dusty closet for a week.

Tally said, quite loudly, "Ashby police. We're looking for a Mr. Aleksy Bacik."

Two dozen well-coiffed Realtors stopped what they were doing, stood up, and got terrified looks in their eyes that reminded Serrano of a teenager about to take their first driving test.

Realtors were hawks. They had to be. They were competing against dozens of other firms and often their own colleagues, and even the hint of impropriety could lose them business. So when a pair of cops walked into the office unannounced, they could all see commission checks flying out the window. Tally knew this and knew it could be used as a cudgel.

Serrano saw a man rise slowly from behind a partition like a child checking to see if there was a monster under the bed. Half a dozen people pointed toward the same cubicle. Bacik raised his hand. Serrano and Tally walked over slowly. No need to make anyone think this would be quick.

Aleksy Bacik was in his early forties, with a thick head of dark-brown hair graying at the side but so unnaturally evenly that Serrano got the sense he dyed it gray on purpose to appear more mature and experienced. He was a shade under six feet, with tanned, heavily moisturized skin. Birth records showed that Bacik had emigrated from

Slovakia with his family at the age of five and graduated from Loyola and currently lived on Barrister Avenue in an apartment that he had purchased four years ago for $2.2 million.

His career was on the upswing. He was making money. He was good at his job.

But this was the kicker: He had spent four years after college working real estate in Darien, Connecticut. Just two blocks from Franklin and Rosato Associates, the firm that represented Rachel Marin.

Bacik worked in a cubicle barely wide enough for Tally to lie down in. Tally took a seat. Serrano went to the adjacent cube and asked a petrified thirtyish redhead if he could borrow a chair. She nodded, just glad he didn't want to question her. Serrano carried the chair into Bacik's cube and took a seat next to Tally.

Bacik sat down. "How can I help you, Officers . . ."

"I'm Detective Tally; this is Detective Serrano. We spoke on the phone earlier."

"Yes?" Bacik said, as though he'd been asked a question.

"We're here about Jim Franklin," she continued. "And the home you sold to Rachel Marin."

"It was a standard home purchase," he said, voice trembling. "I didn't do anything wrong."

Serrano looked at Tally. She laughed.

"You know," Tally said, "anytime I'm talking to someone and they start off by saying, 'I'm not a racist,' well, guess what. You can bet the house that at some point during the conversation, they're going to drop the n-word or talk about how some black guy stole *his* job. See what I'm saying? Nobody says 'I didn't do anything wrong' unless . . ."

Tally waited.

When Bacik said nothing, she continued, "Unless they did something wrong."

"I have an NDA," Bacik said.

"Excuse me?" Serrano replied.

"I signed a nondisclosure agreement. I can't talk to you."

"You signed a nondisclosure agreement when you sold Rachel Marin her house?"

Bacik nodded.

"I've never heard of an NDA for a home purchase," Serrano said, "unless it's someone famous, like Peter Dinklage."

Bacik looked confused.

"Peter Dinklage? Tyrion Lannister? *Game of Thrones*? You need to stay more current with the culture, Mr. Bacik."

"I can argue my partner's definition of 'culture,'" Tally said, "but the fact is, nondisclosure agreements are between two parties regarding a civil matter. They are subject to warrants and are not protected by law."

"Meaning your NDA will not protect you in court," Serrano said.

"Court?" Bacik said, the color draining from his face.

"US law stipulates that NDAs, or nondisclosure agreements, cannot lawfully prevent people from reporting claims to law enforcement or government agencies," Serrano said.

"So the question is," Tally said sternly, "why did Jim Franklin require you to sign an NDA when you sold Rachel Marin her house?"

"I didn't break any laws," Bacik said convincingly. "I sold a house. Plain and simple. It was a routine transaction."

"Buying a home for 800 grand in cash is not a routine transaction," Serrano said. "How many homes in the $800,000 price range have you sold without the buyer procuring a mortgage?"

Bacik was silent.

"Wow, that many," Tally said. "Doesn't sound like a routine transaction."

"Routine or not, it was a legal transaction. You have no right to come in here and bully me," Bacik said.

"Bully you?" Tally replied with mock surprise. "Trust me, Mr. Bacik, if we were here to bully you, you'd know it. We just want to know why so much secrecy was necessary for this 'routine' purchase."

"And we want to know the extent of Jim Franklin's relationship with Rachel Marin," Serrano added.

"He was her lawyer," Bacik said, confident that relaying this piece of information couldn't get him in trouble. "He handled the negotiations and reviewed the contracts for the purchase."

"Did he draw up the NDA?" Serrano asked.

Again, Bacik was silent.

"How many properties have you sold where the buyer required an NDA?"

Again, silence.

"This is sounding less and less like a routine purchase," Tally said again.

"Listen, Mr. Bacik," Serrano said gently. "We have no interest in hassling you. Or messing with your livelihood. And that's real. But we're going to find out the truth. Whether you help us or not. And while we don't *want* to harm your business, if you impede our investigation by refusing to cooperate, well then, I'm going to renege on my promise. So tell us. Point blank. Why did Jim Franklin require you to sign an NDA?"

"You're not going to the press with this?" Bacik said. "I can't have my name in any stories that are *undesirable*."

"If it's like you said, Mr. Bacik," Tally replied, "if you're on the up-and-up, your name stays as clean as a granite countertop the first day of its listing."

"OK," Bacik said. "Her real name isn't Rachel Marin. That was part of the agreement. Marin is the name she used on the contract, and it's the name on the deed, but it's not her given name. I think part of the reason she paid all cash is so there wouldn't be any record of a bank transaction in her legal name. No mortgage, nothing on her credit."

"What is her real name?" Tally asked.

"I don't know," Bacik pleaded, and they both knew he was telling the truth. "Because she didn't need a mortgage, we didn't have to go through all the background checks necessary when a bank gets involved. And the payment was made via certified check from Franklin and Rosato Associates, rather than the buyer. In a weird way, it was kind of like selling to a guarantor."

"You're saying the check came from the law firm rather than the buyer because they were protecting their client's identity."

"I'm not *not* saying that."

"Why would they want to hide her identity?"

"I don't know that either," Bacik said. Again, he seemed to be telling the truth.

"You spent several years in Darien at a small real estate firm called Front Door Associates," Serrano said.

Bacik nodded. "That's right." He liked this line of questioning. It seemed innocuous, and he didn't have to lie.

"Is that where you met Jim Franklin of Franklin and Rosato?" Tally said.

Bacik cocked his head, as though unsure why that question was being asked.

"Because it's fairly random, don't you think—a lawyer from Darien contacting *you* of all people to buy a house in Ashby for an anonymous client in Connecticut? So you *had* to have known Jim Franklin previously. Which is why he and Rachel Marin—or whatever her name is—came to you. Jim Franklin knew you would perform an all-cash transaction, no questions asked."

"Like I said," Bacik replied, "I haven't broken any laws."

"No, but Jim Franklin and Rachel Marin might have," Tally said sternly. "And either you work with us, and we can all be friends, or you can work against us, in which case I will make sure you'll be selling porta potties by the end of the year."

Serrano could see beads of sweat forming at Bacik's temples. He didn't need to look around to know that Bacik's colleagues were listening to every word or that the constant opening and closing of the front door meant prospective clients may have suddenly changed their minds upon seeing a police presence. Every moment Bacik hesitated, he was costing the firm money.

"I don't know all the details," Bacik said, "but something very bad happened to her. *Very* bad. I've known Jim Franklin for twenty years. I sold him his first house."

"I can't imagine the Ashby real estate market is more lucrative than Darien," Serrano said. "Why did you move out here?"

Bacik said, "I got into trouble. I had a bit of a cocaine problem. Front Door hired me, and I was making a solid six figures within two years. Well, there's nothing worse than having a burgeoning drug problem and money to throw at it. So I showed up one day at an open house, high out of my mind, and got in a fight with a buyer. Front Door fired me within twenty-four hours. Jim Franklin paid for me to go to rehab. And when I got out, he set me up here. I've been clean for fifteen years. So, yeah. I owe Jim Franklin. He saved my life. But he also wouldn't ask me to do anything illegal for him. Not after what I'd been through. This was a favor, sure, but a legal one. Whatever that Marin woman did in Darien, I had nothing to do with and have no knowledge of, and that's the God's honest truth. You can talk to Jim Franklin, if he'll talk to you, but that's the extent of my involvement. I sold a house, took a commission, and that's the end of it. Now, please, Detectives. That's all I know."

Serrano looked at Tally and nodded. He believed Bacik.

Tally placed her card on the desk. Bacik looked at it like it was a poisonous frog.

"If you remember anything else, call me. And if we find out you're holding back, it's porta potties for you."

Serrano and Tally left Aleksy Bacik and headed out. But as Tally opened the door to the Irongate office, another woman came barreling through the entryway, careening into Tally and sending them both sprawling to the floor.

"I'll be goddamned," Tally said, picking herself up off the street. "Funny running into *you* here, Ms. Marin."

# CHAPTER 36

Rachel knew why they were there even before Tally said a word. Tally and Rachel both stood up. Rachel brushed past the detectives and walked swiftly toward Aleksy Bacik's cube.

When she got to his desk, Bacik was sitting down and dabbing his forehead with a handkerchief and yet looked relieved. Until he saw her.

"Ms. Marin," he said. "I—"

"What did you say to them?" Rachel demanded. She heard the ruffling noises of a dozen brokers popping their heads up to witness the commotion. Bacik had a look on his face that said *Oh hell, not again.*

"I did nothing illegal," he said. "You *know* this."

*"What did you tell them?"*

Aleksy looked to be on the verge of a heart attack. His face was pale, and dark blotches of sweat dotted his blue shirt.

"I didn't tell them anything," he said.

He was lying.

Rachel could guess what he'd told them. It wasn't everything—Bacik didn't *know* everything—but he knew enough to cause serious problems. She had to assume he'd told the detectives all of it.

Rachel turned around, her purse knocking a pile of papers off Bacik's desk, and ran back to the front door. She flung it open and found the detectives still outside. Waiting for her.

"Why are you looking into *me*?" she said, eying Serrano like she could rip his throat out with her fingernails.

"Your involvement in the Wright murder has been bizarre since day *one*," Tally said.

"The only reason you even know it's a murder is because of me," Rachel shot back.

"Maybe, maybe not. You give yourself far too much credit," Tally said. "Regardless, then you show up at the press conference. And at the Drummond residence. And at Sam Wickersham's office, where he just *happens* to shoot himself."

Rachel said nothing. At this point, the truth was lodged in her gut like a searing-hot ball of lead. Even if she wasn't a suspect, she was certainly a person of interest.

"I had absolutely nothing to do with Constance Wright's death," Rachel said. "I'm trying to help."

Tally shrugged. "Funny how in your world helping is synonymous with lying. Guess we'll find out the truth one way or another."

She turned to face Serrano. A cold, bitter wind was blowing from the north. It stung her cheeks. She felt anger and desperation, fear roiling up inside of her.

"John," she said. "You know I had nothing to do with this."

"Then you have nothing to be afraid of," he said.

"That's not true. I have plenty to be afraid of."

"Then tell us," Serrano said, his voice sympathetic, reminding her of the way they'd spoken that night at the baseball field. "What happened back in Darien? Why did your lawyer have Bacik sign an NDA? What are you afraid of?"

Yes, full of care and compassion. But he was still a cop. And she kicked herself for believing a cop could do right by her. They knew about Jim Franklin. About Aleksy Bacik and the home purchase. That she'd lived in Darien. It was only a matter of time before they pieced it all together.

"Right now, I'm afraid of *you*, Detectives," Rachel said. "Because if you're looking at me, then you've strayed very, very far from the path."

"Have we?" Tally said. "Because if I had a brick for every convict who told me I had the wrong person, I could have built a mansion by now."

"Tell us the truth," Serrano said. "And we can help you."

Deep down, Rachel knew that at some point, someone would learn the truth. She had only hoped that *she* would be the one sharing it with someone who'd earned her trust. A friend. A partner. Someone she loved and cared about. It was not meant to be found by someone overturning rocks looking for pay dirt.

But the fact that they were looking at her meant they didn't think they had Constance Wright's killer in custody. Which meant the cops were essentially investigating two separate crimes: the conspiracy to drive Wright from office and ruin her life and her actual murder several years later. And the possibility that the crimes were committed by separate people with different motives.

"Am I under arrest?" Rachel said.

Tally eyed Rachel like she was dying to say yes. "Not at the moment," she said. "But I promise, if you had anything to do with Wright's death, we'll find out. And you'll wish you had the creature comforts of the holding cells."

"So if I'm not under arrest, I'm going home to my children. It's movie night, and we're watching *The Polar Express*. Good luck, Detectives. I hope you find the actual killer before they get the bright idea to do it again."

Rachel walked away, not letting the detectives see the panic in her eyes. But she knew two things:

One—whoever had killed Constance Wright was *not* a serial killer. He'd targeted her specifically. That she was sure of. Her comment about finding the killer before they struck again was total BS, just to give the detectives something to chew on.

Two—she needed to find out who killed Constance Wright before the detectives found a way to pin it on her.

She would not lose everything she had fought so hard for.

Her children.

Her sanity.

Her new life.

And if Serrano and Tally were looking under the wrong rocks, Rachel had to find the right one.

# CHAPTER 37

Megan watched the entire movie with her head resting on Rachel's chest. They laughed and squirmed and ate enough popcorn to sate an entire theater. Eric spent the majority of his time playing some game where sprites with battle-axes massacred other sprites with larger battle-axes. But still, he stayed. She couldn't remember the last time the three of them had watched a movie together. For one hundred minutes, Rachel forgot about Constance Wright, Detectives John Serrano and Leslie Tally, the Drummonds, Sam Wickersham, and Darien.

The popcorn feast had Megan wired. After the movie ended, she frantically wrote six more pages in a new Sadie Scout story, reading it to Rachel as she went along. Rachel sat on the carpeted floor of her daughter's bedroom, a smile plastered to her face as Megan created tales of Sadie Scout's bravery in the face of danger.

"Sadie always gets the bad guy," Megan said. "I know it's not always like that in real life. But I can do whatever I want in my stories."

"Yes, you can," Rachel said, kissing her daughter good night. She tucked Megan in, then went to see Eric. He was typing on his computer, focused.

"Still working?" she said.

He nodded without turning his head from the screen. "Paper on ancient Mesopotamia due next Wednesday."

"You know I'm proud of you."

"For what?" he said.

"For working so hard. For being you. You're the best son a mom could hope for."

"Dennis Lewiston's dad got arrested a few years ago," Eric said. "He was a dentist. Dennis said it was bogus, but I found the newspaper article. They said he was *doing* things to his female patients while they were unconscious. He lost his medical license and spent two years in Pinckneyville. Dennis said the other inmates did stuff to him while he was inside. Now Dennis and his dad don't talk."

"Eric, that's terrible. What made you think about that?"

He shrugged, the kind of shrug that let her know he knew exactly why he'd thought of it. "Dennis's dad got arrested. You got arrested."

"Eric, that was a big mistake. And I was released right away."

"Dennis said his dad's arrest was a big mistake, too, and now he said his dad probably has two assholes."

"Eric!" she shouted. "I will not have you talking like that."

"Why not?" he said. "You've been telling me what to say and who to be for so long now. Telling me to move on past Dad. But *you* haven't moved on past Dad. You have his picture in the basement, but you won't allow us to have his picture in our rooms. You're a hypocrite."

Rachel didn't even know Eric knew what that word meant. But he'd used it correctly.

"Yes. Yes I am," she said. "And I'm sorry."

Eric seemed unnerved by her honesty. He'd expected a fight, not a white flag. Rachel took a seat on the floor next to Eric's chair. He swiveled to face her. He didn't seem to know how to react, looking down at his mother in such a way.

"When everything happened back in Darien," Rachel said, "my world collapsed. Like yours. I didn't know how to handle it. All of a sudden I'm alone with two young children to raise, after being with your father pretty much my whole life. And not just two children to raise but figuring out how to move on after one of the most awful things imaginable. I know what it did to you. What finding him like that did to you. It changed my outlook on everything. Protecting you and your sister became my only priority. That doesn't mean I always did the right thing. But I *tried*. And I'm still trying."

"I know you are," Eric said softly.

"And now you're old enough to see that I make mistakes. We live strange lives, our family. I think it was a little bit easier on Megan. She was so young. She didn't have the memories you did. But you, you're one of the smartest kids I've ever met. And to be here, now, after everything . . . your father is smiling at you from up there. He's proud of you just like I am."

Rachel saw a tear slide down her son's cheek.

"I miss him," Eric said. "I miss him so much it hurts."

Rachel stood up. Wrapped her arms around her son. She could feel the wetness of his face against her arm, and she remembered the day she'd taken him home from the hospital, so impossibly tiny but so beautiful. His skin slightly bluish, as his blood circulation began to mature. Just the slightest scruff of blond hair. He'd always had her hair coloring. But the proud chin, bright eyes, and high cheekbones—those were his father's.

"I miss him too," Rachel said. "Every single day. And I promise, from now on, we'll find a way to properly remember him."

"I'd like that," Eric said.

It took every ounce of strength she had not to weep.

"Finish your work and get some rest, sweetie," she said.

"I will." Rachel turned to leave. "Hey, Mom?"

"Yes, hon?"

"Please don't get arrested again."

Rachel laughed. "I'll do my best."

◆◆◆

When both children were asleep, Rachel went down to the basement. She switched on the monitor bank. It was the same feed that was connected to the television in her room and simultaneously displayed a dozen cameras throughout the house. She watched her children sleep for a minute, then turned to the job at hand.

Since she'd left Serrano and Tally, Rachel hadn't been able to stop thinking about Christopher Robles. She had assumed Robles had gone to the press conference and subsequently attacked her in order to protect Isabelle and Nicholas. But she couldn't shake the look he'd given her when she bumped into him leaving the bathroom at the Drummond house. Like he knew something, had seen her snooping around. But now, with Nicholas in prison for the Albatross conspiracy, Rachel had a hard time believing Robles would have been willing to kill to hide simple financial impropriety on his brother-in-law's part.

She thought back to the night he broke into their home. Robles had been muttering under his breath. She'd dismissed it before as the rantings of a drugged-out lunatic, but now . . .

Rachel booted up the Microsoft Surface Studio desktop, upgraded with an Intel Core i7 processor, thirty-two gigs of RAM, and two terabytes of built-in memory. She also had six wireless Seagate external hard drives with five terabytes of memory.

Each hard drive contained files from one calendar year. She opened the drive containing files from the previous month and selected the folder "SecCam."

Inside the folder were hundreds of video data files, each marked with a date. She found the folder marked the day of Robles's break-in and opened it. There were twelve files, each corresponding to one of the home's security cameras. She opened seven of the files. Seven different videos popped up on the screen, each from a camera recording a different part of the house.

She enlarged the video from the kitchen feed and scrubbed it to 9:29 p.m. About two minutes before the gunshot. The feed showed Robles skulking around outside the property, looking for a way in.

Rachel opened the other six videos and brought them all to 9:29 p.m. Then she pressed play.

She watched Christopher Robles enter and exit every camera. He tried to open the sliding back door. Then each window around the house. And, of course, he checked the front door. While Robles was testing her security, Rachel was up in Eric's room. Oblivious. It was fortunate Robles had not been of sound mind. A smarter man might have done real damage.

Finally, Robles seemed to get frustrated, pulled the gun from his jacket pocket, blasted out the back window, and climbed through. Just as Rachel thought. The break-in had been spur of the moment. Robles had not exactly been a planner.

Then Rachel watched each monitor as Robles wandered through the house, the SIG Sauer clear even on the grainy feed. She turned the volume all the way up. Robles was muttering. And now, for the first time, Rachel could hear what he was saying. Some of it, at least.

"Told Isabelle not to trust him," Robles said. "Money talks and bullshit walks. He wants her money after he took his wife's money? Bitch, please. He won't protect Sis, then I will."

Rachel listened. She took out a notepad and transcribed Robles's words.

"I know it's his. Has to be."

Rachel paused the videos. *What* had to be his? Robles had clearly been referring to Nicholas Drummond. He was worried that Drummond would go after Isabelle's money. Not an unreasonable concern, given his history of draining his wives' bank accounts.

*But what had to be his?*

Then, it hit her.

The baby.

Constance Wright had been pregnant when she died. And Robles had thought Nicholas Drummond was the father.

She leaned back in her chair, thinking. Early on, she had pegged Drummond as the number one suspect in Wright's murder. But surely Serrano and Tally had run Drummond's DNA against the fetal tissue. And if it had come back a match, they would have had enough probable cause to charge him with Constance's murder.

Even Robles had thought Drummond was the father. But he'd been wrong. But how had Robles known that Constance was pregnant?

Rachel recalled her conversation with Serrano and Tally at the Drummond house. Serrano had said Constance Wright had called Nicholas Drummond just prior to her murder. It was possible Robles eavesdropped on Nicholas and Isabelle or simply listened to Nicholas's voice mails. If Constance told Nicholas she was pregnant and going after his money, Christopher may have assumed Nicholas was the father.

Rachel was convinced that Constance was making a play to get restitution for Nicholas's $1.2 million fraud. That money was rightfully hers. And her baby's.

Christopher knew *something*. His death at the hospital was beyond suspicious. Someone wanted him out of the picture. But Nicholas Drummond had neither the stomach nor the smarts to off his brother-in-law in a hospital. Especially since Robles, charged with breaking and entering and attempted murder, would have been heavily guarded by—

Rachel bolted upright.

Cops.

Robles would have been guarded by cops. There was only one way someone could have gotten to him.

Of course. How could she not have seen it?

*Serrano.*

# CHAPTER 38

She cursed herself for being so blind. Serrano said it himself at Voss field: Wright singlehandedly torpedoed his play to make sergeant. Kicked him when he was down. Added insult to injury when Serrano was at the lowest point in his life. And grudges died hard.

It explained why Robles was at the press conference looking terrified. He must have seen Serrano kill Wright at the bridge and then had to watch the man who killed Constance Wright investigate her death.

And the night she shot Robles—Serrano himself said he was heading to the hospital. And the next day Robles wound up dead.

*Goddamn it.* How could she have missed it?

That speech about his son. The kindness he'd shown toward her children. Her vision had been clouded by her sympathy for Serrano's loss.

*Sometimes behind the kindest eyes lay the darkest hearts.*

She remembered the kindly-eyed man who, years ago, had installed the security system in her family's home. The way he made googly eyes at baby Megan and made her fantasy-obsessed son laugh with his impression of Gollum. *My precious.* The way he shook her husband's hand and told him how he took pride in protecting a nice young family from those who might do them harm.

And then that man had ripped their family apart.

And now Serrano was looking to pin Wright's murder on her. And if he couldn't do that . . . Rachel knew what he was capable of.

She turned off the lights and monitors in the basement and went upstairs. She took the Mossberg shotgun from the safe and made sure it was loaded. She hadn't touched it since the night she shot Robles.

Rachel crept downstairs. She took a chair from the kitchen and set it down facing the front door. Then Rachel took a seat, the shotgun on her lap, and prayed she would not have to use it tonight.

◆◆◆

Rachel stirred when she heard music playing upstairs. Panic swept through her. She'd fallen asleep. The gun was still on her lap. She couldn't bring it upstairs; the kids could burst into the hall at any moment to see their mother carrying a loaded shotgun.

She ran into the living room and tucked the gun underneath the sofa cushions.

"Morning, Mom!" Megan sang, bounding down the stairs.

Her hair was a delightful mess. She bounced into the kitchen, hopped onto a stool at the counter, and said, "Eggs, please."

"Coming right up," Rachel said. Eric joined them a few minutes later, rubbing his eyes. "Morning, sweetie. Finish your paper?"

"It's not due until next week."

"Did you make good progress?" He shrugged. "Right. You're not a morning person. You know who else wasn't a morning person?"

Eric shook his head. "Who?"

"Your father."

Eric's head snapped up. "Dad?" he said. Rachel never talked about Brad so casually.

"That's right. Your father *hated* waking up in the morning. Before you came along, he'd usually wake up for breakfast around lunchtime."

"That's silly," Megan said. "Why would anyone skip breakfast?"

"Beats me," Rachel said, cracking two eggs into a pan.

Eric was beaming, wistful. "Can you make me some eggs too?"

Rachel smiled back. "Of course, hon." She cracked two more into the pan.

While the children ate, Rachel kept sneaking looks back to the living room, where a loaded shotgun was hidden just feet from her kids.

*How did it come to this?* she thought. *Hiding loaded weapons from my children?*

When they finished, Rachel cleaned the kitchen. John Serrano's smiling face stuck in her head like a piece of rotten fruit on a clean white plate. Most days, she felt like she never had enough time to spend with her children. This morning, she couldn't wait for them to leave. And the secrecy made her feel terrible.

Finally, after she had given Megan an extra ten hugs and kisses and patted Eric on the arm (she'd hit her teenage son hug quota early this week), they were off to school. When the house was empty, Rachel ran into the living room, grabbed the Mossberg from under the cushions, and deposited it back in the safe. Then she sat on her bed and tried to regain her composure.

Now, she had to think of a plan. Serrano was a cop. Not just any cop. A detective. He was smart. He was thorough. And he was clean.

But with Sam Wickersham, Nicholas Drummond, and Louis Magursky in prison facing felony charges, it was only a matter of time before they found probable cause to pin the murder on one of them. Rachel was convinced they were all innocent. But Serrano could plant evidence. Doctor reports. Force confessions.

She thought about going to Tally. Serrano's partner surely knew him better than anyone. But they were also tight. Tally would protect

Serrano. Not to mention that Tally seemed to have as much fondness for Rachel as one had for flesh-eating bacteria. No. It couldn't be Tally.

She knew who it had to be.

Rachel picked up the phone and dialed.

"Ashby Police Department."

"Yes, I'd like to speak with Lieutenant Daryl George. Tell him it's Rachel Marin. And tell him the future of the department depends on him taking my call."

# CHAPTER 39

She waited on hold for five panicked minutes. Finally Lieutenant George came on the line.

"Ms. Marin, I really don't have time for you today, so this had better be important."

"Lieutenant George, before you hang up, you need to listen to me. Because if you don't, your department and your career will be over before this phone call ends."

There was silence on the other end. For a moment, Rachel was terrified the lieutenant would hang up.

"Lieutenant?"

"I'm still here," George said.

"Lieutenant, there's a killer in your department. I need you to meet me in person."

"How dare you disparage my officers, who have gone out of their way to show you courtesy and professionalism despite your insane stunts. I have personally gone to great lengths to shelter your own children. Your accusation is totally absurd."

"What's absurd is that if you don't take this seriously, I'll go to the press. And you'll have to answer to them instead of me. And I think you'd like to hear what I have to say before you see Nancy Wiles reporting it on Channel 14 tonight."

More silence.

"Come in to the precinct," Lieutenant George said finally, exasperated. "We can meet in my office."

"Absolutely not. The person I'm talking about cannot be permitted to see me at the station, and I don't trust that you won't concoct a reason to toss me back into holding. You come to my home. Alone. Today."

"I have a budget meeting in half an hour."

"Skip it."

"I'm not going to let this department fall behind because of some crackpot. Believe it or not, I have matters to attend to during the day that do not involve you."

Rachel gritted her teeth. She didn't have much leverage. And if Lieutenant George skipped the meeting, people would ask questions.

"Fine," she said. "But you need to be here before my children get home from school."

"What time is that?"

"Three thirty."

"I'll be there at two."

"Great. And Lieutenant, if you tell anybody about our meeting, or if you don't come alone, Nancy Wiles is on my speed dial. And I hear she's angling for a national anchor spot. Taking down a corrupt police department would be one hell of a story to put on her promo reel."

"I'll be there, and I'll be alone. But think long and hard about this, Ms. Marin. If you're pulling my leg, I will drag you down to the precinct myself, and this time you won't be out the next day."

"Looks like we both have a lot at stake then. Be here at two, Lieutenant."

Then Rachel hung up. And breathed. There was no turning back.

◆◆◆

Rachel was sitting in the kitchen when the doorbell rang. She checked her watch. One fifty-three. Lieutenant George was seven minutes early. She appreciated punctuality.

She went to greet the lieutenant. The window shades on either side of the door were open. She could see him standing on her front step, looking impatient and cold, irritated. Understandable. He wore dark jeans with black boots and a brown coat with a fur-lined hood. She checked the surrounding area. His car was empty. He appeared to have come alone. Rachel opened the door.

"Well?" he said. "You dragged me down here. This better be good."

"Thanks for coming, Lieutenant. Come in."

Upon entering, he removed his shoes.

"Wow. I didn't even have to ask," Rachel said.

"My daughter used to be the same age as your kids," he said. "I remember how hard it is to keep a clean house."

"I appreciate that."

"Don't get used to it. It's probably the only time I'm going to be nice to you today."

"Fair enough."

Lieutenant George dropped his boots by the front door. Rachel took his jacket and hung it in the hall closet. Then she led him into the living room. She took a seat in a gray armchair, and George sat across from her on the green velvet-tufted sofa.

"Can I get you anything?" she said. "Coffee? Water?"

"You threaten me and then offer me coffee? No thank you, Ms. Marin. I just want to know what I'm doing here."

"Cutting to the chase. I admire that. It'll look good in a mayor."

"Come again?"

"Your exploratory committee has been in the works for almost a year. You've been trying to keep it under wraps."

George laughed and sat back. "You really are something," he said.

"Am I wrong?"

George smirked and said, "My campaign manager wants to wait until the spring to make it official. She says people tend to equate good news with good weather."

Rachel nodded. "Makes sense."

"You didn't want me to come here to talk politics," George said. "You told me I had a killer in my department. That is *not* a statement to make lightly. So please, Ms. Marin. Elaborate."

"Detective Serrano," Rachel said. "He killed Constance Wright."

George gave a dismissive snort. "If John Serrano is a murderer, then I'm Charles Manson. John Serrano is one of my very best detectives."

"Which is why he nearly got away with it."

George's smile evaporated.

"If not for me," Rachel said, "Constance Wright's death would have gone down as a suicide. The scene was staged well. The trajectory from the bridge would have been impossible for someone at that height to calculate. And the oddly chipped tooth wouldn't have been noticed if it wasn't being investigated as a homicide."

"Detectives Serrano and Tally told me they ran into you as they were leaving the Irongate Properties offices," George said, unfazed. "They spoke to Aleksy Bacik. I know about the NDA. They also told me they contacted a lawyer in Darien, Connecticut, who appears to have represented you. In fact, if Detective Tally had her way, you'd be held for questioning right about now. They seem to think *you* should be investigated."

"I had nothing to do with Wright's murder, and you all know it."

George shrugged. "They're doing their job. And now all of a sudden, a person of interest in this investigation is pointing the finger at a cop? That sounds like the desperation of a person with something to hide."

"You don't know what desperation is," Rachel said. "Desperation is seeing the police department investigating the wrong person while a killer walks freely."

"We have three people in custody, all of whom had a hand in the fraud perpetrated on Constance Wright. Nicholas Drummond, Samuel Wickersham, and Louis Magursky. Maybe you're telling the truth, and you're innocent of wrongdoing. But those three are not. Bottom line is we're getting justice for Constance."

"You haven't charged any of those three with Wright's murder."

"Yet," George clarified.

"Serrano was passed over for sergeant personally by Constance Wright," Rachel said. "After his son died. He told me."

George shook his head. "That was a long time ago," he said. "And to be honest, I think the mayor made the right call. We nearly had to boot John from the force, his drinking got so bad. I'd never wish what happened to him on anybody. But I have a department to run and a hundred and twenty law enforcement officers under my command."

"Serrano blamed Constance Wright for being passed over. He believes that promotion is the one thing that could have helped him move on from the loss of his son. He never forgot and never forgave. That's motive right there, Lieutenant. And Constance was a much easier target as a civilian."

George furrowed his brow and sawed his teeth back and forth, like he was chewing on an undercooked piece of meat. Rachel could tell he was being persuaded.

"I remember when Evan died," George said softly. "I've seen humanity at its best and worst. But I've never seen the light leave a man's eyes like it did John's after Evan passed. That boy was his world."

He paused.

"I don't know if that promotion would have led John down a different path. Maybe, maybe not. But the man went through some dark times after his promotion was rejected."

"And if he was ever going to get back at her for it," Rachel said, "he knew he'd be better off waiting until she was out of the public eye. And given her personal and professional implosion, her suicide would seem understandable."

"I have no reason to believe you or to trust you," George said.

"But you're still here."

George said nothing. "I'll look into it. But this will need to be treated *very* delicately. John and Leslie are good detectives. And they've both been with the department long enough to know when something is out of whack. You can't tell *anybody* what you've told me today."

"My lips are sealed. As long as you actually begin an investigation," Rachel said. "I'll give you forty-eight hours. If I don't hear from you on any movement on Serrano . . ." She waved her cell phone threateningly.

"You are a piece of work, Ms. Marin," George said. "But like you said, I can't potentially have a killer under my nose and expect people to pull a lever for me come Election Day."

"Thank you, Lieutenant. I just want justice for Constance Wright."

"So do I," he said. "She was a spectacular woman and a good mayor. And I'm glad the monsters who ruined her are going to rot."

"Me too," Rachel said. "For what it's worth, you have my vote."

He smiled. The lieutenant's eyes were a sparkling blue, the color of a lake on a sunny day, and the crow's feet on either side made him look distinguished.

*He'll win,* she thought. *Men who look like that and have a good head on their shoulders don't lose elections.*

"I need to be going," George said.

"My kids will be home soon too. Don't need them asking why another cop is in our home."

George stood up. "Don't call me. I'll call you. Serrano and Tally pick up scents quickly, and they could catch a whiff of this if you call the station again."

"You got it."

"Mind if I use your bathroom before I go?"

"Sure." Rachel pointed him to the bathroom down the hall. She hoped he wouldn't judge the dirty children's clothes overflowing from the hamper. Doing laundry for two children was a Sisyphean task.

When she heard the bathroom door close, Rachel went to the closet and took the lieutenant's coat out for him. She could smell a faint whiff of eau de toilette—Yves Saint Laurent, if she wasn't mistaken.

Out of habit, Rachel felt the inside pocket of George's jacket pocket. A pen, a crumpled dry cleaning bill, and a parking stub. Nothing more. Then she checked the outer pockets.

One pocket had nothing. The other held a plastic bag with something blue inside. She took out the bag, unzipped it, and removed the items.

And her heart skipped a beat.

Her mind went back to the night she'd waited outside of Stanford Royce's house. Before approaching his front door, she'd slipped on a pair of blue plastic shoe covers so as not to leave any imprints in the dirt.

The Ziploc bag contained a pair of the same type of shoe covers she had worn, coated in melted snow and caked in dirt.

Before she could turn around, Rachel felt a shockingly strong arm wrap itself around her chest and then a stinging sensation as a syringe was plunged into her neck.

"You had the wrong cop," he said as Rachel's world spun into black.

# CHAPTER 40

John Serrano had a six-pack of Dogfish Head 60 Minute IPA waiting for him in the fridge at home. It had taken a long time to get control of his life to the point where a six-pack wouldn't turn into a twelve-pack and then into a case and then a bottle of Jim Beam. Besides, sitting in his old maroon La-Z-Boy downing a few cold ones and a bag of pretzels while watching a movie was the perfect way to end a long day. He was in the mood for something a little old school. Maybe *Stand by Me* or *Gremlins*. He was leaning toward *Gremlins*. A very underrated Christmas movie. *Gremlins* and beer. A light snow was falling. It was a beautiful early evening, and he couldn't wait to get home and let the day slide away.

His head was swirling after the talk with Bacik and the confrontation with Rachel. There was something dark in her past she was trying desperately to conceal, but he had a hard time believing she was capable of murder. Or maybe he just didn't want to believe what she could be capable of.

Serrano had pulled into his driveway and was opening the car door when his cell phone rang. *Speak of the devil.*

The Caller ID read *Rachel Marin*.

Serrano swiped to answer the call. "Rachel. I'm guessing you want to talk about today."

"Detective Serrano?"

It wasn't Rachel. Serrano recognized Eric Marin's voice.

"Eric?"

"Detective Serrano, hi."

"Eric, is everything OK?"

"I don't know. I'm at home with Megan, and our mom isn't here."

A knot tied itself in Serrano's gut.

"What do you mean? Tell me what's going on, exactly."

"The school bus dropped me off at home about two hours ago. Megan was sitting on the front step, alone. She said Mom wasn't answering the door. I have a key, so I let us in. But our mom isn't here. I don't know where she is. This has never happened before."

"Did you try her cell phone?"

"It goes right to voice mail. I had your card in my backpack. You said to call you whenever, no matter what. I'm sorry for calling, but . . . we're scared."

"Don't apologize for a second," Serrano said. "I meant it. I'm glad you called."

He mounted the phone into the hands-free on his dash and put it on speaker, then started the car.

"Just stay there," he said. "I'm on my way. Stay on the phone with me. Can you do that?"

"Yes. Please hurry, Detective."

◆◆◆

Eighteen minutes later, John Serrano arrived at the Marin home. Rachel's car was parked in the driveway. There was another set of tire tracks next to it. Serrano frowned. He parked at the curb so as not to disturb the other set of tracks. If her car was still here but Rachel wasn't, that probably wasn't a good sign.

The snowfall was growing heavier. The tracks would disappear before long. Before knocking on the door, Serrano took a dozen photographs of the second set of tracks. Then he surveyed the house and surrounding area. Nothing appeared to be disturbed. No broken branches on the shrubs lining the front steps, no broken glass, no blood. No sign of a struggle.

The front lawn was blanketed by a thin layer of powder. There were footprints but no shoe treads to make out. If necessary, he could have forensics down here to sift through it to study the soil underneath. But he didn't want to jump the gun in case this was a misunderstanding. But something about the scene disturbed him.

Serrano knocked on the door. Seconds later, Eric appeared at the window. Serrano waved at him. Eric opened the door and said, "Thanks, Detective Serrano."

"Of course," he said. "Can I come in?"

Eric nodded. Megan was sitting on the floor in the living room, four books splayed out on the floor in front of her. But there was fear on her face, the books a clear attempt to divert her attention, which didn't seem to be working very well. She looked like she was about to cry.

"It's going to be all right," Serrano said, closing the door behind him. "Walk me through what happened when you got home."

"I came home, and Megan was sitting outside. I have a key, she doesn't, so I let us both in. It was starting to snow, and she was shivering. I made her some chunky veggie soup."

"You're a good brother. Are you OK now, sweetheart?" Serrano asked her. Megan nodded. She definitely was not OK.

"Then what?"

"I called for my mom. She didn't answer. I thought she might have slipped and hurt herself, so we checked every room. Bathrooms too. And she wasn't here."

"There's a basement, right? Could she be down there?"

"I checked there," Eric said, but there was hesitation in his voice. "She wasn't downstairs."

Serrano took out his phone and called Rachel's cell. It went straight to voice mail.

"Do you have the Find My Friends app?" he asked Eric. The boy nodded.

"Yeah, but it's turned off on her end."

*Not a good sign,* Serrano thought. Eric's lower lip was trembling.

"When was the last time you spoke to her?"

"This morning when I left for school."

"And was everything normal then? Did she seem like anything was on her mind?"

Eric thought for a moment. "She's been weird the last few days. More emotional than usual. More huggy, if that makes sense."

Serrano nodded. In his experience, parents tended to become more emotional than usual when they'd either done something wrong or were anticipating something *about* to go wrong. Children knew their parents better than anyone, and Eric was a perceptive kid. He knew something was up.

"Could she have gone anywhere?"

"I don't know," Eric said. "I suppose. But her car is still here."

"Yeah," Serrano said, thumbing his chin. "Her car is still here."

Serrano went over to Megan. A picture book was open to an illustration of a dragon eating a smorgasbord of tacos.

"What book is this?" Serrano said.

"It's called *Dragons Love Tacos,*" Megan said. "I'm too old for it now, but my mom used to read it to me. I brought these out in case she was here and wanted to read to me tonight."

"Did your mom tell you anything, sweetheart? Anything that might let us know where she is?"

Megan shook her head. "Is my mom OK?"

Serrano didn't know how to respond.

"Listen, kids, give me a minute, all right? Eric, did you clean anything before I got here? Glasses? Dishes? Food? Anything at all?"

"No. There wasn't anything to clean. The place was like this."

"OK. Do me a favor, and read that dragon taco book to Megan. I have some things I need to check on."

Eric nodded.

"Where's your mom's room?"

"Upstairs, last door on the left."

Serrano went upstairs and opened the door to Rachel Marin's room. The bed was made. The room was clean. He opened the closet. There were no empty hangers. It didn't appear anything had been disturbed, and it didn't look like Rachel had packed up and left in a hurry. He noticed a large safe in the closet, checked the door out of curiosity, but it didn't budge.

Then he called Leslie Tally.

"John, what's up? Anything the matter?"

"Got a problem," he said. "I'm at Rachel Marin's house."

"Oh hell, what now? Did she dig up Elvis's grave to make sure he's really dead?"

"Not quite. She's missing. Kids came home from school, and she wasn't here. Her phone is off, the car is still in the driveway, and clothes are where they should be."

There was silence on the other end. "What do you think?"

"I don't think she'd run. Not without her kids. I'm going to check with the cab companies and Uber to see if they have a record of any pickups at this address. But something isn't right."

"I'm coming over."

"Good. But keep it to yourself. I don't want anyone else involved in case she's just down at the bar throwing back Jägerbombs."

"Should I call the lieutenant?"

"Not yet. Let me see what I can find here before we officially report her missing."

"I'll be there ASAP."

Serrano hung up. He searched the rest of Rachel's room. Nothing seemed out of place or extraordinary. He went into the kids' rooms. Messy, but nothing suspicious.

He went back downstairs. Eric said, "Megan's hungry."

"You guys haven't eaten?"

Eric shook his head. Serrano was already in a bad spot. He had no idea if this was a crime scene, so he needed to use his best judgment. He opened the fridge. Not much. Some cold cuts and bread, vegetables, yogurt, and chicken thighs. He opened the freezer and got lucky. A frozen pizza.

"You're in luck." Serrano preheated the oven and went back into the kitchen. Megan's eyes were red. "It's going to be fine, sweetie," Serrano said.

"How do you know?" she asked, her voice so plaintive and terrified that it broke his heart.

"I'm not going to leave until we know where your mom is. I promise."

Megan nodded. Twelve minutes later, Tally pulled up. Serrano let her in.

"Kids, you remember Detective Tally, right?" They nodded. "Eric, go check on the pizza. Let me talk to my partner."

When the kids left, Tally said, "No sign of a struggle I can see. No forced entry."

"Nope."

"And nothing out of place in the home?"

"Far as I can tell."

Tally opened the coat closet. She flipped through the jackets.

"No empty hangers," Tally said. "No coats missing."

"This is goddamn bizarre," Serrano said. "You think somebody took her?"

"That woman is no pushover. For her to be nabbed without a struggle, it would take one smart son of a bitch."

"Yeah," Serrano said. "Means whoever took her, she didn't see it coming."

"Trusted them. Maybe even let them in the house," Tally said.

Serrano went to the front door. “She lets him in. No struggle.” Serrano knelt down, touched the hardwood flooring by the door. “Floor is dry. So he takes his shoes off before entering.”

“A boyfriend?” Tally said.

Serrano shook his head. “Doubtful. No sign of any food preparation. No dirty glasses or crumbs, nothing out of place, and the bed is made. This get-together was business, not pleasure.”

Serrano went into the bathroom. Looked around.

“Now this is interesting. The sink handles are wiped clean,” Serrano said. “Our friend used the bathroom and then wiped his fingerprints.”

He checked the toilet lid and flush handle. Same thing. Wiped down. Which meant the children hadn’t used this bathroom. The sink basin was still damp, but the hand towels were dry. Towels might have picked up trace evidence, loose fibers, moisturizer, dead skin. He sniffed the air. Then he did it again.

*Was that . . .*

“Hey, Leslie, come here.”

Tally joined him in the bathroom.

“Smell that?”

She inhaled deeply.

“Not sure,” she said. “Something *kind of* sweet, maybe?”

Serrano nodded. “There’s a scent. Definitely not a woman’s perfume. And I doubt Rachel’s thirteen-year-old son wears cologne to school.”

Serrano left the bathroom. Went into the kitchen. Sniffed the air. Tally joined him.

“That pizza smells good,” she said.

“Hold on a second,” Serrano replied.

Serrano entered the living room. Sniffed again. Went to the sofa. Knelt down. Sniffed. “Come here,” Serrano said, motioning Tally over.

“What?”

“Down here.”

She knelt down. Sniffed.

"What is that?"

"Yves Saint Laurent," Serrano said. His heart began to pound.

"You recognize it?"

Serrano nodded. "Lieutenant George wears it all the time. He bathes in the stuff."

Tally looked at him askance, cocked her head. "You don't think . . ."

"Someone she knew," Serrano said. "Someone smart enough to get the drop on Rachel. Maybe even someone strong enough to—"

"Toss a body from a bridge. Jesus Christ," Tally said. "You're not saying what I think you're saying."

Serrano ran to the front door, threw it open, and sprinted to the adjacent house. He could see a couple sitting on a faded yellow couch through a side window. The window had an unobstructed view of Rachel Marin's driveway. Serrano went around to the front door and knocked repeatedly.

"Ashby PD!" he shouted, continuing to knock.

A minute later, an older man with a handlebar mustache wearing blue pajamas answered the door.

"Ashby PD," Serrano said, holding up his badge.

"Christ, I stopped dealing weed in 1977," the man said.

"What? No, I'm not here to investigate you. Have you been home all day, sir?"

"I have. Wife and I are retired and content to watch our soaps during the day. Unbelievable how many evil twin brothers there are on these shows."

"Did you happen to see another car in the driveway next door while you were home?"

The man scrunched up his face and thought. "Well, saw a blue car pull up earlier in the afternoon. A man went inside and stayed there awhile. Only noticed because other than the cops recently, Ms. Marin hasn't had too many visitors."

"What time was this?"

"Two o'clock? Around then? *General Hospital* was about to come on, and that's when I turn my brain off."

"Did you happen to get a look at the man?"

"Not really," he said. "Looked like a man."

"What about the car?"

"The car I saw good," the man said. "A little too flashy for my taste."

Serrano scrolled through the Camera app on his cell phone and showed the man a picture that had been taken at a police fund-raising barbecue the previous year. Serrano and Lt. Daryl George leaning up against George's blue Camaro. "Did the car look like this?"

The man nodded. "Car that color, it's a speeding ticket waiting to happen."

"Did you happen to see the man when he left? Was he carrying anything?"

"Like I said, once *GH* comes on, I turn my brain off."

"Thank you, sir; you've been a huge help."

"You'd better not give me a hard time about that weed!"

Serrano went back to the Marin home and knelt down next to the second set of tire tracks. He pulled up the photo from the barbecue and zoomed in on the Camaro's tires. The make was Goodyear Eagle F1 Asymmetric All-Season. The tread matched the tracks in Rachel Marin's driveway.

Serrano barged through the front door, breathless, nearly knocking over Tally. He called dispatch at the precinct and said, "I need LoJack on a 2015 Chevy Camaro, registered to Lieutenant Daryl George. Yes, *that* Lieutenant Daryl George. I need GPS on his cell phone and all available street-camera recordings in the Lawrenceville neighborhood of Ashby from 2:00 p.m. today onward."

Tally said, "You can't possibly think—"

"Lieutenant Daryl George killed Constance Wright," Serrano said breathlessly. "And he's going to kill Rachel Marin, if he hasn't already."

# CHAPTER 41

Rachel was jolted awake by her head slamming against something flat and metallic. She tried to scream, but her mouth was taped shut. She tried to pull the tape off, but her hands were bound together by a plastic tie. As were her ankles. She was locked in a car trunk. Every bump and bounce and pothole sent shock waves up her spine, making her cry out in agony. Her fingers scraped against some sort of cloth or burlap sack. The material scratched her face.

She was zipped up in a large canvas bag.

Panic set in. She had been restrained, stuffed in a sack, and thrown in a trunk. She didn't have a jacket on, and the cold was penetrating her bones.

It was pitch black. Rachel took even breaths, calming herself. Her air supply was limited. If she hyperventilated and passed out, she was as good as dead.

Eventually the ride became smooth. Fewer bumps. The car was on a highway or interstate. She didn't know how long she'd been out. She still had circulation in her hands and feet, so it was likely minutes rather than hours.

The trunk had a chlorinated smell, like a swimming pool. She closed her eyes, listened close. Based on the sound of the cars around them and the vibrations from the chassis, Rachel estimated they were driving at about thirty miles an hour. Too slow to be on the highway but too fast for residential streets. She could hear cars passing them in both directions but no horns, which meant traffic was minimal. She tried to think about the layout of Ashby. Which streets permitted such speeds. And no doubt Lieutenant George would be driving at the speed limit.

Lieutenant George. Images swam through Rachel's head of her children playing in the lieutenant's office. His hand tousling Megan's hair. Her daughter laughing.

*Monsters in our midst.*

The lieutenant had done a thorough job restraining her. The plastic bit into her wrists. And the bag prevented her from attempting to pry the trunk open. The lieutenant didn't want her dead—at least not just yet. If she expired, she would involuntarily loose her bladder and bowels, giving him a whole new mess to clean.

Rachel kicked herself for allowing Daryl George into her home. She had been so fixated on Serrano that she'd overlooked any other possibilities. *That* was why Constance had been dressed up the night she died, why she'd had on heels and willingly drunk some alcohol. She'd been meeting her lover: the already-married future mayoral candidate and father of her unborn child, Lt. Daryl George.

It had been the last date night of her life.

The rage against Serrano had blinded her. She'd *wanted* it to be him. And because of her overzealousness she had put herself and her children in danger.

*Oh God, my children.*

Panic set in. She wriggled and writhed, but her bonds were secure. Eric and Megan were surely both home from school by now and likely worried sick. Eric at least had a house key and could let them in from the cold. He was smart. Resourceful. Rachel's car was still in the driveway. He would realize something was wrong. He would call the cops.

Serrano.

He would call Serrano.

Then Rachel felt a hard jolt, and the roadway changed. She heard a muffled, metallic sound underneath and realized they were crossing a bridge. The Albertson Bridge. Where George had thrown Constance Wright over the railing to her death.

They were traveling east over the bridge, toward Woodbarren Glen. That's where he would kill her and dispose of her body. April through October, Woodbarren Glen was a bustling park filled with families, hikers, campers, runners, and bird-watchers. Rachel had taken Eric and Megan there last summer. She remembered beaming as she watched Eric clamber-jump off a tire swing at Crystal Glen Lake and plop feet-first into the water, Megan giggling in her adorable pink two-piece bathing suit. But in the winter, the Glen was cold, desolate, and largely deserted. Camping trails and running paths were covered in snow and ice and would be largely abandoned until the thaw.

A body buried in the Glen would go undisturbed for months, at which point natural decomposition would destroy most, if not all, forensic evidence.

Then, with horror, Rachel realized what the smell was. Chlorinated lime. George had brought it with him to dispose of her body. Chlorinated lime had the same tissue-altering properties as quicklime and would destroy any trace evidence, but the chlorinated scent would mask the natural decomposition smell. It would keep animals—and humans—away.

Lieutenant George had planned to kill her the moment he'd hung up the phone.

Then, as quickly as it had begun, the metal humming ended. They'd crossed the bridge. Rachel could picture the landscape. About a mile down the road, there was an entrance on the right into Woodbarren Glen. After that, the road branched off into several forks, leading to campsites and Crystal Glen Lake. The Glen itself was over a thousand square acres. It was possible she'd never be found.

Soon enough, the car made a right, and the smooth road gave way to the rocky dirt path leading into Woodbarren. With nothing to brace herself, Rachel bounced around the trunk. She kept her teeth clenched to prevent accidentally biting and possibly severing her tongue.

She memorized each turn the car took, estimated the speed, and calculated the distance between each turn. But deep down, she knew it probably wouldn't matter.

Finally, after about half an hour of driving, the car slowed and pulled to a stop. Rachel tried to twist her body in the direction of what she thought was the trunk opening. She heard the front door open and then slam shut. Then the crunching sound of boots on snow. Then another door opened and quickly closed. And then . . . nothing.

Rachel waited. The air supply in the trunk was thinning.

She prayed her children had gotten into the house and called Serrano. She regretted her brief, ill-advised vendetta against the detective and prayed that no matter what happened, he would know what to do to take care of them. It ripped her heart open to think she was on the verge of leaving her children orphaned.

After what seemed like an eternity, Rachel heard the same crunching sound as George returned from wherever he'd been. She heard a key inserted into the trunk lock, and then the trunk itself opened.

Rachel still couldn't see anything. She felt arms wrap around the bag, and Lieutenant George hoisted her up like she was nothing. He then tossed her to the ground like a side of beef.

The drop knocked the breath from her body. Rachel gasped for air. With her mouth covered by tape, she began to choke. Then the zipper came undone, and light seared her eyes. The frigid air bit into her skin. She could do nothing to warm herself.

Lt. Daryl George was staring at her. He appeared to her upside down. He wore large latex gloves that were duct-taped over his mittens and covered in dirt. His breathing was labored, his face bright red from the cold and exertion.

He'd just dug her grave.

"Hello, Ms. Marin," the lieutenant said. Rachel tried to curse at him but ended up swallowing her own spit. She lay on her back, staring up at the darkening sky. Bare oak and hickory trees loomed above her, the oak branches gnarled and twisted, the hickory tall and grand. There was a terrible, frosted beauty to the cold, wintry forest.

"Here's what's going to happen," George said. He drew a large gleaming knife from his coat. She could see a bulge by his ankle, the outline of a gun. But gunfire would alert anyone who happened to be in the woods and possibly draw law enforcement. A knife was quieter. "You're going to walk where I say you're going to walk. If you don't, I'm going to go back to your home and open up your children. And then I will bury all three of you in these woods. Do you understand me?"

Rachel nodded.

"You see those footprints to your left? You're going to follow those as far as they take you. Got it?"

Rachel nodded again. George walked over to her and cut the plastic tie between her ankles.

"Now stand up."

She did.

"We both know how this is going to end," George said. "The absolute best thing you can do is make it easy and quick. If you do as I say, the worst thing that'll happen to your kids is they'll need therapy. And who doesn't these days, am I right? But if you don't do exactly as I say, I will bury their bodies on top of yours. Get me?"

Rachel nodded.

"Let's go, Ms. Marin."

Rachel began to walk. She was shivering uncontrollably. Her hands were tied in front of her. She stumbled among the drifts and fell forward, unable to brace herself, and came up coughing into the duct tape, her face covered in snow and dirt. She could feel a warm trickle seep down her cheek. Blood.

The snow was coming down harder now. By this time tomorrow, their tracks would be gone.

"Move," George said.

She pushed forward, following his footsteps. They were heading deep into the wooded glen. The sky was growing dark. A flashlight popped on behind her, illuminating the snowy trail ahead.

After ten minutes of walking, Rachel's feet were growing numb. Her hands were losing circulation. If they didn't arrive soon, and she fell, she would be unable to pick herself up.

Then, up ahead, Rachel saw the final destination. A hole about six feet long, two feet wide, and four feet deep. A shovel lay beside the hole. She would be buried with it. At the foot of the hole were several bags of chlorinated lime, as she'd suspected. With this snowfall, by tomorrow her grave would be nothing but a part of the landscape.

Then, as Rachel stood at the lip of her own grave, she began to laugh. Lightly at first, then hysterically. She coughed and gagged but continued to laugh.

Lieutenant George walked up to Rachel and placed the knife against her throat, point first. She stared at him and continued to laugh. Then, through the tape, she said two words.

"Scuse me?" George said.

She repeated the words. And laughed.

"You scream, I make your children scream."

He ripped the duct tape from her mouth. Behind it, Rachel was smiling. And she repeated the two words. Slowly.

"You're fucked," she said.

This time, George smiled. "That right?" he said. "Seems to me you're the one in a bit of a bind here. You know, I was debating getting rid of you the moment I heard that you went to the Wickersham kid's office. But I figured you were just a rubbernecker. Bark worse than your bite. But when you fingered John as a suspect? Well, I knew you might just be crazy enough to go to the media, create a big damn mess for me. And I couldn't have people digging into the department. Not with so much at stake."

"Because they'd eventually find out you were the father of Constance Wright's child and that you killed her and Christopher Robles," she said.

George looked down. Tapped the knife with his finger.

"We had a good thing, Connie and I. I cared about her. Truly did. But there was no way I could let that child be born. Of course, she was set on having it. She called it her second chance. And, well, if you knew Constance, there was no convincing her otherwise."

"And nobody gets elected mayor having a love child with the disgraced former holder of that very same office," Rachel said.

"Most folks don't care about a man's personal life if he can cut their taxes. Keep shooters out of their schools. But she wanted to go after Drummond and the Wickersham kid. Get back the money they swindled from her. And, well, between that and the kid, that's just too much of a scandal for even me to clean up."

"And yet here you are," Rachel said. "Digging graves in the woods. What about Christopher Robles? Why did he have to die?"

"He was at the bridge that night," George said solemnly. "I nearly had a heart attack when I saw his face on the news that morning. My guess is after the phone calls from Constance, he figured Drummond was stepping out on Isabelle. So I think he followed Constance, figured he'd catch her with Nicholas. I can't say for sure that he saw what happened that night, but I couldn't take that chance. And once he was in police custody, an opportunity presented itself."

"And nobody questions an embolism in someone with a history of intravenous drug abuse," Rachel said. "At the press conference, he was terrified. I think he knew you killed her."

"Well, it's just bad luck for Chris that you had to go and shoot him. You don't shoot him, he's not in the hospital, and who knows what happens. Funny, isn't it?"

"What's really funny," Rachel said, "is that everything you did in my house today was recorded."

George's smile disappeared.

"Bullshit."

"Look in my eyes, Lieutenant. Am I lying?"

George hesitated. He brought the knife back a millimeter.

"No way," he said. "Only a crazy person videotapes their house."

"Well, guess what?" Rachel said. "I'm damn near certifiable."

"All right, enough. Time to go, Ms. Marin."

George held the knife sideways across her throat, the steel colder than the air.

"Harwood Greene," Rachel whispered.

George paused.

"What did you say?"

"I said Harwood Greene."

George hesitated. "Harwood Greene. The Connecticut Carver. I've heard of him. What in the hell does he have to do with anything?"

"Harwood Greene killed my husband, Bradley Powell. My name is Olivia Powell."

"You're a sick woman, Rachel Marin. Or whoever you are."

"Harwood Greene cut my husband into pieces," she said. "Left his remains in a sack on our front porch. My son found it. I can still hear my boy screaming."

George listened, the knife quivering in his hand, unsure what to believe.

"Harwood Greene was a home security installation technician," Rachel said. "While installing a system for a Darien PD deputy named Jimmy Plotkin, Greene found a kilo of heroin under a kitchen floorboard. So Greene gave Plotkin a quid pro quo. Greene would keep quiet about the drugs, and Plotkin would use the police database to put together a list of homes that had recently been burglarized. Plotkin figured it was for Greene's business, so he could sell them home security systems. But what it really did was tell Greene which houses weren't monitored. He used it to case his victims. Find the blind spots in their homes. Our house was on that list. My husband, Bradley, was Greene's seventh and final victim."

Rachel could tell that George knew she was telling the truth.

"The cops found Greene by accident a few months after he killed Brad. He got pulled over for a busted taillight, and the officer decided to search Greene's trunk. Didn't like the cut of his jib, or something. Greene was smart. He knew the cop had no probable cause for the search. The traffic cop's body cam clearly shows Greene reciting the Fourth Amendment, which protects against unlawful search and seizure. The cop found a spot of blood on the tire jack. It matched one of Greene's victims. They got a warrant for Greene's home, found blood and fibers from the other victims and dozens of horrific photographs. Including one of my son and I the moment we found my husband's remains on our doorstep. He took photographs of the moments the victim's families discovered what he'd done. But since everything they found on Greene was predicated on that traffic stop, there was a mistrial."

"I remember that," George said. "But they would have retried Greene."

"They *would* have retried him," Rachel said. "But some of Greene's sick followers found out where three corrections officers lived and threatened their families. And so Greene disappeared somewhere between superior court and the Bridgeport Correctional Center. And so the monster was loose. We couldn't stay in Darien. Not with him still out there. We moved to another town in Connecticut, but we needed to cut our ties to everything we used to know. I came here to keep my children away from that monster. I changed our names. Our lives. Now, tell me, Lieutenant George, am I lying?"

George eyed her for what seemed like minutes but was only seconds. He was breathing faster. Rachel could hear the knife loosening in his gloved hand.

"No," he said. "You're not."

"And as it turned out, the department *knew* Plotkin had given that list to Greene. But they kept it quiet to save face. When department emails were subpoenaed and released to the public, I sued the city and the Darien Police Department. So ask yourself: Would a woman with two young children, whose husband was brutally murdered by a man who vanished into the wind, a woman who had already been betrayed by law enforcement, lie to you about keeping her own home secure? She would want every *inch of her life* guarded. Because of people like Harwood Greene. Because of people like you. So no matter what happens here tonight, somebody will find that video and see what you've done. So, like I said, *Lieutenant*. You're fucked."

The calm on George's face turned to confusion, then turned to rage.

"God*damn it*!" he shouted. He looked back at the grave, and Rachel saw her one chance to get out alive.

In the split second that he took his eyes off her, Rachel swung around behind the lieutenant and draped her bound hands around his throat. And then she pulled, as hard as she possibly could.

The cop made an *urk* sound as the plastic bit into the soft of his neck. They both toppled backward into the hole. Rachel landed on her side. Her head bounced off a rock, and her world went fuzzy. But she held on. She dug her knees into George's back to get better leverage and *pulled.*

George bucked violently on top of her. His free hand clawed at the plastic. He beat his fist against her arm. It hurt like hell, but she held on. She could feel the breath leaving him. His kicks were losing strength. But then she saw a glint of metal as he raised the hand holding the knife, and the next thing she felt was a searing pain in her thigh as he plunged the blade into her flesh.

Rachel cried out. She could see the knife handle protruding from her leg. But she held on. George ripped the blade from her thigh. Rachel swung her legs around his body, trapping his arms against his chest. She squeezed with every bit of might she had. Slowly, he managed to slide the knife upward. Toward his neck. Toward the plastic cuffs.

Then, with one stroke, George slid the blade between the plastic ties and severed the bond. Rachel's hands fell away. The lieutenant was free.

She scrambled out of the grave and saw the knife plunge into the hard earth where her hand had just been. She could hear George wheezing. She didn't look back. Just ran, her leg throbbing. She could feel the blood pouring down her leg, pooling in her shoe.

Then a crack filled the air, and a tree branch next to her head exploded. He was firing at her.

Rachel slid behind a large oak tree and looked back. Another shot rang out, this one whistling wide of the mark.

George was stumbling toward her, swaying, struggling to breathe. She might have crushed his windpipe. But he had enough to go on. Enough to finish her off.

"Rachel!" George shouted. His voice was raspy, like he'd chain-smoked four packs of cigarettes. "Come out, or I swear to God I'll flay your children from head to toe."

Another shot. The bark shattered above her, raining wood on Rachel's head.

She leaned against the tree, trying to catch her breath. She could feel blood pumping down her leg. By the sound of it, George was firing a Ruger LCR. It had a five-round capacity.

He had two shots left.

Rachel looked around her. She saw a palm-size stone on the ground and picked it up. Rachel felt the cold in her bones. Her hands were shaking. She took one breath, poked her head to the side of the trunk to get a sliver of a view, and sidearmed the rock at Lieutenant George.

The rock missed him by six inches, but he flinched, and that caused him to fire. The shot was nowhere near Rachel.

One round left.

"Olivia," George said. "Only one of us is leaving here alive. You're either going to bleed or freeze to death. Your choice."

She threw another rock at George. He ducked but kept his stride. She could hear his footsteps. He was just ten feet away. She tried to even out her breathing.

"All right," Rachel shouted. "Swear that you'll leave my kids alone."

"I give you my word," he said.

*Like you gave it to Constance.*

She thought about Eric and Megan, when they were younger. Back when they were still Sean and Chloe Powell. When they were a young, full family with lifetimes of happiness ahead. Brad would come home and wrestle with his young son, Rachel's heart melting as he kissed his infant daughter gently on the head. She remembered the way he'd taken care of her during and after each pregnancy, bringing her water, massaging her feet, rubbing her sore hips. Telling her she was beautiful even when she felt anything but and knowing that he'd meant it.

But Brad was gone. It was her duty to take care of their children now.

She was not dying here tonight.

"As long as I have your word," Rachel said, "I'm coming out."

She stepped out from the left side of the tree, but the instant she saw George raise the gun, she spun around back behind the tree and ran at him from the right side.

The gun went off, the bullet piercing the air where her head had been a millisecond before. The final bullet. George was empty.

He reached into his pocket to reload, but before he could, Rachel was on him. She threw a punch at his injured throat, which George barely managed to deflect, but it caught him hard enough to make him stagger. Then she kicked at the side of his left knee and heard a crunch as she dislocated his kneecap.

George screamed in pain and went down. Rachel jabbed an elbow into the side of his head. She threw another elbow, but this time George caught her arm and punched her square in the stomach.

Rachel doubled over, unable to breathe. She fell to her knees, wheezing. George stumbled to his feet, dragging his injured leg. He kicked her in the side, and she felt a rib snap. He kicked again, but this time she caught his foot and thrust her palm into his bad knee. George screamed again and fell over.

Without hesitating, Rachel slid behind the lieutenant and wrapped her right forearm around his neck. She pulled her right wrist toward her body with her left hand to tighten the choke hold. He beat madly at her arm. She then wrapped her legs around his torso, pinning his arms to his sides. He kicked and spit, but Rachel squeezed his throat and held on for dear life.

George's breathing began to slow. His kicks had little strength behind them. The gun fell from George's grasp, and Rachel kicked it away. His breaths came out as choked gasps. She could feel the pulse in his neck slowing. He was dying.

She thought about what Myra had said. About the night she'd gone to Stanford Royce's house. She'd done exactly what she'd gone there to do. And it had haunted her ever since.

No more.

Rachel took her arm off the lieutenant's neck and stood up.

"Nobody dies tonight," she said. She reached into George's coat and found his cell phone. It was off. She pressed the power button, and the screen illuminated. She prayed her children were safe.

She dialed 911 and put it on speaker.

When dispatch picked up, she said, "My name is Rachel Marin, and, hell, where do I start. I'm in Woodbarren Glen with—"

Just then, Rachel saw a glint of gray reflect off the phone screen as George raised the knife. She didn't have time to move. In a second, it would be in her heart.

Two shots rang out. A spurt of blood erupted from George's shoulder. The knife went flying from his grasp and disappeared into the snow. George writhed on the ground, clutching his shoulder, blood seeping from two gunshot wounds. Rachel spun around and saw John Serrano and Leslie Tally standing twenty feet away, their guns raised.

Serrano ran over and aimed his weapon squarely at George's chest.

"Lieutenant Daryl George," Serrano said. "You are under arrest for the attempted murder of Rachel Marin. And the murder of Constance Wright."

George gritted his teeth as his face grew pale. Serrano looked back at Tally.

"EMTs are on the way," she said. Tally jogged over to Rachel, saw the blood staining her pants. "Here. Lie down. Let's raise that leg and put some pressure on it."

Tally helped Rachel to the ground. She took her coat off and wrapped it around the knife wound, pulling it tight. Rachel grimaced.

"Thank you, Detective."

"It's my job," Tally said. "But you're welcome. I will send you the dry cleaning bill, though."

Rachel laughed. She looked up at John Serrano, his gun still trained on Daryl George.

"I think you two have this under control," Rachel said. "I'm gonna take a nap now."

Rachel closed her eyes, prayed she'd get to hug her children soon, and let the darkness envelop her.

# CHAPTER 42

***One Month Later***

The doorbell rang, and Rachel limped over to answer it. The rectus femoris muscle in her quadriceps, sliced neatly by Daryl George's blade, was still healing. Eric was helping out with the laundry, and Megan did her best to set and clean the table after meals as their mother recovered. But tonight, Rachel felt no pain.

Standing on her front step was Detective John Serrano. He was wearing dark blue jeans, a green flannel shirt, and three-day-old scruff. In one hand he held a twelve-dollar bottle of merlot, and in the other, an unopened box of movie-theater-flavored popcorn. His hair was neatly combed.

"Wine and popcorn. Best dessert ever," Rachel said. And she meant it. "The only thing that might make it better is—"

Serrano pulled a bag of peanut M&M'S from his pocket. Rachel smiled.

"You are a god among men," she said.

"Candy and booze. That's a mighty low god bar you've set."

"And you'd still be shocked how few manage to hurdle it. Come on. They're waiting."

She hung up Serrano's coat as he removed his boots. Eric and Megan were sitting in the living room. Eric had a paperback copy of *A Storm of Swords* open in front of him and was reading it to Megan.

"Eric, what did I say about reading violent books to your sister?"

"Aw, Mom, it's not violent."

"Are there any decapitations in that book?"

Eric hesitated. "Yes."

"Flayings?"

"Yes."

"Then put it down. Find a Baby-Sitters Club or something."

"Those are boring."

"Boring is being locked in your room until you're twenty-one."

Eric saw the popcorn and candy and lit up. "Baby-Sitters Club it is."

"Do us a favor, hon," Rachel said. "Bring over the ottoman, and put a tray on it for the food. I need to show John something."

"John?" Eric said. "He's not Detective Serrano?"

"Tonight, I can be John," he said.

"OK, *John*," Eric said with a wry smile. "I'll go get it, *John*."

As Eric went off, Rachel motioned for Serrano to follow her. She led him to a door locked by a keypad. She plugged in the code and opened it.

"Come with me," she said. Rachel flipped a light switch on and led Serrano downstairs. They came to a metal security door. Rachel plugged in another code.

"What do you keep down here, gold bullion?" he said. Rachel didn't respond. She opened the security door and led him into the pitch-black basement.

"Why do I feel like Jodie Foster at the end of *Silence of the Lambs*?" Serrano said. "If there's a body decomposing in a bathtub, this is the last time we hang out."

There was a click, and the basement was illuminated.

Rachel stood underneath a single seventy-watt light bulb with a pull string. Serrano looked around the basement.

"What is . . . what is all this?"

"My work. My *real* work," she said.

The basement floor was lined with rubber mats. Free weights were stacked neatly against one wall, along with medicine balls, jump ropes, plyometric trainers, a treadmill, an elliptical machine, a BoxMaster Tower bolted to the floor with a dozen striking pads of varying heights and positioning, a mounted pull-up bar, and half a dozen other training machines and devices.

On another wall was a bookshelf filled with dozens of forensic, psychological, sociological, behavioral, and law enforcement texts. The *DSM-5*, *Fundamentals of Forensic Science*, *Forensic Science and Toxicology*, *Pharmacology*, *Biology*, *Criminalistics*, *Forensic Psychology and Criminal Behavior*, *Homeopathy*, *Police Procedure & Investigation*, *The Law Enforcement Officer's Bible*, *Proving Federal Crimes*, and *Law Enforcement and Justice Administration*. And that was just one shelf.

"I was a different person before Brad died," Rachel said. "A simpler person. And after he was gone, I couldn't afford to be that person anymore. I had to be stronger and smarter than ever for the sake of my children. Because I didn't trust that anyone else could protect them."

Serrano went over to a six-foot-long ebony wood desk topped with a powerful desktop computer, a bank of monitors, and numerous external hard drives. A notepad lay open to a fresh page, next to a jar filled with pens and pencils.

Then Serrano noticed the framed photograph hanging above the computer. He pointed at it.

"Is that . . . ?"

Rachel nodded solemnly.

"That's Bradley," she said. "He died a week before his thirty-fifth birthday. When I was younger, I hated how everyone said our kids looked like him. For some reason it felt like a jab at me, an insult. Now, knowing our kids look like him is what gets me through the day. They have his eyes. His chin. I'm thankful for how they remind me of Brad. Thankful that monster couldn't take all of him."

"Harwood Greene," Serrano said. Rachel nodded.

"He'd already killed six people by the time he got to us. Can you imagine what it's like, to sue the police department, the city where you raised your family? People had sympathy for us at first, but once I sued, they turned their back. They said I was profiting off my husband's death or blaming the whole department for one bad egg. Meanwhile, our lives had been shattered. Harwood Greene left Bradley's remains in a dirty sack on our front porch. Eric found it, saw his father literally torn to pieces. He didn't speak for a month. It was years before he stopped waking up in the middle of the night screaming. That boy upstairs, he went to hell and back."

She felt Serrano take her hand. A great well of emotion rose up in Rachel. She allowed one audible sob, like he'd opened a valve, squeezing Serrano's hand back.

"The police found photographs in Greene's house. Some of the photos were of me and Eric the night we found Bradley. Greene sat in a car half a dozen blocks away with a telescopic lens, documenting our horror. He did it with every victim. Like the pictures you get when you go on a roller coaster."

"I can't even imagine," Serrano said.

"That's why I went to the press conference," Rachel said. "I figured the killer might enjoy seeing the havoc they created. Like Greene did. Turns out, the killer was there. Just not in the manner I expected."

"And Daryl George will never set foot on carpeting again," Serrano said.

"Did you know that six people took responsibility for Greene's crimes?" Rachel said. "He had followers. *Followers.* People *admired* that demon. Greene's lawyer presented two witnesses who owned the same camera as Greene. They claimed to have taken those photos and planted them at Greene's house. Then one of the jurors leaked to the press. Between all that and the unlawful search, it was easy for the judge to declare a mistrial. And then Greene was gone. Every *single* day, for I don't know how long, I waited for him to show up on our doorstep.

Our home in Darien had been violated. So I brought my kids here, and we became different people. I became an angrier person. I was angry that the Harwood Greenes of the world could destroy lives and get away with it."

"That's why you got involved in Constance Wright's murder."

"Constance Wright was kind to me," Rachel said. "That was enough reason to try to give her justice."

"You should know," Serrano said, "the city council voted unanimously to rename the Albertson Bridge the Constance Ella Wright Bridge."

Rachel looked up, tears in her eyes. "Really?"

"She deserves to be remembered. Besides, Augustus Albertson was *kind* of a terrible racist. Lot of folks have been petitioning the council to rename that bridge for years. I guess once they found someone who deserved it, it was easy to push it through."

"That makes me happy."

"Me too. Know what else will make you happy?" Serrano said. "The carabinieri in Italy found Caroline Drummond."

"You're kidding."

"Nope. She was shacked up with a widowed cheese maker in a villa in Pitigliano. She's being extradited as we speak and should be stateside in about two weeks. And then she'll stand trial with her brother."

"I hope Constance knows all this, somehow," Rachel said. "You know, I've been thinking. About doing more of this. Helping people."

"It would be kind of a shame if your talents were confined to this basement," Serrano said. "I can even speak to the new lieutenant. The force is perpetually understaffed. I'll see if they could use an occasional consultant."

Rachel beamed. "I could kiss you."

Serrano motioned to the photo above the desk. "Not with him watching."

"OK, let's go upstairs. If these kids don't get some sugar and butter into their bloodstreams soon, they might mutiny."

"Just so you know," Serrano said, as Rachel turned off the light, "I never thought you were involved in Constance Wright's death. You might be a protector, Rachel. But you're not a killer."

Rachel smiled and moved closer to Serrano. She stood on her tiptoes and kissed him lightly on the lips.

When she finished, Serrano said, "But what about . . ."

"The lights were off," she said. "Bradley didn't see anything."

They went upstairs to find Megan pulling Eric's hair and walloping him with the remote control.

"Megan!" Rachel said. "Release your brother, or the next movie I let you watch will be the introductory video for college freshmen."

Megan let her brother go and crossed her arms sullenly but with a smile underneath. Serrano took a seat on the couch, with Eric and Megan at either end. The children burrowed into the corners of the sofa. Eric grabbed a handful of popcorn and added a few M&M'S to it, then shoved the mixture into his mouth.

"Know what I have at home?" Serrano said to Eric. The boy shook his head, popcorn kernels spilling onto his shirt. "The Lord of the Rings extended editions on Blu-ray. Four hours each. Plus bonus features."

"Shut *up*," Eric said. He turned to his mother. "Mom, I'm going to live with Detective Serrano."

She laughed and said, "I promise we'll watch them one day. Just not in a row."

Serrano patted the seat next to him. "Saved you a seat."

Seeing the three of them together made her heart soar. She had no idea where things might go with John Serrano, but she was eager to find out.

"Just give me one second; I'll be right back."

"Hurry back," Serrano said. "Movie's starting."

"I'll be quick."

Rachel went upstairs and into her bedroom. She shut the door gently, opened the closet, and entered the combination to the safe. She removed the cardboard box, slid off the rubber bands, and opened it.

Atop the pile was Reginald Bartek's driver's license. She flipped it over, read the inscription, then placed it back inside. Then she took a small plastic bag from underneath the various ID cards, unsealed it, and dropped a piece of jewelry into her palm.

She thought about what Serrano had said in the basement.

*You might be a protector, Rachel. But you're not a killer.*

It was a men's bracelet adorned with brownish-yellow Tiger Eye beads. She ran her fingers over the bracelet, thinking about the night she'd removed it from a lifeless wrist.

*No more.*

Then she gently placed the bracelet in the box, put it back in the safe, and went downstairs.

She nestled in next to John Serrano. She felt his fingers close around hers. Rachel smiled and leaned her head against his shoulder. And for the first time in a very, very long time, she felt at peace.

# ACKNOWLEDGMENTS

Ever since I was a child, people have accused me (usually with good reason) of being off in my own world. For a writer, that's a compliment, provided you come back down to earth from time to time. Thankfully, once I leave my fictional worlds behind, I have an amazing family to come back to.

I'm fortunate to live with three strong, beautiful, amazing women. My wife, Dana, and our wonderful daughters, Ava and Lyla. My family keeps me grounded, keeps me sane, keeps my priorities in order; they're endlessly patient when I *am* off in my own world and never let me forget that the most important job I have is Dada.

I was fortunate to grow up in a book-loving household and can thank my mother and father for encouraging the crazy notion that I could write. And as most will attest, my sister, Allison, is the funnier sibling, so if you happened to find any humor in this book, you can assume I learned it from her.

A sincere thank-you to Hoboken chief of police Ken Ferrante and lieutenant John Orrico for letting me pepper them with questions about the job—and life outside the job. I have tremendous respect for the men and women who put their lives on the line to protect us day in and day out, and you won't find two better public servants.

As you might guess, I am not, in fact, a single mother. But I wanted to understand Rachel Marin inside and out, and for that I thank the people who shared their lives and stories with me, especially

Zoe Quinton, who helped me understand the unique bond between mother and child in a way that enriched the book and my own appreciation for people raising children under often difficult circumstances. They are true warriors.

Thank you to everyone I work with at Polis Books for their understanding as I delicately balance being both author and publisher. Wearing two hats may look silly, but there are no better jobs in the world.

The team at Thomas & Mercer has been everything I could have hoped for in a publisher. Thank you to my editor, Jessica Tribble, who was passionate about this book from the start and pushed me to make it even better. Thank you to Grace Doyle, Sarah Shaw, and everyone else at T&M who supported this book and got it into the hands of readers. Kevin Smith, Miranda Dunning, and Carissa Bluestone made this book infinitely better, helped make sure all the pieces fit together snugly, and corrected my improper capitalization of Nerds candy.

A great agent is a business partner, a sounding board, and an unflappable, indefatigable, bookish consigliere. Amy Tannenbaum is all of that and more. Here's to the first of many.

And to the readers, old and new: Whether you've read my previous books or you're reading me for the first time, thanks to each and every one of you for allowing my characters to enter your lives for a little while. I hope you'll invite us back soon.

# ABOUT THE AUTHOR

*Photo © 2017 Jason Rhee*

Jason Pinter is the bestselling author of six novels: the acclaimed Henry Parker series (*The Mark*, *The Guilty*, *The Stolen*, *The Fury*, and *The Darkness*), the stand-alone thriller *The Castle*, the middle-grade adventure novel *Zeke Bartholomew: SuperSpy*, and the children's book *Miracle*. His books have over one million copies in print worldwide. He has been nominated for numerous awards, including the Thriller Award, Strand Critics Award, Barry Award, and Shamus Award.

Pinter is the founder of Polis Books, an independent press, and was honored by *Publishers Weekly*'s Star Watch, which "recognizes young publishing professionals who have distinguished themselves as future leaders of the industry." He has written for the *New Republic*, *Entrepreneur*, the *Daily Beast*, *Esquire*, and more. He lives in Hoboken, New Jersey, with his wife, their two daughters, and their dog, Wilson. Visit him at www.JasonPinter.com, and follow him on Twitter and Instagram @JasonPinter.